GANTHIS WAS JUST STANDING THERE, LOOKING down this corridor and then that one and then this one again.

"What is it?" Koliander demanded.

Ganthis frowned. "We have run into a bit of a dilemma, my lord."

"What sort of dilemma?"

"I am . . . of two minds as to which way to go."

Two minds? "I thought you were an expert in negotiating these passages."

"I am indeed."

"Then how can you make such a mistake?"

"The passages are always changing, my lord. And they never assume the same configuration twice."

"Then why did you say you were an expert?"

"An expert at *change.* Knowing what they have done in the past, I cannot predict what they will do in the future. However, since the changes are never the same, I can predict what they will *not* do. And that is a valuable tool indeed."

Koliander was not entirely certain that Ganthis' words made sense. Then again, what *did* make sense in the Keep?

He waited for Ganthis to make a decision. But after what seemed like a long time, they still had not budged from the spot. "We cannot stand here forever," Koliander snarled.

Suddenly one of the corridors vanished—and another one appeared behind them. It did not seem to help. Ganthis continued to look perplexed.

Feeling useless, Koliander made his way partway down the corridor that had just appeared. Not so far that he might risk losing sight of Ganthis, of course. Just far enough for him to feel that he was *doing* something.

Not that the demon expected to see anything worthwhile. That would have been asking a lot. But as luck would have it, he *did* see something.

Something completely and utterly unexpected.

Tales of the Crimson Keep

NEWLY RENOVATED EDITION

EDITED BY

ROBERT GREENBERGER

CRAZY 8 PRESS

CONTENTS

INTRODUCTION

by Kevin Dilmore

THE GREATEST EPIC TALES BEGIN WITH UN-forgettable words.

"*Gallia est omnis divisa in partes tres.*"

"It was the best of times, it was the worst of times."

"Come and listen to a story 'bout a man named Jed."

Each opening line snares one's attention, starts one's imagination rolling and intentionally sets the stage for all that is to come. That last one even carries its own snappy tune that you are sure to enjoy in your mind for the next hour. (Glad to help.)

And so it was with the first line of the first story ever to chronicle the mysterious and magical world of the Crimson Keep.

"There's no way we're going to get all of this mopped up in time!"

One might say it was an opening so strong that it required not one but five writers to pay it off.

The true differentiator of that opening from others above is not simply its arguable comparative quality. That was not an opening chosen for its ability to begin an already plotted tale. It began as a line without any story at all. Any indelibility, any evocative power, any meaning at all that a reader might now find in that line did not even originate with its writer. The line matters only because of the interests Peter David, Michael Jan Friedman, Robert Greenberger, Glenn Hauman, and Aaron Rosenberg (with kibitzing from Howard Weinstein) harbored in making it matter.

To that end, the six writers created "Demon Circle," the original novella that inspired the anthology that awaits you.

That initial work carried its share of creative baggage, too. It began as a fundraising project for the Comic Book Legal Defense Fund spawned with no initial plotting at a weekend science-fiction convention. The story opened with a line written by a random attendee at a panel to introduce Crazy 8 Press as a new publisher. Authors worked independently, crafting their words and creating a world that the next successive writer would discover only when the previously written pages were handed to him. And all the work was done in plain view of convention attendees and passers-by with writers hunched over their laptops and toiling in a brick alcove smaller than the average public toilet stall. Few stories have been born of such fresh hells.

Through all obstacles they hurtled, building on each others' ideas, sculpting characters that earned reader interest and keeping a narrative on track despite whatever plot twists and let's-see-you-top-this moments each writer served upon the next. And in the face of it all (undisclosed deals with any devils notwithstanding), they delivered not only a fun read but a whole new universe in which to explore and play.

Here we are today, a few years down the road, and the mind-boggling Crimson Keep with its wise and wizened Master, his pupils in magic and mysticism, and a surrounding host of demons at war with humanity remains alive in our imaginations. The world they created as a bit of a lark has proven enduringly interesting enough not only to them but to other writers as well that we now are able to return to it in the pages to come.

Prepare yourself for more adventure, more laughs, more thrills and, yes, more demons in seven all-new tales of the Crimson Keep. But as far as opening lines go, this time the guys are on their own.

A LESSON LEARNED

by Aaron Rosenberg

"ASK AGAIN AND I'LL TURN YOU INTO A NEWT!"

"Truly?" Jocomo shrugged and scratched at his beard. "Can you actually do that? A newt? How would that work?" He looked down at his beefy frame and thick, permanently tanned arms. "Where would the rest of me go?"

"It wouldn't go anywhere, you idiot!" The stocky, white-bearded wizard known only as the Master retorted. "It's magic! It just— oh, why do I bother?"

And he slammed the door in Jocomo's face.

All in all, it was the longest conversation Jocomo had managed to elicit out of the crotchety old wizard yet. He took that to be a good sign. Whistling, he lowered himself into a seating position against the door, closed his eyes, and settled in to wait again.

◼ ◼ ◼

"Wha— argh!" The Master managed to catch himself before he pitched forward on his head and turned to glare down at Jocomo, rubbing his shins where they'd barked up against the younger man. "You again!"

"Me again," Jocomo agreed.

"What do you want now?"

"Same as before," Jocomo answered as calmly as ever. "For you to teach me."

"I don't do that sort of thing!" the Master screamed at him. "I'm a wizard! I work alone!"

"Lots of wizards have apprentices," Jocomo pointed out.

"Then go bother one of them!"

Jocomo shook his head. "They already have apprentices," he explained. "And most of them wouldn't want one as old as I am." Typically apprentices were mere boys, whereas Jocomo was a full-grown man and actually approaching middle years, which is what happened when you were already an established tradesman but then decided to do something completely different. "Besides," he added, "everyone says you're the best. And you should always learn from the best."

"Humph." He could tell the Master was trying not to look pleased at the compliment. "What makes you think you can even learn magic to begin with? It's not like farming or baking or whatever you did before this—"

"Carpentry," Jocomo offered, still lounging against the door with his legs stretched out before him. "House-building, mostly. Furniture too sometimes."

"Yes, well, magic isn't like that," the Master snapped. "At its heart it's a talent, not a craft. You either have it or you don't." He glared down at Jocomo for a minute. "Well? Do you?"

Jocomo smiled. Slowly he levered himself up from the ground. He stretched his arms and cracked his knuckles. He took several long, deep breaths. And then he raised his thick, long-fingered hands, the fingers laced together, before spreading them wide—

—and releasing the small, pale yellow butterfly that fluttered and flapped its way clear of the two men, arcing unsteadily up into the wide blue sky.

A butterfly that most certainly had not been there a second before.

"Yes. Well." The Master watched the small insect's departure. "All right, you've got the gift, fine. That still doesn't mean I want anything to do with you." He turned and started down the path from the keep. "And keep the form fixed in your head next time," he warned over his shoulder. "Its right wing was smaller than the left, that's why its flight was so wobbly."

Jocomo watched the master wizard stomp off, and smiled to himself. Then he went to find some food for himself, something he could eat quickly so he could be waiting when the Master returned.

■ ■ ■

"Don't you have anything better to do?" The Master demanded when he trudged back up the long path, a large sack slung over his broad shoulder.

Jocomo, who was whittling a small chunk of wood, shook his head. "Nope."

"No family to tend to?" the Master pressed. "No shop to maintain? No sick old relative to spoon feed soup? Nothing?"

"No family," Jocomo answered. "No shop—I was a traveling craftsman, went from town to town, all I ever needed was my tools and my pack. No old relatives." He grinned beneath his thick reddish-brown beard. "No soup, neither." He held up the fruit of his whittling efforts. "Got this, though."

The Master took the object from him and studied it carefully. It was a small wooden ship, complete with two sails that had been carved as if the wind were filling them. "Yes, very nice," he agreed reluctantly, handing it back. "Why don't you go carve more of them and sell them to small children the world over?"

"Because," Jocomo replied, "I'd rather do this." He cupped both hands around the ship, leaned in close to it, and breathed out a hefty gust upon the carving.

And, as they both watched, the wooden sails creaked and billowed in earnest, and the tiny ship lifted off from his hands and rose into the air, sailing forward as if the sky were water and it a true ocean-going vessel.

After a minute, however, its forward progress slowed, and it began to dip lower and lower, its sails stiffening as the magical wind that animated them faded. Finally the tiny ship came to rest upon the ground perhaps ten feet away, now once again a lifeless carving.

"Focus," the Master commented reflexively. "It's all about the focus. That and investing the ship with some of your own energy—if you do that, it can sustain its own motion rather than having to continually draw from you." Catching the slow smile upon the carpenter's face, the Master scowled. "There, I've taught you something," he all but snarled. "Are you happy?"

"It's a start," Jocomo agreed quietly as he pulled his legs in to let the other man stomp past. The door slammed just behind his head, but he didn't mind. After a minute or two, when he was sure the Master wasn't coming back out right away, Jocomo rose to his feet, walked over, and lifted the little ship out of the dirt. Then, with it cradled in one hand, he returned to his post.

Focus, he thought.

∗ ∗ ∗

"Your castle is growing."

"What?" The Master glared at him, same as he did every day when he had to step over Jocomo to go in or out.

"Your castle. It's growing," Jocomo repeated.

"Yes? So?" Turning, the Master glanced up at the massive, sprawling stone structure behind them. "It does that."

"Really?" Jocomo scratched his nose. "Never seen a building do that before."

"Of course not!" Now the old wizard puffed up with pride. "This is the Crimson Keep! It's unique among all the kingdoms and all the realms! Its very stones are woven from the stuff of magic!"

"That's why it grows?"

"That's why it grows."

Jocomo studied the looming walls. "How old is it?"

"At least a century now," the Master huffed. "To tell you the truth, I'm not entirely sure exactly how old—I forget the year when I started it." Catching himself, he glared at his unwelcome companion again. "Why?"

This was how it was now. Jocomo had worn the Master down a little over the past few weeks, simply by always being underfoot and by never getting ruffled. Whenever the Master left the keep, Jocomo was there by the door. And when he returned Jocomo was still there, waiting. Only, each time it seemed the Master paused to talk just a little bit longer.

And each time he paused, Jocomo showed him a new magic trick he'd figured out.

And each time, the Master gave him tips on how to improve it.

This time, though, Jocomo didn't do any tricks. He was still too busy studying the keep. "It's speeding up," he said.

"What?"

"Your castle, its growing. It's speeding up."

"Don't be ridiculous," the Master said. "I'd know if that were the case."

Jocomo shrugged, eyes still on the castle before them. "It's five stories tall," he pointed out.

"Yes, and?"

"It was four last week."

"So?" The Master tugged angrily at his own beard. "Is that supposed to mean something? Or do you just prefer the number four to the number five?"

"That's an entire floor in a single week," Jocomo answered, ignoring the jab as he had already learned to do with each of the Master's barbed comments. "If it normally grew at that pace, and you built it a hundred years ago, it'd be thousands of stories high." He squinted up at the top of the keep. "It's not."

The Master looked at the Keep, then at this infuriating stranger with his sturdy frame and strong hands and calm face and steady voice, then back at the Keep. Finally he shrugged. "So what?" he asked. "Time is wonky within the Keep, there's no reason space wouldn't be as well."

Then he brushed past Jocomo and through the open door, slamming it shut behind him.

Jocomo didn't watch him go. Not this time. He was still studying the Keep instead.

※ ※ ※

"It's going to collapse," was how Jocomo greeted the Master as the old wizard stepped outside two days later.

"What? Don't be ridiculous," the Master snapped. "It's magic—it can't collapse."

But the former carpenter shook his head. "I don't think that's true," he said. "Maybe it takes a lot more for that to happen, but I think it could. And it will."

"Oh? And why is that, exactly?" The Master set his hands on

his hips and glared at the younger man.

"It's growing too fast," Jocomo replied. "The joints and joists and beams can't keep up."

For once the Master was honestly confused instead of just irritated. "What?"

"Those are all connection points and structural supports," Jocomo explained. "The Keep is growing them along with these rooms and floors and towers. Not fast enough, though. It should really be laying in the joists and beams first, then assembling floors and walls, then ceiling, and finally tightening up and sealing all the joints. Near as I can figure, though, it's actually just creating whole rooms and slapping then down on top of each other." For just a second a smile split his thick beard. "It doesn't seem to have a lot of patience—just like its master." The Master scowled at that, but Jocomo's mood had also shifted to the somber. "Problem is, it's trying to add joints and joists after the fact, and that doesn't really work. They have to be there from the beginning. So it's shoving these in and actually creating more problems than it's solving." He rose to his feet, dusting his pants and shirt from the dirt all around, and gestured to the Master. "Here, I'll show you."

Together they traipsed around the side of the Castle, the Master grumbling about how much time he was wasting on this.

Until they stopped beside one of the newer additions to the magical dwelling and Jocomo gestured for the Master to have a look.

"See there?" He indicated the spot where a new turret had begun to form at the outer corner of the building. It wasn't fully shaped yet, though, and so they could see into the walls themselves. Right where the new met the old, there was what looked like a mad flurry of thick wooden beams jutting forth at all angles like someone had rammed a piece of bread onto a pin cushion. "It's trying to line things up," Jocomo said, "but it can't. And with those beams like that they can't support the tower's full weight—it'll hold for a little while, longer thanks to your magic, but eventually this whole piece is just going to pull away and collapse under its own weight."

The Master studied the situation, stroking his long beard.

"What do you suggest I do about it?" he asked finally. For once he wasn't sneering or snapping or shouting at Jocomo. But then, at the moment he wasn't a master wizard trying to turn away a would-be apprentice. Right now he was just a homeowner with a problem, consulting an expert carpenter.

Of course, Jocomo was sure no carpenter had ever faced a situation quite like this. "I'm not really sure," he admitted. "Normally, I'd say fire whoever you have building this place like that and hire me, and then I'll tear out this whole section and lay the beams out properly and start over." He shrugged. "But the Keep itself seems to be the builder here, and I don't think it's going to listen much."

There was a moment of quiet, and then Jocomo realized with a start that the Master was now eyeing him speculatively, still stroking his beard all the while. "What?" Now that he actually had the wizard's attention, Jocomo wasn't entirely sure he really wanted it.

"It does listen, somewhat," the Master answered slowly. "Not to my words, perhaps, but to my thoughts and desires. That's because my magic is bound up within it, and thus it is bound up to me." He frowned. "If I let you in, and teach you magic, you'll be bound to the Keep as well—and it could draw upon your knowledge of structure and building to assemble itself properly."

Jocomo stared, unable to believe he'd just heard that. "Are you saying you'll teach me?"

"Yes, yes," the older man snapped. "But not for you, you understand. You did not win here. I'm doing this for the Keep. That's all!"

"Of course." Jocomo fingered his own beard to cover the smile he was unable to quell. "I know you never would have given in otherwise."

"Quite right." And with that the Master gestured at a nearby section of the wall. The rough-hewn stone there shimmered as if it were melting in the sun, and then a large patch of it rippled and faded away, pulling back to create a circular gap. Jocomo could see through it to a comfortable sitting room beyond. "Well, don't dawdle," the Master warned, and stepped through and into the Keep proper. Jocomo quickly followed.

As the stones slid back into place behind them, it occurred to him to wonder something. Apparently the Master could exit anywhere along the Keep's walls whenever he wanted, just as he had done now. But if that was the case, why did the cranky old wizard always use the door? The same door Jocomo had planted himself beside for all these weeks?

Jocomo bit back another smile. Perhaps he hadn't been losing after all.

⁎ ⁎ ⁎

"I brought you a present," Jocomo announced, causing the Master to look up—and to start at the skinny, gawky boy standing there just outside the entrance to the Master's study.

"Who is that?" the old wizard demanded. "And what is he doing here?"

"That is Alfast," Jocomo answered, weathering his mentor's anger as calmly as ever. "He is your new apprentice."

"What?" The Master eyed the boy, who was gazing all about him, eyes wide, mouth open. "I didn't ask for an apprentice!"

"No, but you need one all the same." Jocomo smiled. "He's a bright lad, and eager to learn. I think he'll do fine here."

"I won't take another apprentice!" the Master declared, rising to his feet. Thunder began to rumble ominously outside the Keep's walls—or perhaps within them—to match his gathering rage. "You don't get to tell me what I need!"

"No," his student agreed, "but I do tell you what the Keep needs. And it needs for you to have an apprentice." He gestured around them. "Look at this place. What do you see?"

"Wonders untold," came the immediate reply, followed by the slightly more considered "it's an ever-expanding magical building, of course. The biggest and the best of its kind, all the rest are pale imitations."

"All of which is true," Jocomo agreed. "But look around. Really look." He laid an affectionate hand on a nearby support column, his long fingers resting in the grooves around its sides. "Since you took me on the building has stabilized. Its joints and beams are sound. It's sturdy, well built." He smiled, glancing all around. "No more joist issues."

Which was true. The Master's theory had proven correct, and once Jocomo had entered the Keep it had begun feeding off his thoughts as well. Now it was all tightly built, steady as a rock even though it was bigger and more fanciful than ever. "I need to go off and do my own wizarding," he reminded the Master gently, "and without me or at least some other apprentice this place will start to crumble and pull apart again. It's too big for any one mind to support now. Even yours."

"And you really think he can help?" The Master eyed Alfast skeptically. "What does he know about beams and joists?"

"Probably nothing," Jocomo admitted. "But that's not the problem. The building has gotten enough of me over the years that it now understands the basic principles of house-building. What it needs is youthful energy, unbridled enthusiasm." His smile threatened to become an evil grin. "And the bigger it gets, the more help you'll need to keep it all together. Which means sometime in the next few years you're going to have to take on additional students." Jocomo did laugh then, he couldn't help it. "If you're not careful," he warned, "you could wind up with a regular magic school!"

"Hmmph!" The Master scowled at his first pupil's obvious glee at this horrible concept. "It was bad enough having you around cramping my style," he grumbled. "And now you expect me to take on this beanpole, and then whoever else wants to come out?" He shook his head, glared at Alfast, then at Jocomo, then repeated the process. "This'll never work," he insisted. "I know myself—I'm not a teacher. And I hate the idea of so many younglings invading my privacy."

"This Keep is so large you could set five people loose here only a few minutes apart," Jocomo argued, "and they'd never encounter each other again within these walls. You know that. This place isn't going to stop growing, so your choices are to kill it somehow, to try holding it together on your own and possibly destroy both of you, or to take on more students."

"Fine!" The Master ground his teeth together under his beard. "I'll try him out and see how he does. No promises, though. I may decide I can't stand him, and turn him—"

"I know, I know," Jocomo cut his mentor off, grinning as he shouldered his pack where he'd set it, all cleaned off and repaired and refilled, earlier this morning. "You'll turn him into a newt." He shook his head. "I'm still not convinced you can actually do that." Then he shrugged. "Take care of yourself," he told the Master fondly, offering his hand. They shook. "I'll try to swing back by sometime in the next few years to see how everything is here."

The Master sighed, carefully extricating his hand from Jocomo's. It was already obvious that this was the start of something, something both wizards might continue for a long, long time. As Jocomo slid past the boy and created an exit in one of the outer walls, the Master turned to his new pupil. "Vey well," he declared, trying belatedly to take some of the thunder from his words. "Alfast, was it? Come here, boy, and let me tell you what magic is—and how you will someday use it."

Awestruck, Alfast hurried over to his new master—

—and the Crimson Keep sent forth a wave of contentment as it began to learn and grow once more.

THIEF IN THE NIGHT

by Russ Colchamiro

THEY ROAMED THE CRIMSON KEEP.

And on this night, of all nights, they were keenly alert. But of course Plick knew this. He came prepared.

Twin brothers Mandor and Candor, the hounds, ran sentry; Mandor starting in the North wing, Candor in the South. Burly beasts, they surveyed the various layers and stairwells, checked each room, every hidden passageway, and, on a rotating schedule only they knew, ensured that no creature, dead or alive, breached The Keep's perimeter.

Of course, Plick knew this, too.

And it wasn't because Plick was the smartest charge flushed out of The Keep's Wizard training program, nor was he the cleverest, most creative, nor even downright lucky. No siree, Bob. Plick was, in most respects, what the ancients called a *creadadaaoo*. Or, in layman's terms, a boob.

But *creadadaoo* or no, he was in fact a darn good cat burglar, and on this one night, of all nights, particularly well informed. He had Dunbar to thank for that.

"Okee dokee," Plick whispered as he shimmied open a second floor bathroom window. To bypass the wards of security he used a clever little entrance spell that didn't force secured locks to open, but convinced them it was unnecessary to remain locked, and thus opened of their own accord.

Short and slight of build, Plick was, if nothing else, agile with a knack for soft landings. Slipping inside The Keep, his foot took hold of the cast iron toilet, and then onto the cold stone floor.

Mandor howled in the distance. Or was it Candor? Plick

couldn't tell. But then, he didn't care. Plick had plied a cat mimicking spell that, under ordinary circumstances, was nothing
more than a novelty prank, but when infused with a potent mix-
ture of feline pheromones he bartered for in Old Town, would
keep the hounds chasing phantom cats all night. More than
enough time to retrieve the *Occupacala* spell.

Ten years he'd been waiting. Ten years since they kicked him
out. And ten years to plot, consider, and wait. Opportunities to
re-enter The Keep were far and few between, even for a skilled
cat burglar, so Plick jumped at the chance.

Once each year The Keep cleared out for a cleansing ritual in
the deep Nangorian Woods. Magic carries with it various impu-
rities that collect in the system, and lest they be purged in an
ancient rejuvenating ceremony, they settle like sludge at the base
of the neck, interfering with the flow of enchantment. Even the
Master himself had cause to clear out the ole noggin now and
again, just to remain sharp.

The Master never chose the same night two years in a row,
but thanks again to Dunbar, the trader of secrets—and almost
two years of burgling profits used as payment for that crucial
piece of information—Plick knew that tonight, of all nights, was
the night.

Using an ancient light crystal, he shone a thin beam along
the floor, illuminating a path through the cook's bathroom,
bedroom, and, after sliding open the door, into the side hallway
leading down the main foyer.

Yet with Mandor and Candor prowling the grounds, Plick
wasn't about to take chances. He curled his right hand up to his
mouth, pursed his lips, and using his left hand to mute the call,
recited the next phase of the cat mimicking spell.

"*Felonious erroneous* call through the night. *Felonious erroneous* . . . take flight!"

Plick checked his timepiece. He counted down. "Five . . .
four . . . three . . . two . . . ."

On cue Mandor or Candor began to howl in the distance, the
deep, guttural snapping of two large beasts with an appetite for
intruders, particularly cats. (Mandor once picked his teeth with
a tabby's dismembered front paw, while Candor turned the poor

feline's teeth into dice, and got a craps game together that lasted most of the night. Ironically, he lost the teeth in a bet).

But with the hounds now occupied, Plick continued his prowl through The Keep. The existence of the *Occupacala* spell was nothing but legend—nobody but the Master could confirm if the spell was real—but Plick knew for sure that it was. During what turned out to be his last year of study, he discovered the ancient parchment it was written upon, folded up in the inside jacket pocket of Elisa the Round, a nasty ghoul who had been stuffed and mounted, and put on display in what was usually the East Hallway. That no one had bothered to check all the pockets was a staple of Plick's burgling. Most of what he had stolen over the years was in actuality forgotten in plain sight.

Nevertheless, the *Occupacala* spell contained incredible power. He'd have it soon.

Down through the main foyer, illuminated by oil-lit lamps and moonlight shining through the windows, Plick ducked beneath three gargoyle statues, around the stone hearth, and then, with some deft balancing, unlatched a secret bookcase that led behind the main kitchen.

Clasped between his teeth Plick shone his light crystal down the spiral passage, guarded by a dozen black widow spiders, perched on a web, stretching across the damp and musty stairwell. Plick quickly neutralized the critters with an arachnid spell he had mastered during his very first month at The Keep, hypnotizing the spiders into believing they had already feasted, and were now ready for a long period of digestion.

Yet the next part was going to be tricky. The hidden pathway narrowed and corkscrewed such that even a skinny fellow such as Plick would have to shift himself sideways—and suck in his gut—in order to maneuver through the tight space. The stairwell had been originally designed for various animals, shapeshifters, and creatures of the night to act as covert messengers through The Keep, a tactical advantage if one had the capacity to utilize it.

But physically contorting oneself through the crevice was actually the easier component, made obvious by the various skeletons sprawled along the descending stairwell. Unbeknownst to most, the passageway had been constructed from *Taborian* lime-stone, which, when doused with black pepper, elicited intense, paranoid hallucinations from any whom passed through. It rarely ended well.

Unless you knew the counterbalance spell, which Plick did.

"*Chillious bilious* calm and true, *chillious bilious* not me, but you." Beneath his feet was a skull cracked near the forehead. "Definitely for you, though, bro. Ouchie."

Plick then came to the bottom of the stairwell, scraping his wrist on a jagged edge. He bit down on the light crystal, and then tapped his foot against the bottom stone, in the proper sequence. *Tap, tap-tap, tap, tap-tap-tap.*

With the sound of a belching demon the stone wall slid open, sending Plick tumbling to the floor. But when he popped back up he found himself exactly where he wanted to be—inside the carpenter's shed, adjacent to Nola's bedroom.

That alone was reason enough for optimism. Still, Plick repeated the cat mimicking spell once more, just to be safe.

But then he stopped

Above the carpenter's work bench was a small window. It creaked. Plick ducked down, curled next to an iron stool, and listened. Wind blew. Leaves rustled. A branch tapped against the glass. And still, Pluck listened. He listened.

Okay, he thought. *You've made it this far. Keep it together, Plick. You're almost there. You're almost . . .*

It was then he felt a tickle on the back of his neck. Possibly a stray leaf blown in from the grounds. Or a twig.

Or a spider. A black widow.

His timing would have to be impeccable. He eased up, slowly . . . slowly . . . slowly, so that his neck was even with the workbench, tilted his head ever-so-slightly, and, praying that the bead of sweat inching down his temple wouldn't spook the deadly arachnid, let the creepy crawly scurry off his external jugular vein and into the shadows.

Plick let out a long, heavy sigh. "Oh, thank the spirits," he said. "I don't—"

A two-armed beast knocked Plick to the ground, and with a heavy object, *klonked* him on the noggin. Face down on the dirt floor, Plick let out a groan. But having anticipated a potential scuffle—it was The Keep, after all—he pulled off a cloth pouch bag tied to his waist, and tossed illuminating dust into the air—a burst of light in the dark—temporarily blinding his attacker.

Plick grabbed a heavy tin bucket off the table, about to swing it. He held his arm, mid-swing, and then squinted, hoping his eyes would better focus. "Gamble? Is that you?"

"Wait," the wounded attacker said. "P-Plick?"

"Dude," Plick said.

"Dude," Gamble said.

Plick fumbled along the desk. He found a kerosene lamp, lit it. He held it up. "G. What are you doing here?"

Beefier and almost a half foot taller than Plick, Gamble sported pasty white skin and a thicket of red hair, with matching goatee. He had been kicked out of the wizard training program the same time as Plick. And for the same reason. "What am *I* doing here? What are *you* doing here?"

"I'm . . . you know . . . looking."

"Looking for what?"

"You know. This and that."

"Right." Gamble gave a squint. "This and that."

Plick nodded. There was no chance that Gamble being here tonight was a coincidence. In any case, Plick needed to keep his cool. There was a lot at stake. "So . . . ? It's been, what . . . five years? How've you been?"

Gamble shrugged. "Ups and downs. The usual. Went by fast. Kinda slow, too. But fast. Fast and slow. I don't know."

"Don't I know it. You still hanging out at McGregor's? I heard you left town." He lied.

"Nah, not really. Been here. Mostly down at The Elgin Pub. In Old Town. North side."

"Oh, yeah," Plick said, trying to sound casual, but inwardly doing all he could to suppress a panic attack. "Been by there, but never went in. I hear they have good wings."

"They really do. A few too many feathers—you need to pluck a few—but those Grelia birds have juicy drum sticks. Plus they give you carrot sticks, and lots of blue cheese. You'd like 'em."

There was an awkward silence, the two thieves separated by

far more than just time and distance. Knowing they'd been in close proximity all these years only amplified their absence from one another. But Plick was a here-and-now kinda guy, and seeing as how he hated awkward moments, tried to fill the silence, as he so often did.

"The Keep. I forgot how big it is. Never been here when it's so quiet. Everybody's gone."

"The cleansing ritual," Gamble said, revealing that his timing indeed was intentional.

"Yeah. Right." Plick chuckled. "The cleansing."

Simultaneously recalling the last cleansing ritual they participated in more than a decade ago, the old running mates—and former best friends—broke out into laughter.

"Wait . . . wait . . . wait," Gamble said. "Remember the Master?"

Plick cleared his throat and hiked up his pants, to get into character. His voice boomed, mocking the ancient one. "Reeee-member, lit-tle ones. The cleansing ritual is for . . . the body . . . the mind and . . ."

Gamble finished the story. "And then Insley ripped the biggest fart ever! Classic!"

Plick smiled. "It's good to see you, G. Seriously."

"Yeah," Gamble said. "You, too."

They hugged it out.

Before long it occurred to them both that they should secure the room, verifying that Mandor and Candor were nowhere to be found.

Gamble went to the window. "Don't worry. I used the floating rabbit spell. They'll be chasing ghosts all night."

"*Good* one. I've been using the cat calls."

"Ohhhhhh." Gamble seemed impressed. "*That's* what it was. I heard it, but wasn't sure. I forgot all about that spell."

Plick smiled, revealing his vanity. "One of my favorites. Pretty simple, but it doesn't last too long. In fact," he re-checked his watch, "I'm probably due for another round. Hold on." Plick renewed the spell. "That oughta hold 'em for awhile."

"Good," Gamble said. "Let's get out of this room. It's giving me the willies."

"Agreed. Even for The Keep." A giant rat scurried along the floor just then, with a dead critter dangling from its mouth. "Hey," Plick said. "You hungry?"

The husky redhead nodded. "I could eat."

* * *

The corner galley was one of the smallest in The Keep, yet the most fun to pillage. Originally set up for the maintenance workers, over the millennia it shifted to a de facto party alcove, stocked with drink and snack foods of every sort.

On opposite sides of an island in the middle of the kitchen, Plick opened the cast iron ice box. "Whoa. This thing is loaded. Ale?"

Gamble already had his arm extended across the island, holding a large stein. Plick did the honors. The kitchen had several wood cabinets, two large cutting boards, a white, porcelain sink, and a slate floor. A yellow bird shot from a cuckoo clock next to the pantry. Eleven p.m.

"To old friends," Plick said.

"To being cuckoo."

Ale dribbled down their chins. Gamble then filled the room with a massive belch. Not to be outdone, Plick forced one out, but instead of a full-blown burp he drew up foam and bile, throwing up a little in his mouth.

Feeling that he had lost some stature, Plick tossed his stein into the sink, leaned against the counter, hand rolled a cigarette, then drew his finger along the slate, bringing up a flame. He lit the cigarette, inhaled, held the smoke, and then pushed out four rings, which dissipated into the words *Smoke 'em if you got 'em*.

Gamble chuckled.

Plick held out his cigarette pouch. "Want?"

"I quit."

"Really? Since when?"

"Since . . . I got busted on a job along the Yulberry River. One of the low rise castles. Had a beautiful diamond necklace and earrings set that would have carried me for six months. So I light one up in the mark's living room, to celebrate. Rookie mistake. Smoke tipped off the neighbors. Speaking of which . . . you should probably put that out."

Once again Plick felt like he was losing ground, trying too hard to impress Gamble when he should have been focused on the task at hand. He needed to course correct. "How long you do, after the bust?"

Gamble shook his head at himself. "Grenmore. Eight months. It would've been five, but I got into it with Smithy."

"Smithy! Oh, man! Wait . . . Smithy with the third eye or Smithy with the bad leg?"

"Bad leg."

"Right. Okay . . . . How is ole Smithy?"

Gamble surveyed the kitchen, then drew his hand along his red, spiked goatee. "Dead."

Plick froze. His mouth went dry. Smithy bailed him out of a jam once in Nady Heights, a debt he had intended to repay, and now never would.

Gamble exploded with laughter. "Nah . . . he's fine. We were playing *Run the Ghoul*, and I caught him with a *Power Lord* card up his sleeve. We got into a beef, tossing some spells back and forth, and next thing you know I'm in lock-up for an extra three months."

"Smithy," Plick said, smiling, relieved that Smithy was still alive and kicking. But he was still unsure if he could trust Gamble. A lot had gone down between them.

"Smithy," Gamble repeated, and then gestured toward the fridge. "Hey . . . they got any meat pies in there? I'm starving."

"No idea. Lemme check. I don't see . . . yep. Here we go. We got goat cheese, lamb, or batwing and olives."

"Mmmmm . . . batwing and olives. That sounds interesting."

"Hey. Dumbass. Kidding," Plick said, evening the score. "It's plain or Rump steak."

Gamble blushed, dropped his head. "Yeah, okay. I knew that."

With lamb pie and another stein of ale in their bellies, Plick finally asked a question that was lording over them. "Why'd you bail on me, G? Where'd you really go?"

Gamble's smile drew serious. His mouth hung open before

answering. "I . . . couldn't do it anymore, Plick. I just couldn't. It was one thing we got booted from The Keep, we were in it together. And then after that . . . yeah, we had a good run, me and you. How many jobs we pull? Two dozen? Three?"

"More. Forty at least."

"It wasn't a bad set-up, right? We'd make a score, live it up, go broke. Over and over." Gamble cupped the stein. "But ask yourself, Plick. How long could it last? How long before we ended up right back here, where it all began?"

Plick's heart began to thunder. "I . . . I don't know. It's just . . . you left me hanging, G. I was on top of the Arkney Caves with the three silver raven eggs in my satchel. We planned that heist for months. You were supposed to take the hand-off from me and fence them to Doris the Spindle, under the swamp. But you never showed. I lost the eggs, barely got out with my neck, and then had to go underground."

"Sorry, man. I just . . . I was on my way. I really was. But sometimes you just know it's over. I knew if I went out that night I'd screw up, and we'd get busted. And it would have been a long stretch for us both. I had to chance that you'd be okay. I'd been going through the motions for too long. I just didn't know how else to end it. Come on, Plick. We both knew it was time."

As much as Plick wanted to push back, he couldn't. They were twenty years old at the time, just twenty-five now, yet he felt closer to fifty. "I . . . I know, I know. It's just . . . I wanted it to last a little longer."

"Yeah." Gamble nodded. "Me, too." But then he stepped forward, hunched his shoulders, and rose up. The overhead light caught his red mane, which glowed behind his head. "So are we really gonna talk about this . . . or what? It's getting late."

Okay, Plick thought. *Here we go.* He nodded. "Let's do it."

Gamble nodded as well. "You're here for the *Occupacala* spell. So am I."

"Yes," Plick said. "It looks that way."

"We've some choices, then."

Plick offered him a smirk. "You could always walk away."

"So could you."

"Or . . . we both could. But that's not going to happen, now is it?"

"No chance," Gamble said.

"Right," Plick said. "No chance. So."

"So."

Plick would admit to being a fool in many respects, but he was no Fool. He knew that Gamble was bigger and stronger, with an unpredictable streak that had always made him difficult in combat. But he was also a half step slower than he thought he was, just enough to make him vulnerable. Still, it wouldn't be an easy contest, one that Plick could easily lose.

"Or," he proposed, "we could go halfsies."

Gamble tensed up at first, seemingly caught off guard at the proposal, but then shook his head, offering a chuckle. "Same ole, Plick. These aren't raven eggs we boosted. There's no haul to split. It's the *Occupacala* spell."

"You're right. It is."

The *Occupacala* spell wasn't just any spell. If utilized properly, it provided the ability to occupy and control another's mind, indefinitely. It was one of the most dangerous spells within The Keep, but also one that had gone missing at the time Gamble and Plick had been expelled from the order. That was no coincidence.

Plick saw opportunity here. "Here we are, G. Together again. Say whatever you want, but it was always supposed to be you and me. Partners. Like we started."

Gamble leaned forward on the island. He let his head bob a few times before looking straight ahead. "Listen, Plick. I've been waiting ten years to reclaim that spell, and so have you. It was always just a matter of who got here first. The thing is, I . . . owe you an apology. I . . . shouldn't have bailed on you that night. I can blame on it being young and stupid and completely burned out. And all of that is true. But I should have just told you I needed to go my own way. I handled it badly. I'm sorry."

Plick very much had the urge to jump into Gamble's burly arms and cry his eyes out. But that would have to wait. "Thanks, G. I appreciate that."

"Yeah, well . . . don't appreciate me too much. I actually owe you another apology."

"Okay." Plick exhaled through his nose. "Lay it on me."

Gamble was now standing upright. Firm. "I never should have partnered with you in the first place."

Plick tensed up. "Come again?"

"We were both in love with Nola, Plick. And because of it, she's gone."

The room began to rumble with pent-up magic just waiting to be unleashed. It would take very little for things to go real bad, real fast.

A cat burglar's first move is to leap off the ledge, and then hide in the shadows. But Plick didn't have that option. He recalled three spells he used to escape danger. Two of them were for distractions; the other was deadly. "We're going there, then?"

"Yeah." Gamble's hands started to glow orange. Tainted magic. "We're going there."

Plick raised his hands as well. They, too, were ripe with magic, glowing green. Had Plick followed the Path, his future held potential for greatness. "You had the parchment in a roll. You were supposed to meet me in Nola's room. We agreed."

"No-no-no," Gamble said. "*You* had the parchment."

"Did not."

"Did too."

"Dude." Plick tossed a magic bolt at the floor, scorching the tile. "Did. Not!"

"Did," Gamble retorted, and blasted a hole in the ceiling, followed by debris dropping to the floor, "too!"

They shifted into attack stances, at five paces. The oven was still hot. A half-eaten pie crust shifted to the edge of the island, about to fall over. The cuckoo clock struck. Eleven thirty. On the night they lifted the *Occupacala* parchment ten years earlier, about to conjure the spell—Nola went missing within The Keep. She hadn't been seen since. Nor had the parchment.

That the Master couldn't prove their involvement was the only reason Plick and Gamble were expelled from the Order rather than suffering a fate far worse. The Master, not one to easily accept blame, in this rare case blamed himself—for his negligence. He'd never gotten over it.

"Hold a second," Plick said. "Just wait a minute."

"Don't mess with me, Plick. I'm serious."

"I'm not, G. I'm not. Just wait a minute. Just *wait*. Let me think."

Breathing heavy, with glowing hands still extended, Plick glanced toward the hallway off the back bathroom, just beyond the kitchen. Gamble did the same. They looked at each other. Then back at the hallway. And then simultaneously they realized a critical mistake they had both made ten years ago, and as such had been harboring the same false assumption ever since.

"Nola," Plick said.

Gamble nodded. "*She* had it."

■ ■ ■

Nola's room was just as they remembered.

Known at first as the groundskeeper's daughter, Nola hadn't come to The Keep expecting to join the Order. But when she picked up levitation spells just by overhearing loose chatter, the Master invited her into the program.

Her skills advanced quickly despite the late start, and had all gone according to plan—which it most certainly hadn't—the Master envisioned Nola as perhaps one day becoming one of the more gifted wizards in his charge.

Plick and Gamble stood in the doorway. They stared into the large, half-moon mirror secured to her dresser, reflecting their images back at each other. They hadn't been in that room since they were fifteen years old, and though they internalized the decade that had transpired since, they were nevertheless stunned to see just how much the years had caught up with them. By biological standards they were both still young men, but in their unique context within The Keep, they were now old and beaten down, looking every minute of it.

They had gotten by after their expulsion from the Order, but living with broken dreams, and a broken heart, had taken its toll.

Gamble was the first to cross the threshold into Nola's room. He went to the dresser, and picked up Nola's hair brush, silver plated with three dragons twirled around the handle. "She was always brushing her hair with this." He let out a half smile. "Always."

"I remember. It was so long. Blonde."

"Brown," Gamble corrected. "Her hair was brown."

Plick ran his fingers along her bookcase, lined with all manner of fairy tales, adventures, spells, and potions. "Really? Are you sure? I always remembered it being blonde."

Gamble shrugged. "The years," he said. "My memory . . ."

Plick nodded. "Mine, too." He then went to her closet door, wood, like the walls. He put his hand on the silver, Cerberus-plated doorknob, to look inside, but stopped himself. "Stupid, right? I feel like if I open this door her skeleton will fall out."

"It won't."

"Yeah?" Plick was moderately suspicious. "How do you know?"

"Because if that happens I'll freak out, and I don't think I can really handle that. So, no, there's no skeleton in there."

Plick decided to take his word for it. He nevertheless inhaled, deeply, and closed his eyes as he pulled the door open.

"No!" Gamble shouted. "Holy crap cakes! Ah!"

"What? No!" Plick jumped back, and in doing so tripped over his own feet. He collapsed to the floor. But when he opened his eyes, all he saw in the closet were various shoes piled up at the bottom, dresses, pants, and blouses on hangers, and boxes stacked haphazardly on the upper shelf. "You jerk. You scared the ghoul out of me."

Gamble chuckled. "Batwing and olives, dude. Batwing and olives."

"Yeah, yeah. Help me up. I need to . . ." Down on the floor Plick could see underneath the bed. Mixed up with dirty socks, roller skates, two sweaters, and a scattering of papers he found a red box with a black, iron-clasp lock. He retrieved it, and then set it on top of the bed. But down on his knees, it occurred to Plick that he was vulnerable, if Gamble wanted to go that way. "Look at this."

Gamble approached. He raised his large hand. "Is that . . . ?"

Unsure which way Gamble was headed, Plick nodded, rolled to his side, and then shot up, with magic right beneath his palm.

"Yeah. I think so." He took a deep breath, exhaled, and reached for the metal buckle. The box was empty. But then Plick instinctively dug out the false bottom, which revealed a secret compartment underneath. Folded over were three parchments, marked in feather pen ink, in scripture, one each with the names *Nola*, *Plick*, and *Gamble*.

The night before their lives changed forever, before Nola and the *Occupacala* parchment went missing, they each made a list. And with it, a triangulated pinky-swear that they wouldn't reveal the name on their lists until they all graduated from the Order. A day that never came.

Plick announced the header: *"The person I love most."*

Gamble worked his wrists, and without further instigation grabbed the parchments from Plick, pushing him aside. "She said she wouldn't do that. She said she would never tell."

"Tell what, G? Tell what?"

"I can't let you read this. I just can't."

Plick put his hands up. "It's okay, dude. It's okay. Let's put them back. That's all. We'll stick them back in the box like we were never here. We can even hide them in the . . ." All the magic Plick had ever learned suddenly shot through him. "The leg! That's it! The leg!"

Gamble jerked back, and extended his hand, magic at the ready. "Leg? What leg? What are you . . . ?" His mouth hung open, the parchment still clenched in his tight fist. He looked at Plick, and then, with him, down at the floor. At the leg of the bed. The front left leg.

The Master was not what anyone would call touchy-feely, but he did mandate that every resident of The Keep was entitled to their own personal space, and did not tolerate violators of that edict. Teenagers were, however, teenagers—in their cases wizards-in-training—which meant that maintaining privacy was at best, tricky, and at worst, a futile endeavor.

To counteract the various eyes—and spies—lurking within The Keep, Nola hollowed out the center of the left front leg of her bed. Though just a few millimeters, it was still wide enough to hide pages from her diary, or notes she wanted Plick or Gamble to find.

Without further discussion, falling into their old cat burgling partnership, Plick peeled back the flat pouch around his waist, and removed the necessary instruments. Gamble got down on the floor, and lifted up the left side of the bed.

Plick knelt down, let out a long breath. "Okay," he said. "Here I go." With his left hand he deftly inserted the tip of his silver lock pick into the nub of wine-bottle cork that filled the end of, and thereby concealed, the hallowed-out bed leg. And like a surgeon removing shrapnel from a delicate artery, with his right hand Plick manipulated a set of tweezers to shimmy the cork free, careful not to let it splinter, or crumble into pieces that would be all but impossible to remove.

"Easy . . . easy . . . eaaaa-zeeeee . . . got it!"

Wide-eyed, Gamble smiled. "You always had good hands, Plick. Nice."

"Don't thank me just yet. But thanks." Plick laid on his back, popped the light crystal in his mouth, and shone it up the bed leg. "Yeah," he mumbled, "something's definitely here. Let me see if I can . . ." He inserted the tweezers into the leg, and with just the slightest nip was able to clasp onto the very tip of whatever was inside. "I'm there. I've got . . . something . . ."

He retracted his hand, slowly, and with it the edge of a parchment.

Gamble's breath drew heavy. His eyes bulged. "You got it, Plick. Oh, my heavens. After all these years. The *Occupacala* parchment. It's ours, it's ours, it's . . ."

Plick withdrew his arm. With it came a tightly rolled parchment, as thin as a pipe cleaner. He put down the tweezers and light crystal, wiped the sweat from his nose. He blinked deliberately, and then put his finger tips to the parchment, to unroll it. Until Gamble took his wrist.

"I think that's mine, Plick."

Plick looked up at the much larger Gamble, who had encroached upon him, to cut off the angles, leaving Plick, on the floor, unable to shift in place—a true logistical disadvantage. And, as Plick knew all too well, a classic Gamble move.

Gamble dropped the bed, which slammed down on Plick's ancient light crystal, cracking the core. It splintered.

"Halfsies," Plick said. "Like we said."

"Actually." Gamble squeezed Plick's hand until his fingers trembled with pain. "*You* said halfsies. I never said boo."

"But, G. Dude." Plick was wincing, his wrist about to snap. "We had a deal. Come on."

"You never learn, do you, Plick? That was always your problem. Still is. So desperate to be a team. You could never be on your own. Not then . . . and not now."

"Ah . . . ow. G. You're really hurting me. Please." The parchment fell from Plick's nearly broken fingers.

Using his boot, Gamble drew the parchment closer. "Don't worry, Plick. It'll all be over soon." He raised his massive fist, his free hand, about to club Plick across the jaw. "And you'll know exactly what hit you."

Yet before he could strike, a mist began to leak out from the hallowed out bed leg, which had a slight exposure thanks to being caught on the light crystal. And from that mist came a swirl, slow at first, but picking up in intensity until it formed a mini-tornado, tossing Plick and Gamble across the room, knocking books and picture frames from the shelves.

The tornado then morphed into a whirlwind of hair and arms, until, finally, it began to slow again so that before them both was the cause of their guilt and fear.

"Nola," Plick said. "Wow. Look at you . . ."

Nola stood, no longer a gawky teenage girl with a slight overbite and no bust, but a beautiful, fully developed young woman. She held out her arms, looked herself over, and nodded, impressed with her physique. "I know, right?" She stretched her arms up, clasped her hips, and bent forward. "Oh, *man* I need to do some pilates."

Gamble dashed for the doorway. But Nola tossed binding rings at him, slamming him against the wall, and secured him there, his mouth clasped shut. And with a levitation spell, Nola drew the parchment off the floor. "I'll take that."

Plick clasped his throbbing hand. He winced. "N-Nola. W-what happened? We looked for you *everywhere*."

"Not everywhere. Duh." Nola unrolled the parchment. "Ohhh . . . so that's what the whole thing looks like. I could only study it in fragments." She gestured to the bed leg. "Obviously."

Plick shook his head. "I . . . how? When? We were . . ."

"What, Plick? Going to steal the *Occupacala* parchment? Show the Master how clever we were? Impress everyone? Be the cool kids on campus?"

Plick whet his lips. "Well . . . yeah. Kinda."

Nola chuckled. "You know, Plick? It's like they say. 'The more things change the more it's just a shame.'"

"Uh . . . it's 'stay the same.'"

"What's the same?"

"The saying. 'The more things change the more they stay the same.' It's how it goes."

"Yes, Plick. I know. But in your case, it's really just a *shame*."

Plick didn't know what she was implying, but he was pretty sure that, whatever it was, it wouldn't be going his way.

"Being alone gives you time to think. And time to figure out who you are. Which you might find amusing, because . . . I loved you, Plick. I really did. As purely, naively, and dopishly as a fifteen-year-old girl could."

Unsure how to respond, Plick was all smiles—and fear.

"Go ahead." Nola clasped her fists, growing stronger by the minute. "Open the box. Take a look. I wrote your name there. You were so worried it might be Gamble, but that was never in the cards. Right . . . G?"

Fastened to the wall by magic, Gamble could do nothing but grunt.

Nola offered him a mock smile. "Thanks, G. Good chat." She drifted around the room. Her room. "That's the truth, Plick. I spent a year learning the misting spell. It was a surprise. I was going to teach it to you, so we could slip off whenever we wanted. Just you and me, and drift into the night sky, all the way to the clouds, and maybe even the moon. It was going to be so romantic. It's all I could think about. You were so nice to me back then. You weren't trying to *get* with me. You wanted to *be* with me." Nola drew her finger under Plick's chin. "But me being the teenage dolt that most teenagers are, I thought I knew more than I did."

Plick had waited a decade to find Nola, and even longer to know for sure whether or not she really did love him. And now that he knew, he wished that he didn't.

"You were a nifty little thief, Plick. That's what I loved about you. You knew how to be sneaky, but not mean. Always so mischievous. You brought me out of my shell." Nola smirked. "Which is ironic, actually, since I got stuck inside this one." She tapped the edge of the bed. "I practiced misting and de-misting hundreds of times. It got so easy I tried it in every room I could find. So finally I planned to mist up and squeeze inside the leg, pull the cork, from the inside, to keep the space secure, and then pop it right back out. Only . . ."

"You got stuck."

"Yeah. Stupid, right? I got stuck. I had the bed tipped back, but I guess not far enough, because it fell back on its spot, and jammed the cork in there. And with the weight of the bed, I couldn't move it. I was trapped."

Plick took a tiny step closer, the teenage boy in him still pining for his lost love. "We must have looked for you in here a thousand times. More even."

"I know. I heard. And *unnnn*fortunately . . ."

Plick's shoulders slumped. "We couldn't hear *you*."

"No," Nola said. "You couldn't. It was funny at first, ha-ha-ha, stupid me. Get me out and we'll all laugh about it later. But after a few hours . . . ? Not so much. Then after a few weeks, a few months . . . a few *years*, it was decidedly unfunny. How about you, Gamble? You think it's a joke. You think it's *funny*?!"

Her bellow startled Plick. But Gamble legitimately trembled.

"But you know what I realized, Plick? And I thought about it for a looooong, long time. Because trust me, there ain't nothing to do in that hallowed out leg. Nada. Nothing, except go over the details of your last day over and over and over until finally it all just," she snapped her finger, "clicks. The bed didn't just fall back down on the floor, now did it?"

"I-I . . . I don't know," Plick said. "I wasn't there. I wasn't—"

"Not you, Plick." Nola moved in on Gamble, who squirmed against the wall. "Him."

"Him? What do you mean? . . . G? What does . . . ?"

Gamble shook. "Mmmm . . . mmm . . ."

"Go ahead, G?" She flicked her wrist, removing his gag. "We're long past that now, aren't we? You never saw it, Plick? Did you? You don't see it now. The name? On our love lists? I wrote *your* name . . . you wrote mine. And G? Well . . . he wrote yours."

White light flashed before Plick's eyes. "W-wait. W-what?"

Nola chuckled. "It was so sweet, really. Here you two were, best friends in all the world, partners in crime. You with schemes, Gamble the muscle. Yet deep down so afraid that you were competing for my heart, when really . . . it was Gamble competing with me . . . for yours. I kept his secret, as I promised. But G? He knew I'd been practicing my misting spell, and knew what I had in mind. *You* pulled the bed down, didn't you, Gamble? You trapped me in that bed."

Plick put his hands up to his eyes and pressed until all he saw were swirls of black. "Oh, no no no." He shook his head, crushed beneath the weight of it all. "No. Oh, no."

"Oh, yes. But not to worry. While I was in that leg with our stolen parchment, I had loads of time to practice. So I did. And it was only last week that I finally had my chance. Don't know how, but a dust mite found its way in there with me. I wasn't sure if it would work . . . but I occupied his mind. It didn't turn out to be much of a challenge, let me tell you. There is seriously *not* a lot going on in there. Nevertheless, I got him to shimmy out of the leg . . . my first taste of freedom in a decade. And then I had him grab hold of a mouse, who was a little tougher to wrangle, but the longer I conjured the spell, the stronger it got. I went from a mouse to a hawk in the woods, a hawk to a golden retriever named Peaches—again, not a real thinker. And from Peaches . . ."

"You got to Dunbar," Plick said.

"Not bad, huh? A five transfer occupation . . . from inside this leg! Give it up, boys. Can I get an amen?" Nola lifted her hand, waiting for a high five. It didn't come. "Anyway . . . occupying Dunbar, I tipped you guys off about the parchment and the date of the cleansing ritual, and trusted that if you two put your itty bitty brains together you might form at least one coherent thought, and know where to look. Even the Master didn't know, so . . . kudos, boys. It reminded me of the old days. But still . . ."

"Ten years?" Plick said.

"Ten long, long, looooong years," Nola said. "*Long* years."

Still pinned to the wall, Gamble showed some fight. "So what now, Nola? Is this *really* how it ends?"

"The end of one chapter, the beginning of another." Nola conjured an owl clock just then, let the second hand tick along, about to strike twelve. "Nearly midnight, boys. The witching hour. The delight of devils, and ghouls, and . . ."

From the distance came two disturbing howls.

Plick turned to the window. "The hounds."

Nola nodded. "The hounds. Indeed."

Plick and Gamble turned to Nola. Their eyes filled with terror.

Nola offered them a smile, like that of a child pulling the wings off a butterfly. "What? Did you really think The Keep would be unguarded? That the hounds would be distracted by your dopey little tricks? Cat calls? Rabbit ghosts? Seriously? You thought the two of *you*, could infiltrate *The Keep*? Without help? Wow. Even for you."

"But why are you doing this?" Plick said. "You loved me. I loved *you*!"

"Yes. You did. And I really did, too. But you gave up on me, Plick. You left me here to rot. Stuck in the one secret place only you could know to look. And you *didn't*! You have any idea what that did to me? Trapped . . . *in the leg of this bed!* . . . with you just inches away, ignoring me, while I suffered. Not knowing if I'd ever get free."

"I didn't know! I swear! Please! Nola. I'm begging you."

"Begging time's over, Plick. It's time to say goodbye." With the flick of her eyebrows she released Gamble, who fell to the floor.

The burly redhead—her former friend—looked up at her. "What about the hounds, Nola? What do you want?"

"First . . . I need to pee, like . . . so bad. Then I'm going to order take-out. I've got a craving for ginger-sautéed Brodan noodles with the roasted hazelnuts. After that I'm going to put the *Occupacala* spell to really good use. Really. Good. Use. In the meantime . . . I'm back and I'm free and I'm gonna have me some *fun*. The Master and crew should be back within the hour. You could hang with me until then. Catch up."

Plick and Gamble stared at her.

"No? Didn't think so. You're definitely not getting the parchment, and you want no piece of the Master. And if my timing is right—and I'm pretty sure that it is—the hounds should be outside right . . . about," she turned to her conjured owl clock as the hands struck midnight, "now."

Plick couldn't be sure, but it felt like every clock in The Keep binged and bonged with a frequency designed to rattle his soul. With it, the howl of the hounds were upon them.

Nola pulled her hair back into a ponytail, then let it drop over her shoulders. It was brown after all. "So what happens next? That's entirely up to you. But might I make a suggestion?"

Reluctantly, they both nodded.

"Do right now what I couldn't for such a long, long time." Nola kissed Plick flush on the mouth. It was a kiss from a time long gone, transporting Plick to that distant, magical place, where he had been happiest of all. She ran her hand along his cheek, smiled wistfully, and took a step back. Then, as she had done in secret, drew back into a mist.

The howls grew louder. Mandor and Candor were right outside. Plick and Gamble went to the window. Their eyes, met by two pairs staring back at them, lit up with fright.

"Run," Nola said from the ether. Both a warning and a plea. "Run."

DEMON CIRCLE

by Peter David, Michael Jan Friedman, Robert Greenberger, Glenn Hauman and Aaron Rosenberg

from a first line contributed by Kevin Dilmore

"THERE'S NO WAY WE'RE GOING TO GET ALL OF THIS mopped up in time!" screamed Belid.

Athis had to admit to some small measure of satisfaction. After all, Belid was their master's star pupil, the one their master expected would carry on the glory of his mages' den. Belid was the handsome student, the charming student, the student their master showed off when prospective clients came to visit. Belid was the one who could already cure the blight—for a few weeks, at least—and fashion reliable love charms—for those already predisposed—and make someone invisible—if no one was looking too hard.

And yet, it was Belid who had screwed up.

Again.

"We're dead!" he groaned. "Dead!"

Athis might have sat back and enjoyed his fellow student's grief if he weren't in as much jeopardy as Belid was. The mess that they had made wasn't just going to be Belid's undoing. From all appearances, it was going to be Athis's as well.

But how did one clean up such a mess? It wasn't as if they had dropped a bowl of porridge on the floor, though Athis had done that often enough, much to the dismay of his master. No, this was a lot more than just porridge, and a lot uglier, and a lot smellier as well.

And porridge didn't need to be cleaned up in any particular

amount of time. In fact, if Athis's master was out of town on an assignment for some wealthy noble as he was today, a mess of porridge could sit there for hours without repercussions. Except for the smell, of course.

This mess, the one spreading across the floor at the moment like a red and yellow tide, was different from spilled porridge in that this mess apparently had an older brother. And that older brother would be arriving in a matter of minutes unless Belid could figure out a way to send the mess back where to the arcane otherworld it had come from.

"Don't just stand there," Belid yelled, "do something!"

"Me . . . ?" sputtered Athis.

"Yes, you! You're the one responsible for all this!"

Athis didn't quite see it that way. Summoning the demon Koliander had been entirely Belid's idea, as he remembered it. What Athis had done had merely been a consequence of that summoning, and an accident at that. Nonetheless, he studied the unholy pool of slop on the floor and tried to think of a way to get rid of it.

The most disconcerting aspect of the situation wasn't the stench, though that was certainly enough to get Athis's stomach churning. No, to his mind the worst part was that certain parts of the demon hadn't decomposed completely. Was that an arm sticking out on the side near the window? Athis thought so but couldn't be sure.

Meanwhile, Belid had cupped his face in his tanned, graceful, well-manicured hands. He was trembling, paralyzed with fear. If they were going to survive this, it was going to fall to Athis to step into the breach and get something accomplished.

Unfortunately, he wasn't the world's best student. A lot of his spells backfired, or had side effects, or just didn't work at all. When he tried to come up with a spell to help dissipate the odor, it only mostly worked. A sour smell still lingered. And when he attempted a containment spell, slowly pronouncing each word in order to manage the tongue-twisting syllables that normally tripped him up, it worked so slowly he thought it would go on forever.

Still, a slow haze finally covered the goo that was once

Koliander, a demon whose name Athis recognized but for the life of him couldn't recall a thing about. The haze solidified in stages and eventually became an opaque membrane, indicating that the spell was complete. That done, Athis rolled up the sleeves of his robe, not wishing to get them any dirtier than he had to, and crouched down to lift the demon's magically bagged remains.

"Damn, this is heavy," he said with a groan. "Give me a hand."

Belid pulled one hand away from his face and waved it before him.

"Not funny," said Athis. "Now get down here and help me lift it."

It was the first time he had ever given Belid an order, so it was surprising—even under the circumstances—when the more accomplished student obeyed it. Belid took his hands away, opened his eyes, and approached Koliander's remains. Then he sighed, bent down, and reached under the membrane-contained glop.

"Together now," said Athis.

He got a good grip on the demon's remains and made sure Belid had a chance to do the same. Then he nodded and lifted, and together they hefted the literal dead weight off the age-worn stones of the floor.

"Now, what?" asked Belid, still pale with fear. "Where do we put it?"

"I don't know," Athis said angrily. "I did the spell. Maybe you can figure out where to dump it."

"Dumping it's not going to do any good," said Belid, his voice rising in pitch. "We need to send it back where it belongs."

"Which neither of us knows how to do, right? So for now, we put this . . . stuff in the supply closet. At least until we come up with a better, more permanent solution."

Belid groaned. He was lazy by nature, the kind who always sloughed off hard work, more interested in looking like he knew what he was doing than actually learning all his lessons. And now this was the result.

"Fine," Belid said through gritted teeth, obviously not wishing to handle the awkward weight any longer than necessary.

Together they lugged their burden toward the heavy oak door that led into the walk-in supply closet. Upon arrival, they placed the remains of the one-time demon on the ground and opened the heavy door. Within, a brazier cast a flickering light on the shelves that were cluttered and piled deep with the tools of the mage's trade.

With a sigh, Athis directed Belid to go in and find a space for their burden. The star student stepped in, lifting his robes to keep from getting dust on the hem. He made his way into the back and Athis heard him moving things around as bottles clinked together and metal scraped against metal. After several minutes of this, Belid emerged, a fine sheen of sweat marring his perfect features, and dropped to his knees to help pick up the solid object.

"Your spell is faulty," Belid complained.

Athis tapped his toe atop the containment membrane and shook his head. "Seems fine to me."

"Not that. The smell."

Athis bent down and took a whiff. Sure enough, there was a nauseating tang filling the air. The demon's remains were starting to stink even through the containment skin.

"Figures," said Athis.

His enchantment to stop the smell, imperfect from the start, was wearing off even faster than he had anticipated. And that was why, in his master's oft-expressed estimate, he was still years away from the final tests that would let him leave the mage's school—and Belid—behind.

There was only one spell Athis had really mastered. Well, mostly mastered. He glanced down at the demon's remains again. If only he could get internal and external reduction rates to match!

But that was something to figure out some other time. Right now he needed to concentrate on the task at hand.

"Never mind that," he told Belid. "Let's lift."

They lifted. Athis backed into the room, letting Belid direct their path. Once they had shoved the demon's remains as far back as possible onto a seldom-used shelf, they began taking vials and jars from the other shelves and using them to conceal their burden from sight.

"Ewww, what is that stench?"

The two students started and looked around guiltily, but fortunately the question had carried from out in the hall. Their first inclination was to remain in hiding but with the door open, the speaker would surely come and find them.

"Go," Belid hissed. "I'll finish covering it up." Athis nodded and all but ran toward the door and the questioner beyond.

As he exited the closet, he found himself face to face with Klaria, one of their fellow students. Klaria's hair was always kept closely-cropped, giving her a martial appearance despite the curves and robes. Hands on her shapely hips, she stared at him piercingly and asked, "What have you done this time?" she asked. "No, wait, you never start trouble. You're usually left to clear up Belid's . . . messes."

The youth in question emerged from behind Athis, brushing dust from his deep blue robes, smiling brightly at the attractive brunette despite the turmoil he had to be feeling. "Klaria my dear, so good of you to join us."

"What did you do?" she asked.

Athis gave her his wide-eyed "what me?" look, the one he usually used on their teacher.

"Yes, you. Spill."

When Athis hesitated, Klaria moved past him and then past Belid as well, and bent to examine the floor for the source of the hideous smell. A moment later, she stood up triumphantly, a fingertip smeared with a bit of the demon.

"What's this?" she demanded.

"We were talking about the demon war," said Belid, his voice little more than a whisper. "The master was saying that news is sparse, and that we need to learn more. So I thought . . . that is . . ."

Klaria's eyes opened wide. "That you'd summon one of the combatants and quiz him? You're an idiot. Where is he?"

Athis couldn't help but glance towards the supply room, its door still ajar.

"Oh, really? Hiding him in the broom closet? How original!" Klaria sneered. "Fine, let me at him." And, before either of the youths could stop her, she'd shouldered past and flung the door open. "Hello?" she called out, stepping into the supply room. "Mister Demon?"

Athis followed her in, shaking his head. This was bound to not go well.

"What do we do?" Belid hissed at him, falling into step. At least he had the presence of mind to shut the door behind him once they were all inside. No sense inviting still more people to the party!

"How the hell should I know?" Athis hissed back. "This is your problem, you fix it!"

"My problem? You killed him!"

Athis winced and tried to hush the other apprentice, but it was too late.

"Killed? Killed who? Who killed him? What?" Klaria spun around and, with two quick steps back, was in their face. "You killed the demon?"

"We didn't mean to!" Athis protested.

"It was all his fault!" Belid whined at the exact same time.

They glared at each other.

"I can't believe you two!" Klaria shook her head. "All right, what happened?"

"Well, we summoned Koliander—" Belid started, but her gasp stopped him.

"Koliander? You summoned a Koliander? Are you insane?"

"What?" Belid managed to look embarrassed, annoyed, and blasé, all at the same time. "His name was handy!"

"Handy? Of course it was—it's only in every demon history text EVER!!!" Klaria's eyes had grown a little wild, a condition which Athis couldn't help noticing looked remarkably attractive on her. Not many people could pull off the panicked look and still be that striking, but on her it worked. Then he started to focus in again on what she was saying.

"Wait," he said, "what?"

"I said, which Koliander was it?" She pronounced each word slowly and clearly, as if she were speaking to an idiot or a child. Which was probably exactly what she thought of her fellow apprentices right now. And Athis suspected his answer wasn't going to help that any.

"Um—I dunno," he asked. "How can you tell?"

The glare she gave them both could have frozen a firebeast in its tracks. "The horns? Hello? Do you remember anything we learn in class? Ever?"

"Oh, right," said Athis. Demons measured their rank by their horns, not only according to length but also color and shape. Athis frowned and tried to remember what this demon's had looked like. It was all a bit of a blur. "Um, they were about this long"—he held his hands up maybe two feet above his head—"and sort of reddish-brown, with a faint sheen to them like they were glass."

Belid nodded in agreement.

Klaria stared at them, her face now gone completely white. "This long?" she asked finally, her voice barely a squeak now as she matched Athis's estimate, "or THIS long?" She moved her hands up a bit higher in the air.

"Oh, yeah, I guess that could be right too," he admitted.

Belid nodded again. Klaria got even paler. For a naturally dark-complected girl, she could get really fair really quickly!

"Koliander the Undying," she whispered. "You summoned Koliander the Undying. And you KILLED him?"

"Um. Yeah. I guess." Athis tried desperately to remember any of those lessons. "Is that bad?"

"Where did you put him?" The words were sharp as cut glass.

"Over this way." Belid leaped into action, probably just as an excuse to get out from under Klaria's eyes. He led the way into the shadowy depths of the storage room, Klaria stalking right behind him and Athis reluctantly bringing up the rear. Finally they reached the shelf where they'd set the demon's remains—

Only the space was empty.

"Oh, come on!" Belid turned and glared at Athis. "Can't you even get a simple containment spell right?"

"What? Like any of this is my fault!" Athis lunged forward and would have wrapped his hands around the other youth's perfect neck if Klaria hadn't stepped in between them.

"Enough!" Her cry echoed off the rough stone walls. "We need to find him. Now."

"Absolutely!" Belid nodded vigorously. "If our master finds

those remains before we do—"

Klaria grabbed him by the front of his tunic and literally shook him, punctuating each shake with a word. "There. Are. No. Remains!"

"What?" Athis wasn't sure whether to stop her or help her, but he did want to know what she meant. "Of course there are— we killed him. Well, I killed him. I didn't mean to—I meant to make a mouse." That didn't sound right. "What I mean is—what do you mean, no remains?"

"Argh!" One hand detached from Belid's tunic and latched onto his. "He's called the Undying for a reason, you dolt! He can't be killed!"

Athis didn't get it. "But—we killed him!"

"No, you just disrupted him for a moment! And as soon as he recovers, he'll come back even stronger! And kill whoever did that to him, plus anybody else in their immediate vicinity!" As if just now realizing what she was saying, Klaria released both of their robes and thrust them away for her, taking a step or two back for good measure.

"So he's not dead?" Belid brightened. "Excellent, then we didn't kill him after all!"

Now it was Athis's turn to shake his fellow apprentice. "Didn't you hear her, idiot? He's going to kill us!"

"But," said Belid, "at least his brother won't be mad anymore."

Athis hadn't thought Klaria could get any whiter, but she was now almost the color of a fresh linen sheet. "His . . . brother?"

"Yeah, he said something about a brother," Athis told her. "Right before we apparently didn't kill him. Something about his older brother coming after him to avenge him."

For a second he thought Klaria was going to claw her way through the outer wall with her bare hands. "His brother is com- ing here?"

"That's what he said." Belid was brushing a bit of dust and lint off his garments. "Why, is that a problem?"

"A problem?" Klaria said. "Is it a problem? I don't know, do you think having the supreme commander of the entire demon army show up here looking for his brother, whom you just tried to destroy, is any sort of a problem?"

Her voice had gotten louder with each word, and by the end Athis's head was ringing from the shouting. Shouts that apparently jarred loose a memory or two—maybe he'd listened to a few of those demon history lectures after all!

"Markindo?" He dredged the name out of those hazy recollections. "Markindo the Dragon? He's coming here?" He gulped. He couldn't remember much, but he was fairly sure that descriptor wasn't a reference to the demon's favorite tattoo.

"Apparently, yes," Klaria agreed. "Because you summoned his brother Koliander the Undying, his second in command. And then killed him, or at least made the attempt. Do you even have a brain, or did it all dribble out onto your robes during potions practice?"

Athis wasn't sure which answer would be safer there, so he just let that go.

Belid, however, had finally realized the gravity of their situation. "The demon commander? Coming here? For us?" He gulped. "That's bad, right?"

"Well it's sure as hell not good!" Klaria snapped back.

"What're we going to do?" Almost as an afterthought, Belid slapped Athis across the chest. "This is all your fault!"

"It is not!" Athis hit him back.

"Is too!"

"Not!"

"Too!"

"ENOUGH!!!" cried Klaria.

Athis stopped in his tracks, as did Belid, and turned back to Klaria.

"It doesn't matter whose fault it is," she told them, her voice going surprisingly low and calm, "because the bottom line is, when Markindo arrives, he's going to kill all of us out of hand, just for being in his path."

"Okay," said Belid, looking like he was thinking fast for a change, "so we get as far away from here as we can. I think I've just about got that flying spell down now, and that should get me at least as far as Tirano Castle, and from there I can—" The slap knocked his head back and shut him up in mid-panicked sentence.

"We need to focus," Klaria warned, shaking her hand. Athis wondered if it stung half as much as Belid's cheek, which was reddening. Probably not.

"We need to find Koliander," Klaria continued.

"The one who wants to kill us?" Belid shook his head. "Nuh-uh. Bad idea."

"We need to find him," Klaria repeated slowly, "and explain that it was an accident. Get him to call off his vengeance, then convince him to stop his brother from showing up at all."

"Nice!" Athis gave her a quick one-armed hug, but backed off when she looked like she might tear his arm off at the shoulder. "Great idea, Klaria! We'll do that!"

"Sure, sure," Belid agreed. "How hard can it be, right? We're only looking for one demon, after all. And this castle isn't that big—we should be able to find him in no time!"

Both Athis and Klaria looked at him like he was nuts. "Not that big?" Athis echoed. "The Crimson Keep?"

The place renowned for its thousand rooms and hundred staircases? Reputed to never stop growing or shifting as the result of an old spell gone slightly awry? The wizard's castle that, it was said, apprentices could get lost in forever, and where it was rumored that servants could reappear after months gone to explain that they'd only been heading down to the cellar for another cask of salt?

Athis himself had gotten lost once, during his first year, and had wandered for what felt like months but turned out later to only be three weeks before following a well-fed rat back to the cheese cellar and from there up to the more familiar and more stable portions of the castle.

This was the place that Belid thought would be easy to search?

He looked at Klaria and shrugged. Did they really have a choice?

"Where should we start?" he asked, as they retraced their steps through the storage room door. "Should we split up to cover more ground, or stick together in case we get lost—or the demon finds us first?"

"What about a spell?" Belid asked instead. "Can't we just

whip up a locator, find the demon, and then use a translocation to take us there?"

"Sure," Klaria answered. "You do that." She crossed her arms and started tapping her foot. "Well? Go ahead!"

"Um, well, right. Athis, take care of it," Belid instructed.

Athis just snorted and shook his head. He knew the basics for a locator spell, but the last time he'd tried it to find a wayward sock he'd turned the sock purple and unraveled it as well, spreading the yarn all across his room. He didn't think that was going to help endear them to Koliander or his brother, and that was assuming it worked on demons the same way it did on stray footwear.

As far as a translocate, he wasn't even about to try one of those! He shuddered at the memory of Randall, a student who'd thought he was ready for that particular feat. They still avoided the third corridor on the fifth level, where his face peeked out from one of the columns.

"We stick together," Klaria declared. "It's the only way I can be sure you two imbeciles don't get into any more trouble."

Athis wasn't about to complain. Even with her sharp tongue, he'd still rather spend time with Klaria than with Belid. At least he thought so. If she slapped him the way she had slapped Belid, though, all bets were off.

"Fine, fine," he agreed. "Now, if you were an undying demon that had just been mistakenly summoned and then accidentally sort of killed and had just returned to life, where would you go?"

The three of them stared at each other for a second. Then they all answered at once:

"The kitchen!"

Belid took off at a dead run, feet flying as he raced down the corridor like the legions of Hell were behind him—which they very well might be, before too long. Athis sprinted after him, and Klaria kept pace easily, her long, shapely legs eating up the distance.

The kitchen was at the castle's center, one of the sections that got daily use and thus rarely shifted, and they had all long since learned the quickest route there, so they were able to navigate the corridors and stairs and courtyards with ease—at least, until they passed through the small secondary rear courtyard and reached the kitchen itself.

What they saw there stunned them all to a standstill.

■ ■ ■

Their Master was seated at the table, eating a sandwich.

He had prepared it with his usual meticulousness. The Master, it was generally conceded, could easily just wave his hand and the food would miraculously appear in front of him. But he was old-fashioned in some respects, and when it came to food preparation, he typically preferred to attend to such matters himself.

There were crumbs on the table where he had meticulously sliced the bread. A leg of mutton was on the sideboard from which he had carved several thin strips of meat that he had laid between the two slices. Some fruit was carved up as well; the Master typically preferred to carve his food into as small pieces as possible. He said it enabled him to prolong the experience that way. A stein filled with what could safely be assumed to be mead from his private store was on the table next to him, with a nicely foamy head atop it.

None of the apprentices knew the Master's actual name. It was a closely held secret, for names had power and the Master was disinclined to give anyone that degree of power over him. "These are dangerous times," he would say, "and caution must be our watchword." That was what he said, at least. There were those of his students who contended that he had simply forgotten what his name was because he was so damned old, and even a few who privately thought that the Master's birth occurred before the whole "names" thing came into style. Back when there were so few people around that names simply weren't a necessity because people could just say, "Hey! You! Over there! With the brown hair! Come here!" and you just knew they meant you.

Whatever the reason, be it power, old age, or lack of precedent, the Master was simply referred to as "Master." It just seemed the simplest way to go.

The fact that the Master was there was not the only surprise before Athis and his companions, however. Even more astonishing was the stunning young woman seated directly across from him. A young woman Athis had never seen before.

She was quite possibly the most exotic woman that he had ever beheld. Her skin was nearly as pale as a candle, and the comparison was furthered by the orange-ish yellow sheen to her eyes, as if they were flames burning on wicks. Pale blonde hair, so light that it was almost white, cascaded around her shoulders and her head in copious amounts. She was wearing a pale blue dress that, for some reason, looked vaguely familiar to Athis, although he couldn't quite figure out why.

Then he caught Klaria's urgent glance. She looked concerned for some reason, and his eyebrows knit in an unspoken question. Indicating the woman seated there, she mouthed the words, *That's my dress. She's wearing my dress.*

"Master!" Belid said, his voice ascending an octave in his nervousness. He cleared his throat and started again, trying to sound casual. "Master, we . . . ah . . . we weren't expecting you. We had thought you were out of town. Working for a noble. A wealthy noble."

"You thought correctly," said the Master mildly. He brushed some of the crumbs from his thick white beard.

"You're back early," Athis said.

"Wizards," the Master replied archly, "never arrive early or late, but instead precisely when we mean to." He studied their expressions, the way they were staring at him. "You seem rather tense over the notion that I've returned before you were expecting me. Is that the only matter of any substance before us? Is it possible that there is something you are not telling me?"

The three young wizards cast nervous glances between each other. No doubt Klaria would have been happy to rat out the other two, but she was clearly too distracted by this woman outfitted in her garb. It made no sense to Athis. Why would some woman have shown up out of nowhere and grabbed a dress out of Klaria's closet? What was she, someone who had arrived unexpectedly naked in the midst of—

Oh no. Oh, gods no . . .

"Something such as," the Master continued, indicating the young woman with a nod of his head, "who this charming young woman might be? She is, I assume, a friend of one of yours?"

Athis tried to speak but his mouth was completely dry. Belid didn't seem to be having much better luck in uttering a word, much less forming a coherent thought. Seeing that her two fellow students were having trouble speaking, Klaria quickly said, "Me. Mine. My friend, I mean. Master, this is . . ."

"Lia," said the blonde woman, extending a slender hand in a most delicate fashion. The Master, ever the gentleman, took it and kissed it suavely on the knuckles. "My friends call me Lia."

"Delighted, my dear," the Master said. He held her hand a moment longer before reluctantly relinquishing it.

He's flirting with a demon. We're all going to hell for this, thought Athis desperately. *Straight to hell.* He looked toward Belid, having no idea how they were supposed to handle this.

That was when he heard a voice in his head that wasn't his own thought: *What's he playing at?* He jumped slightly and then glanced at Klaria, who was nodding almost imperceptibly. Of all the students in the wizard's class, Klaria had always been the most proficient when it came to thoughtcasting. Full credit to her that she was able to maintain the focus required to thought-project in such a situation such as this one.

"He" meaning the Master? Athis thought. He had no talent for projecting thoughts himself but Klaria had opened up the connection between them, so he was effectively coasting upon her abilities.

No, you idiot. "He" meaning the demon!

He's a she at the moment, Athis pointed out.

I noticed that. Something about the ripe bosoms tipped me off. Where are his horns?

He switched genders, thought Klaria, *and that's the only thing you're wondering about?*

Oblivious to the heated exchange of thoughts that was going on, the Master was leaning forward toward Lia. His voice was softer, his body language was different. Was it possible that he was actually smitten with "her"?

Athis was appalled by the notion that the Master even cared about such matters. Wasn't he incredibly ancient? Didn't ancient men stop caring about such things at some point?

"And what," Lia inquired in a low, seductive tone, her large eyes fixed upon the Master, "is your name?"

"Ah," the Master said, "I'm afraid I can't tell you that."

"Whyever not?"

"Oh, there are reasons."

"Well," said Lia, "that's very unfortunate. And here I thought we were getting along so well." She rested her hand atop his and the Master smiled in a way that Athis had not only never seen before, but wished he wasn't seeing now.

Oh my gods, said Klaria in his head. *I'm getting it.*

Getting what? Nauseated? Athis thought back at her.

No! Don't you understand? Koliander is going to try and seduce the Master into telling him . . . telling her . . . his true name. If he does that, the demons can use it in their castings to control or even kill him somehow. And with him in their clutches . . .

There's no limit to the damage they can do, Athis realized in horror.

At which point "Lia" ran her fingers through the Master's beard and said softly, "Perhaps we can take this conversation somewhere more . . . private."

"No!" the three apprentices shouted in unison.

The Master turned his head, surprised that they were still in the room. "I beg your pardon?"

"Sir, you couldn't possibly leave yet."

The Master's brow furrowed, and his eyes sparked dangerously. "And why not, pray tell?"

"Because . . ." said Athis.

"Because . . ." said Belid.

". . . because dinner will be ready in a few minutes!" Klaria blurted out.

"Yes, of course," said Athis, "we couldn't possibly let our guest go hungry!"

"Right," Belid added, "anything she wants to ea—ouch!"

Athis could hear Klaria's thought to Belid as she took her weight off his foot. *You idiot, don't give the pretty demon a standing invitation to eat anything . . . she'll start with us.*

"Good!" said the Master. "I expect a wonderful dining experience for us tonight."

"But you've just eaten," Koliander said, using a voice that could have made a priest rend his robes to ribbons.

"I'm a man with a large . . . appetite."

"Oooo, I just knew you were. Very large, I'll wager."

"I look forward to showing you. More wine?"

"Oh, I really shouldn't . . . but you talked me into it, you smooth devil."

"You have no idea."

I sincerely hope this is some effect the demon has on him, Athis thought.

The Master picked up the wine bottle, then shook it—clearly empty. He turned to Klaria. "Girl, fetch me some more wine."

"Uh . . . Master, I don't know what I should pick."

"Whatever goes well with the dinner you're preparing, child. Get on with it."

"But, sir, I would want to choose something very special for your very special guest, and you have much more knowledge of the wines in the cellar. Could you come down there with me and help me choose something appropriate?"

The Master muttered under his breath, then slowly got to his feet. "My dear," he told Lia, "if you would pardon me for just a moment, I will endeavor to return with something exemplary for you. Something very . . . full bodied."

"And sweet and smoky, I hope."

"As the lady requests." He turned to Athis and Belid. "Boys, keep our guest company, and stay on your best behavior. Any . . . offense . . . will be dealt with harshly. Come, girl." The Master gathered up his robes and left the kitchen, with Klaria looking back over her shoulder . . . as if she might never see them again, Athis thought to himself.

Lia/Koliander looked at the departing pair, then slowly turned back to Athis and Belid. "Sooo . . ." she purred, "here we are. Alone at last." Her gaze smoldered even more. "It's a shame I'm no longer . . . horny."

"Listen," said Athis, "I'm really, really sorry we killed you—"

"We didn't kill her," Belid rasped. "I mean him. We didn't kill him."

"Ah," said the demon, "but you did."

"But you're still here," said Athis.

"You're deathless," Belid added.

"Doesn't matter," Lia insisted. "The intent is what counts. You tried to kill me, actually thought you killed me, and would no doubt have killed me if it were even remotely possible to do so. In case you were wondering, this puts me in a rather testy frame of mind."

"Understandably," said Athis, jockeying for an angle though verbal maneuvering had never been his strong point. "But if you please, put yourself in our place. There you were, all unexpectedly, since we had never really summoned a demon before, and we panicked, miserable creatures that we are. And then that went wrong, so very, very wrong, and things just got a little out of hand. We made a mistake. Surely you have made a mistake in the course of your long, long life?"

The demon shook her head from side to side. "Never. And I am thinking it would be a grave mistake indeed to allow you two to get away with what you did to me. It would give others the idea that such an affront could be tolerated. I'm sure you understand that I'd want to eliminate such a precedent."

"Of course," said Athis, trying to be reasonable.

Belid elbowed him in the ribs. "What are you saying?"

Indeed, thought Athis, *what am I saying?* "Er . . . while I see your point," he told the demon, "I think there is another way of looking at the matter."

"Really?" said Lia. "I would be curious to hear it. It will amuse me while I consider the most satisfying way to rend you limb from limb."

"Right," said Athis, thinking harder than he had ever thought before in his life, "you see . . . um, that is . . ."

"You don't want anyone to know about this!" Belid blurted out.

Pale blonde eyebrows rose in confusion. "Don't want them to know about what? That you killed me? True, but once they see the manner in which I responded everyone will know better than to try the same thing themselves."

"No, not that." Belid was sweating, but Athis thought he saw an all-too-familiar gleam in the other apprentice's eye. "This."

And he gestured at her bosom.

"What, this?" Koliander laughed. "Why ever not?"

Yes, why not? Athis wondered, but Belid had a response ready. "Because how would it look if word got out that Koliander the Undying, one of the most fearsome demons in existence, was forced to disguise himself as a mere woman in order to escape detection?"

"I am not disguised to escape detection!" the demon snapped, and Athis saw the hint of horns pushing out from her fair forehead as rage started to distort the shape-change. "I have altered my form to elicit the name of our ancient enemy, your Master, the better to destroy him!"

"That's not what people will think," Belid pointed out. "That may be what you meant, but when people hear that you turned yourself into a pretty little girl—"

"Young woman," the demon interrupted, "thank you very much!"

"—little girl," Belid continued, ignoring the correction, "everyone will assume it was out of fear. You were helpless in the Crimson Keep, after all, surrounded by deadly foes, unarmed, unclothed even, and so all you could do was cower and hide. In a little girl's body."

"I. Am. Not. Hiding!" As she rose to her feet her form began to shift, the shoulders bulking out, the arms lengthening, the forehead distending in two sharp points, the jaw widening, the skin darkening. Athis took a step back, and grabbed Belid's arm when his fellow apprentice didn't budge. Was he mad, goading the demon like this?

"No, you're not," Belid agreed, and his voice was surprisingly calm. "But that doesn't really matter, does it? It's all about what people think. And that's what they'll all think when they hear about this."

"Not when I raze the Crimson Keep to the ground!" Koliander's voice had changed as well, the dulcet tones gone, the lilt turned gravely, the words distorted by the prominent fangs that were starting to sprout from upper and lower jaw. Athis didn't remember the demon looking this fearsome when they'd first summoned him, but then again it had all happened so fast. He was getting a good look now, though, and wished he weren't.

Yet Belid, who normally was so useless, remained uncowed. "It won't matter," he insisted, and his tone was the same snotty one he used when he was lording it over Athis and Klaria and some of the others, after he'd done something stupid and they'd been forced to help him cover it up. "No matter what you do, if word leaks out about the form you took, everyone will laugh about it. Forever. You'll be a laughing stock. Koliander the Little Girl, they'll call you."

Koliander leaned in, his heavy face looming down on them, most traces of the lovely young woman now vanished, and his breath stank of decay and death and damnation. "And how, pray tell, would they hear of this, little human? When I shall rend the flesh from your bones and the light from your soul, and do the same to all of your little friends?"

And, amazingly, Belid had an answer for that as well. "Thoughtcasting."

"Thoughtcasting?" Athis asked it just as Koliander did, but no one seemed to notice.

"Yes. Specifically, the sort carried out by our friend and fellow apprentice, Klaria. You remember her, don't you? You should—it's her dress you're wearing." A dress that was now badly stretched, and splitting in several places. "She's with the Master, in the wine cellar. By now she's told him all about you, but that's not the really important part. What is important is that she's also been linked in to the two of us the whole time, and has heard this whole conversation. And right now she's thoughtcasting to everyone she knows, all over the kingdom. And telling them all about your pretty little guise." And he grinned—actually grinned!—up at the crazed demon. "I can almost hear the laughter already."

Amazingly, the demon actually paused. He straightened, his face no longer inches from theirs, and his horns even shrank back a bit. His features smoothed and his skin paled as he thought Belid's argument over. Athis held his breath.

Finally, after a second that seemed to last an eternity, Koliander backed up a step. And shrank back down all the way into his alluring female form. With a decidedly female grace,

"Lia" settled back into her chair.

"What exactly do you propose?" Her voice was still a little deeper than it had been, but almost back to its sexy huskiness— and worlds better than the terrifying growl of a second ago.

"Simple," Belid replied. "We all forget all about this little . . . incident. You depart at once. When the Master returns, we tell him you were called away—a family emergency or some such. We never tell anyone you were here, you never tell anyone you were here, and everyone forgets about it. No harm done, and your reputation is secure."

"But your friend has already thoughtcast everyone about it," the demon noted. "The damage is already done. Or was that simply a feint on your part?" Athis heard the edge to that question, and hoped Belid had done so as well.

He needn't have worried. If there was one thing Belid excelled at, it was getting out of trouble. "Oh, she did," he answered readily, and Athis couldn't tell if that was the truth or not. He hoped the demon couldn't either. "But she's planted it as a subliminal thought, to be released upon news of our death and the keep's destruction. If that never happens"—he shrugged—"the thought will never surface."

Clever, Athis was forced to admit. And the demon clearly thought the same, judging by her nod. "Very well," she said, though it was clear the words pained her. "I will depart, and we will speak of this nevermore." For an instant, her eyes flared with a painful light, and smoke seemed to rise from her temples. "And know that if you do speak of it, I will return, and my vengeance will be fearsome indeed."

"Oh, absolutely," Athis agreed quickly, his knees threatening to collapse on him from sheer relief. "Trust me, we won't say anything. We know better." He glanced at his companion, but Belid was already nodding agreement as well.

The demon rose from the table again, though this time she retained her composure and her attractive appearance the entire time. "I will be glad to be rid of this guise," she admitted, glancing down at her form, "and of this entire experience."

As will we, Athis thought privately. *As will we.*

But it seemed that the danger might be past. And that they

might make it out of this alive.

Which was when he noticed the kitchen's back wall. And the fact that it was starting to shimmer as if an intense heat were radiating from it.

Now what?

Belid followed his glance, his jaw dropping as he spotted the heat shimmer. And his expression made Koliander turn to study the phenomenon as well. When the demon's lovely eyes went wide and her mouth formed a soundless gasp, Athis knew they were in trouble. Again.

"No, not now!" Koliander cried, her voice exactly that of a fair young maiden suddenly confronted with a terrible, almost unbearable horror. "Not now!"

"What?" Athis didn't really want to ask, but he knew he had to. "What's happening?"

The gaze she turned upon him showed sheer terror, and the words that followed made him feel faint. "My brother. It's my brother. He's coming!"

"Markindo?" Athis found he could barely speak through the wave of fear washing over him. "Markindo the Dragon is coming?"

"Yes!" Somehow Koliander had made her way around the kitchen table, and now she clutched Athis by the shoulder. "You can't let him find me! Not like this!"

"Why?" He was confused. It didn't help that his brain felt like it was made of grape jelly. "He's coming to rescue you, right? Or avenge your death?"

"Yes! When I die, he senses it, and he eventually arrives to ensure that my body is still intact enough for me to revive, and that my vengeance is complete! But he can't find me here! Not now!"

"But you're okay," Belid pointed out. "You're fine. Can't you just tell him it was some kind of mistake, and convince him to leave, too?" The entire wall was aglow now, the rough stones there practically invisible, but Athis thought it looked as if they were melting. He could feel the heat radiating from that section of the room, and on the table the Master's lunch was beginning to smoke and smolder.

"It doesn't work like that," Koliander was explaining, her tone still desperate. "He sensed my death. He'll know it was real. He's primed and ready to attack. And once he realizes this is the Crimson Keep, nothing will be able to hold him back. Plus, if he sees me like this—" she waved a hand at her curvaceous body. "—I'll never hear the end of it!" Then the demon said the last thing Athis would ever have expected:

"You've got to help me!"

Over her head—her beautiful, silken-haired, sweet-smelling head, he couldn't help noticing—Athis locked gazes with Belid. His fellow apprentice looked as shocked and confused as he felt.

To make matters worse, Athis heard the unmistakable sound of footsteps approaching from the lower stairs. The stairs that led up from the wine cellar. Klaria was on her way back up. With the Master. The Master, who was smitten by the disguised Lia, and who was the mortal enemy of the demons Koliander and Markindo. The Master, who had no idea what was going on, and would attack the demons if he recognized them, with the resulting magical conflict most likely causing all their deaths. The Master, whose lunch was now fully aflame on the table behind them.

What were they going to do?

Athis, Klaria's voice sounded in his head.

Where the hell have you been!?

They spoke very quickly then, since mental communication tended to transpire far more quickly than normal speech: literally as fast as the speed of thought.

You know where I've been! In the wine cellar! I was out of range.

Thoughtcasting has range?

When you're still learning the ropes? Yes. She sounded irritated. *I'm holding a conversation with you and I'm still five hundred feet away. You'd think that alone would be sufficiently impressive for you.*

Did you tell the Master everything? Tell him Lia's true nature?

Of course not! He'd go berserk if he found out. Between the demon's fury and the Master's wrath over your actions, to say nothing of his being openly smitten with a creature of evil, you'd probably have better luck taking your chances with mercy from the demons. Plus he would probably smack the daylights out of me for failing to ride herd on you.

He moaned inwardly. *And the whole thing about the subliminal thought trigger . . .*

Subliminal what? What in the name of Hecate are you talking about?

Dammit. So Belid was bluffing.

About what?

Another advantage of mental communication was that one could shorten the process of recounting things. Athis simply recalled the entire exchange between Belid and Koliander and effectively dumped it all into Klaria's head.

Oh my gods, Klaria's appalled reaction came back. *Your survival is hinging on a stone cold bluff?* Then a reluctant touch of admiration came through. *Remind me not to play poker with Belid. Anyone who can deceive a demon under those circumstances . . .*

Klaria! Can we focus?

Okay, okay. During the time that Athis and Klaria had been communicating, barely a second had passed. Koliander was still standing there, looking petrified at the prospect of his oncoming brother. Belid looked as if he was regretting that he had not taken the time to prepare a last will. *If what we're focusing on is our collective impending death, then I'm pretty much in the right frame of mind.*

Athis bit his lip. Something Koliander said had been bothering him. *Here's what I don't understand. If he can shapeshift back into a more demonic form . . .*

Despite being left out of the current telepathic exchange, Belid had apparently reached the same puzzle as Athis and now turned to face Koliander. "Come to think of it, why are you worried about your brother seeing you like this?" he asked. "Why can't you just change back to your demonic form?"

"Because this is my new permanent form!" the pretty demon raged. "I can transform to my true form for a few seconds, but otherwise this is what I look like until I—"

"Get killed again?" Athis suggested.

"Yes!"

Got it! Klaria's voice sounded in his head.

And because they were sharing thoughts, the exact same thought went through Athis's head as well. Later it would be impossible for them to decide who came up with what. Assuming there would be a later.

Meanwhile, Markindo the Dragon was nearly there. He wasn't simply burning his way in, though. That was far too plebian a way for an entity of his magnitude to make an entrance. Instead, Athis knew, he was using an Infurnace spell, one that generated heat up until it hit a certain point and then would create a formidable but contained explosion.

"I have a plan!" he shouted over the building whine of accelerating power. "You'll have to trust me!"

"Trust you to do wh—?" Koliander started to ask.

Levitation was one of the very first spells they learned at the Crimson Keep. Like most of his other spells, Athis wasn't very skilled at it—but he was good enough to give it a shot. Stretching out his hand and shouting above the scream of energy being unleashed, he intoned, "Levito!"

A moment later Koliander was lifted off her feet, her arms flailing, and sent sailing through the air right toward the wall that was about to erupt. She slammed up against it, pinioned like a butterfly on a board, and had just enough time to screech, "Oh, you son of a—" before the wall around her erupted in a massive explosion. She was briefly silhouetted against the eruption of fire and light, and then her high-pitched screech was overwhelmed by the boom of the energy detonation.

Athis tried to brace himself, but there was no time. He was lifted off his feet and propelled backwards, all the while insanely trying to grab a handhold from the air itself. He crashed into the kitchen table, overturning it. Food, plates and cups clattered to the ground around him. The large knife that the Master had been using to cut the bread stuck in the floor point down, between Athis's legs, right below his crotch. Fortunately, he could barely see it because he had been partly blinded by the flash of energy.

Something was dripping into his eye. He wiped it away and realized that it was blood oozing from a gash in his forehead.

Belid was lying a short distance away. The larder had been jolted loose by the energy discharge and had fallen atop him. There was a week's worth of food piled on him, apples and vegetables and beef jerky from the look of it.

There was also a gargantuan hole where there once been a solid wall. Standing framed in it, his red eyes burning with cold fury, was Markindo the Dragon.

Athis blinked several times, unsure of what he was seeing and thinking that perhaps the manner in which he had struck his head had somehow addled his senses.

Markindo was three feet high.

He looked like a dragon, all right, with scaly greenish brown skin and horns and claws and sweeping leathery wings upon his back that were stretching and twitching. But he barely came up to Athis's waist.

Belid likewise looked flummoxed. "I was expecting someone taller," he said.

Markindo strode forward. Impossibly, the floor trembled with every step he took. He went straight for Athis, probably because he was closer, and grabbed him by the front of his garment. Then, without hesitation, Markindo lifted him over his head as if he weighed nothing. "You," he snarled, "killed my brother."

The door to the basement suddenly banged open and the Master was standing there, a bottle clutched in his hand, his eyes widening as he saw the damage and who was responsible for it. "You dare!" he bellowed. He glanced around with sudden concern. "Where is the girl? What's her name . . . ?"

"She fled, Master," Belid said quickly, trying to get to his feet. He was still dizzy and only managed to fall in another direction. Finally, he simply remained on the floor. "She is safe. The more immediate concern is . . ."

"The more immediate concern is your impending death for the high crime of killing my brother!" said Markindo. He tossed Athis aside with as much concern as he would brush away a flea. Athis hit the ground, rolled, and bumped up against Belid.

Klaria was standing just behind the Master, as pale as if every drop of blood had drained from her face. But seeing her reminded Athis of their conversation, and their idea, and he forced himself upright enough to play his last card.

"We didn't kill your brother!" he shouted, his voice little more than a croak. "You did!"

Markindo looked at Athis as if he'd lost his mind. "What are you talking about?"

"Just now! When you made your entrance. He was standing in front of the wall, trying to perform a counterspell to prevent your entrance. See for yourself!"

The Dragon's face twisted into a scowl of distrust as he looked where Athis was pointing. Then his expression became one of disbelief as he saw the twisted, burned out, nearly incinerated husk that had been Koliander. "What . . . but . . . this is impossible! A trick! I felt his death earlier . . ."

"Echoes!" Belid said.

"What?" Markindo's voice raised to thunderous levels.

One had to credit Belid. No one came up with nonsense faster. "Truly monumental deaths can actually have ripples backwards in time! His death just happened, but you sensed it and came here and, ironically, caused it!"

"That's absurd!" Markindo said, but he sounded a bit uncertain. "I've never heard of such a thing."

And to Athis's and Belid's utter shock, the Master said, "I actually have. But that's beside the point. You, demon, have trespassed here and now—"

"Why would my brother be trying to stop me?" Markindo demanded.

The Master looked annoyed that the Dragon had interrupted him, but then his curiosity clearly got the better of him. He turned to Athis and said, "Yes, why was he trying to stop him?"

"Because," Athis said quickly, "he had just arrived here. Just now."

"Yes, he most definitely wasn't here when you were here, Master," Belid added.

"And," Athis continued, "he had just enough time to tell us that he was here to sue for peace in the Demon Wars."

"Peace?" The Master looked amazed.

Markindo trumped amazed and went straight for outraged. "Peace? Between us and them?"

"That was the offer he was bringing us," said Athis, "hoping to use our Master here as an intermediary, until you came crashing in and killed your own brother."

"He was?" asked the wizard, eyes narrowing.

"Absolutely," said Belid.

"Well, then," said Markindo, "we have a choice." He directed his attention to the Master and the young wizards all at once. "We can do battle right now and I can bring this cursed castle down around your ears. Or we can wait for my deathless brother to reconstitute, and he can tell us exactly what he was doing here. It's your decision."

* * *

The lady or the dragon, Athis thought. *Can't we just start this day over?*

The Master spoke. "You do realize you may be here a while, Markindo."

"Ridiculous," said the demon. "My brother takes no more than an hour to regenerate."

"In any other place, perhaps. But this is the Crimson Keep."

Markindo looked at him askance. "So?"

"This place is a mystical tesseract. Time folds on itself here in strange ways. Perhaps that was the cause of the ripple effect whereby you detected his death. He could recreate himself in a minute, or it could take a millennium."

"Then why shouldn't I just destroy you all now?" Markindo's nostrils began to flare . . . literally.

He's not just blowing smoke, Klaria couldn't help but broadcast.

"Well," Belid replied, "for one thing, there would no one here to keep you comfortable while you're waiting for your brother to reassemble."

"That's true," Athis agreed. "Dying is one thing, but dying with the shame of being inadequate hosts is quite another."

The Master harumphed but finally nodded. "You are our guest," he admitted grudgingly. "Allow us to treat you as such."

Markindo considered the suggestion. "I am not uncivilized," he announced at last. "Very well, I will accept your hospitality."

"Then we're agreed," said the Master. "I offer you my finest suite"—he gestured, and a portal opened in space to a magnificent bedroom, lavish and perfectly proportioned to the demon's diminutive size—"and a bottle of my best wine. We will have a banquet ready for you shortly. Why don't you avail yourself of the accommodations? I am sure the constant warfare allows little time for luxuries."

"That it does not," Markindo conceded. He followed the wizard into the bedroom. "Besides, you should never slaughter on an empty stomach. You end up killing more than you need, and the corpses go bad before you can finish eating them all."

"I've heard that said. Here. Enjoy." The Master offered the bottle of wine he'd been holding. The demon sniffed at the cork, then looked at the label. "Don't worry," the wizard assured him, "it has neither gone bad nor is it enchanted. It's actually quite subtle, and the finish lingers for a long time."

Markindo considered the bottle some more. "It does smell delightful, but I've never heard of the vineyard. Klein?"

"It's unique," said the wizard, leaving the demon alone in the bedroom. "Very unique."

"I would expect nothing less." And Markindo pulled the cork out of the bottle, whereupon Athis's master returned to his students and closed the door behind him, leaving the demon alone in the room.

But not before placing a sound-dampening spell across the portal. That way, Markindo wouldn't hear what they were saying.

"Quick," Klaria whispered, "seal the door, sir!"

"Whatever for?" the Master asked. "A demon of Markindo's stature can't be contained by a simple door-sealing spell."

"But," said Athis helplessly, "we can't just let him sit there."

The wizard cocked an eyebrow. "Because Koliander, when he regenerates, will not support your story?"

Athis heaved a sigh. "That's right."

The wizard scanned the faces of his charges. "Clearly something has gone very wrong today, and if I had to choose among the three of you for someone to blame, I would start with you, Belid."

Belid started to protest, but seemed to think better of it.

"Beneath your polish you are vain and lazy," his Master told him, "while you," he turned to Athis, "are merely not terribly smart." To Klaria, he said, "You really should choose better friends, my dear."

Athis was sure the idea had already occurred to her more than once that day.

The wizard's brow furrowed. He stroked his beard, a sign that he was thinking deep thoughts. "We cannot simply send Markindo back where he came from. Now that he has found the Crimson Keep he can bypass its defenses at will. He would simply come back again and destroy us—unless we destroy him first."

"And let's not forget Koliander," said Athis. "He's certain to regenerate sooner or later."

"Most likely sooner, knowing the way today has gone," Klaria said.

"Well, then," said the wizard, "we have our work cut out for us, and not a lot of time." He pointed a long, bony finger at Athis. "You're with Klaria. You need to impede Koliander's regeneration—not just for a little while, but forever."

"How can we do that?" asked Klaria.

"I have a thought in that regard," their Master answered. He explained, and they both nodded. Then he turned to Belid. "You remain here with me. We will deal with Markindo—and I have an idea on that as well."

■ ■ ■

Klaria and Athis carried the remains of the once-attractive demon between them as they moved through a twisting stone corridor of the castle. For some reason, the husk was heavy than it looked. But then, magical events often had unforeseen results.

"Sorry about your dress," Athis said in a sheepish voice.

"Trust me," said Klaria, "after seeing it in that, I'd never wear it again."

"Too bad," he said. "It was quite fetching on you."

She seemed to soften a bit at the praise. "Thank you for that, but let's focus on our task, please. You can drool on me later."

Abruptly, Athis heard a popping sound. Looking down at

the husk of Koliander, he saw that a seam had opened in it, and deep in the seam he could see a yellow liquid. It was that liquid that was blubbing and producing the popping.

He and Klaria looked at each other. "He's coming back to life," Klaria said, her tone flat with fear, and Athis didn't need to ask which "he" she was talking about.

"We have to pick up the pace," he told her.

And they did, not quite running because Koliander's remains were too unwieldy for that, but moving as fast as they possibly could. The problem was that as Koliander regenerated, he got heavier, and more gelatinous. A containment spell would have helped, but what they really needed was . . .

A bucket!" Athis told Klaria. "Now!"

It wasn't her way to take orders. "Why can't you get the bucket?"

"Because," he said, "you can't carry this thing any farther on your own. But I can."

Klaria looked skeptical. However, it was clear that she didn't have the muscle to lug Koliander anywhere on her own. So, grabbing her skirts, she rushed off to find a bucket.

In moments she was back, holding the largest bucket she could find. Meanwhile, Athis had slung the demonic mess over his shoulder made some progress down the corridor. But even in that brief time, the bubbling sounds had grown noticeably louder. And when Athis dumped the regenerating demon into the bucket, he saw that the bubbles were growing in size. They had a few minutes, tops, to accomplish their goal.

There were rope handles on either side of the bucket. Each taking hold of one, they hefted it as high as they could manage, which turned out to be just a few inches off the ground. With shuffling steps they trundled forward, noting how much heavier Koliander was becoming second by terrifying second. Inside the bucket, muscle and sinew were taking shape. Athis thought he could even see an eye glaring up at him from the bubbling mess.

Finally, they turned a corner and came in sight of their destination—a waste shaft.

The Crimson Keep had a carefully maintained network of

service sluices into which the staff emptied befouled bedpans. The tunnels and channels and pipes were all heavily enchanted to prevent anything dumped inside them from reforming—Athis guiltily remembered a young fellow apprentice named Ganthis, who had accepted a very silly dare his first week here. They hadn't known about the enchantments then, and afterward, well, it was simply too late. For centuries or more those spells had been reinforced, for one purpose and one purpose only—nothing that went into those shafts ever came back out.

They had even been told stories of would-be invaders who had thought they could access the tunnel by entering through the moat and then climbing back up the shafts to the interior proper. They had never been seen again. It was the waste disposal system that had saved the castle's occupants in those days and, if the Master was right, it was the waste disposal system that would save them now.

Athis had barely completely the thought when a half-formed talon reached over the bucket's lip and grabbed him by the wrist.

The grip was tight, with serious muscle behind it. Athis let out a high-pitched scream, especially when he saw the scaled, hairy green arm attached to the talon, which was beginning to produce droplets of blood where it broke his skin.

"Hurry," Klaria urged him, as if the wounds were her own.

Athis gritted his teeth and walked faster, trying to ignore the pain in his wrist. Blood dripped down his hand and left a trail on the floor. The metal door in the wall that gave access to the nearest waste disposal sluice was just ahead, but it seemed so far away . . .

Athis's shoulder ached from carrying the demon's growing weight. On her side of the bucket, Klaria grunted with effort. It will all be over in a few moments, he assured himself. Just a few more seconds . . .

A small metal door loomed in front of them, getting closer, ever closer. Finally, it was close enough to reach out and touch.

"Now!" Athis groaned.

With his right hand, the free one, he opened the metal door and pulled it down, slamming the demon's talon hard enough to make it release its grip. Then he used the same hand to reach underneath the bucket. On her side, Klaria did the same. And together, they lifted the bucket as high as they could.

An inchoate cry burst from the partly formed throat in the bucket: "Arrrgh!"

Despite its protests, Athis and Klaria tipped the bucket's roiling contents into the muck-encrusted slide that led down into the shaft itself. The odors coming up and filling their nostrils made Athis gag but he continued to focus on his task. Little by little, the increasingly chunky slime that was Koliander ran down the shaft.

Finally, the bucket was emptied. But out of nowhere, two scaly green talons rose up and gripped the edges of the opening, refusing to give in to gravity. Gurgling noises that weren't quite words emerged from the unformed vocal chords, deep noises that turned Athis's already overworked knees to jelly.

He wondered if Koliander was merely repelled by the notion of winding up in the pit, or if it sensed the potent spells waiting there to thwart its continued resurrection. Either way, it was putting up a fight. Left unscathed, it would haul itself out of the opening and become a fully formed demon again.

They couldn't let that happen.

Klaria stepped back and gestured for Athis to follow her move. He was only too happy to comply. When she lifted a booted foot he grasped her meaning and did the same. She thoughtcast to him: *one, two . . . three.*

They kicked with all their might, hard leather heels grinding into the still unfinished talons, cracking the as-yet fragile bones and causing the demon to let out his own cry of anguish and pain.

The talons opened and the glop that was Koliander the Undying slid out of sight.

Klaria stared at Athis, who looked back at her. Neither could think of a word to say, nor would they have had the strength to utter it if such a word had occurred to them.

Numbly, Athis wondered how the Master and Belid were doing.

※ ※ ※

"Markindo is a most formidable demon," the Master observed.

"I would say so," Belid agreed.

"Which is why there is only one way to destroy him."

"One way?" Belid echoed.

"It will require a great sacrifice. The sacrifice of a human life." The Master looked pointedly at Belid.

The student didn't like the way this conversation was going. "Wait a minute. You mean—"

"The only way to destroy Markindo is for someone to die in the process. And you know who has to do the dying."

Now Belid really didn't like the way this conversation was going. "Master," he said, his voice breaking, "I'm too young to die. And too charming. You said yourself that I—"

The master scowled. "Not you, Belid. I meant me."

Belid stared at him. "Oh. Right."

He couldn't help thinking of the implications. If the master were to perish, Belid would be the highest ranking student in the mages' den, and therefore the one to inherit it. Mages' dens were known to make their owners wealthy. And powerful. And—

Wait a minute, he thought. *What am I thinking?* He didn't want his master to die. Hell, he liked the old fellow. As much as Belid wished to get ahead in the world, he didn't want to do it at his master's expense.

At least not yet.

"No," he said. "That is unacceptable."

His master seemed to look at him with a new respect. "You mean . . . it is you we should sacrifice? Why Belid, I am touched. I—"

"Isn't there a way for us both to survive?" Belid asked quickly.

"Both?" The wizard shrugged his bony shoulders. "I don't believe so."

There must be, Belid thought. *There must be . . . .*

But in the end, he couldn't think of any.

"Here is what we must do," he said, producing a small knife from within his robes. "As you know, a wizard's blood is invested with magical power. And the older and more powerful the wizard, the more potent his blood. To make a charm against disease or blind an enemy from afar, a few drops will generally suffice. But to destroy a demon the magnitude of Markindo . . ." The wizard pulled his sleeve away from his wrist and used his knife to slice into the exposed vein. "That is a different story."

Belid gasped as he watched his master's dark red blood well up, and slide down his hand onto his fingers. Before it could drop from his fingertips, the wizard pronounced a single word that Belid had never heard before—and created an invisible vessel right there in the middle of the air.

Slowly, it filled with the Master's blood. "When there's enough of it," said the wizard, "we will do a little shaping. Then we will call Markindo out of his luxurious suite and present him with the unexpected."

"But, Master," said Belid with genuine sadness, "you—"

"Will not live to see the result of my handiwork," the Master agreed. Even for one of my strength, it will take nearly all my blood to destroy the Dragon. Which is why you must pay attention."

Then he told his student what he must do.

As Belid watched, repeating the wizard's instructions to himself silently, the vessel filled. And as it filled, the ancient wizard grew pale and weak. Finally, he was unable to stand anymore. Sinking to his knees in his robes, he looked up at his student with glazed eyes.

"Don't blow it, boy," he said in little more than a whisper.

"Don't worry," said Belid, "I won't." Though he didn't feel as confident as he made himself out to be.

Finally the vessel was full. With the last of his strength, the Master closed the wound in his wrist, lest he lose consciousness too soon. Then he reshaped the vessel into a long, pointed spear—a spear made of his enchanted blood.

"I'm calling Markindo," he rasped—and collapsed.

A moment later, the portal to the demon's luxurious accommodations opened, and the Dragon walked out. "Is it time?" he demanded loudly. "Has my brother reformed?" He must have been full of wine, because he didn't notice the dark red spear in Belid's hand at first. Then he spotted the Master on the floor.

"What's this? What's happened?"

"Your death," Belid replied, steeling himself for the task at hand. He lifted the spear, drew back his arm, and hurled the weapon with all his strength, aiming straight for the demon's heart.

Markindo's eyes went wide as the magical missile sped across the intervening space, but it struck him full in the chest before he could react.

"Urk!" he cried out, the sound fading to a gurgling gasp as the spearhead burrowed deep into his flesh and then sprouted from his back, between his wings. He flailed at the shaft but his fingers slid from it, their strength already fading as the Master's blood destroyed him from the inside out.

The light was already dimming in the demon's eyes as he toppled backward, striking the stone floor with a thunderous boom. He twitched once, twice, then stiffened and collapsed— as still as his ancient rival, laying not more than twenty feet away.

■ ■ ■

Athis turned the corner just in time to see the demon Markindo fall, something long and red protruding from his chest. A moment later, he saw Belid and their Master. Except their Master was lying on the floor, unmoving.

What happened to him?" Athis groaned, rushing to their Master.

"He used his own blood to fashion the spear that killed Markindo," said Belid, his voice flat and without emotion. "He sacrificed himself to save everyone else."

As Klaria caught up with him, Athis knelt at the wizard's side and felt his neck for a pulse. He could barely find one.

"It's no use," said Belid. "It took almost all his blood for the spell."

Almost all his blood, Athis thought. Suddenly, he had an idea.

The spell he had studied for so long—the same one he had used mere hours before, to disastrous effect. But this time, if he was right, it could save the wizard's life. Holding his Master in his arms, he began to pronounce the required incantation.

"What's he doing?" Belid wondered.

"I don't know," said Klaria, her voice wracked with sorrow.

Athis continued the incantation, word by word, until he came to the end of it. As he finished, the wizard began to change. To shrink. And after a few moments, to disappear into the folds of his robes.

"Where did he go?" asked Klaria.

Athis smiled to himself. Exploring the pile of robes, he found what he was looking for and fished it out.

"A mouse?" said Belid.

"Not just any mouse," the mouse intoned in a familiar voice, though pitched a bit higher now.

Belid stared at it. "Master?"

"Indeed," said the mouse. "Still alive, thanks to Athis here. He recognized that for me to survive with so little blood in my body, I would have to be a lot smaller. And unbeknownst to us, he had perfected a spell that would allow me to become so."

Klaria looked at Athis with new respect. "Really?"

"Really," Athis said proudly. Of course, he didn't mention that he hadn't exactly mastered it. It was supposed to be a standard transmogrification, after all. He just couldn't seem to get the outside and the inside to line up. The body shrank, but the blood within didn't. When he'd tried it on Koliander, hoping to change the menacing demon into a harmless mouse, well—too much blood, not enough flesh, and *boom!*

This time, however, it had worked perfectly. Or rather, its failure had been the perfect solution. The Master's form had shrunk, but his remaining blood had stayed the same. What had been barely a trickle for a full-sized man was more than enough for a plump and healthy rodent.

"Now," the Master continued, peering at one student after the other with his little, black mouse eyes, "if you don't mind, could one of you take me up to my study? It's going to take some doing for me to become a healthy, fully-formed human being again, and I'd rather start sooner than later. Plus there's the matter of the Demon Wars—with both Markindo and Koliander destroyed, it should be a simple matter to end this conflict once and for all. Tedious, but simple." His little whiskers twitched. "I wouldn't mind some company, however. Do you think your lovely friend Lia would object to spending time with a mouse . . . ?"

THE SEEMING

by Michael Jan Friedman

EVEN IN THE GUTTERING BRAZIER LIGHT, WHICH cast an army of marching shadows throughout the stone corridor, the demon had no trouble spying the mouse. The tiny creature was peering out from a crack in the wall, apparently weighing the chances of its making it across the floor to the opposite wall without being molested.

At the demon's present pace and stride, which was brisk and very demon-like, the issue would be close. *Too close for the little bugger to chance it*, he thought. And the mouse could not possibly have been in such a hurry that it would cross the corridor at any price.

After all, the opposite wall would be just like this one. No better, no worse. All it offered the mouse was the *illusion* of progress, the seeming of it rather than the reality.

However, it was in the demon's interest for the mouse to venture forth despite everything. So he slowed his progress down to a crawl. No—*less* than a crawl. In fact, he nearly stopped altogether.

Then he thought, *Come. See how much room I've given you. Gauge the distance between us, and then between you and whatever opening you spy in the opposite wall. And note that I am moving as slowly as a living thing can move, naturally or supernaturally. Whatever trivial thing you desire on the other side of the corridor, it's yours—yours for the taking.*

The mouse hesitated.

Proceed, the demon thought, giving the tiny creature's mind a nudge. *Proceed as if it is your own idea and no one else's, as if there is no hungry demon manipulating your intentions. Proceed as if you are in complete control of your circumstances.*

Suddenly, the mouse scurried across the corridor, moving as quickly as its little gray body could move. As the creature would discover in short order, it had made the worst decision it was possible to make.

Because no sooner had the mouse shown itself than the demon pounced on it with fearsome quickness and determination, grabbed the furry little body in his clawed hands, and stuffed the thing whole into his mouth.

The mouse squirmed to get out, of course. Its kind was inclined to do that. But the demon clamped his teeth together, denying it egress. Finally the demon opened his jaws and chomped down, snapping the mouse's diminutive spine and putting an end to its struggles.

The power of illusion, he thought. *Not the worst talent to have.*

He sat down, placed his back against one of the stone walls, and took his time grinding the mouse's pulpy little carcass between his teeth, feeling its bones crunch and its warm juices slide around his long, forked tongue. Certainly not the tastiest morsel he had ever devoured, but not the least tasty either.

Besides, it wasn't as if sustenance was plentiful in this place— this maze of winding, twisting, looping corridors known widely as the Crimson Keep.

It seemed to the demon that he had been wandering its precincts for as long as he could remember, following one stone passage after another without the slightest hint of progress, until the monotony threatened to turn his mind to paste. But even worse than the monotony was the knowledge that his wandering had availed him nothing.

Of course, it might have been worse. When the mages who inhabited the upper reaches of the Keep sent him sprawling headlong down one of its slick, slimy, waste sluices, they had meant for him to keep on plummeting that way forever. He had no doubt of that, no doubt whatsoever.

And for a while, it had seemed they would get their way.

For every time he tried to slow his descent, pressing half-formed elbows and knees and even the side of his nearly amorphous head against the rough, stone walls, he failed in his objective. And as if that weren't bad enough, he lost a layer of flesh into the bargain. So he wasn't just an inchoate mess of arrested development, kept that way by the spells in the sluice. He was also bloody and tattered and shredded in places he hadn't previously known he had.

With no end to his frustration in sight.

Then he came to a place where the sluice had fallen into disrepair, where the stones were loose and the mortar had begun to crack away and there were holes into which he could sink his claws if he angled them just right.

And to his surprise, the spells in that spot—the charms that had kept him from regaining his proud, demon-like form—had fallen into disrepair as well. He didn't know how or why, but quite clearly they had done so. So there was an opportunity for him there, to say the least.

But he was falling so quickly, it would be difficult to gain purchase. He would need to put forth a maximum effort and ignore what promised to be an insane amount of pain if he were to capitalize on the opportunity, the likes of which he might never see again.

So the demon thrust out every raw, partially formed body part he possessed, and endured the agony that resulted. And bellowed, inasmuch as he was capable of bellowing with his lungs so incomplete and therefore ineffectual. And gnashed his teeth, insofar as they could be called teeth. And cursed his enemies, to the extent that his mouth was equipped to utter curses.

Until finally, his blood and gore and bits of bone smeared along the stones of the sluice for thousands of feet, he brought himself to a final albeit unceremonious stop—and with what rudimentary limbs he had, dragged himself out of the sluice into one of the Keep's narrow, serpentine corridors.

Victory, he thought at the time. And more than that, a chance to find the thrice-cursed mortal mages who had stuffed him into the sluice in the first place, no doubt thinking they had seen the last of him.

But they *would* see him. He would make certain of that. He would find them and he would make them pay dearly for what they had done. And then he would stuff their remains into a sluice so they could wallow in agony for the rest of their wretched lives.

He would do all that, just as sure as his name was Koliander the Undying.

Since his emersion from the sluice, he had healed, he had come together, he had grown out his limbs and his horns until they were as they should be. He had become himself again.

Except for one thing—his ability to shift his shape. For whatever reason, he had regained everything *but* that.

It was disconcerting, to say the least. He had been shape shifting all his life, ever since the dark, dismal night he crawled out of his mother's grisly womb.

The Master had a hand in this, he thought. *When I see him again, I'll make him regret it. Oh, how he'll regret it.*

But for the time being, Koliander would have to rely on his other powerful attributes. He could still create illusions in people's minds. He could still escape death. He would get by.

I'm still Koliander the Undying, he thought proudly, defiantly. *Let my enemies beware.*

The demon was reveling in the prospect of punishing those enemies—particularly the mages who had put him in the sluice system—when he felt the floor tilt recklessly beneath him, slamming his raw, ravaged shoulder into the nearest wall. It was all the warning he would get before the floor fell away altogether.

Because that was how it was in the Keep.

Floors tilted and fell away all the time. Once-promising-looking corridors came to an abrupt end, or became so narrow as to be impassable, or turned back on themselves to form an endless circle from which one could not escape.

Until everything changed again.

Unfortunately, Koliander didn't have time to ponder the problem—because a pit was opening beneath him, a yawning hole big enough to swallow an army of Kolianders. He cursed volubly. He hadn't escaped the sluice system only to be dumped into an abyss.

Frantically, he cast about with his claws for something to hang onto. But to no avail. The braziers on the walls were all that protruded from them, and the closest of them was well out of reach.

He had already begun sliding helplessly into the pit when, out of nowhere, something clamped around his wrist. He felt the strain from claw to shoulder as he stopped short.

Dangling above the darkness that was widening below him, he looked up—and found himself peering into the face of a fair-haired, lightly bearded human being with uncommonly large ears.

The fellow didn't look strong enough to have arrested Koliander's descent. Nor, for that matter, did he look strong enough to hold onto the demon for long. And yet, Koliander's fate appeared to dangle from the human's slender, rosy-pink hands.

Oh joy, the demon thought.

A few pieces of debris fell into the bottomless darkness below him and were swallowed up almost instantly—just as Koliander himself would have been if not for the human's intervention.

"Please," the bearded fellow grated from between tightly clenched teeth, "I cannot hold you much longer. Can you find purchase among the stones?"

Koliander scowled. If there had been purchase, he would have arrested his descent on his own. Then he spotted a stone sticking out a bit further than the others—one that hadn't been there before, and might possibly bear his weight. He placed his heel on it, tested it. It held.

With the help of that stone, he pushed himself up the vertical surface that had been the floor a scant few moments earlier. Then, still clinging to the human's hand, he found a niche with his free claw and wrestled himself up to the brink of the pit.

"Excellent," the human grunted.

"You may let go now," Koliander told him, and shook his wrist free of the fellow's grasp.

"I am grateful," said the human. With an audible sigh, he sprawled backward across the stones behind him.

Puny weakling, Koliander thought. But then, weren't *all* humans puny, frail things? It was a miracle that they had survived as a species as long as they had.

Using his claw hold and his foothold together, he hauled

himself out of the hole.

On safe ground—for the time being, at least—Koliander got to his feet and dusted himself off. Had he been a human, he would have felt compelled to thank his benefactor. As it was, he barely resisted the urge to take a bite out of the fellow, which would have at least temporarily assuaged Koliander's rampaging hunger. After all, he had not eaten anything except that measly mouse since . . .

He frowned. Since a juncture he could not remember. *Curse this keep . . .*

"I am glad," the human said, sitting up, "that I was able to lend a hand. *Literally.* It is dangerous in this area, you know. Pits like this one are opening and closing all the time. In fact—"

He peered more closely at Koliander in the brazier light. "You're a demon."

Koliander snarled. "Reached that conclusion all by yourself, did you?"

The human frowned. No doubt, the gravity of his situation was sinking in. "In weighing what you will do with me," he said in a remarkably even voice considering his circumstances, "I hope you will take into account the fact that I saved your life."

"You expect gratitude? From a demon?"

"Not at all, my lord. But I may hope for it, may I not?"

Koliander glared at him for a moment, waiting for his indignation to build. It didn't. Sometimes he just wasn't in the mood to destroy an innocent being.

It happened.

"Your hope has been realized, human. Count yourself lucky."

"Indeed I do, my lord."

Koliander looked around. There were no less than five passages radiating from where they stood, two of which skirted the edges of the newly formed pit. "I don't suppose you know where we are? Or how to get out of here?"

"Well," said the human, "as for where we are, we're in the Crimson Keep."

The demon rounded on him. "Do you think I'm an idiot? I *know* we're in the Crimson Keep. I meant *where* as in which *part.*"

"Yes, my lord," the human said. To his credit, he flinched

only a little bit. "I was about to address that very question—but it is not a simple one, primarily because every *where* in the Keep sooner or later becomes some other *where*. Fortunately, it is not necessary to know where you *are* in order to reach a place where you are *not*. That is to say, where are not *yet*."

Was it possible that the human was more slow-witted than the rest? Koliander had never learned enough about the species to make an accurate distinction.

"I apologize if I have been the cause of some confusion," the human said. "What I mean is I can get us out of here, if that's what you wish. In fact, in the time I have spent in this keep, I have become a veritable expert on the subject of getting out of here."

The demon eyed him. "If that's so, why haven't you escaped this place *already*?"

"Because one does not become an expert overnight. It takes time and dedication. But now that I feel I have achieved said expertise, I can find us both a way out. In fact, I was well on my way toward that goal when I noticed your difficulties."

"From which I would have extricated myself even without your assistance," Koliander was quick to point out—even if he wasn't sure he believed it. He had a reputation to uphold, after all.

The human lowered his gaze. "I have no doubt, my lord."

The demon pulled down on the front of his tunic. "Then what are we waiting for? I have revenge to wreak."

"Indeed," the human said, straightening again. "Let us proceed without further delay. If you would be so kind, follow me."

If you would be so kind. Koliander liked the phrase. There was no obeisance quite so satisfying as a well-spoken obeisance.

Not that there was even the remotest chance of Koliander's being kind. He *was* a demon.

The human chose one of the corridors that led away from the pit and Koliander followed. *Eagerly.* Because it wasn't just revenge that propelled him. It was something even more important, even more compelling.

Koliander's elder brother, Markindo—widely known as The Dragon for his incendiary breath—had led their family's armies in the Demon Wars ever since their sire, Kalikhorian the Magnificent, spilled his last, black drop of ichor on the Field of Twisted Iron, just south of the Falls of Flame. For a time, it seemed that Markindo would fare no better than Kalikhorian.

Then, ever so gradually, the tide had begun to turn in Markindo's favor. He had won battle after battle, small ones at first and then larger ones, gaining in stature and confidence with each successful encounter. Until finally, he arrived within reach of the unthinkable—a decisive victory in the Demon Wars. Not just *a* victory but *the* victory, the one that would bring an end to a strife so old that no one could remember the beginning of it.

But as terrifying and puissant and demanding of respect as Markindo could be even on his worst days, he was—it had to be said—not the canniest of demon overlords. It was to his brother Koliander that he turned time and again, whenever he needed to outwit the enemy. And of course, that need arose with unerring regularity.

In short, Markindo would accomplish *nothing* without his brother's counsel.

And where am I when my brother needs me most? Koliander asked himself. *Where am I when the ultimate triumph is there for the taking? Trudging through an endless, stinking maze, no closer to finding egress than I was when I extricated myself from that thrice-cursed sluice.*

"Delightful," he muttered.

The human glanced back at him. "I beg your pardon, my lord?"

"Nothing," Koliander said. "Nothing at all." He just hoped the human was as good at negotiating the Keep as he claimed to be.

"I must say," said the human, "it is a great relief for me to have made your acquaintance."

The demon's eyes narrowed. "And why is that?"

The human shrugged. "There are more dangers in these corridors than there are shifts in architecture. But if anyone can defeat these perils, it is Koliander, son of Kalikhorian."

The fellow's confidence was flattering, but Koliander wanted to know more. "Dangers of what *sort?*"

"A great many things have gotten lost here, my lord. Not just men. Not just demons. There is more to the Keep than anyone knows—at least until one has walked its halls as long as I have."

The words were hardly out of his mouth when the wall on their left seemed to vanish, revealing a mismatched group. The first one in line was a tall, wrinkled individual with a wide-brimmed hat, a flowing, grey beard, and a long wooden staff. Wizardly, but not the wizard who owned the Keep. This one was more austere, wearing but a coarse, gray robe.

Next came a couple of grizzled individuals with steely expressions and handsomely wrought blades in their fists, followed by a fair-haired, ethereal-looking archer and a short, squat specimen wielding a double-edged axe. Koliander thought the axe-wielder the last of the entourage when he saw four others show up, scurrying along behind their comrades.

Halflings, the demon observed. Halflings with hairy, over-sized feet and children's swords.

Koliander turned to them, claws extended, prepared to do battle. After all, he didn't know them or their intentions. But the group didn't respond to him in the least. It moved on as if it hadn't even noticed him.

"What—" he started to say.

"The wall is transparent," the human explained. "At least from our side. From theirs, I would say, it is opaque."

Koliander grunted. "Transparent walls?"

"It is the Keep, my lord."

Abruptly, the wall became opaque again on their side as well. All Koliander could see were mortared stones, and he was glad of it. The idea of seeing those who couldn't see him in turn made him more than a little uncomfortable.

Suddenly he remembered something, and turned to his companion. "You haven't answered my question, mortal. What *sort* of dangers?"

Again, the human averted his eyes. "I am not trying to be elusive, my lord. That would be disrespectful, and disrespect is the last thing I have in mind. In fact—"

"The dangers!" Koliander growled.

"Yes, my lord, of course. It is just that none of these creatures has ever been seen outside the Keep, so they have never been given proper names. To be sure, parts of them would look familiar to you—teeth, claws, tails, and so on. But they are composed of those elements in . . . unusual combinations."

The demon saw he wasn't going to get anywhere with this line of inquiry.

"But as I say," the human continued, "you are Koliander, Son of Kalikhorian. You will be equal to any danger."

The demon tilted his head as he considered his companion. "You appear to have a healthy respect for me."

"I have ample reason, do I not? The name of Koliander rumbles like thunder in the halls of demon kind, inspiring awe in every black heart within earshot. Is there a whelp anywhere in the Shadow Realm who does not know and fear Koliander's ferocity? Koliander's justice? Koliander's greatness?"

"Now that you mention it, not that I know of," the demon conceded.

"Well then, there you go."

Koliander knew the human was sucking up to him. It didn't matter. He liked it.

"What is your name, human?"

"Ganthis, my lord."

"And how did you end up wandering the Keep, Ganthis? Did you somehow displease its Master?" He spoke the last word as if it were a curse.

"I did not, my lord. Though if I had, it might have been easier to accept my imprisonment. You see, I was a mage-in-training. An apprentice, you might say."

"An apprentice to the damned *Master?*"

"Indeed. But not long enough for me to learn a decent spell. Before that could happen, I accepted a dare from my fellow apprentices. They said I could not make it to the kitchen and return with a goose's egg before they could count to fifty."

"And *why* would you want to bring back a goose's egg?"

"It was a silly dare, my lord, made even sillier by the fact that the kitchen *had* no goose eggs—only chicken eggs. Of course, being new to the place, I was unaware of that fact. And I had always been fleet of foot, so much so that there was not a youth in three counties who could beat me. So I agreed to the bet."

Fool, the demon thought.

"Had I gone directly to the kitchen, I would have been all right. But I thought I saw a shortcut and I took it. Unfortunately, it didn't lead to the kitchen as I had expected. It led into the bowels of the Keep. Before I knew it I was lost, and I have remained so ever since."

"But not for much longer," Koliander reminded him.

"Not for much longer," Ganthis agreed.

Just then, Koliander caught sight of something. Something small, down by the base of one of the walls, barely visible between the stones up ahead. *A mouse.* Just like the one he had devoured earlier.

How long had it been since he did that? It felt like minutes. But time in the Keep might take on a slew of different shapes. Sometimes it seemed to stretch, at others to bunch up.

Only one timepiece had proven reliable since Koliander escaped the sluice, and that was his stomach—which was growling now, telling him that it wouldn't balk if he were to swallow another fleshy morsel like the last one.

"Is something wrong?" Ganthis asked.

Koliander turned to his companion and held a finger to his mouth—the human signal for silence, or so he had come to learn. Concentrating, he reached inside the mouse's tiny brain and pushed as he had pushed before.

Go ahead, he thought. *Venture forth. There's no danger to you, none whatsoever . . .*

"I beg your pardon, my lord," said the human, even louder than before, "but if there's something that causes you consternation, you have but to—"

Suddenly, the mouse looked up at them, no doubt alarmed by the sound of the human's voice. Then it retreated deeper into the wall. Koliander swore beneath his breath and glared at his companion.

"*Now* see what you've done!" he grated. "Did you not see me put my claw to my mouth?"

Ganthis's brow furrowed. "Yes. But I did not know what the

gesture meant. A demon putting his claw to his mouth . . . why, it could signify *anything*. Or nothing at all."

It occurred to the demon that he could eat Ganthis instead. After all, the human had more meat on him than did a mouse. Not a lot more, but some.

No, he decided, resisting the temptation. *He is too valuable to me. At least for now.*

The human's brow furrowed. "You are not upset, are you?"

Koliander rounded on him. "Why would I be upset? It was only food you scared away. The only food I've seen in . . . I don't know, hours? Days?"

Ganthis smiled. "I get it—you're *hungry*. Why in the name of the sun and stars didn't you say so?"

"Why?" the demon echoed.

Because, he thought, silently answering his own question, *there is no point in complaining when your complaints will not get you anywhere. Because all such complaints do is remind you why you felt the need to complain in the first place.*

"Yes," the human said. "Because if it is food you want, I can be of assistance in that regard."

Koliander chewed the words over. "What kind of assistance?"

"The food kind, of course. And more palatable than mice— at least when it comes to *my* palate. As a demon, you may have more exotic tastes. Still, I cannot imagine that—"

Trying hard to contain his impatience, Koliander leaned forward until his nose and Ganthis's were touching, and barked two words. The first was "Food." The second was "Where."

Ganthis leaned back to disengage himself from contact with the demon. Then he looked around for a moment. "That way," he decided at last. He pointed for good measure.

Koliander followed his companion's gesture and found himself looking down a long, high-ceilinged corridor, more poorly illuminated than most. "And what will we *find* when we go that way?"

"Vines," said Ganthis, making his way down the corridor.

Vines? The demon made a sound of disparagement deep in his throat. As if vines might grow in this sunless place . . .

"Here we are," said his companion. Ganthis knelt by the wall on his right and plucked something from it.

As Koliander caught up to him, he saw that Ganthis hadn't lied. There were indeed vines climbing the stones of the wall. And depending from them was a collection of dark, purplish fruit—fat, juicy-looking globes, each the size of a human head.

Ganthis took a bite of the fruit, then held it out to the demon. "Take some," he advised.

Koliander took it. Holding it up to his nostrils, he sniffed it. The scent was pungent but far from unpleasant. He bit off a piece, crushed it between his teeth. The taste was not unpleasant either.

"What is this fruit called?" he demanded.

"I wish I could say," said Ganthis. He wiped the dark juices around his mouth with his sleeve. "All I know is that it provides sustenance. And it grows plentifully in the Keep."

"Why have I not encountered it before?"

The human shrugged. "You have to know where to look. And as long as I've been here, I have at least learned that much."

Koliander was about to take another bite when he saw something move in the shadows farther down the corridor. Something *big*. He threw the fruit aside in order to be ready for whatever happened next.

A moment later, he saw the big thing unfold—for like Ganthis, it had been kneeling. And unfolded, it was even bigger than it had seemed. *A giant*, Koliander thought.

Of course, there were giants and there were giants. This one was as enormous a two-legged creature as the demon had ever seen, and he had personally engaged the towering Sodelath of Wreckenhearth on the rocky banks of the River Twilight.

Koliander wasn't going to let anyone stop him from reaching his goal, no matter *how* big the bastard might be. He flexed and unflexed his claws, ready to rend giant flesh and spill giant blood.

But far from offering Koliander and his companion an obstacle, the giant pressed himself into the stones of the wall—in what must have been a painful and humbling experience for him—and gestured for them to pass.

"Much obliged," said Ganthis, "but we are not quite ready to depart." He glanced at Koliander. "My companion here has yet to eat his fill."

"I understand," said the giant in a deep, coarse voice.

"Excellent," Ganthis said. "So how are you holding up, my friend?" He plucked another dark, purple fruit. "Your muscles ache?"

"They are much the same," said the giant. "And your quest to escape the Keep?"

"No real progress, I am afraid," said Ganthis. "But as ever, I remain optimistic."

The giant didn't reply to the remark. Instead his gaze flickered over Koliander. "Your companion is a demon."

"As luck would have it, yes," said Ganthis.

"Curious," the giant rumbled.

His presence in the corridor made Koliander anxious. As soon as he had stuffed enough fruit into his maw to assuage his hunger, he turned to Ganthis and said, "Let's go."

"As you wish," said the human.

They walked past the giant, who again pushed himself into the wall as far as he could. Even then, it was difficult for them to work their way past his bulk.

"Well, take care now," said Ganthis.

"You as well," said the giant, his words mangled by the fact that his face was jammed against the wall.

As Koliander passed the fellow, he caught an ample whiff of his body odor. What was it about giants that made them smell so bad? Was it simply that there was *more* of them to smell?

The demon waited until he and Ganthis had vanished around a bend in the corridor. Then he said to the human, "you seem to know him rather well."

Ganthis nodded. "Him and a great many others who wander the Keep."

"Yet he shows no inclination to travel with you."

"Actually, the feeling is mutual. Not that Cleggik back there is a bad sort. Quite the contrary. He has a beautiful singing voice, more beautiful than you would ever imagine. In fact, that is what got him lost in these corridors in the first place."

Koliander didn't ask to hear the story. Nonetheless, Ganthis embarked on it.

"He came here to sing for the Master—some solemn occasion, I forget exactly what. Just before he was scheduled to begin, he felt the urge to visit a garderobe."

"Too much wine," Koliander suggested.

"Too many pastries," Ganthis said. "Being a singer, he didn't have much money for food, much less for sweetmeats. His engagement here was a rare opportunity to devour as many of them as he could. It proved his undoing. Oh, he made it to a garderobe—eventually. But it was not the close, convenient one to which he had been directed by the Master's staff. And when he tried to find his way back . . ."

Ganthis's voice trailed off. He didn't have to say any more.

Koliander laughed at Cleggik's misfortune. "He got lost looking for a *bathroom?*"

"Indeed, my lord. But the experience never soured his disposition. In fact, one can often hear him singing if one listens closely enough, even if finding the singer is not always as easy. And contrary to his appearance, his song is always a joyous one. As I say, not a bad sort at all."

"Then why does he not seek egress with you?"

"Because he has given up, my lord. He will tell you that there is no way out of the Keep, no matter how hard one tries to find one."

"In stark contrast to your own belief."

"As I have said. It is only a matter of time and perseverance." Ganthis winked at the demon. "And a certain native intelligence which, I must humbly admit, I am fortunate enough to possess."

Koliander didn't like being winked at. He was tempted to pluck the offending eye from its socket then and there. But he reminded himself that Ganthis could be of help to him, immense help, and the possibility would be diminished if the fellow had one eye instead of two.

"And then," said Ganthis, "there is the saddest story of all."

Not wanting to encourage him, Koliander remained silent. It didn't help.

"His name," said Ganthis, "is Isthal of Arrondemere. You have heard of him, no doubt?"

Koliander had indeed. The fellow's stupidity was as legendary among demons as it was among human beings. Maybe even more so.

"The one," said the human, "charged with guarding Krayken of Wellingrog?"

Koliander scowled. He could see he would have no peace until he acknowledged his companion's questions.

"Yes," he said irritably, "I know the story as well as anyone. Krayken was the bloodiest of us demons, the most vicious in battle. Eager to get rid of him, the forces of humanity hatched a plan. When they met Krayken the next time, they executed it.

"Subtly, gradually, they separated Krayken from the main body of his armies. Then they hacked away at his Demon Guard, at great expense to themselves, until they reached Krayken himself. He fought with insane fervor, dispatching one warrior after another, but at last the human beings took him down and bound him.

"This Isthal fellow was given the responsibility of keeping watch over the captive. After all, he had a special talent—the ability to paralyze any living thing, demons included, for the space of several heartbeats. All he had to do was see the creature and he could freeze it in its tracks. But once he used this ability, he could not use it again for an hour or more.

"All of which seemed to make the task of watching Krayken rather easy. Especially since the demon had been chained and manacled."

"Or so it seemed," Ganthis chimed in enthusiastically, seemingly incapable of keeping his mouth shut. "Krayken—who could cast illusions—had merely given his captors the *impression* that he was chained. In fact, their chains lay in a pile at his feet. The only restraints he wore were his manacles.

"Still," the mortal continued, "Isthal was watching over him. And though Isthal was unaware of the state of Krayken's fetters, he knew the demon was an illusion-caster. He was ready for Krayken to fashion a deception.

"In the end, ironically, that was the very thing that proved his undoing. For when Krayken stood up and started to walk away, Isthal did not respond. He mistook the reality for a deception—one that might work against him if he fell for it.

"He could have frozen Krayken in place, of course. But what if his captive *wanted* him to do that—so he could not do it again any time soon? What if the whole point of the illusion was to force Isthal to expend his lone magick?

"It was the plentitude of such questions—and the dearth of any answers—that impaired Isthal's judgment. He allowed Krayken to continue to walk away unimpeded. And he did so until the demon was well out of his captor's sight.

"For a long time, Isthal stood his ground, certain that the demon was simply casting an illusion. It was only when his relief arrived and saw that Krayken was gone that the truth—a painful one for Isthal—began to come out. In the investigation that followed, conducted by human wizards, it was determined that Krayken was not just apparently gone—he was gone in *fact*.

"It was the worst turn that could have befallen the mortal armies. For as Krayken had made his way back to the demons' lines, he had disguised himself as a series of bushes, and in the process taken note of his enemy's positions. By the time he reached his tent, he knew more about the strengths and weaknesses of the mortals' forces than the mortals knew themselves.

"Before dawn, he rode at the head of the demon armies—and overran the mortals. Many a human being died in that battle. And though it was clear to most that Isthal had acted reasonably, even astutely, one man insisted on pointing an accusing finger at him.

"That man, of course, was Isthal himself. He even made up a name for himself—a name which has, unfortunately, stuck with him ever since: Isthal the Unseeing."

Koliander snorted with some satisfaction, for Krayken's victory was a sweet one. "A great moment in the Wars."

"Yes," said Ganthis as they came to another junction of multiple corridors, this time six of them. "At least from your point of view. But from Isthal's, it was anything but that—which is why he came to the Keep uninvited and proceeded to get himself lost. And he is said to wander here still, shunning the humanity that he believes he has betrayed."

Koliander chuckled. "*His* problem."

He was not sure what kind of response he expected from his companion. As it turned out, he got no response at all. Ganthis was just standing there, looking down this corridor and then that one and then this one again.

"What is it?" Koliander demanded.

Ganthis frowned. "We have run into a bit of a dilemma, my lord."

"What sort of dilemma?"

"I am . . . of two minds as to which way to go."

Two minds? "I thought you were an expert in negotiating these passages."

"I am indeed."

"Then how can you make such a mistake?"

"The passages are always changing, my lord. And they never assume the same configuration twice."

"Then why did you say you were an expert?"

"An expert at *change*. Knowing what they have done in the past, I cannot predict what they will do in the future. However, since the changes are never the same, I can predict what they will *not* do. And that is a valuable tool indeed."

Koliander was not entirely certain that Ganthis' words made sense. Then again, what *did* make sense in the Keep?

He waited for Ganthis to make a decision. But after what seemed like a long time, they still had not budged from the spot. "We cannot stand here forever," Koliander snarled.

Suddenly one of the corridors vanished—and another one appeared behind them. It did not seem to help. Ganthis continued to look perplexed.

Feeling useless, Koliander made his way partway down the corridor that had just appeared. Not so far that he might risk losing sight of Ganthis, of course. Just far enough for him to feel that he was *doing* something.

Not that the demon expected to see anything worthwhile. That would have been asking a lot. But as luck would have it, he *did* see something.

Something completely and utterly unexpected.

It cannot be, Koliander thought, his head swimming as if he had been struck by an especially powerful thunderbolt. *And yet . . .*

"Is everything all right back there?" Ganthis called.

"Just fine," Koliander said.

He moved closer to the object of his scrutiny. Close enough to touch it, if he so desired. Close enough to be certain beyond any doubt as to what he was looking at.

A human. Stuck in the wall, half-in and half-out. His expression one of shock and terror.

But not just *any* human.

For this unfortunate one, this slender, fair-haired, large-eared son of Man, was *identical* to the specimen that had been leading Koliander through the maze of the keep. Every feature, every *hair* was exactly the same.

How can this be? the demon wondered.

He had no trouble understanding how the fellow had gotten himself stuck in a solid wall. Clearly, he had screwed up a translocator spell. *It happens.*

But how was it that the victim of the spell was so much the image of Ganthis? *So very much the image?*

Were they twins? If so, would Ganthis have failed to mention as much? For the love of pain, he seemed determined to mention everything else.

"Lord Koliander!" Ganthis cried from up the corridor. "There is another change coming! We must—"

"In a moment!" Koliander bellowed.

He continued to study the imprisoned human, his demon brain grinding the facts of the situation like bones, and slowly but surely sucking out the marrow of a conclusion.

An *inescapable* conclusion—that the Ganthis up ahead was not Ganthis at all, but an imposter.

Why? Koliander demanded silently. *Why would he—if he is in truth a "he" at all—pretend to be someone he is not? What kind of trouble is he leading me into?*

And who is he really?

"Lord Koliander!"

The demon cast a glance at the passage behind him, which

indeed was beginning to change—to shiver like something seen through wind-driven water—right along with the other passages that converged at the junction. Koliander had no idea what the change would leave in its wake. All he knew was that Ganthis was standing his ground, gesturing frantically for Koliander to join him.

The demon scowled. Was the imposter truly trying to help him? Or was this a trap—one he had meant to spring on Koliander all along, waiting only until the time was most propitious?

He cursed as only a demon could curse. In a few moments, the passage would transform itself into something else. *Do as the imposter says—or not?* He had to choose, and quickly.

Grinding his teeth, he moved to join Ganthis—the one that was still alive, and not frozen in the fabric of the wall. Suddenly, a long stretch of floor in front of him began fading away. If Koliander tried to set foot on it, he would certainly find himself plummeting into the Keep's nether-regions.

So he took two steps on what was still solid—and then leaped as far as he could.

Emptiness gaped below him like the maw of a gargantuan beast. For a moment Koliander was sure that the maw would claim him. Then his scaly, gray heels came down on the far side, where the floor was still intact.

Close, he thought, looking back at the abyss. In fact, it could not have been any closer. And if he had chosen to ignore the human's advice . . .

Clearly, Ganthis—or whoever he was—had not been ready yet to spring his trap. *But he will be, I'm sure. Otherwise, why go to the trouble of carrying out such a deception?*

"Why did you not heed me?" Ganthis asked as he rushed to Koliander's side, his tone just short of a demand.

Koliander looked into the imposter's eyes. *So innocent-looking,* he thought. *So empty of guile—or so they seem.* He hated deceivers, especially when it was *him* they were trying to deceive. He felt an urge to drive a horny-knuckled claw down "Ganthis'" gullet and rip out the fabricator's organs one by one.

But if he did that, he would never find out why he was being deceived—or by whom. And he desperately wished to obtain those bits of knowledge.

So he lied to the liar—which, he supposed, was only fitting. "I am not a follower by nature, mortal. I am a leader."

"Of course, my lord," said the imposter. "But in this instance, when my understanding of this place is superior to yours, forgive me for saying so . . ."

"Even then," Koliander insisted. "But I will make an effort in the future to . . . trust . . . your instincts."

"I am honored," said the human. He glanced this way and that at the corridors around them, which were writhing like serpents. "And rest assured, my most puissant lord, I will do everything in my power to justify that trust."

I am sure you will, Koliander thought. *Until the time comes when you finally betray me.*

They stood there a few moments longer, waiting for the changes around them to cease. At last, they did so—leaving but one passage open and accessible.

The demon scowled. It looked like they had no choice but to proceed in that direction. But Ganthis—or whatever he was called in truth—didn't seem nearly as disappointed in their lack of options.

"This is it," he said, an undercurrent of laughter in his voice.

"This is what?" Koliander asked.

"The way out. That is, not the exit itself, but a passage that will lead us to it."

"Really? How do you know?"

"As I indicated earlier, my lord, I know what these passages will *not* do. And what *this* one will not do is fail to lead us to an exit."

Koliander was not convinced of the logic. "What if it changes again, denying that which we seek? Is that not the vast likelihood?"

Ganthis shook his head from side to side. "It is not. At least, not until we have had ample time to take advantage of it."

The demon scowled. *I can refuse to follow him. Or just kill him. But there is a chance he means what he says about this passage. After all,* he *has to find egress too, does he not?*

"This," the human announced, "is a great stroke of luck. An

incredible stroke of luck. I cannot say how long I have wandered these corridors without encountering a stroke of this magnitude."

And he set off along the corridor.

Koliander considered his options for a moment. In the end, he decided to take his chances and follow the imposter. He did not know what the fellow had in mind for him, and that was a concern, but it could not be much worse than wandering the Keep for the rest of eternity.

As "Ganthis" had promised, the corridor did not undergo any significant changes as they negotiated it. Only at one point did a wind come out of nowhere and sweep through, and send the brazier flames—and the shadows they made—jumping all over the place. Outside of that, the passage remained as straight and true and solid as a passage might remain *outside* the Keep.

Until they came to a place where one of its walls had fallen away, revealing the dirty, brown maelstrom of swirling detritus just beyond it. Koliander knew what it was, too. After all, he had spent a fair amount of time in it.

The sluice system, he thought.

The one that inexorably carried the Keep's garbage down to its nether-regions. The charmed network into which the Master's mages had dumped the helpless, half-formed Koliander, hoping never to see him again. And if not for a fortuitous flaw in that network, they would almost certainly have gotten their wish.

The demon saw the imposter's plan unfolding before his eyes. Which was why he would not fall for it.

"All we have to do," his companion said as they came up alongside the maelstrom, "is ignore what is going on there and move past it."

Koliander looked at him askance. "I thought you said this corridor would remain unchanged."

"And so it has," the human said genially. "If I am correct, it has always been this way—exposed to the maelstrom. And as far as I can tell, it always will be."

"I see," said Koliander. "And our chances of accidentally falling into the maelstrom? And becoming part of the garbage descending into the bowels of the place?"

"I would not worry about it, my lord. As you can see, there

will be plenty of floor underneath us."

"Unless," said the demon, "one of us happens to give the other a gentle shove in the direction of the whirlpool. Then no amount of floor will be enough."

"Ganthis" smiled uncertainly. "Why would one of us wish to do *that*, my lord?"

"Perhaps *you* can tell *me*. After all, it is *you* who are the deceiver."

The remark brought "Ganthis" up short. His brow puckered. "I beg your pardon. I thought you said *deceiver*."

"Precisely," Koliander snapped. "Which is what you have been from the moment you pulled me from the jaws of that stinking pit."

"Ganthis" turned pale. "I assure you, my most powerful and terrifying lord, you are mistaken."

"Am I? You still claim, then, that your name is Ganthis?"

"Of course," said the human. "It is the name I was given at birth."

Koliander decided the time for talking was past. "Here," he said, grabbing the imposter by the wrist, "perhaps it is time *you* were introduced to the sluice."

The demon didn't intend to actually throw his companion into the maelstrom. At least not until he knew who the fellow was and what he was up to. He meant to drag him only as far as the hole in the wall, where "Ganthis" might be encouraged to reveal certain truths.

But as it turned out, the human was not easily dragged.

As hard as Koliander tugged at him, "Ganthis" managed to stand his ground. And before the demon could express his surprise at the fact, his companion yanked his wrist free. So powerfully, in fact, that it made Koliander's own arm go numb up to his shoulder.

What the—? "You seem rather puissant for a human," the demon spat. "And a slender one at that."

"Ganthis" looked perplexed. "No one is more surprised by my display of strength than I am, I assure you. Though I must say, as surprises go, this one is certainly a *pleasant* one."

"For *you*," said Koliander. "For me, it is rather inconvenient."

"No doubt. I do not suppose you have an explanation for it?"

"Me? You are the one who is posing as a dead man."

"A dead—?" The human's expression of surprise widened. "What in the name of the Seven Sisters are you talking about?"

"There's a mirror image of you stuck in a wall we passed back there." The demon jerked one of his claws over his shoulder to indicate the direction—not that directions meant much in that place. "And don't bother claiming it was your twin brother."

"I have no brother," the human said. "So, clearly, that is not the answer."

"Clearly," the demon agreed.

Hoping to surprise his companion, Koliander took a swing at him with a clawed appendage. The fellow's parry was so quick, so hard that it made the demon's arm lose feeling again.

"What *is* it with you?" Koliander demanded.

"I told you," said the imposter, "I do not know."

The demon began to feel something cold and unfamiliar uncoil in his gut like a waking serpent. It was *fear*.

This human, whoever he was, was suddenly a good deal stronger than Koliander had imagined. Stronger, in fact, than Koliander himself. And if that were so, the human no longer had to fawn over the demon lord.

I am imperiled, Koliander recognized. He needed to do something about that fact—and quickly. *But what can I do?*

Then he saw it—the opportunity that would remove him from danger. Of course, it would also deprive him of his guide. But if "Ganthis" had spoken the truth, all Koliander needed to do now was follow this corridor and he would find his way out of the Keep.

In the end, he did what any self-respecting demon would have done in such a circumstance. He *struck*.

In this case, that meant lowering his scaly shoulder and plowing into his companion with all the force he could muster. But even then the human did not go sprawling as Koliander had hoped. For a moment, in fact, it looked as if "Ganthis" would not budge at all.

Then something strange happened. He didn't fall, exactly. Rather, he *toppled* in the manner of a tree.

And in doing so, he fell into the maelstrom behind him.

As the fellow disappeared into the churning, brown waters of the whirlpool, Koliander thought he saw his companion's face change—become something not unlike the demon lord's own countenance. Then "Ganthis" was washed down the sluice, along with his newly discovered strength.

Funny, Koliander thought. He would have expected a bellow of rage, of horror . . . something. But his companion met his fate silently, without so much as a whimper.

Would he escape the disposal system as Koliander had? As it happened, the demon did not care. All that mattered to him was that he still had a chance to escape the Keep.

And the glimpse he had had of what looked more like his own face than the human's? That too was of little moment.

Until he heard a voice in his head. A *human* voice, unless he was mistaken.

He looked that way, said the voice, *because he is Koliander the Undying. And you, by contrast, are not.*

I do not understand, the demon thought.

You are not Koliander. Not a demon at all, in fact. Which is why you were unable to alter your appearance earlier, when you tried to do so—because you are not even remotely a shape-shifter.

The being who had formerly believed himself to be Koliander shook his head. *Then who am I? And while we are at it—who are* you?

I am the fellow whose Keep it is, said the voice. *You know, the Master. The one you've been itching to sink your claws into.*

Which was no longer an issue, now that he knew he was not Koliander. Or was it? Clearly, the Master had duped him. Maybe he *did* have a reason to sink his claws into the fellow.

The question is moot, actually, the Wizard told him, *because you do not have claws. Not really.*

Then what are these? the one who was not Koliander asked, holding his claws up as if the Master were standing in front of him and could see them.

An illusion, the Master said. *Like the rest of your appearance. Only an illusion.*

Like the one he had created in the mouse's mind, to encourage the thing to venture out of its hiding place. *Only an illusion.*

Actually, said the Master, *that was not an illusion at all. It was just a coincidence. The mouse went scampering across the stones of its own volition, as mice often do. Were you truly Koliander, you could have exerted some influence on the creature. But since you are not . . .*

So to sum up, thought the one who was not and had never been Koliander, *it is because of you that I believed myself to be a demon. Which I am not.*

That is correct.

And it is also because of you that I believed my companion to be something other than a demon. Which was also wrong.

Correct again.

But . . . .why? Why deceive me into thinking I was something I was not and my companion was something he was not? Simply to amuse yourself?

Far from it, came the Master's response. *You see, your companion was supposed to have been an untidy mess, descending for all of eternity, or at least the greatest part of it, through my enchanted sluice system. But something happened.*

Somewhere along the line, he hit a stretch that wasn't enchanted enough. Listen, it's an enormously long and complex sluice system; there are bound to be a few dead spots. In any case, as Koliander flowed through this regrettably un-enchanted stretch, his body remembered its true form and resumed the job of reassembling itself.

Once I realized what was going on—and don't ask how I knew, I am the master of this place, remember—I had to do something about it. Somehow, I would have to get Koliander back the sluice system again—a branch that would not pour him into the un-enchanted stretch a second time.

Not an easy task. It would only be even remotely possible if I befuddled him—confused him, distracted him, made him think he was someone else—and, as if that weren't challenge enough, also gave him a reason to want to reach this juncture, where the sluice system was open and easily accessible.

So, using one of my wizardly powers, I made him think he was someone else. A former student of mine called Ganthis, who had gotten lost in the Keep long ago.

A fellow who had every reason to reach this part of the Keep. And you . . . I made you part of the picture as well. Because without you as my agent, I would have neither the constant, compelling distraction of a hungry, impatient, and irascible demon nor the opportunity to insert Koliander back into the sluice system.

As luck would have it, you caught sight of the real Ganthis—a most improbable event, but there you have it—and nearly bollixed up my scheme as a result. Fortunately for me, and all of us who would have suffered if the demons got the upper hand in the wars, you managed to keep your mouth shut until my trap was sprung.

Now, you may be wondering why Koliander—in his guise as Ganthis—did not exhibit his demonic strength until the end there. That is the result of my magicks, which so thoroughly convinced him that he was Ganthis and not a lord of the demon hosts. It was my choice to let him remember his strength at just the right juncture, causing you to feel threatened.

And, feeling so, to take action. In particular, the action of returning Koliander to the sluice system. Not a bad plan by half, if I say so myself.

The one who had believed he was Koliander, albeit mistakenly, mulled over what the Master had imparted to him. He agreed—it had been a good plan, if a perhaps unnecessarily complicated one. But the Master's explanation left one seriously big question unanswered . . .

If I am not a demon, the one who was not Koliander thought, *then—*

Then who are you? The Master chuckled—a strange sound, to be sure, when it was rolling around in one's head. *Funny you should ask. Remember Isthal of Arrondemere?*

The one who allowed that bound demon—Krayken of Wellingrog—to escape? Isthal the Unseeing?

The same.

Not-Koliander shook his horned head. *I am . . . Isthal?*

Indeed.

And as if by magic—in fact, very much by magic—the fellow who was not Koliander or, for that matter, a demon at all, began to change. His horns shriveled away. His hide lost its scaliness, became softer and smoother. He narrowed, straightened, assumed what might be called the proportions of a human being.

And not just any human being. Specifically, the fellow who had endured such shame that he could no longer live with himself: The warrior Isthal.

"It's true," the fellow said out loud. "I'm Isthal." And as he said the words, Isthal's memories came flooding back to him. Not just the painful ones, but the cherished ones as well.

In that same moment, he understood why he had been chosen to serve as the Master's pawn. For Isthal possessed the ability to freeze a demon for just a few moments. And it was only because he had frozen Koliander, albeit out of instinct rather than conscious purpose, that he could shove the demon back into the sluice system without meeting a bit of resistance.

You are Isthal, all right, the Master thought. *And in my estimate—which, let us not forget is a widely respected one—you have at long last redeemed yourself. Once you let a particularly dangerous demon escape, much to the chagrin of your comrades in arms. Now you have doomed another demon—one who might well have turned the tide of the Demon Wars—to eternal imprisonment. The scales, it seems to me, are balanced once more.*

Isthal lowered himself to the stones of the floor and pressed his forehead against them. *I owe you more than I can ever repay,* he told the Master.

Of course you do, came the reply in his head. *Which is why you will return to the Demon Wars and make us all proud with your exploits. And eat a lot better than you have eaten recently.*

Isthal recalled his consumption of the mouse, and not with gusto. It was a meal he would not care to repeat any time soon.

I beg your pardon, he thought, *but there is still the matter of my escaping the Keep.*

Of course, replied the Master. *Fortunately, it is a matter easily addressed. The corridor in which you find yourself, the one Koliander told you would take you to an exit? It will do no such thing. Instead, make the next one hundred and seventeen lefts that present themselves, all the while resisting the temptation to make a right. The egress will be right there—you cannot miss it.*

Thank you, Isthal said. But before he could complete the

thought, he realized he was talking to himself. The wizard was no longer present.

He looked around—first at the stone passageway, with its ruined wall and its open view of the ensorcelled sluice system. Then at himself, very clearly a human being and not the least bit a scaly, clawed demon. Then he marveled at how quickly the narrative of his life had rewritten itself.

And he resolved as fervently as any man could resolve any thing to keep from being blinded by illusion ever again.

Whereupon he set out to make the next one hundred and seventeen lefts that presented themselves, all the while resisting the temptation to make a right.

POOR WANDERING ONES

by Russ Colchamiro, Peter David, Mary Fan, Michael Jan Friedman, Robert Greenberger, Glenn Hauman, Paul Kupperberg, and Aaron Rosenberg

CLEGGIK THE GIANT FELT LIKE SINGING.

It had been a long time since this was so. A monstrously long time.

At first, when Cleggik got lost in the sprawling, ever-changing Crimson Keep—simply looking for a bathroom, to his enduring desolation—he held out hope of eventually escaping the place. In this regard, he was not unlike the others he came across in his wanderings, men and women and beings of all stripes and descriptions, and even worlds.

Despite the Keep's diabolically shifting corridors, despite its appearing and disappearing stairs and anterooms, Cleggik and his fellow wanderers doggedly sought an egress. If they didn't find it one day, they thought, they would find it the next.

So they followed corridor after corridor, swam pools, climbed ladders—whatever seemed likely to bring them closer to their goal. But they never reached it.

In the Keep, there was no sunrise and no sunset. But time still had a weight to it, and some bore it better than others. Despite his size, Cleggik was a simple singer. He had never faced adversity the way a warrior might have. And little by little, he had fallen into despair.

To be fair, the Keep had ground down Cleggik more than it did its other prisoners. After all, it hadn't been designed for someone his size.

As expansive as the Keep's passageways could be at times,

they could at other times be exceptionally narrow, forcing Cleg-gik to slide sideways in order to make his way through them. Or when the ceilings got too low, to crawl on his belly. Or when they twisted this way or that, to twist along with them.

Sometimes he had no choice but to kneel and endure the crushing pressure of stone walls coming together, grinding his elbows and his shoulders and his knees, painfully contorting his neck, and even threatening, on occasion, to snap his bones. And he had to continue to endure such agonies until the pressure relented and his environs transformed themselves into something more tolerable.

It was a nightmare, one from which he could not wake. He went on from breath to breath, consuming whatever odd, fungus-like sustenance the Keep provided in this wall crack or that one, moving forward out of inertia more than anything else. But he harbored no hope of regaining his former life.

He had been a singer of great repute before he came to the Keep, the owner of a voice that made men and women and even house pets groan with a joy they had never known possible. He no longer sang—not so much as a note. What for?

Until now.

Cleggik looked out at the corridor that stretched before him straight as an arrow. It looked like hundreds, maybe thousands of other corridors he had encountered in his travels, with one significant difference: It had not changed in all the time he had been looking at it.

He hadn't meant to study it, only to sit and rest from his last crushing, twisting ordeal. But after a while, he'd noticed that it hadn't changed. Not even a little.

The more he noticed, the more he continued to watch it. And the more he continued to watch it, the more he marveled at it.

A corridor that remained the same? For so long? In the Crimson Keep? It was unheard of.

And that was why he suddenly felt like singing.

And in fact, *sang*.

His voice sounded like someone else's. After all, he hadn't used it in so long. But it was a lovely voice, even if he said so himself.

It wasn't until he'd reached the end of his song that he realized someone was approaching him from behind. The stranger—for Cleggik had never seen her before—was a small, slender woman with dark hair and clothes that had, it seemed, once been rather elegant. Now, of course, they were threadbare and torn.

"That was beautiful," the woman said in a voice as petite as she was. "Truly beautiful."

"Thank you," said Cleggik. "It would have been better, I think, had I not been so out of practice."

"I cannot imagine it being better," the woman said. "And now that I think about it, I don't want to. Because my heart almost burst as it was, and had it been any more touching I would likely not be standing here now, talking to you."

"In that case," said the giant, "I am glad that it was what it was."

"Agreed."

"Who are you?" Cleggik asked. "And how did you come to be trapped here in the Keep?" It was a question he used to ask a lot, when he had first gotten lost. Before he stopped caring enough to ask.

"My name is Aurelia," the woman said. "And to be honest, I don't know how I arrived here. One moment I was asleep in my bed, in my father's house. The next I was . . . here. Feeling groggy, as if I'd been drugged."

"Perhaps you were," said Cleggik.

"It's possible. My father is a wealthy fellow, and I may have been kidnapped. But if I was, and it was the intention of my kidnappers to trade me for a ransom, they bungled the job, as you can see."

Her eyes began to well with tears. However, she blinked them away. Not for the first time, Cleggik imagined.

"Pleased to meet you," said the giant.

"And I you," said Aurelia.

Cleggik pointed down the corridor. "It's the most remarkable thing," he said. "This passageway . . . it hasn't changed in the longest time. It has remained a passageway. And even more remarkably, it has remained *this* passageway."

She followed his gesture. "That's odd. What do you think it means?"

Cleggik shook his head. "I don't know. For that matter, I don't know if it means *anything*."

"The Keep is always changing. At least, that has been my experience. If it's stopped . . . " Her voice trailed off.

The giant shrugged. "It may *still* be changing. It may simply be doing so more slowly, in increments so tiny that we're incapable of noticing them. And perhaps only for the time being. At any moment, it may transform itself into something very different."

"Would it not be a good idea," Aurelia asked, "to proceed further? To see if the passage *remains* unchanging? After all, this may represent something of an opportunity."

Cleggik knew what she meant. "To escape the Keep."

"Yes. To escape."

The giant's renewed sense of hope began to waver like an oasis seen across the desert. What if this development was only a tease? What if the corridors of the Keep suddenly began to close in on him as they had done before, forcing him into configurations his body was not meant to assume, shaving the flesh from his bones?

Then his heart would be crushed along with the rest of him. Because like it or not, he had already embraced the possibility that this change in the Keep—or rather, this lack of change— was not only permanent but also widespread.

"I suppose," said Cleggik, "we can explore a little further. There is no harm in that."

"None," Aurelia said.

So they moved down the passageway.

And to their continued surprise, it didn't twist or drop or ascend or change shape. It just remained what it was.

As did the next passage. And the next. And the one after that.

Each time Cleggik and Aurelia waited for what seemed like a goodly time before they declared a passage unchanging. And each time, unchanging was what it was.

Cleggik shook his head—and wondered if this new development had anything to do with the Wizard.

❦ ❦ ❦

"Where is he?" Athis demanded, slamming the door shut and then spinning about and flattening himself against it. The door shook violently, nearly throwing him to the floor as he wrestled to shove home the iron bolt near its upper edge, though he already suspected that restraint and the matching one at the bottom would not be enough to keep the portal secure.

"How should I know?" Klaria replied, crouching down and slamming the other bolt in place. "Move out of the way," she instructed, her tone as crisp as ever, and Athis hurriedly did so. He slid to the side just in time as his fellow apprentice gestured, incanted, and then flung both hands toward the buckling door— and a wave of magical energy washed forth, coating the door and its frame and forming a shimmering surface that instantly quelled the pounding that had been occurring on the door's other side.

"Thanks," Athis told her, brushing a bit of dirt and some splinters from his robes. "I should've thought of that." He had mastered the sealing spell just a few weeks before, but in his panic it had slipped his mind. Fortunately, Klaria had maintained her cool, as usual. "That ifreet was really upset about the water."

"It was an accident!" a voice insisted from behind them, and Athis and Klaria both turned. Belid, the third of the Master's most senior apprentices, was standing, wringing his hands. His usual handsome features were slightly marred now by the fact that his pale hair was singed and his eyebrows had been seared away completely. "It's not like I meant to spill that on her!" Belid continued, his tone rising to a near whine.

"Well, you try explaining that to her," Klaria suggested, arching one eyebrow. "Meantime, we've got a bigger problem."

Athis nodded. "The Master," he agreed, resting his lanky frame against the nearest wall. "He should've been back ages ago." He sighed and shoved his hair out of his face, not for the first time contemplating trimming his hair close the way Klaria did. "If he had—" He didn't need to finish that statement. The ifreet had come to speak with the Master about something important, magical, and highly confidential. The fiery creature had grown more and more irate as time had passed, which was why the apprentices had decided to placate it by bringing it something to eat and drink.

Which would have been fine—if Belid hadn't slipped and emptied nearly the entire carafe directly onto the startled ifreet's lap.

The resulting column of steam had nearly blinded Belid. And the ifreet's bellows of pain and rage had come close to deafening him. But at least he had still possessed enough presence of mind to run for the door. Athis and Klaria had beaten him there, but had lingered to distract and delay the ifreet, which had been entirely focused on Belid.

Now, with the door locked and bolted and sealed, there was no way the ifreet could get loose, at least for a while.

And hopefully the Master would be back before that could happen.

In the meantime, "What's next?" Athis asked, rubbing one hand over his face. He was tired, so tired these days. He had actually considered casting a spell to keep himself awake, but had decided it against it. You never knew what sort of side effects a spell might bring, and he'd felt it would be better to be tired but sane and intact than to be ensnared in some strange cascade of magical maladies.

After all, none of the three of them were yet full-fledged wizards in their right, a fact that continued to gall them to no end. But they were still the most senior of the Master's apprentices, which meant it fell to them to maintain the Keep during his absence.

Even if that included dealing with an irate and deadly—and sopping wet—ifreet.

Klaria considered a moment, then made a face. "Cleaning the cage," she replied, and both Athis and Belid groaned. But for once Athis was quicker to recover.

"Not it!" he shouted, and giggled at the look of horror crossing his peer's face. "Yes!"

Belid turned pleading eyes toward Klaria, but she had been immune to his so-called charms from the moment she'd set foot in the Keep and he'd tried telling her that it was his job to inspect all new entrants for any concealed weapons. The weapon she'd used in response, her knee, hadn't counted as concealed at all.

"Not a chance," she told him now, a grim smile touching her lips. "The cage is all yours. I've got to prep for class." The three of them took turns teaching the newest group of apprentices, and this week it was her turn. She was actually the least inclined toward teaching of the three, and the most brusque in class, though she was also the most clear and direct in her instructions and the most adept at simple, practical spells, which made her the students' favorite. She turned to Athis. "Which means you get kitchen duty."

He smiled. "Done!" The kitchen was one of his favorite places in the Keep, both because he loved food and because it was at the very heart of the castle and, as the single most-used room here, rarely shifted or changed. And there was something comforting about cleaning dishes and preparing meals. It was clean, simple, straightforward work, with clear instructions and an obvious and valuable conclusion. All in all, Athis couldn't have asked for a better chore.

At least, that's what he thought as he set out for the kitchen, whistling to himself. Behind him Klaria smiled, shook her head, and then turned and headed off toward the classrooms, leaving Belid to grumble and curse under his breath until a dull thump from the ensorcelled door made him yelp and hurry away himself.

Which meant that none of them were there to see the spell-sealed door slowly vanish into the wall—and a new door appear a few feet to its left. A door that did not have any sort of magical lock upon it.

A door that slowly, carefully, creaked open.

* * *

Being the smaller of the two, Aurelia peeked from behind the door, looking about the now empty room. She looked left and right, up and down, slowly craning her head until satisfied the space was devoid of people.

"Do you see what made that noise?" Cleggik asked.

"No one's here and there's just the one door but the thump came from another direction, of that I'm sure."

"It was a minor chord," Cleggik noted and Aurelia turned, fixing her pretty pale blue eyes on him. "I was taught music before I could walk," he shrugged. "I think of everything musically. Your voice, for example, is a lovely alto. Do you, perchance, sing?"

"Only when I bathe," she said and gingerly stepped into the room. She sniffed the air, studied the space for some clue as to where they were. It was simple, unadorned, and devoid of information.

"You did hear the voices, right?" the giant asked.

"Of course. Three, maybe a little younger than me, but they were bickering."

Cleggik eased himself into the room, ducking his head and studying it for himself. Seeing nothing remarkable, he reached out for the door before Aurelia's hand swatted him away.

"Who knows what is out there? My captors? Those magicians? Something worse?"

"Staying here seems pointless," Cleggik said. "I am hungry and the lichen does a very poor job of sustaining me."

"Tell me about it," Aurelia admitted. "I have absolutely no idea how long I've been wandering these halls."

"Me either," the giant agreed. "I have actually heard the Keep crack and groan with growth so I know it has been some time. They are not happy noises, not at all."

"What do you mean?"

"I mean, when I first arrived, the corridors, rooms, halls all shifted when I wasn't looking. It happened so silently, it took me a while to realize what was happening. But now, it changes and makes noise. Reminds me of my father when he tries to get out of his favorite chair."

That distressed Aurelia deep inside herself although she had no idea why. It did, though, give her the conviction to go exploring and now it was her turn to try for the door. She gripped the iron handle and gave it a tug, pleased to find it silently open. Beyond the doorway was a long corridor, similar to all the others she and no doubt Cleggik had encountered. About one-third of the way down, there was a branching corridor to the left and further down there was a door on the right.

"Which way?" he asked.

"This corridor fades into darkness with no light so I would think we go left."

"Very good. It is getting a might warm in here."

Aurelia led the way and as they left the room, neither noticed the stone walls emitting wisps of steam, condensation beginning to form on the very stone itself.

Neither heard a sound as they walked but paused just before the juncture and she bent low, peering around the corner. After studying it for several moments she turned back to her oversized companion with a smile.

"Someone's cooking! I mean genuine food. I can smell the onions and mutton from here."

Cleggik inhaled deeply and his grim demeanor instantly altered, his broad, bearded face breaking into a smile. His stomach rumbled. After a moment, he whispered, mostly to himself, "A minor third, C, and a perfect fifth, E." She had no idea what he meant but concluded they were both hungry enough to risk following the enticing aroma. One step after another led the unlikely pair towards the next door where the cooking was underway. As they neared it, the clatter of pots and pans, of running water, and of a single male voice could be discerned. This caused Aurelia to pause and carefully listen, attempting to discern what was happening. Her companion, for his part, had put his hands over his ears, disliking the discordant noise.

"He's cleaning," she finally concluded.

"Well, make him stop. I haven't heard such noise in an age and it hurts," he said, attempting to whisper but being louder than she would have preferred. Still, whoever was behind the door might know why she was brought to the famed Crimson Keep. Or, at least, *when* it was and how to get back to her father's estate.

She mentally calculated the risks and decided to chance it. With measured steps, she walked the rest of the way to the broad wood and iron door and grasped the handle. Looking over her shoulder she shot her companion a look to make certain he was ready.

"Whoever is behind the door may be powerful; can you protect us?"

He flexed his hands, wiggling his fingers, and formed fists the size of twin suckling pigs. Then he furrowed his brow and nodded in agreement.

With that, she swung open the door, which moved noiselessly, and she stood in the doorway ready for anything.

Well, anything but the sight of a teenaged male, simply attired in a robe, in the process of falling to the ground. He landed with a *sploosh*, droplets of water rising high above him before settling back atop him.

"Fedgegloop," the male said.

The sight made Aurelia chuckle aloud and her hand flew to her mouth to stifle the sound. But it was too late as she heard the other splash about, struggling to his feet.

"Klaria, if you think that's funny, well, it's not . . . " The words died in his throat as he cleared the island between them and his mouth dropped open as he took in the sight of the young woman and the giant.

"*Gagh!*" he screamed, his voice going high.

"Alto," Cleggik said.

"Fedgegloop and Gagh—I don't speak your language," Aurelia said very slowly, and very loudly in the hopes he would somehow understand her.

All the male did was stare at her, his eyes darting back and forth between the two, but mostly, they settled on her and his mouth hung open.

Behind him, there was a large porcelain basin filled with soap suds and portions of various copper pots. Along the table were racks where already cleaned cooking items were hung to dry. To her right was a huge fireplace where the aforesmelled mutton was roasting over a low, steady fire. Beside it, over a small fire, hung a huge black pot where vegetables simmered.

Now Aurelia's stomach rumbled at almost the exact same pitch as Cleggik's had moments earlier.

"You . . . you're a girl," the male finally said.

"Yes I am," she agreed, delighted he could speak her tongue.

"He's a giant," he said.

"Yes I am," rumbled Cleggik. "A hungry one."

"Please don't eat me!" the male said.

"Okay."

The male blinked at that and began to slowly collect himself. He straightened, schooling his features and resumed speaking, his voice now measured and more assured.

"I am Athis, a student of the Master. Welcome to the Crimson Keep, where we offer protection and hospitality."

"We have been 'guests' here for some time, I think," she said. "I am Aurelia, daughter of Wilder and Blaise, keepers of Stonecraft Mansion."

"And I am Cleggik, from the Corwain Valley, a simple singer."

"What are you doing here?"

"I was hoping you could tell me," Aurelia said. She flashed him a smile, hoping to encourage him to tell her something, anything that might help her get home.

"Wait, were you two among the Lost?"

"The Lost?" Cleggik asked.

"The Keep is old and constantly growing and changing. It is not uncommon for people to go missing for days or months at a time," Athis said, wiping up the mess he left on the stone flooring.

"Months?"

"Yes, Aurelia," he said, clearly testing her name on his tongue.

A loud, deep rumble interrupted their conversation. It was similar to the sounds she had heard earlier but this was more sustained, deeper in tone, and she shuddered.

Athis, for his part, let out a scream of fright.

"Definitely an alto," Cleggik said.

"Do you know what's making that noise?" Aurelia asked.

"I don't know, it sounds like the walls are moving again. I've been told that sometimes the stones shift, though I've never been close enough to see it happening myself."

"Sounds like you're not very observant," said Cleggik.

"Excuse me? I'll have you know I'm very *oh my word* where are my manners? You say you've been in the Keep for a long while, you must be starving! Um . . . here, start with these!" Athis grabbed two goblets, dunked them in the bucket of clean water and handed them to Cleggik and Aurelia. "Drink, drink, while I check on the food!"

Cleggik looked at the goblet, tiny in his giant hands. "Do you mind if I just drink the bucket?"

"Please, go ahead!" Athis was at the fireplace, stirring the vegetables. "The meat should be done shortly, and I can offer you this now— and here, something stronger to drink! I've been saving this for a special occasion!" He reached for the wine rack and pulled out a bottle, waved his hand, and the cork popped off with a spray of effervescence. "I believe the locals called it champanyah." He poured into three fresh goblets.

"Is it supposed to be that pink?"

"Madame, I've never had any other kind," said Athis.

Cleggik looked down at the two. "Look, we thank you for your hospitality, but we have been inside the Keep for a very long time. We have not seen the sky in a very long time. Can you lead us to the front door, so that we may take our leave and return to our lives?"

Athis looked up at Cleggik uncomfortably, as if suddenly reminded of the great difference of size between them . . . and how hungry the giant was. "Well . . . that might take some time."

Behind him, the rumbling started again. Closer than before. But not as close as the rumbling from Cleggik's stomach.

■ ■ ■

Belid scooted along to catch up to Klaria, expecting to have to hurry to make it to the classrooms at the same time as her. He was wrong. After turning left at the end of the corridor, he found Klaria stopped in front of an unexpected brick wall, muttering.

"Oh dear," was all he could say.

Klaria turned and faced him. "'Oh, dear'? That's all you have?"

"Oh dear, the walls have moved and we should have turned right and taken the long way to class?"

"Look behind you."

Belid looked and saw the hallway to the right had also become suddenly truncated. "Oh." Off in the distance, he could hear rumbling. "It's going to be one of those days in the Keep."

"Or one of those weeks. I just hope all that rumbling isn't some sign of mutiny." As if on cue, the rumbling started to get louder and rhythmic. *Rumble rumble rumble* . . .

"Stop that rumbling!" Belid said sternly. Oddly, the noise stopped with a single silent *rumble*. Belid didn't like that at all, and turned to Klaria.

"Klaria . . . what was the sealing spell you used to lock up the ifreet again, exactly?"

"*Sigelu interne dala kastelo*, of course."

"Oh, no."

"'Oh no' what?"

"It's *sigelu interne dala kambro*, not *kastelo*. You sealed him inside the castle!"

"Yes, he's sealed in."

"No. He's. INSIDE. THE. CASTLE."

RUMBLERUMBLERUMBLERUMBLE . . .

♦ ♦ ♦

Athis could not quite believe it.

He had found the main door.

Let me say that again, he thought smugly. *I found the main door.*

What might have seemed a rather routine accomplishment in any other building was a feat of some consideration in the Crimson Keep. Athis was continually frustrated by the way the shifting hallways, corridors, and stairs of the Keep seemed to single him out most of all as he endeavored to get from Point A to Point B with as minimal difficulties as possible. The fact that it seemed to be cooperating with him as he led Aurelia and Cleggik toward the castle's exit was filling him with joy. Indeed, perhaps this was a symbol of something. Maybe he was reaching the end of his tenure as a student and was on the verge of becoming a full-fledged wizard. Anything was possible.

Suddenly the ground under him trembled so violently that he almost lost his footing. The only thing that prevented him from hitting the ground was the massive hand of Cleggik that reached out and snagged his arm. Indeed, for once the giant's size was of benefit to him. Rumbling walls and a shaking floor might be incredibly inconvenient and challenging to someone of normal height, but Cleggik was so large that either shoulder was touching the walls, helping him to remain easily braced.

The length of the rumbling was increasing, it seemed to Athis, and he had zero idea why that would be. He didn't think it was an earthquake of any sort. He had experienced quakes once or twice in his youth, and it was a completely different sensation. The most obvious was that the force of the shaking didn't seem to be emanating from the floor. Instead it appeared to be originating from the walls themselves. But how in the world could that be?

"How could *what* be?" asked Aurelia

"How could the quaking be originating from . . . ?" His voice trailed off and his head whipped around as he stared at her in confusion. "I didn't say that aloud."

"Yes, you did," Aurelia said firmly. "I heard you."

"Did I say that out loud?" Athis asked Cleggik.

"I wasn't paying attention," Cleggik said less than helpfully. "I was trying to figure out the pitch of the trembling. It's odd because it keeps shifting . . . "

"Never mind," and Athis let out an annoyed sigh. "Anyway . . . I was just wondering where this shaking is originating from. It seems to be coming from the walls themselves. I don't—"

"Can I be honest?" said Aurelia. "I don't really care why the walls are shaking. I am just desperate to get out of here. I've been wandering endlessly. I am not sure if I've been here for weeks or months or . . . I don't know . . . years. If something is going wrong with the castle, please solve it on your own time. Just let me out."

"Yes, of course," Athis said sympathetically. "That shouldn't be a problem. It's right up here."

He pointed and she stared ahead in confusion. "That . . . isn't what I was expecting."

There was a fairly normal looking door at the end of the corridor.

"It isn't?"

"It's a castle. I was expecting some sort of massive gate."

Athis smiled at that. "Oh, we have one of those. It's quite large and we always lower it when we are expecting guests. It impresses them immensely. But we also have this nice, ordinary one that we use to enter and exit."

"That's lovely," she said and she started to head straight toward it.

That was when there was another rumble, bigger than ever, and there was a sound as well. Insanely, it sounded to Athis as if someone was screaming.

It was not the only scream that Athis heard at that moment, because the other one was coming from Aurelia. She howled as if she had been stabbed. She clutched at her chest, her eyes widening, and Cleggik was able to prevent her from collapsing to the ground. All the blood drained from her face and for an instant she looked to Athis as gray as the castle walls.

"What's wrong?" said Athis urgently. He dropped to the ground, taking her chin in his hand and lifting her head up so that he could gaze into her eyes. "Aurelia, *what's wrong?*"

"I don't know," she managed to gasp out. "I . . . I was in so much pain. I've never felt anything like it in my life." Her color was starting to normalize. "It was like . . . like a hundred icicles carving into me."

"But it's gone now?"

She managed to nod. "Yes, thank the gods. Help me out of here."

"Of course."

He stood and helped her to her feet. She smiled gratefully and took two more steps forward, and she cried out again.

"What's wrong with her?" Athis demanded of Cleggik, although he had no idea why he was asking him. There was no reason that he would have an answer.

At that moment the walls once again rumbled fiercely, and yet again Aurelia cried out while at the same time there was another shriek that ripped through the air around them.

Cleggik reached down and lifted Aurelia into his arms. Most of her body was balanced on his forearm.

"Get me out," she whispered.

But Cleggik didn't move. Instead he was staring down at her, and when he spoke his voice was thick with curiosity. "The scream. The scream from around us . . . it's the same pitch as yours."

"So?" she whispered, still clutching at her chest. "Please, Cleggik, just get me out of here . . . "

"I mean the exact same pitch," said Cleggik. "Like . . . the same voice."

She clutched at his arm. "I don't care. I don't know where the scream is coming from, and it doesn't matter. Carry me out of here, Cleggik. I'm begging you. I just want to go home. I won't scream anymore, I swear."

Cleggik seemed to hesitate and then he nodded. Athis barely managed to get out of Cleggik's way as the giant strode past him, heading for the door.

And Athis could see that Aurelia's promise was having a horrific effect on her. Her body was not only shaking furiously, but she was biting down on her lower lip to contain the screams that were slamming around, determined to erupt from her throat. Blood was trickling down her chin and her eyes were tightly shut to help contain her agony.

"Put her down! Stop!" cried Athis, but Cleggik ignored him. Instead with one massive step after another, he approached the door, drawing closer and closer, and suddenly the door banged open.

A figure was standing in the doorway.

"She can't leave," it said.

■ ■ ■

"You mean *in the walls?*" said a stunned Klaria.

"Yes! In the walls! We have to let him out!" Belid told her.

"Okay!" She paused and then said, "How exactly?"

"You sealed him in!" Belid shouted. "You must know the counter spell!"

"*Why* would I know it?!" Klaria demanded. "The whole point of the sealing spell is to prevent something that wants to kill you from doing so! Why would I want to learn how to let *out* something that I've sealed away?!"

"Maybe there's something in the library . . . "

"You're kidding, right?" she said skeptically. "We've got a pissed off fire demon trapped in the walls, and you think we're going to be able to find our way to one of the hardest rooms in the place to locate?"

Then Belid put up a hand. "Wait. The walls stopped rumbling. That's good, right?"

That was when flame erupted from the walls. Within seconds the hallway under them was burning furiously.

"It's trying to kill us!" Belid cried out.

"Worse," Klaria said grimly. "If it wanted to kill us fast, it would light up the floor. Instead it's keeping it confined to the walls. It wants us to die slowly."

"That's terrific! Let's not help it cooperate! Come on!" and he desperately pointed at a door at the end of the corridor.

Belid and Klaria sprinted toward it, and for a moment it seemed as if they were definitely going to make it, right before the door began blazing.

■ ■ ■

"*Master!*" Athis cried out.

The Master strode into the corridor and the door, entirely on its own, slammed shut behind him. "You cannot leave," he said again.

Aurelia began to sob. "I just want to go home to my parents . . ."

"You have no parents."

"Yes, I do! I'm—"

"No, you're not," said the Master. To Athis's surprise, his voice dropped to what seemed an almost sympathetic tone. "Everything you believe you remember is a falsehood. You are not who or even what you believe." He glanced up at Cleggik. "Don't worry. You are. You had no way of knowing, I'm afraid."

"Knowing what?" demanded Cleggik. "I don't understand!"

Aurelia took a deep breath and let it out slowly. "I am Aurelia, daughter of Wilder and Blaise, keepers of Stonecraft Mansion."

"No, you are not. That is just something you fabricated because you were so determined to leave. But you cannot. Ever. Because of what you are."

"What . . ." She stared at him as if seeing him for the first time. "What am I?" Her voice sounded like an eggshell about to break.

He took her hand in his. "You *are* the Crimson Keep, my dear."

"What? I'm . . . I'm what?"

He squeezed her hand tightly. "You are its heart, its soul, its essence. You cannot leave because if you do, all this will crumble. Although it seems to be in the process of crumbling right now. I wonder why."

Meanwhile, at that exact moment, in the depths of space, the sun began to go nova.

❦ ❦ ❦

The ifreet was confused. The ifreet was also angry, although in fairness, as beings of the fire persuasion the ifreet as a whole had a tendency towards hotheadedness, even at rest. But in this instance, iFrita believed she had ample cause for anger. She came as a representative of her people to speak to the old Wizard of the Keep on a matter of great urgency, but not only was she left to wait for hours in a drafty anteroom, but then insult was followed by injury when one of the Wizard's whelps assaulted her with water. Water! The nemesis of her race!

But this imprisonment was the last straw . . . the straw that she would use to burn the offenders. She felt the spell hit just before the world went dark, and when she finally regained her senses, she found they had been somehow altered. iFrita no longer had eyes or ears, yet she could see and hear all things at once within the Crimson Keep. Her arms and legs were gone, yet she felt every inch of the great castle, both within and without. She had become something different, something far more than even the oneness that connected her with the ifreet, making her aware of everything, from the tiniest dust mites in the unswept corners of the great dining hall to the glorious heat of Mother Sun, whose voice iFrita now heard calling out to her.

She had become the Crimson Keep.

The Crimson Keep had become her.

And together, they were infinite!

With that realization, iFrita began to laugh and the walls of the Crimson Keep shuddered and shifted while the tiny, little humans inside scurried about in fear.

* * *

The flames in the great fireplace in the massive entryway of the Crimson Keep suddenly flared to life and exploded from the enclosure. Cleggik lunged between the rush of fire and Aurelia and the Master, prepared to sacrifice himself for a girl he was no longer sure was even real.

"You must go back, Aurelia," the Master said, recoiling from the heat. "Without you, I don't know how long the Keep can hold together."

The girl cried out and tore herself from the old sorcerer's grasp. "I don't care . . . I can't go back, not now, not after feeling what *living* is like! Let this cursed old place fall and make me free of it!"

"That's impossible!" the Master insisted, stepping towards her. "The Keep cannot fall!"

As if to prove him wrong, the walls began to violently shake and the flames danced wildly about. Above their heads, the plaster ceiling heaved like swells on the ocean and inside the walls they could hear timbers creaking and snapping.

"It falls *now*," Cleggik sang out, raising his hands above his head to keep the ceiling from coming down on them.

"Then we've no more time," the Master said. His cold, analytical eyes looked into hers. He saw no awareness in them, only fright, and for an instant, he thought he might hesitate in pity, but he reminded himself she wasn't real. At least not in a human way. And even if she were, wouldn't the salvation of the Keep have warranted this small sacrifice?

"No, please," Aurelia whimpered.

"Don't make her go," Cleggik begged.

The flames rose higher and the shuddering walls were starting to crack and shatter, showering them in dust and debris.

"If the Keep goes, the whole world is doomed," the Master said. "I *am* sorry, my dear. Truly."

And then the Master spoke the words of a spell that reminded Cleggik of a night lark's song while Aurelia's sobs sang behind it, and then the flames were blasted back by an explosion that stank of sulfur and Aurelia was gone.

A moment later, the breathless Klaria and Belid came crashing through a door.

"Master! Thank the gods you're back!" Klaria gasped.

"There's been an . . . accident," Belid cried. "There was this visiting ifreet, you see, and she . . . "

"What have you done this time, boy?" the Master snapped.

"*I* didn't do anything, but Klaria cast a spell that—"

"Excuse me, but I wouldn't have had to cast a spell in the first place if *you* hadn't spilled the water on her and—"

"So because I'm clumsy, that's an excuse for you to screw up the spell?"

"Somebody had to do something and it sure didn't look like it was going to be you, so I stepped up while you were wetting yourself and—"

"Children," the Master interrupted, trying to maintain his calm.

"I didn't wet myself. That was just splashback from the water I spilled on the ifreet."

The Master's eyes went wide and when he spoke again, his voice blasted through their bickering. "You did *what?*" he thundered.

Even the shuddering walls seemed to pause for an instant at the Master's wrath.

"It was an accident?" Belid squeaked. "Anyway, that's not the worst of it."

"How does it get worse than pouring water on a fire demon?" the Master demanded.

Klaria grinned weakly. "By casting a spell that . . . *also* accidently, I should add, *bound* the ifreet into the walls of the Keep."

The Master's mouth opened and moved but no sound came out. He could only stare at them with an expression unlike any Belid had ever seen before. It was a look that made him frightened to be alive at that particular instant in time.

Finally the Master screamed, "You did *what*, you fools?"

The flames answered him: "They have assured the supremacy of the Flame!" the fire crackled.

"Observe!" the Crimson Keep rumbled in agreement and a part of the western wall and ceiling disappeared, revealing a swollen, crimson sun above the horizon, spewing tendrils of superheated gases from its bubbling surface.

"Okay," Belid said in an awed whisper. "This is even worse than I thought."

■ ■ ■

Aurelia gasped, "Who . . . who's there?" but of course no words were spoken. Castles could not speak and stone and mortar possessed no thought. But awareness is a thing measured differently by different entities. The tiny, soft form that her need for humanity had created had barely any awareness at all, hardly enough to stumble through the dark, while the Keep was at the heart of the All and woven together with the real and unreal, the waking and the dreaming, aware of everything.

Just as she was aware now of another, separate consciousness where there should have been just the one, just the Keep. Perhaps it was merely the last, fading echo of Aurelia, the momentary dream, the transitive instant when the flesh is forgotten and the Keep is once again the All and the Only.

But then something not her said, "The Keep belongs to the Flame now," and it was Aurelia who started to scream.

■ ■ ■

The floor of the great foyer heaved under their feet and the very air was vibrating as though with a force barely contained, straining to be released. The Master stared straight into the roiling sun and spoke like one in shock: "The sun. The fire demon's using the power of the Keep to encompass the world in flames."

Belid and Klaria exchanged looks, then turned back to their master, saying, "What do we do?"

"That is an excellent question, but one to which I have no ready answer." The old man turned eyes blazing almost as hot as the sun on them, "You see, never before in the history of . . . of . . . of *history* have two powerful opposing magical forces ever been contained within the same locus of infinite power at the same time. All commonsense tells one that such a happenstance *should* be fatal to the very fabric of existence." The Master pointed up at the expanding sun on the horizon. "Oh. Look! I guess there is still some sense left in the world after all!"

As much as Belid usually appreciated the Master's ironic sarcasm, he interrupted this shining example of it with, "Master, please!"

"Shut up! I'm going to try and take care of . . . *that*," the Master said, pointing again to the sun, then he shifted his gaze to Klaria. "Can you reverse your spell?"

She shrugged. "I . . . I . . ."

The Master cut her off. "Do what you can. And try to keep this damned place on its foundations until I get back."

Cleggik watched the old sorcerer disappear and shuddered. The world was falling apart around him in a cacophony of discordant sounds and vibrations, some that sounded like Aurelia and tears, others like pain and death. Even clamping his massive hands over his ears didn't block the sounds, so in desperation and despair, Cleggik began to sing as loud as he could.

♥ ♥ ♥

iFrita stirred.

Not just because her power was expanding, which it was. And not just because Aurelia was whimpering, weakening, desperate, and humiliated—powerless to reclaim the human form to which she had grown attached, impotent in her battle to stave off possession of the Keep, of *her*—which was also true.

No, the fire demon was basking in its own glory, feasting on the magical bone marrow of the Crimson Keep itself. Like fungus overtaking a forest, with each waking moment iFrita fused her very essence with the Keep, just as the Keep's essence fused with her.

A sadistic cancer with limitless appetite—and no cure.

"You have no idea how much I've delighted in watching you walk the halls of the Crimson Keep," iFrita said to Aurelia, still struggling to accept her lot as the one true Keep—and the grand responsibility that came with it. "It took millennia . . . perhaps longer . . . it can be difficult to tell, as time here is as ever-shift-ing as the walls themselves. Your walls. You."

"Took?" Aurelia whimpered, coughing, her spirit-self lost between states of being—no longer a woman able to experience the tactile world in human form—to feel and sense and *be*—yet also unable to reclaim her place as the Keep, lost in the amor-phous state of *once was* and *might never again be*. Her walls were breaking apart. Her very self was crumbling into dust, into *not being*. "Took? To do what?"

"Ha! You really are a fool, aren't you?" The ifreet's embers curled deeper and farther through the stones of the Keep, its magic-cancer tentacles mutating the Keep's essence, eroding Aurelia's capacity to concentrate. To think. To retain her con-sciousness. "Do you think I just showed up one day, by chance, and burrowed into your soul? Do you think you began walking the halls of the Keep—unaware that you were the Keep, walking through yourself—simply because it *happened*?"

"No, I . . . ," Aurelia said, aching like a mother whose child is dying in her arms, without knowing why it was even happen-ing, or what, if anything, could be done to stop it. "I didn't think about it, I didn't realize . . ."

The ifreet chuckled, a smarmy chuckle of self-congratula-tory conceit. "Yes. I know. You didn't think at all, did you? Since the beginning of time itself—maybe even before then—you, the Crimson Keep, have declared yourself the gatekeeper between worlds, the membrane between existence and not, between life and death. Between the time before time and time immemo-rial. Or . . . at least you as want to define it. But that's your true arrogance, is it not? So in love with your purpose that the *myth* of you became more important than *being* you. Your need to be *needed*—your ego—has tossed away the very nature of your exis-tence. To give shape and meaning to the world."

"I . . . I don't understand. Why . . . ?" Her clarity disintegrat-ing, even as Aurelia felt herself transmogrifying back into the Keep, she felt the ifreet's poison overtaking her, absorbing into her soul. "W-why are you doing this? Why now?"

"Because I *hate* you," iFrita said. "Because once upon a time when the Keep was still young—when *you* were still young—me and my kind discovered a purpose within the Keep. We wanted to be part of something bigger than life itself. We wanted to contribute. To serve. But in that booming voice of his—you know that voice more so than any other—the Master laughed at us, shunned our very existence. He said we were like a virus that needed to be contained, if not eradicated, that all we could ever do was poison the world. Poison the Keep."

Aurelia seized, feeling the infection within her soul, within the stones that gave shape and boundaries to the Keep.

"Our dreams destroyed, we realized our new purpose. To become what the Master deemed us to be. We've watched, and waited. Our resolve ran thin, I won't deny that. There were times when we thought all hope was lost. That we would never find our way into your pores. And then . . . and here is the greatest irony of all . . . it was only after the Master's new charges thought they were the smartest to roam that Keep—destined for greatness—did we know our time had come. An act of selfishness—of arrogance—made it possible for you to become Aurelia, to roam the halls. And your roaming the halls—roaming you—made it possible for me to enter your soul. And to make . . . you . . . mine."

"N-n-no," Aurelia eeked out in her ever-weakening state. But truth put to words cannot be ignored, or denied. "The Master would never allow that. No one would ever . . ."

"Ahh . . . wait. Do you hear that now?" iFrita said. "Breath. Listen. It is distant, but pure. Your withering stones are crying out for mercy. They are singing the song of their demise. Of your demise. Good night, Aurelia. Goodnight Keep. Your end in this life has come."

* * *

The song echoing throughout the Keep was not, however, of death, but a lyrical spell of hope. Cleggik breathed, allowing all the beauty and sadness and pain and love he had stored within his very essence channel its way through his voice, echoing through the halls of the Keep, even as the stones began to tumble and fall around him.

Belid heard the notes, felt them wash over him. As did Athis, Klaria, and all those who roamed the Keep. The Master, too.

The hallway surrounding Cleggik shrank and twisted, the ifreet's cancer-magic about to extinguish the most beautiful voice the Keep had ever known. But the love that flowed within those notes, like a scent in the wind, rolled and curled around the edges of the cancer-magic. The bricks and stones were carried along the air as if turned to pollen, awaiting a winged creature to make sweet nectar.

So Cleggik sang, as if those notes he shared were to be the very last he would ever sing. The very last notes that would ever be sung—or heard—by anyone.

Cleggik released his mind, gave himself to over, to his voice, a gift he had not known until then was a gift at all. Even as a boy he questioned why life had mocked him so. Why would he, a giant—a massive physical being who, if the need be, could crush a stone in his bare hands—also carry within his chest a river of gentle tones?

A giant who did not wish to smash, but to sing, to share the tenderness in his heart, could only be seen as weak. How could he be respected as a giant—have a reason to even be—if all he desired was to sit quietly be a stream, and through his honeysuckle voice express what roamed in his heart?

Giants do not whisper love. They smash. They destroy.

But only now, he thought, that perhaps he had been given such a massive form to protect this very gift. That his body—and thus his brute strength—was the cast iron safe within which he stored his most precious possession, to be set free only as the Keep rumbled into dust.

So Cleggik sang. Oh, yes, he sang. The walls trembled . . . but they held. The ground dipped . . . but it stabilized. The doors that shifted and shrank, yet returned to form. The walls themselves began to leak, dripping with tears, the poison being squeezed from their veins.

"Keep singing," Cleggik heard, and though no voice was present, he knew certainly from where it came. Aurelia. The Keep. She—it—they—were getting stronger, beginning to heal, purged of the cancer-magic.

"Your voice is the cure," the voice said, its power—and vigor—returning. "I told you when I first heard your tones that yours is the most beautiful, soothing song I'd ever heard. It is so much more than that, my dear Cleggik. You will save me. You will save us all. You are—"

"Ooof!"

Cleggik's song went dark and cold. Silent.

His massive body dropped to the floor, landing face-first on the cobblestone. Blood leaked from the back of his head. Which is what happens when with great force you are smashed in the skull with an iron goblet.

"I told you to be quiet," his attacker said. "I didn't want it to come to this. I warned you, Cleggik. You are a Giant, with a singular purpose. But you wouldn't listen. You left me no choice."

❦ ❦ ❦

Drops of red trickled down the gleaming goblet, and Athis, Belid, and Klaria stared in shock at the one who wielded it.

"M-Master?" Athis stared wide-eyed at the old man, who stood over the unconscious Cleggik with a malicious smirk on his lips. "Why did you do that?"

As the Master glanced at him, a flash of green lit his eyes.

"Because he's not the Master!" Klaria exclaimed. Magic crackled through her arms as she prepared an unmasking spell.

"There's no need for that, my dear." The Master's voice was no longer the gruff, male one they'd become so accustomed to, but rather a low female tone. His—her?—face warped and stretched, elongating into the sharp, green face of a demon. "Now that I know what's going on, there's no need for me to wear that old codger's face. I do believe he's still on the road, though it's possible he's been trying to get into the Keep, and iFrita's been keeping him out."

"Who are you?" Belid demanded with a bravado he certainly wasn't feeling, as evidenced by his buckling knees.

"I was supposed to assist iFrita in our mission to take over the Keep, and we decided it'd be more strategic if I kept my presence unknown. That's not difficult with so many disguises to chose from." As if to prove her point, the demon abruptly shrank and sprouted wings, becoming a raven. The iron goblet clattered to the floor.

"A shapeshifter," Athis murmured.

"Indeed." The raven then morphed into a mirror image of his own face, and he jumped back in astonishment. "Unfortunately, this cursed place separated us. I couldn't have been in the bathroom for more than a minute, but by the time I emerged, the corridor was entirely different, and iFrita was nowhere in sight. I spent hours looking for her, and when the walls started rumbling, I knew something important was happening and took the Master's form to find out what." The demon shifted back into her green-skinned form. "Now I know: iFrita infiltrated the Keep as planned, and soon, she shall be triumphant."

Around them, the walls trembled and swayed, flames leaping across the stones. Without Cleggik's calming song, the Keep rumbled more violently than before. Corridors twisted into spirals, and windows and doors shattered.

"You fool!" Klaria pointed emphatically at the shapeshifter. "If the Keep is destroyed, you'll be destroyed with the rest of us! Why did you attack Cleggik?"

The demon arched an eyebrow and looked disdainfully at the unconscious giant at her feet. "On the contrary, iFrita knows I'm here and will ensure my safety once she's defeated that whimpering ninny who inhabited the Keep before her. I sent Aurelia back into the walls so that iFrita could destroy her once and for all. As for Cleggik—I sent him here years ago to weaken the Keep, and instead, the idiot forgot his mission, then got himself lost. And then he had the audacity to aid Aurelia with his song. He's a failure and a traitor. Good riddance to him. And good riddance to you."

The demon's body grew into that of an enormous beast with long claws and protruding fangs. Red scales glittered down her back, reflecting the wall's leaping flames. She filled the entire corridor, but the burning walls appeared to have no effect. Opening her wide jaws, she lunged at the three humans.

❦ ❦ ❦

You are a Giant, with a singular purpose. Cleggik fell through the clouds of his dream, those words whirling through his mind. *Giants do not sing. They destroy. This is your chance to redeem yourself.*

A proud woman in a black cloak stood over him. He now sat against a tree at the side of the road, depressed and miserable after being cast out of his clan. By choosing song over strength, he'd brought them shame.

Help us destroy the Crimson Keep. Green light flashed across the woman's piercing eyes. *Smash its walls with your fists and bring terror to those within. You will be helping us complete a great quest, and your deeds will become legend. Your clan will be proud.*

Through the fog of the dreamscape, Cleggik recalled the memories he'd tried so hard to bury. How, desperate and alone, he'd accepted the task. How he'd arrived at the Crimson Keep intending to destroy as much as he could, but found himself too fascinated by its strange beauty and wondrous magic. How he'd decided he'd rather remain true to himself—a simple singer—than rejoin his clan. And how he'd been ashamed that he'd ever considered destroying such a magnificent place and tried to forget why he'd come in the first place.

He recalled majestic, breathing hallways. And at the end of one—a lovely young woman named Aurelia. She smiled and reached out one hand to him. And though he knew she was a dream, he opened his mouth and sang to her.

❦ ❦ ❦

"You've forgotten who you are." The ifreet's cackling voice tumbled through Aurelia's ears.

Except . . . she had no ears. Somehow, she existed without form. Confusion and panic spiraled through her mind, and her heart trembled. Frightened, chaotic thoughts bombarded her. Not words—just emotions. She felt as if the terror and alarm of a hundred people were enveloping her consciousness.

Then, all that ceased as a song burrowed into her soul. One

that calmed her with its placid, cascading melody. It almost sounded like—but no. It couldn't be Cleggik. She'd been aware enough of what was going on within the Keep's walls to know he lay unconscious.

Yet the sound was undeniable. More than the sound—the serenity. She felt as if *she* were the one singing, letting the music flow through her body, possess her senses, and carry her into a transcendent place.

"There, there." The ifreet clucked mockingly. "It will all be over soon." Her flames wrapped around more and more stones, bit by bit swallowing the Keep whole, and with it, Aurelia.

But that song—it anchored her mind. And through its peace, a realization dawned on her. She wasn't *hearing* Cleggik—she was absorbing the emotions and thoughts he experienced in his dream.

The Keep grew by feeding on the knowledge and desires of those who dwelled within, but in her human state, she'd forgotten. Filled with the terror of those trapped within the crumbling, burning hallways, she'd been unable to focus. But with Cleggik's song soothing her mind, the awareness returned.

Once, it had been only her and the Master. As she'd grown, the Master had brought more and more students into the Keep to satisfy her growing appetite for human experiences. They'd strive and desire and rage and grieve, and after generations of students had passed through her walls, she'd found herself mixing herself up with them more and more, until she came to think of herself as one of them and yearned to join them.

The yearning had become so strong, she'd forgotten her purpose and abilities and become Aurelia. But now—now she remembered.

"What's the matter?" the ifreet taunted. "Aren't you even going to try fighting back?" The magic-cancer wound its burning tendrils into the Keep's core.

She ignored the pain and searched her mind. She held the collective knowledge of so, so many. Surely, one of them knew how to defeat this demon.

The answer came from an unexpected place: The mind of the shapeshifter demon who'd accompanied the ifreet in disguise. Somewhere in the hallways, it was terrorizing three of the Master's pupils. But though it worked with the ifreet, it didn't entirely trust her. And, for insurance, it had learned of a way to banish the fire demon from this realm.

The Keep drew the knowledge from the shapeshifter's mind and was surprised by what she found. Not a complex spell full of dark magic, but an incantation calling upon the gods of old. It was more than magic. It was a supplication, a prayer.

"What are you doing?" The ifreet's voice grew alarmed. The magic-cancer slithered faster and faster through the Keep, as if it knew its time was running out.

The Keep concentrated on reciting the incantation. With Cleggik's melody still rolling through her mind, the words emerged as a song.

The notes echoed through the Keep, smooth and tranquil as a rippling brook. The hallways ceased to twist, and the stones grew still. The flames spiraled upward as a great force sucked them into the sky, past the clouds, and into the great vacuum beyond.

"*Stop!*" the ifreet screeched. "How—"

The words melted into a bone-shattering scream.

A column of fire rose from the entire Keep as that almighty force drew tendrils of flame out of every crevice, until none remained.

■ ■ ■

"The ifreet must be gone!" Athis had never imagined he'd find such comfort in the sight of boring walls, but at present, boring was the best thing they could be.

"That's wonderful." Beside him, Klaria spoke through clenched teeth. "But in case you've forgotten, we still have a shapeshifter to deal with!"

She, Athis, and Belid were taking turns shooting spells at the demon, which kept morphing into various monstrous forms. It had only grown angrier after the flames were somehow sucked from the Keep and was now clawing at them in the shape of a mighty manticore.

It reared to strike, then abruptly froze in place. Spasms

wracked its body, and the three students watched in surprise as it abruptly shrank into a tiny mosquito.

Clap! A pair of wrinkled hands smashed the bug.

"How unpleasant." The Master wiped his green-stained hands on his robes. "Can't I go on a simple trip to the bookstore without someone trying to destroy this place?"

"Master!" Belid exclaimed, grinning widely.

Athis nudged him. "How do we know it's *really* the Master this time?"

The Master turned to Klaria. "How's that unmasking spell of yours coming along?" He spread his arms. "Go ahead."

Klaria narrowed her eyes, then called upon the spell. Magic crackled through her veins and burst out of her hands, forming a shimmering blue cloud around the Master. When it dissipated, the old man remained unchanged. Exhaling, she lowered her arms. "It's him."

"Fantastic." The Master stroked his chin. "Now that we've gotten that over with, would you mind explaining what happened?"

A low groan rose from the ground. Athis, Belid, and Klaria whirled in alarm to find Cleggik, whom they'd all forgotten about, stirring on the floor.

The giant blinked groggily. "What did I miss?"

"Just the ifreet getting sucked out of the Keep," Belid replied.

"An *ifreet?*" The Master glared. "What have you done this time, boy?"

Belid flinched. The shapeshifter had used those same words; it had been very thorough in its disguise. "It wasn't me! Klaria—"

"Oh, don't you dare try to pin this on me again!" Klaria snapped. "You spilled water on a fire demon, and—"

"That's not important! What matters is that *you* bound the ifreet to the walls of the Keep, which somehow came to life as a young woman named Aurelia!"

"You did *what?*" The Master bellowed. The very walls held their breath as he glared at each student in turn. "Do you realize what could have happened?"

"Yes—the shapeshifter version of you explained it quite vividly." Belid gave what he imagined was a disarming smile in hopes of deflecting the Master's wrath. He was, after all, the favorite. "Encompassing the world in flame, death and destruction and mayhem—"

Pop! Belid vanished in a burst of smoke. In his place, a little brown newt crawled on the floor.

"Master!" Klaria stared. "What—"

Pop! Just as abruptly, she, too, was turned into a newt.

Athis widened his eyes and spun to face the Master. "None of this was my fault! I didn't—"

Pop! A third newt scurried up to the other two, which were running around in panicked circles.

Cleggik gaped at the Master. "A bit harsh, don't you think?"

"Thanks to them, a fire demon almost burned the world to a crisp. I'd say the punishment is lenient, all things considered." The Master waved his hand dismissively. "Don't worry, they'll figure out how to turn themselves back soon enough. Call it an accelerated course in transmogrification." He peered at Cleggik's wound. "Now, let me do something about that head of yours. I rather enjoy your songs and would hate for you to drop dead. Follow me."

As Cleggik followed the Master down the hallway, careful not to step on the three panicked newts scurrying alongside them, he ran his hand along the Keep's stones and recalled the young woman who had emerged from them. A light tune emerged from his throat, almost of its own volition. Humming, he let the melody envelop him.

Around him, the walls creaked softly, as if the Crimson Keep were sighing with contentment.

THE WEE FOLK AT THE END OF THE HALL

by Paul Kupperberg

BELID DECIDED IT WAS TOO NICE A DAY TO SPEND IN class.

It didn't matter that the temperature outside the Keep hovered perilously close to the freezing mark or that the sky was dark with roiling, thunderous clouds that had been flinging icy rain and stinging sleet at the sodden landscape below for several days now. It made no difference that the penalty for blowing off one of the Master's lessons was a sharp reprimand, a long and tedious lecture on the virtue of hard work, and two weeks of three-times-a-day kitchen scutwork to drive home the point.

Because as much as Belid detested peeling potatoes, scrubbing trash bins, and having to stay awake through one of the Master's endless lectures on personal responsibility, he hated one thing even more:

Falling flat on his face in front of his fellow students.

Which was exactly the position he was going to find himself in if he attended today's class.

The subject was alchemy. The assignment was the transformation of simple elements into compounds. It was, according to the Master, as easy as tripping over one's own feet. Which was no easy task for the Master these days, now a four-legged mammal ever since one of the aforementioned fellow students, Athis, had had to turn him into a mouse after the old man had given up most of his blood in their battle with Markindo the Dragon, the Supreme Commander of the Demon Army. But even as a tiny rodent (albeit one slowing working his way back to humanity), the Master had spoken, and Belid, ever the contrarian and often the literalist, decided to take him up on that challenge and had spent a considerable amount of time trying to trip over his own feet. He hadn't been able to do it. Knowing what was coming, he had repeatedly failed to catch himself by surprise and trip himself up. Even when he tried distracting himself, he couldn't make it happen. He finally concluded that if the alchemic assignment was even half as difficult as tripping over his own feet, it was too tough a task to tackle. What didn't occur to him was that if he had spent even half the time he had put into trying to send himself sprawling to the floor into studying instead he might have actually learned something.

But the truth was Belid was not a believer in work. Especially hard work. Especially hard work imposed on him by others. Sure, he had meant to study, he had even tried. Well, once. That evening when he dug the spellbook out from under the mountain of dirty clothes piled in the corner of his room and started to read up on elemental transmutation. Was it his fault the material was so dull that he fell asleep after just a few paragraphs? Sure, the Master had demonstrated it in class, but his presentation was even duller than the text and Belid's mind had quickly wandered off to more pleasant thoughts, like being massaged by the thousand-taloned sloth of Siggertoth or having his private parts tattooed by a blind man with a nervous disorder.

So here it was, the morning of the test and he knew as much about alchemy and elemental transmutation as he did animal husbandry, a fact was soon to be embarrassingly demonstrated to his teacher and his peers. Unless, of course, he never made it to class and therefore couldn't, ironically enough, trip himself up, metaphorically speaking, before them.

Having reached that conclusion—and thinking, not for the first time, that it was too bad the Master didn't offer a class in rationalization, which he was certain he would ace—Belid, as was his wont, took the easy way out, inclement weather notwithstanding.

He spun himself around three times and then took a walk down the corridor he found himself facing.

≣ ≣ ≣

Unlike run of the mill castles, the Crimson Keep was not, as it were, set in stone, even if it looked like it was from outside. It was constructed of stone, of course, and sported the requisite drawbridge, moat, towers and turrets, but inside the standard issue castle exterior was a place of infinite possibilities. It was said to possess a thousand rooms and a hundred staircases, very few of which stayed in the same place for any appreciable length of time. The story was that a long ago spell gone wrong was the cause of the Keep's endless shifting through time, space, and rationality. It wasn't unknown for a quick trip to the sanitary to result in weeks' or months' long absences during which the unfortunate wanderer tried to retrace a route back to their starting position that had changed in the blink of an eye or the emptying of a bladder.

The inhabitants of the Crimson Keep knew to keep to the best traveled routes in order to avoid this circumstance. Whatever the spell was that caused the shifting and folding of its inner reality seemed to be weakened by familiarity, so their sleeping quarters, classrooms, kitchen, and connecting corridors were the least susceptible to change. But diverge from the beaten paths and who knew what would happen.

In this case, Belid was hoping for the worst.

It wouldn't be the first time he had found himself lost in the Keep, just the first time he'd deliberately set off to lose himself. A day or two wandering through the ever-changing maze, even a week—there was, he remembered, another test first thing in the morning after the rest day that he wouldn't mind missing as well—would serve him just fine. He figured if he didn't go too far, exactly how lost could he possibly get?

Except, he quickly realized, "lost," like "pregnant," wasn't exactly a matter of degree. You either was or you wasn't.

And Belid was.

What felt like a walk of maybe thirty yards had brought him to a space that was as alien to him as the living quarters of the King's palace. Which he might have been in for all he knew. He turned to look back the way he had just come, but that part of the corridor was no longer the same as it had been just moments earlier when he had passed through it. And when he looked ahead of him again, that too had morphed into something entirely different as well. What had been a straight corridor now branched off in three separate directions.

"Enny-meeny-miny," he said stepping into the center corridor. "Moe. As in mo' lost."

The corridor was lined on either side with doorways that were spaced about twenty feet apart. At the far end was a small window through which bright sunlight shone. The window was set at about eye level in a solid wood door.

"Just *where* have you brought me?" Belid said under his breath. The weather had been unrelentingly stormy at his starting point. A tempest like that didn't blow over in a few minutes.

The sorcerer's apprentice hurried over to the door and looked through the window at an enclosed courtyard overgrown with lush foliage and dotted with a riot of colorful blossoms. Weathered brick walls climbed higher than the trees, their close growth making for an almost solid canopy of green through which brilliant sunlight rippled. Brightly hued butterflies with wingspans two hands across flitted past the window and darted here and there beneath the treetops.

Belid smiled, nodding in approval. Prior experiences had brought him to a lot of dark, dank places in the castle, populated, if at all, with creepy crawly nightmarish things, but this was the sort of being lost he could get used to.

There was no handle or latch, just a thick plank held in place by rusted iron brackets embedded in the wall on either side of the door. The old hunk of wood was wedged tightly in the brackets and it took more energy than Belid liked to expend to push and heave it loose. A good old spell of transmutation enabling him to change the wood to something easier to manipulate or to accelerate the rusting of the iron brackets would have been a handy thing to know, but then, a few minutes of physical exertion was way less labor intensive than the hours of memorization it took to learn such spells. It was all about the effort-to-need ratio, after all.

He got his shoulder under the plank and pushed. It took a little perspiration and considerable grunting for him to shove it loose.

Without a handle to pull on, it took a few extra minutes to find finger holds that allowed him to swing the door in and open, but soon enough he was rewarded with a wave of warmth and summer fresh scents that made him forget what it took to get here. Because after the endless days of being cooped up inside the chilled and damp walls of the stormed in Keep, "here" was paradise.

Belid closed his eyes and sucked in a lungful of warmth.

"Oh, man," he sighed on the exhale, stepping out onto the lush carpet of emerald turf. "I've hit the jackpot."

Which, of course, was the moment the butterflies chose to attack.

❦ ❦ ❦

The first one stung him on his shin.

"Ow! Jeez, since when do butterflies sting?"

He hopped aside, swatting at the flittering attacker. It avoided his hand and swept away, back into a thick swarm of butterflies that were, Belid realized with an uneasy feeling, massing in the air just a few feet in front of his face. And that unease multiplied by a factor of, well . . . a lot—mathematics was never exactly his thing—when he saw that brightly colored wings aside, they weren't butterflies after all. They were people. Tiny little people with wings. And spears. And angry expressions on their tiny little faces as a pair of them cried out, "Swarm! Swarm! Swarm!"

And came flapping at him a lot faster than Belid would have thought possible, provided he had the time to think as he screamed and dropped to the ground, waving his hands and kicking his feet to ward off the tiny attackers.

Tiny though they may have been, there were lots of them, someone crying out repeatedly and redundantly "Swarm!" even as they swarmed over him, jabbing him in dozens, no scores of places at once with their spears. Individually, their jabs weren't more than a nuisance, but taken together, they hurt. Plus, he was pretty sure that this was one of those times when those long ago parental warnings about losing an eye due to some activity or other was actually valid. And Belid was at quite a disadvantage seeing as how the butterfly people weren't at all concerned about hurting him, while he was scared stiff he might accidentally squash one or more of them if he flailed too hard.

"Stop it," he shouted. "Ow! C'mon, leave me ow alone! I'm ow not going to ow ow ow hurt you."

They were scrambling up his shirt now, which he quickly pulled off over his head and started swinging through the air like a bullfighter's cape, scattering the "Swarm! Swarm! Swarm!" swarming swarm. He managed to get back on his feet and turned to run back inside the castle, whose dim, cool halls were infinitely preferable to this sunny summer's day in Hell. But the door had somehow closed behind him and, when he ran into it, it stayed closed, no matter how hard he shoved against it. He was locked out.

"Swarm! Swarm! Swarm!"

He didn't know how many tiny little jabs it would take to kill him, and he had no desire to learn the answer right here and now. He needed to do something, quick and non-lethal. As if he even knew anything lethal. Just something flashy to distract the butterfly people and buy him a moment to gather his wits.

A spell of illusion might work. Conjure up an image of something big and scary to frighten them off. Except he was big and, if he was as tiny as them, he would have already found himself frightening. Besides, coalescing dust particles from the air and redirecting light to create the images was too complex a spell, especially while one was being nibbled to death by ducks, as it were. A nice flash-bang, perhaps. A few words to heat up the air quickly enough to ignite the oxygen and hydrogen in a focused area, resulting in a blinding flash and a satisfyingly loud little boom. It was one of those simple but annoying spells students picked up early on in their studies and which they practiced frequently on sleeping or otherwise preoccupied classmates.

Face turned protectively towards the door, shoulders hunched against the stinging onslaught of their little spears, Belid began to briskly rub his hands together, chanting the words of the spell. He drew his hands apart, holding a spherical shape as large as an apricot, then an apple, than an orange, and finally a good sized grapefruit, feeling the warmth growing between his palms until, at last (it was only a few seconds, but time tended to slow down when hundreds of little needles were being jabbed into your back and bottom), it was ready, and he whirled and flung the flash-bang into the swarm.

It flashed.

It banged.

And with renewed cries of "Swarm!" the butterfly people hurtled en masse around the young sorcerer's head and drove him back down to the ground.

* * *

Magic isn't just a matter of mouthing spells, but rather of giving a name to the power that existed inside oneself from which one drew to make the spells manifest. Just knowing the words didn't make things happen, otherwise all Belid or any other student of the arcane would have to do was memorize a bunch of spells to be an adept. If it were that simple, anybody with a halfway decent memory or cheat sheet could become a great sorcerer. The power was in the name. Remembering and naming the name made the power work. But having who knew how many tiny little butterfly people dancing on your skull made remembering even your own name, much less a multisyllabic spell with far too many consonants from a dead language something of a chore, so Belid settled for screaming and begging.

And, much to his surprise, his strategy worked. Once they had him reduced to a whimpering, whining mass of huddled frightened on the ground, the swarm backed off, leaving just four of them hovering by his face with rapidly beating little wings. Of those four, the wings of two of them, both unarmed, were painted in intricate patterns of unimaginable brightness and beauty; the others, who held little spears at the ready, were colorful in their own right, like the rest of the swarm, but they all paled in comparison with the unarmed couple.

"Who are you?" one of the two said in a tiny voice.

Belid squinted. The one who had spoken looked to be female, while her companion was most likely male. They had arms and legs and humanish torsos adapted for wings, and both were entirely hairless. He was basing his assignment of sex entirely on human characteristics, although prior encounters with other magic-based life forms had taught him that the analogy didn't always hold up.

"Well, speak up!" the (maybe) male of the pair demanded in a high-pitched yet imperious tone.

On the spur of the moment, while he pulled his shirt back on over his head, Belid decided a good bluff was in order.

"I am Belid," he said, then quickly added, "the magnificent."

"You? Magnificent?" the female said with squeaky skepticism.

"Why's that so unbelievable?"

"Magnificence is not usually accompanied by screams of terror and begging," the male said.

"Oh, that," Belid said with a little laugh that sounded false even to him. "I'm one of those non-violent sorcerers. I was, you know, begging you to stop so I wouldn't have to hurt you."

They both stared back at him, disbelieving little eyes against a backdrop of fluttering rainbow hued wings.

"Yeah, the screaming . . . that's, uhm, one of my spells. Of protection. For you guys. And see, it worked. None of you got hurt." Then, thinking it best they change the topic, he said, "So, where's this? Who are you?"

"We are People," the female said. "I am called Sphaaaa."

"I am called Chuuu," the male said.

The sounds they made to identify themselves weren't words, but more like the sounds of something infinity lovely and pleasurable. Almost like he imagined certain colors would sound if we heard their vibrations rather than saw them.

"I come in peace, Sphaaaa . . . am I pronouncing that right?"

She gave a minute dip of her chin. "It will suffice from an Other," she conceded. "Your sudden presence was a surprise to us," Chuuu said. "We have never had an Other in the Garden. The Portal to the Otherside has been sealed since the Great Story of the People and the Shadowings began to be told."

Belid took a moment to parse this new information. It sounded to him like Chuuu was saying the butterfly people had been locked in this courtyard for a long time, but weren't totally unfamiliar with humans. And what was that last thing?

"Shadowings?" he said.

"Shadowings," Sphaaaa confirmed in a hushed tone, pointing into the sky.

Correction. Up into the trees, at a pigeon-sized black bird-like shape that sat perched on a branch staring down at them with glowing red eyes.

"I take it the People and the Shadowings aren't exactly friends."

The swarm began to flit and shift about nervously.

"No," Sphaaaa said. "We share the Garden, but nothing more."

"An uneasy truce, huh?" Belid said. "Is it okay if I stand up?"

"Rise," Chuuu said, he and Sphaaaa fluttering to stay at eye level as he did.

"There can be no truce," Sphaaaa said. "The People and the Shadowings have been and must forever remain at war."

Belid eyed the treetops. They rose above the top of the wall surrounding the courtyard. Knowing what he was looking for now, he was able to pick out several more Shadowings on other branches, all keeping watchful eyes on the goings-on below.

"This is probably a stupid question, but if it's so bad here, why don't the People just leave? I mean, you can fly, so all you've got to do is go over the wall and find a new place to live."

"Alas, we can not," Chuuu said.

"The Shadowings," Sphaaaa said with a sigh, as if that explained everything.

"Okay, so maybe you'd have to fight your way out, but that would be just one battle and then you'd be free. Isn't that better than living in a constant state of war?"

Chuuu said, "The Great Story tells us leaving is forbidden."

Sphaaaa said, "The Shadowings are our punishment."

"None among the people may ever die a peaceful death," Chua continued.

"War is our atonement," said Sphaaaa.

Then, together, they sang out, "Thus spake the Omnipotent One."

"Right," Belid said, no more enlightened than before their litany of an explanation. "Uhm, maybe you guys better start from the beginning."

* * *

Stripped of its religious symbolism, flowery language, and general mythic rigmarole, the People's Great Story went something like this:

A long, long time ago, the butterfly people got into a beef with a powerful sorcerer, the aforementioned Omnipotent One. There was the requisite war between them and his forces, which ended in the defeat of the People. But they had so ticked off the sorcerer that instead of destroying the People, he chose to imprison them in the Garden for all of eternity, to be watched over by these magical constructs, the Shadowings. The People ruled the ground; the Shadowings the treetops. Neither side could invade the space of the other, but there was a small zone in which both sides could co-exist, right at the level of the top of the wall.

Unfortunately, it was in that precise zone in the treetops that the People's only sustenance grew, while the Shadowings, wouldn't you know it, fed only on the People, making the mere act of gathering Sunday brunch by the People, in effect, a suicide mission. Every day was a battle for survival. The Shadowings also prevented them from going over the wall. The sorcerer had granted the People life spans that had no natural end, like dying peacefully in bed at a ripe old age or being run over by an ox cart. Their only way of shuffling off this mortal coil was to be devoured live, and horribly, by a Shadowing.

Amen.

* * *

"Wow," Belid said. "What exactly did you guys do to piss off this sorcerer dude like that?"

"Piss? Off?" Chuuu said with a bewildered tilt of his tiny head.

"You know, like, incur his wrath."

Sphaaaa averted her gaze. "We do not speak of our shame," she said softly.

"Sure, I get that," Belid said, seeing as he had a few incidents in own past that he preferred go unremembered, much less spoken of. Like that time when he was new to the Keep and the Master's tutelage and tried skipping ahead in the lessons to translocation. This was before he had heard the story of Randall, an earlier student who had made the mistake of trying out such a spell on himself and whose face still peered out of a column in the third corridor on the Keep's fifth level. Belid had tried the spell on a mouse he had trapped in the pantry, but the results hadn't been pretty and, to this day, he was fairly certain that kin of the poor little rodent still left little . . . *gifts* in his daily meal. It was probably just his imagination—although most of the meals served at the Keep tasted like they were liberally seasoned with mouse poop. It was probably just a combination of bad cooking and a guilty conscience.

At the thought of even the Keep's admittedly mediocre cuisine, Belid realized he was hungry. And, of course, he hadn't bothered to pack a lunch before taking off to deliberately lose himself in the castle's never ending corridors. What had he expected, to find rest stops along the way? Or a fast food franchise tucked into a corner?

Not that it would matter if there were rest stops or burger joints in every other room of the massive old castle. He was, d'uh!, locked out here in a courtyard. The Garden. Whatever.

"Oh crud!" he said.

"You are troubled, Belid?" Chuuu said.

"I'm screwed," Belid said, gesturing helplessly at the door. "I belong in there . . . but it's locked from the inside."

"The Portal to the Otherside has been sealed since the Great Story of the People and the Shadowings began to be told," Chuuu said, stating the obvious.

Belid groaned and shoved his shoulder against the door. When it didn't budge, he shoved harder. Still no budging.

"Isn't there any other way out of here?" he said.

"There is only the Portal," Sphaaaa said, "but it has been sealed . . . "

"Yeah, right, since the Great Story of the People and the Shadowings began to be told," Belid finished for her. "But I mean for me . . . you know, someone *not* cursed by an evil sorcerer to be bird food for all of eternity."

It took him a moment to hear himself through his frustration, making him cringe at his thoughtlessness.

"I'm sorry," he said. "That was mean."

"There is only the Portal," Chuuu said. "And the Wall."

Right, he thought. The Wall.

Belid took a few steps towards it. It looked to be forty, fifty feet high, built of large smooth stones fitted together with mortar filled flush with the surface of the stones, leaving no finger or toeholds for him to climb. Assuming that even with finger and toeholds he could actually have climbed forty or fifty feet up a sheer stone wall without falling and busting his butt or his skull. Or both.

But, here and there the trees grew close enough to the wall that several heavy branches hung close to it . . . and the trees *did* provide what appeared to be ample hand and footholds for climbing. Not that he'd never climbed a tree before. Never had reason to. What was up a tree that could possibly make it worth climbing?

Well, in this particular case, freedom.

🐾 🐾 🐾

Belid was already sweating and breathing hard by the time he was a little more than his own height off the ground. It had taken considerable effort just to leap high enough to grab the lowest branch and haul his own weight up onto it. He really needed to start working out. Or stop climbing trees. He guessed that after he'd gotten up this one, he'd likely go with option B.

Sphaaaa, Chuuu, and the rest of the People fluttered around the base of the tree watching his efforts with interest. Belid wished he could flutter. Or at least knew a good spell of levitation. Maybe there was something to the idea of paying attention to his lessons like the Master was always saying. He might have learned something that would come in handy. The problem was, lessons were always taught in a dry, dull classroom where the urgency to learn anything was nonexistent. Now, light a fire under their butts or trap them in a courtyard of doom while trying to teach them something and you'd have yourself a bunch of motivated students. Something for the suggestion box when—if!—he got back.

After a brief pause to catch his breath, Belid got back to climbing. The distance between branches was shorter now that he was up here, but it was still a slow, hard slog and, truth to tell, he was no big fan of heights. Not that he suffered from vertigo or anything like that, but he was a rational enough human being to know that the higher up you went, the further you had to fall. And as sturdy as the branches looked, they still bent and made menacing creaking sounds when he put his weight on them.

At his next rest stop, a good fifteen or twenty feet above the courtyard, Sphaaaa and Chuuu flew up and hovered at eye level.

"Hey," Belid said, trying not to sounded winded.

"You say you are a sorcerer," Sphaaaa said, trying, out of politeness, he thought, to keep the skepticism from her voice.

"Right. I mean, yes, I am."

"A magnificent," Chuuu added.

He shrugged modestly. "So they say."

"Is it in your power," Sphaaaa said, "to free us?"

Oh crud!

"Free you?"

"From the Garden," Chuuu said.

"Defeat the Shadowings and reverse the spells of the Omnipotent One so that we may leave here and make our way in the world beyond the Wall," Sphaaaa said, just in case he had forgotten the story they had told him.

"Um, yeah, that's an interesting question," he said with a stammer. "I guess that kind of depends, you know?"

They stared at him. They obviously didn't know.

"On the, um . . . kind of spell it is, and . . . and, you know. Other stuff."

Their baffled exchange of glances told him they needed more.

"Well, O.P.S. and all that, you know? Er . . . that's other people's spells. Like," he said, thinking fast. "Okay, without knowing exactly *which* spell the Omnipotent One used to bind you to the Garden, I don't know what sort of counter spell would reverse it."

They lowered their heads and Belid could have sworn that the iridescence of their wings lost some of their brilliance at his words. He was starting to feel guilty for having exaggerated his skills. If he had only told them he was just an apprentice right off the bat they wouldn't have gotten their hopes up in the first place.

"Look, I'm really sorry," he said. Those were the first sincere words he had said since he'd found himself stranded in the courtyard.

"We . . . endure," Chuuu said in his tiny voice, made even smaller by regret.

There wasn't much else to say, so Belid got back to his climbing. The higher he went, the closer together were the branches, making progress much easier. He tried to not look back at the disappointed butterfly people or the ground that kept receding under him.

The Shadowings had been watching him the entire climb, their beady little red eyes glowing from black feathered faces like laser pointers. He thought—hoped—maybe they would take off when he got closer but they showed no sign of moving, much less of fear.

He was still a good ten feet below the top of the wall and the lowest level to which the Shadowings could descend when it occurred to him that they might not know or care about the difference between a person and a People. Deciding it would be a good idea to ask before climbing into their zone, he paused for another breather, settling on a wide limb and wrapping his arms around another. As before, Sphaaaa and Chuuu rose to his eye level.

"So, the Shadowings," he said. "How dangerous are they?"

"They are death," Sphaaaa said.

"Yeah. But what I'm asking is how dangerous are they to *me?*"

"You are not of the People," Chuuu said.

"So they're only a threat to you guys?"

"There is only the People and the Shadowings in the Garden," Sphaaaa said.

"Then you've never seen them attack anything else?"

Chuuu said, "There has never been anything else."

This wasn't helping.

What was it the Master had once told them? "Hope always for the best but plan also for the worst."

In this case, the worst would be getting pecked to pieces by a flock of angry magical birds many, many feet above the ground. But what choice did he have? His only way out was up and over the wall, right through them. He really should have a weapon or a spell of some kind ready to let loose with if they did come for him. He dismissed a simple flash-bang, seeing how it hadn't even phased the People. A fire spell? Maybe if he set the treetops on fire that would scare them off long enough to allow him to get out of their zone . . . except burning the treetops would also destroyed whatever it was that the People ate that grew up there.

Invisibility?

No. That only worked on human perceptions. And the way he did it, not always so well. The Shadowings would still be able to sniff him out. The rate he was sweating, there wasn't a creature alive who *couldn't* smell him.

A shielding spell?

Another negative. He wasn't sure he remembered all the words in the right sequence and he'd hate to find out he'd gotten it wrong while his eyeballs were being pecked out.

How about an earthquake? He could create a localized disturbance for about ten feet around the tree . . . except that was stupid. The Shadowings could fly. The best thing he could hope to accomplish was to shake himself out of the tree.

An infurnace spell then. Something more than a flash-bang but less than an outright fire. It might be just enough to keep the birds at bay long enough for him to get over the Wall. It was probably his best chance . . .

But just to be on the safe side, he reached over and broke off the stoutest branch he could reach, which he tucked into his belt behind his back. Hope for the best, expect the worst, and when in doubt, bash 'em with a stick.

❦ ❦ ❦

The nearest Shadowing was less than a yard above his head and just off to his left, between him and the Wall. So far, it hadn't moved, hadn't made a sound. Just stared.

"Hiya," Belid said, trying to keep his tone friendly despite the stick tucked into his belt.

A second Shadowing flapped down from above and joined the first on its branch. Then another. Followed by two more. The treetop rustled with activity as more of them appeared, grouping on the branches directly above and around him. He didn't bother counting to see how many there were, knowing there were plenty more than enough to do him some serious damage if that's what they had in their little bird brains to do.

"I'm just passing through, okay?" he said soothingly. "I don't want to hurt anybody. And you don't want to hurt me, right?"

The massed Shadowings stared. Silent. Like silhouettes of statues. *Creepy* statues.

Belid took a deep breath and as non-threateningly as he could, reached for the next branch.

The Shadowings stared.

So he tried another step up.

Still staring.

He reached up and grabbed hold of the next highest branch. His hand closed around something slimy. It felt like a thick, loamy moss. Was this the stuff the People fed on? He glanced down. Sphaaaa and Chuuu were still hovering around where he had last stopped, watching. The entire swarm of the People had flown up to join them, but they were keeping their distance from the Shadowings. Belid wished he was down there with them, but it was now or never.

He hauled himself up, into the zone of the Shadowings. He expected that was when they would all come to life and be on him like white on rice, but all they did was continue to stare. Sweet!

There was about a five or six foot gap between him and the top of the Wall, a distance he could cut some by going further out on the limb on which he was now perched. *Precariously* perched, he reminded himself. But he had a pretty good sense of balance—at least in comparison to his talent for leaping across open spaces forty feet in the air—and it was just a matter of making it a foot or two further out on the branch before making the jump. At least the top of the wall was flat and free of obstructions like barbed wire or embedded shards of glass, making it easy to grab hold of if he fell a little short of his goal.

"Don't think about falling of *any* kind," he muttered. Taking a deep breath, Belid slid one foot sideways along the branch. So far, so good. He glanced at one of the Shadowings and said, "Wish me luck."

It didn't. But he slid further out along the limb anyway, feeling it start to sag a little under his weight. For the next lateral move he'd have to take his hand off the comforting trunk of the tree and be balanced on his own. But that would also put him right about where he needed to be. So he took a deep breath, made a silent prayer to whatever superior being watched over idiots who went, literally, out on limbs, and made the move.

Some philosopher or other once said, "Don't look down," and Belid heeded that advice, keeping his eyes straight ahead, focused on the top of the wall that was his ultimate destination. All he had to do now was jump, just a couple or three feet, like hopping over a puddle in the road. Heck, at this distance he could just about topple forward and make his mark. No problem.

Right.

Except for the forty foot drop.

"Stop it," he muttered. "Failure is not an option."

But falling was.

The wind rustled gently through the treetop around him. The Shadowings watched him in silence from above. The People fluttered about below.

And Belid, bellowing a curse that would have gotten his mouth washed out with lye soap by the Master, made the jump.

❧ ❧ ❧

The Shadowings were faster than anything with wings Belid had ever witnessed. They went from stoic immobility to frenzied attack mode as soon as he was airborne, a sudden and startling confusion of wings and beaks and talons that surrounded him in screeching ferocity and almost made him miss the wall. As it was, he only just managed to hook one arm over the top while the other flailed spastically about at his attackers, his toes scraping at the stones in a useless search for a foothold. His confidence in holding on by virtue of his upper body strength alone was somewhere between zero and nil, especially with only one arm and a flock of pissed off ensorcelled pigeons going at him like he was the last breadcrumbs in the park.

It took him forever—well, a couple of seconds, but that's forever when one is dangling from a wall—to remember the stick jammed into his belt at the small of his back. It took him another little forever to reach around and try to tug it loose while being pecked and scratched and flapped at, but, fortunately, in those eternal seconds, everything changed as the People, with their glowing florescent butterfly wings and tiny little needle-sharp spears came flying into the fray.

Correction. Not *into* the fray, but right past it.

While the Shadowings were otherwise engaged with Belid, Sphaaaa and Chuuu lead their people up and over the wall in a mad dash escape run.

"Hey!" Belid yelled, but the little people didn't even look back at him, much less come to his rescue. As it was, several of the Shadowings on the periphery of the attack on him broke off and with loud screeches, dove after the nearest People, catching a couple of them in their beaks and gobbling them up like potato chips. But as Belid had discovered when he first stepped into the garden, the People were swift little buggers and had used the confusion he had caused to make good the escape of the overwhelming majority of their number.

Well good for them . . . and, as it worked out, good for Belid as well. Whatever the motivation for their going after him, the Shadowings were programmed primarily to keep the People from escaping, so once alerted to the butterfly people's bold move, they forgot about him and went for the swarm going over the top.

At the rate the People were moving, Belid calculated he had only a few moments to make it up and over himself, so, ignoring the numerous Shadowing inflicted scratches and lacerations and grunting and gasping like an octogenarian trying to get up out of a beanbag chair, he flung his other arm over the top of the wall and finally hauled himself onto it.

He made it.

And now, sitting astride the top of the wall, sweating, bleeding, and gasping, he took a moment to assess his situation and plan his next move. To one side was the enclosed courtyard. Ahead of him were Shadowings darting after the last of the escaping People as they dove over the wall, which seemed to be a barrier the black birds were unable to cross. To the other side was freedom . . . correction. To the other side was a whole lot of nothing, or at least nothing he could see through the thick, swirling mist rising up from the ground below—if indeed there was ground below—that extended for as far as the eye could see in all directions. For the first time since conceiving his escape, he was confronted with a major flaw in the plan: How the devil to get *down* the other side?

There was nothing close enough to the other side of the wall he could see on which to climb down. Maybe he could tear his clothing into strips and tie them into a rope and climb down that, except (a) he doubted he was wearing sufficient clothing to make a rope long enough to reach the ground or whatever lay beneath the mist, (b) there was nothing up here to which he could fasten the rope even if it were long enough, and, most importantly, (c) even if he could make a rope long enough and had something to which it could be tied, he doubted he could do it in the next five seconds, which was probably the outside limit of time he had left before the last of the People were gone and the Shadowings remembered *he* was still there.

Correction. Not five seconds. Just three. And even that little bit of time was used up now that the People had descended out of reach of the Shadowings' beaks. Without the hors d'oeuvres of flimsy winged People to snack on, they were ready to return to the relatively big and beefy boy sorcerer and the beady little red eyes that turned his way looked, if possible, even meaner than before. He got the feeling that since he was the one who had cost them their main meal they would probably want to fill up on him to hold them for as long as possible.

The Shadowings were regrouping, flocking together and wheeling around the tree to come at him all at once.

So. Get pecked to death by angry birds or die of the broken neck he was sure to sustain from the fall?

"Either way," Belid said with a groan, "this is gonna hurt."

But the broken neck would, at least, be quicker, so he closed his eyes, wishing he hadn't decided to skip class today after all, opened his mouth, started to scream, and let himself topple over the side.

☙ ☙ ☙

Sore, scraped, bruised, broken (or at the very least bruised) of a couple of ribs, and unable to put any weight on his left foot without a lot of pain, Belid leaned against the bottom of the Wall, counting his blessings, principle among which was the treetop he had plunged into about a third of the way into his fall. The dense foliage, hidden in the heavy mist, took him by surprise but broke his fall as he bounced off of one limb and down to the next for the next fifteen or twenty feet. It was like the worst amusement park ride ever, but each impact slowed his descent that much more even as it caused new bursts of pain.

It took him a few seconds to understand that he wasn't necessarily about to die and started reaching desperately for something to grab on to. He was able to wrap his fist around a branch which brought him to a sudden, arm-wrenching stop, the momentum from which slammed him into the tree trunk. He was pretty sure that was what caused the broken ribs, although he had to admit that could just as easily have happened when the branch snapped under his weight and he fell the last half dozen feet to land face down on the ground.

But it was all good. Belid wasn't about to complain about a few cracks in his cartilage or busted bones, as long as they weren't the ones in his neck or spine. Anything short of dead would heal.

He even smiled, despite the pain.

"This is my lucky day," he said out loud, just because he was happy to still be on his feet—okay, foot—and *able* to speak.

The first order of business was to get the lay of the land. He was definitely on the outside of the castle, but not in any place that he recognized. The mist that had blocked his view of the ground while looking down from atop the Wall now blocked his view of the top of the Wall and the castle behind it. It hung like a fluffy shroud high above his head, the Wall and tree top that broke his fall melting into it. But the surrounding landscape was clear and looked every bit as ordinary as any other stretch of ground he remembered from various other parts of the Keep's exterior he had seen. Trees, bushes, grass, flowers, rocks, boulders, and moat. As changeable as the old place was inside, he'd never heard of the exterior shifting or morphing, so it was just a matter of picking a direction and hobbling around the perimeter until he came to the front gate.

Easy, he thought. What could possibly go wrong with that?

■ ■ ■

Even with his dinged-up ribs and an ankle swollen to twice its normal size, the circumnavigation of the Crimson Keep took Belid just minutes before he saw the happy sight of the great gates looming ahead of him. As he limped along, the sky above slowly reverted to the stormy, sleet spitting overcast he had left behind when he'd earlier initiated his escape from that day's studies. He was in pain, soaked to the skin, and shivering from the cold, but he knew it would all be over in just a few minutes. Once inside, he would brew the appropriate herbs into a hot tea to take care of the aches and sip it while floating contentedly in a warm bath, after which he would bind his ribs and ankle, and be if not as good as new, at least on the way to some semblance thereof.

Plus, he had a unassailable excuse for the missed alchemy test. He could rehearse his sincere, heartfelt speech to the Master while soaking in his hot tub. Took a wrong turn, got trapped, freed an imprisoned race of shiny little butterfly people, barely escaping with his life in the doing. If that wasn't a get out of kitchen duty free story, he didn't know what was. And it even had the virtue of being true. Mostly. Except for the "took a wrong turn" part, but why quibble with a good thing?

As he tromped towards the gate, Belid wondered what the People would do with their newfound freedom. And wouldn't it be something if, because of the role he played in helping them gain it, he went down in their history as some sort of legendary figure? A mighty sorcerer who liberated them from captivity by a cruel wizard.

"Or, dare I even think it . . . maybe I'll even be remembered as a god?"

"That seems rather unlikely, Belid," a voice as icy as the wind hissed behind him. "If you are remembered at all, it will be as the Trojan horse who facilitated the invasion of the Crimson Keep and the destruction of the tyrannical Master."

"Oh, come on. He's not that bad. I . . . Hey. Wait," Belid said as he started to turn in the direction of the voice. "I thought I was alone out here?"

"No," said the evilly smirking tall, slender black leathery skinned bat-winged man hovering in the air above him said. "You have company, boy."

But what was even worse than an evilly smirking tall, slender black leathery skinned bat-winged man was the army of tall, slender black leathery skinned bat-winged people armed with great big sharp spears gathered behind him.

"Wait," Belid said. "Don't tell me. You're Chuuu, aren't you?"

The slender wedge-shaped head lowered and raised an inch. Its smile wasn't pretty.

Belid gulped.

"Well, wow. You've, uh . . . changed. Doesn't look like freedom's really agreeing with you guys."

"On the contrary. These are our natural forms. The same spell of the thrice-cursed Master that consigned us to that hellacious Garden stripped us of our true glory," said a second one, flying down to Chuuu's side.

Belid took a wild guess. "Sphaaaa?"

"At your service."

"So . . . when you say 'Master,' I assume you're referring to . . . ?"

"To the Master of the Crimson Keep, the so-called Omnipotent One who left us in the accursed Garden to be eaten alive, one by one, until we cease to exist," said Chuuu. Their transformation hadn't changed one thing, the back and forth way they spoke, almost like they shared a brain.

"I was afraid you were going to say that. So in this long ago war with the Omnipotent One, *you* were the evil guys?"

"It depends on what you consider evil," said Sphaaaa.

"To the People, the sacrifice of every other thing that lives in tribute to our true god, Khaaaa, is a blessing," Chuuu added.

"See, I'd consider that sort of on the evil side," Belid said, quickly adding, "But what do I know," all the time wishing he could shut up. The last thing he wanted to do was antagonize a people whose baseline morality was the death of every living thing.

"It is why we are. It is our holy duty," said Sphaaaa.

"So, just to clarify here, meaning no offense to your duty, holy or otherwise, what you're saying is, if I understand you, that whether or not I get you through the gates, you're going to, uhm . . . kill me."

Chuuu didn't sound the least bit apologetic when he said, "It is our holy duty."

"Okay, then I've just gotta ask if the fact that I'm the one who freed you from the Garden carries any weight?"

Sphaaaa said, "Your reward shall be a quick and painless death."

"Yeah. What I thought . . . well, actually a little better, what with the whole quick and painless death thing," Belid said. "But I'm afraid I'm going to have to decline."

"That is your choice," Chuuu said.

"So it shall be," Sphaaaa said.

The two pie-shaped heads turned briefly to one another, before swiveling back around to look at Belid, sharp-toothed smiles pulling back leathery skins.

"Swarm," they said, in unison.

※ ※ ※

It was some time around the mention of sacrificing every living thing to their true god that Belid started to think he might have messed up here. That, in fact, messing up was more or less his default setting. Okay, messing up and taking the easy way out. So he had two default settings. He messed things up all the time because he was always looking for the easy way to do something. His brain started to flash a kaleidoscope of examples, a lot of examples in fact, but he put a stop to them fast because now wasn't the time to list his failures. Because he knew that all things came in threes, which meant he had a third default setting, which was where he needed to be focused now. Mess up, yes. Laze-about, you bet.

But he also always thought of something.

A way out. The loophole in the contract. The wiggle or the weasel. See. Even examples came in threes.

So now, already running despite the pain in his swollen ankle towards the front gate, Belid got to thinking, largely to distract himself *from* the pain. He could lower the drawbridge with the simple password spell the Master had supplied all the students with, but that would let all the People in with him.

He also got to thinking about how little like a sorcerer he had been thinking and acting since this whole thing started. Talk about lazy. Other than a useless flash-bang to try and scare off the butterfly people, he hadn't once turned to magic to help with his predicament. Like . . . why hadn't his first thought been to actually try the simple password spell on the door that locked behind him and trapped him in the Garden in the first place?

It was too late now for recriminations. If ever there was a time to dig deep down and try, *really try*, it was now . . . although even if he got lucky and survived the People, he was positive the Master would kill him for interfering with the spell that had kept them confined in the Garden and controlled by the Shadowings.

So if only to save a punishment that was worse than being torn to death by the claws and fangs of otherworldly magical beings, he needed to get magical and get there quick. So what did he have to work with? The People. The Garden. The Shadowings.

Yeah. Okay. And what else? It was something that had flashed through his mind earlier, a stray observation then that now seemed like the most important thought in the world. Belid could hear the rustle of their wings as they swooped behind him. They were closing in. The gate was far away. He was never going to beat Sphaaaa and Chuuu and their silent army to them, and even if he did, then what?

What *was* that thing? They were talking, but it wasn't about what they were saying. It was about how . . . something. C'mon, brain, he urged, taking in great big gasps of air to give it all the oxygen he could. Think! Chuuu said something, then Sphaaaa said something, then Chuuu again, then . . . right. That was it. They spoke like they shared a brain. And they were the only ones who spoke. The rest of the swarm was silent. It really was a swarm, the herd mentality in action . . . but unlike a herd of wildebeest, which goes by some sort of common instinct, the herd mentality was personified in Sphaaaa and Chuuu. Like the Queen *and* King bees of the nest.

So that was kind of good. That meant it was only one against two. Without Sphaaaa and Chuuu to direct the rest, the swarm would probably become mindless, harmless individuals. Probably. Maybe.

But he couldn't leave them out here, fluttering about the countryside. What if a new Queen and King emerged from the swarm and reunited them? Then the world would be right back to where it was at this very second. Minus, of course, his own imminent demise . . .

Okay. That meant using some great big spell of containment, which was way beyond anything even close to his skill level . . . or tricking them back into the Garden where they reverted back to harmless little bits of gossamer winged bird food.

Ooo!

The Shadowings.

The gods only knew, well, the Master would know, but the Master was the last one he *could* ask, how long the transformed People had lived under the beady little watchful eyes and sharp beaks of those black birds, but one thing he was pretty sure would be a result of that was a reflexive fear of the Shadowings. Not the pigeon-sized buggers back in the Garden, though, but great big proportionally sized Shadowings. With wingspans greater than the greatest dragon that ever flew.

Belid glanced over his shoulder. Chuuu and Sphaaaa flew lei-surely behind him. They were just toying with him. They could have him any time they wanted. Which didn't leave much time for conjuring up dragon-sized Shadowings even if he had clue one how to do such a thing.

Which left only one alternative.

Belid stopped dead in his tracks, whirled around, and gasped out, "Okay, you guys win. I surrender."

Chuuu and Sphaaaa were back in his face. Their breath didn't smell little anything that should be coming out of a benign little being who subsisted on garden moss.

"The gate," Chuuu said.

"Open it," Sphaaaa said, somehow managing to get a menac-ing sibilance into the words.

"Okay, but I've got to cast a spell to . . . "

"Cast it," Chuuu said.

"Now!" Sphaaaa emphasized.

"Okay, keep your wings on. It takes a minute. The Master doesn't want just anybody wandering inside, you know."

Chuuu ground his teeth together and his wings fluttered con-vulsively. So did the wings of most of the surrounding People.

Belid turned to the gate. He took a deep breath and started to speak the password spell. That was easy. It would lower the drawbridge and reveal the great wood and iron gate, which could be swung open at the pronouncement of another brief spell. Usu-ally though, they just used a small door set into the gate instead of bothering to open the whole thing and, as the Master often reminded them, "let out all the heat" from the drafty old castle.

But the inner doorway was, he hoped, going to stay closed. As the drawbridge began, slowly, to come down, Belid glanced at the expectant Sphaaaa and Chuuu, knowing it was now or never to get them thinking about the thing he needed them to be thinking about.

"How about those Shadowings, huh?" Belid said, spinning quickly on the winged couple.

"Let them come," Chuuu said with a harsh croak that could have been a laugh.

"It would be the People's turn to devour the Shadowings,"

Sphaaaa said, also amused.

"Oh, right," Belid said. "Because now you're so big and not butterflies anymore and they're still so small. Good thing they didn't escape from the Garden too and return to *their* natural forms as well. I mean, for all we know, before the Master snagged them to watch over you, they were, y'know . . . *giant*."

Chuuu's eyes went large for just a split second and then his and Sphaaaa's eyes both glanced to the side of the Keep around which was the Garden. The rest of the People did the same.

"That . . . no, they would have found us by now," Chuuu said.

Sphaaaa buzzed close to Belid and nudged his shoulder in the direction of the castle gate.

"Quiet! Speak only to recite your spell," she said.

Belid threw up his hands in surrender. "Sure, sure. I'm just saying. Giant Shadowings. Yikes," he said, and launched into the spell, as he had been told.

Well, it was *a* spell, but not *the* spell Sphaaaa and Chuuu were expecting.

As earlier noted, Belid was a believer in following the path of least resistance, the road most frequently taken. And, because who didn't like to have a little fun at the expense of others every now and again, the path of the prankster. Like the flash-bang spell used to make classmates jump, there were a few other relatively simple, benign incantations to create havoc and laughter at the expense of another human being's dignity. One of them, Belid's favorite in fact, was a nice little spell of illusion. It had occurred to him to try one on the People when they were tiny but he hadn't know what it was that would frighten them. But now he knew. And, to insure and strengthen the illusion's efficacy on them, he firmly planted the idea of giant Shadowings in their communal mind.

Belid had to admit that it was a pretty good illusion. The dark clouds overhead and the icy rain really gave it the right dramatic touch. There was even a well-timed rumble of thunder and a satisfying peal of lightning right at the moment the gate seemed to swing open and the flock of ridiculously oversized red-eyed Shadowings came flapping from inside, each barely able to squeeze through the massive opening.

The People fell for it. Or rather, Sphaaaa and Chuuu did and the hive minded People just went along with them. They spoke in unison, invoking some deities in rather unflattering terms, and then turned as one to flee the giant-sized birds flapping towards them, forgetting all about Belid in their terror. So, mission one . . . accomplished.

But, he couldn't hold the illusion for long. He'd never tried something this big or elaborate before. Luckily he wasn't dealing with the most sophisticated mind in the world. Still, once the illusion started to fade or they realized that the dark birds couldn't hurt them, they'd remember him again.

Then again, at the rate the People were cutting through the air, he wouldn't need long at all. Just a few more seconds . . . keep the imaginary Shadowings herding them in the right direction, tight to the castle wall. He hopped after them, keeping the People in his line of sight, rounding the side of the castle, being chased by magically induced figments of their primitive imaginations.

The further they got from Belid, the weaker his hold on the illusion, but they were right about where he needed them to be, so he sent the Shadowings circling the People in a tightening spiral. A couple of his giant birds had already dissolved into their true nothingness but he hoped the People were too terrified to notice. Then, the People dove en masse up into the mist obscuring the top of the castle wall, the snapping beaks of the Shadowing shadows dissolving like soap bubbles against the more substantial mist.

Belid waited, holding his breath.

One of two things should have happened.

The bad thing would be Sphaaaa and Chuuu realizing there was nothing really chasing them after all.

The good thing would be that they went back *over* the wall, into the Garden, and reverted to cute little butterfly people who would be eaten by real Shadowings if they tried to escape.

He only had to wait a couple of seconds to find out. If it was the bad choice, the two very annoyed leaders of the group mind would come charging out of the mist at the head of a small army that was going to tear him apart.

And if it was the good one?

From the distance came the faint but frenzied screechings of Shadowings as they fed.

▪ ▪ ▪

Belid hobbled into the Crimson Keep. The icy rain had stopped and the dark clouds parted to reveal a surprisingly warm sun just as he limped inside. The joke, as ever, was on him. As was the irony. As much as he tried to take the easy way out, the easy way always seemed to end up being harder than the hard way was supposed to have been in the first place. His day had started with the fear that he would be embarrassed in front of his classmates. It had ended—almost permanently—with him on the brink of violent death.

Maybe next time, he'll actually attempt the hard way first. It had to be easier than the easy way.

Maybe.

Keeping strictly to the familiar route, Belid went to his room where he stripped off his soaking wet clothes, fell into a hot bath to wash his scrapes and cuts, bound up his ribs and as ankle as best he could, then dressed in dry clothing warmed by the fire before heading to the pantry for something to fill his belly. He laid out some bread and cheese, wondering how long had it been since he had stepped into that Garden, relative to Crimson Keep reality time. The way this infernal place worked, he'd probably been gone days, maybe even weeks. Everyone would be so relieved to see him alive and well missing classes would be forgotten, or at the most, of minor importance.

Belid fell asleep at the table with a smile on his face and a loaf of bread for a pillow.

That was the way Athis and Klaria found Belid, almost an hour later, as they strolled into the pantry for the midday meal.

"So this is where he's been," Athis said in disgust.

"Not a very inventive hiding place," Klaria said. "Think we should wake him up before the Master finds his sorry hide?"

"Well, the Master was pretty annoyed that Belid missed this morning's alchemy lesson," Athis said.

"Mmm, yes. Said something about rendering Belid some new bodily orifices, didn't he?"

"I believe so."

"Good. Then let him sleep. He likes to show off so much, let's see how smug he is when the Master's coming down on him like a ton of bricks. Triple kitchen duty . . . it shouldn't happen to anybody," Klaria said. "Except Belid."

"Look at him, smiling like he's got something to be proud of. He even sleeps smug," Athis said with an annoyed shake of his head.

"He's probably dreaming of new ways to be a sluggard."

"Lazy lout."

"Shh. Here comes the Master. Switch places with me. I want to see Belid's face when he wakes up with the Master's screaming in his face."

"Lazy lout," Athis said again.

But, for the moment at least, Belid slept the sleep of the content, dreaming that he was someplace where classes didn't exist, and there were no such things as evil little butterfly people and mean black birds locked behind doors at the end of impossible corridors.

ASSESSMENT

by Robert Greenberger

"YOUR SPELL IS FAULTY," BELID COMPLAINED.

Athis had grown very tired of that oft-repeated phrase. He heard it every day, every week, and every month during his apprenticeship with the Master. Usually, it came from the Master's raspy voice but all-too-often it also came from his fellow students, none more than Belid the handsome. Belid the perfect. Belid the idiot. After all, it was barely a year ago when the attractive and vain young wizard summoned Koliander to chat him up about the Demon War and all hell broke loose.

Had Athis' transmogrification not gone awry, the Master might have died but instead, he was changed into a mouse with densely powerful blood that let him resolve the crisis. It took months before the Master was restored to something close to his humanoid form but the lessons continued as did the scolding.

"You lack confidence," the Master said to him soon after finally regaining his normal appearance. The comment came during one of their rare one-on-one sessions, when Athis had spectacularly failed to properly use the translocator in sending the baker back to the store rooms, sending him instead to the edge of the nearby cesspool. Only recently did the baker stop glaring at him every time Athis arrived to collect a meal for the Master.

"Your fingers need to be farther apart." Belid said from his position in the training room, a heavily protected space where spells could be worked out and perfected. With the Master now working his way towards concluding the Demon Wars, or so they all hoped, the emphasis had been switched from offensive to healing and constructive spells. The towns and people ravaged by the millennia-long conflict meant there would be much work to do once the longed-for peace was made a reality.

"They're as far apart as I can make them," Athis complained, fighting to keep the whine from his voice. They were standing about four feet apart, each in their deep blue apprentice robes. Belid, by virtue of his status among the current crop of train-ees had a bright blue sash around his waist. He preened with it and more than once, Athis and some of the other apprentices wished to splatter it with mud or worse. There was even one night the sash had been hung by the bed and nearly wound up being translocated to the nearest pub, letting the young man explain its whereabouts to the Master, who would no doubt find this unamusing.

Athis concentrated and strained to spread his fingers, which were of average size and shape, even further but the pale skin felt like it was ready to tear apart. He was already in pain from the straining he had been doing the previous four times he tried the spell, receiving flickers of magical energy rather than a fully-formed spell.

"What you need to is find a way around your limitations," a voice said from behind him and Athis winced. It was Klaria, the sole female apprentice at the time. She had been complet-ing other work and was just entering the training area, her robes nicely displaying curves that kept Athis awake at night.

"You have so many, no doubt you're adept at that . . . finding solutions," she said but there was a twinkle to her eyes. She was teasing him, whereas Belid was just being an ass. "For example, have you tried the other hand? Perhaps that one is more, um, flex-ible?"

"The dolt hasn't considered that," Belid said, concentrating on his own spell and not looking in their direction.

"Have too," Athis automatically responded, hating that he now sounded like a five year old. He bit his lower lip and extended his right hand, spreading the fingers in the same manner and summoned the spell from memory. There was a warm, comfort-ing surge of energy from his chest which seemed to bypass his arms and go right to his fingertips. Golden energy danced on all five fingers and grew brighter, growing nearly bright white, until separate thin streaks of magical energy fired forward, merging a foot before him into a thicker pure-white beam. Its intended target was a ceramic pot that had a web of cracks down one side.

The golden energy caressed the dull brown pot and slowly it began filling the gaps between edges and just ever so slightly, the pot wobbled then vibrated. The cracks were being woven back into a whole unit, the golden light reflecting off the glazed surface.

Athis smiled at the progress and dared look at Klaria for confirmation. She was not meeting his eyes, but appraising his work.

By taking his eyes off the object, however, his concentration wavered ever so slightly and that is when the pot picked up speed and was vibrating so violently it quickly shattered. A nearly perfect circle of debris formed around the stand where the now ruined pot had stood.

"Grife," he muttered.

"You almost had it," she said consolingly. Was there an actual hint of warmth in her voice or was that his overactive imagination at work again? She was rarely at ease, always at the ready, prepared for anything and ready to fight. Belid flirted when they were all together, but Athis could tell she intimidated him, especially after the Koliander fiasco.

"Almost is not good enough," Athis cried out in frustration. "I'm never going to get this!"

"Don't worry about it, Assless," Belid said in his haughtiest tone. "You can always continue on as *my* apprentice." The implications in that stung deep. Athis knew he was nowhere near as accomplished as Belid or Klaria and clearly had years to go before the final test. Still, he was dogged and made positive contributions to life within the Crimson Keep. So he wasn't ready to replace the Master, none of them were, especially Belid, who needed constant reminders to remain humble with his power.

His dark thoughts were interrupted by a new voice with a familiar rasp.

Athis, come to my chambers.

Rarely did the Master resort to thoughtcasting to summon his charges so it came as a surprise. Given the timing, he suspected the old man was well aware of the disastrous spell and was going to scold him atop the criticism from Belid. He needed nothing more to darken his day; he already was thinking the worst things about himself, his abilities, and his place within the Crimson Keep.

As he turned to leave, he was surprised to find Klaria fall into step beside him. They shared a surprised glance and once more, he let himself get lost in her dark eyes, the irises ringed with the most lovely shade of green he had ever seen. That they had been summoned, and no one else, was unusual and no doubt filled their minds with questions that could only be answered by their Master. Stepping into the dimly lit corridor, the two looked left then right, not to check for rushing servants but to orient themselves. After all, the Keep was an ever-changing structure said to have a thousand rooms and a hundred staircases with additions and subtractions by the day or hour. It was rumored the changes reflected the Master's needs or moods while others believed it was a cursed structure. Navigating it, though, was an unending challenge even after all the time the students had spent there.

Klaria had the better sense of direction, as she was better in most things, and gestured to their right. They walked in an uneasy silence which irritated Athis since he hated being tongue-tied around her in private. They were of similar age but the similarities stopped there. She carried herself with a military bearing, always erect, her body tense and prepared for action. She kept her hair cut incredibly short adding to the martial appearance. He was less comfortable in his skin, in need of muscle and probably a haircut. His wiriness did have the advantage of making him fairly adept in some gymnastic battle forms. Other than shaving regularly, he rarely worried about his appearance, focusing more on perfecting his craft and earning the Master's rare praise. They trained together, spent their off hours near one another but their friendship was casual despite his desire for more. Fraternizing among the apprentices was neither encouraged or discouraged and the Master never addressed the issue. There were, of course, unwritten rules: don't get caught, don't get pregnant, don't embarrass the Keep and its Master. So far, he'd honored all of those.

After ten minutes of walking down nearly identical stone corridors, differentiated by wall sconces and dusty tapestries depicting ancient conflicts or distant realms, Klaria slowed down. She actually had hesitated when faced by two staircases, one winding up to the north while another was a straight path to the next level. Closing her eyes, she concentrated her senses no doubt invoking some location spell. He shut his own eyes and tried to remember the words to the one spell he knew by heart. After losing his way for three weeks soon after arriving in the Keep, he was determined never to get so lost again.

His mind went blank and then he sensed the walls and stairs and the Master. A queasy feeling in his belly indicated he was on the right track and ever so slightly the shorter stair sharpened in focus.

"There," he said as she was beginning to point in the same direction.

"See, you're not so hopeless after all," she said with a grin. He started to break into a grin but stopped himself and gave her an exaggerated nod in return. They headed in the same direction while inwardly he was elated the spell worked.

"Why do you think he wants us both?" he asked.

"Maybe an errand," she said.

"Well, it couldn't be about the pot otherwise he'd just summon me," Athis added.

"Could be he wants a witness to your punishment," she said, the jibe being delivered so deadpan he couldn't tell if she was kidding. He certainly hoped it was hoped that was the case.

Several minutes later, they stood before the heavy wooden doors, carved with runes neither could read. It was a dead language, and the Master was believed to be the only one left alive who could read it. They protected his inner sanctum and the pair needed permission to cross the threshold. It came when the door to their left swiveled outward.

The apprentice nodded towards her to go first but she was already striding forward through the opening. He hurried to catch up and then paused. Neither one spent much time in the Master's chambers and no one ever went to the far back where he

actually slept. If he ever slept. That was another point of specu-
lation. The room itself was made from the same dark gray stone;
burning torches ringed the room with additional light thrown
off by a large glass chandelier that seemed to have a miniature
sun in its center. As a result, it was the brightest room either had
ever seen in the Keep. There were chests along two walls, above
them shelving with pristine bottles of powers and liquids in an
order Athis couldn't discern. A writing table was along the third
wall with a high back chair filled with large cushions. Bottles of
colored ink stood at attention atop the table and a stack of blank
papyrus was to the left and beside them were wooden scrolls
waiting to be affixed to the completed documents. A wax candle
was near the ink and quills, ready to affix his ornate seal, which
was in a carved, wooden box on the opposite side.

The Master, though, was nowhere to be seen.

He shot her a questioning glance, daring not to speak and
embarrass himself. She shook her head imperceptibly, clearly not
ready to speculate.

"Good morning," the Master said.

The two whirled around; Athis amazed that so powerful a
sorcerer could merely materialize without either of their height-
ened mystical senses detecting him. He had *so* much to learn.

"Klaria, you have been with me for seven turns of the sea-
son," he said. She nodded in agreement. Then he turned his gaze
toward Athis. "And you have been here for four."

"That's true," he said, feeling he needed to fight the instinct
to flee in terror.

"You continue to train together and are both making adequate progress," he continued. Klaria flinched, clearly hoping
for higher praise while Athis was delighted to hear the word
"adequate". "Still, there come times when you each need to be
assessed, to see how far you have come with your training. While
the war may be nearing an end, we must remain ever vigilant.
And you must perfect your skills. Therefore, I have a task for
you to perform which will enable me to weigh how far you have
come."

Tasks. Tasks he could do. Fetch something from town via
magic, rearrange some furniture perhaps. Having used his magic

just minutes before, Athis was actually feeling limbered up and ready to perform.

A small, red-breasted bird appeared seemingly from nowhere and settled atop a tall cabinet. It seemed to be staring right at him, making Athis feel self-conscious. Bad enough the Master did that, but a bird should not have such power over him.

"As you know, there are other mystics across the land," the Master began as he strode across the room toward one of the shelves. "One in particular, Achrios, stole something from me some time back and the time has come to retrieve it. I am sending you to his castle to find it."

A field test? The last time he was sent out of the castle on a mission he wound up completing the mission a day late and nearly burning down a blacksmith's shop, far from an easy task. This got Athis nervous but he tensed himself so as not to betray his concern. He kept his focus squarely on the Master, ignoring Klaria, who was no doubt thrilled.

He retrieved a scroll and was unraveling it, rolling up one end as the other unspooled until he found what he was looking for. He laid it atop the writing table and a long, tapering finger pointed to a pen and ink image of a multifaceted gem.

"Ruby quartz, infused with hellfire and very dangerous," he intoned. Athis recalled that hellfire was not easily captured and the gemstone was one of the few that could contain not only the heat but also the eldritch energies. Carrying it would be tricky enough; retrieving it sounded nearly impossible.

"Achrios won it from me during a challenge some time back," the Master said. "Some time" could mean years or centuries since no one quite knew his age. But what was known was that he had trained several generations of wizards and was among the most powerful, which explained why he was a focal point in the Demon Wars.

"Why now?" Klaria dared ask.

"Eh? Because if I am to sit at a negotiating table with Demon generals, I will need every trick up my sleeves," he replied. "Bargaining in good faith is not something they are known for and preparation, as you know, is the difference between success and death. These are still dangerous times, and caution must ever be our watchword."

Words, literally, to live by, Athis knew.

"What is being tested," she asked.

"What do you mean?" he asked in return, stepping toward her. She did not flinch while Athis nearly did even though they were still some distance apart.

"Are we to demonstrate the use of a certain set of spells? Certain stealth tactics? By what will we be judged?"

"Ah! Nothing."

She blinked.

"Nothing?"

"Nothing. Was that not clear?" He sounded annoyed.

Athis finally spoke up. "No sir, I think she is looking for a rubric, something by which we can be accurately measured."

She shot him a thankful look but immediately returned her attention to the older man and waited patiently.

"I said nothing and meant it," he explained. "You have spent years honing your mystical abilities so this is a test about *not* using them."

"What?" Athis said, far too loudly for his own ears. The interruption earned him a glare from the others in the room.

"You will use no magic whatsoever. I shall send you there with a charm that will activate and bring you back once the gem is in your possession. Between arrival and return you will expend no magical energy."

"How will you know," Klaria matter-of-factly inquired.

"You will be marked," the Master replied. "You will be covered with runes that will activate and glow should either one of you use magic. All will see your failure long before you return to me. And understand, you will both shine like the sun even if one of you breaks the rule."

Without another word he crossed the room to the shelves and reached but failed to grasp a large jar. Settling on his feet, he gestured with both hands and the jar levitated down to where he could grasp it. Twisting about he held it out to Klaria who cocked an eyebrow at him.

"You will need to follow the rune design exactly for this to work, which you may consider a part of the examination if you so choose." He then retrieved another scroll and held it out to Athis. As he unrolled it, his eyes went wide as he saw how intricate the markings needed to be and how they stretched from forehead to toes, front and back.

"Master, how will these be applied?" he asked.

"Ah, yes, another part of the test," he said and Athis swore there was mischief in his expression. "You are being sent in as a team which requires a level of trust. Consider this your starting point."

Klaria by then had stepped over to study the scroll.

"Surely you jest," she began, but the protest died as he glanced her way.

"This should take you less than an hour if you're efficient," he said breezily. "Report back here by then so you can begin immediately." The two looked at one another in bafflement and by the time they looked up, the Master was gone.

There was no discussion as they left his chambers and the silence grew only thicker as they walked. Athis' mind was a swirl with concerns over the mission, the gem, the runes, and how they were being applied. While he'd kissed a girl or two in his time, he had never been naked with one before and he was concerned with his involuntary reactions. Worse, he knew Klaria, and *liked* her. This was going to be complicated and he was dripping with nervous sweat by the time they stopped walking before the door to her private room.

"Inside and strip," she said with authority, nothing at all salacious in her tone.

He did as she ordered, removing his robe and the shift under it, hesitating as he got to the small clothes beneath. With each layer, he had to control his breathing, using all the exercises he had learned to control magic. He looked in every direction but her's and he focused on another small bird that made lazy circles near the high ceiling. His eyes were mostly closed and his back toward the room's other occupant. The rustling of fabric indicated she was getting ready.

"Klaria, I am sorry . . . ," he began before turning.

"Hush. This is merely part of our study, part of our being magicians. This means nothing more." Her tone was flat and less than convincing. After all, both were still in their teen years, years from being bonded or mated or whatever was to come. He knew others liked her but she was so focused on work, he doubted she had even kissed a single boy. She was perhaps as nervous as he, maybe even more.

She was pulling the rubber stopper from the top of the jar as he turned. The first thing he saw was the scroll spread on her desk, weighted at the edges so the designs were clearly visible. He then dared looked at her.

His breath caught as he saw her in the flesh. She was pale, which made her nut brown nipples even more prominent. Her breasts—god they were gorgeous—were small but suited her lean form. She was hard where he expected her to be soft, well-defined muscles on her arms, torso and legs. And she was bare where he expected something dark and inviting.

That was when he realized her eyes were studying him with a harsh appraisal and he was suddenly very, very conscious of how *not* toned he was. He fought off the instinct to suck in his small gut—too late! Her eyes flicked over his groin and returned to meet his.

With a sigh, she said, "Think you can follow the directions and not muck it up?"

Athis could manage a nod.

"Then go first," she said, positioning her feet firmly on the ground, her legs now slightly parted. "And be quick about it."

Beside the jar was a small brush and he dipped it once, then studied the illustration. He touched the brush to her right temple and slid it down into a curl just above her cheek. Athis continually checked the scroll and applied the ointment. In short order, she was decorated in a way matching the scroll's picture. He nodded confirmation to the silent girl who mostly resembled a statue, barely breathing. Their eyes would not meet.

As he worked faster, he got lower and was thankful the design ran down her breastbone and skipped her breasts entirely. On the other hand, he rounded her waist and drew special markings on her rear cheeks before descending down her thighs, circling them until he was near her sex. He slowed, not to linger but to get it right and remove the need for corrections.

Then he was done.

"It dries quickly, which is good," she said. "And then you don't feel it at all. Did you screw up at all?"

"It does not appear so," Athis said, averting his eyes from the handiwork. She shrugged on a bathing robe to cover herself and then turned to him.

"Then I shall begin. Stand still and no surprises," she commanded. Athis nodded once and tried to imitate her frozen position. His greatest fear alternated between feeling ticklish or coming to attention as she neared his hips. Her strokes were longer, more commanding and faster but she was right, the ointment was at first cool on the skin and then rapidly absorbed.

Her hands made quick work of his face and shoulders, then down his left arm, right arm and she resumed work on his back, from the nape of his neck to his spinal column and then his hips. He bit his lower lip and thought of the Master, the cold, stone hallways, even Belid; anything to keep his mind from where she was touching him; where he had dreamed of her touching him. The brush worked its way back and forth across his own cheeks then around to his navel, encircling it with a flourish with the brush dipping down his right thigh. And so it went until she was adding a series of dots to his toes.

It was suddenly over.

"Get dressed," she ordered and turned her back, which seemed silly after all that . . . closeness. He complied and as he did, she said, "Thank you, Athis, for not embarrassing either of us."

Athis didn't know what to say but knew enough to say nothing than the wrong thing.

Once he was dressed he stepped into the hall, giving her privacy and time for them to each collect their thoughts. His mind went everywhere and nowhere as he fought for control and calm because they needed to begin their mission. Within minutes she stepped outside, locking her door and appeared ready. The markings on her face were fading, being fully absorbed into the skin so by the time they would arrive at their destination; none would see a single mark.

It was a short time later they were standing once more before the Master. He studied their rapidly fading markings as he accepted back the scroll and jar. With a flick of two fingers, they floated back into position as he continued to examine them. "Good work," he said. "I hope this bodes well for you both."

"Master, how long will we have to complete the test?"

"A fair question, Klaria. I could do this in less than a day but then again, I am practiced at this. I will therefore give you two."

"And should it take longer?" she inquired.

He shook his head. "It should take no more than two days." His tone implied the pair had to succeed or coming back would be unpleasant. As incentives went, Athis considered this one not as desirable as others he'd had over time.

"What shall we do for food or . . . ," she was asking as his hands waved in the air.

A flash of bright crimson light blinded Athis and the next thing he heard was her completing the sentence. ". . . money?"

Blinking away the temporary blindness, Athis realized he was chilled. They were outside, standing on a cobblestone street in a village he did not recognize. When he awoke that morning, the Crimson Keep was bathed in warm spring air. This place had the bite of fall and the leaves were withered on the trees, ready to fall. A breeze cut through his robe despite its thick wool and he imagined a whiff of frost as he exhaled.

Klaria was already making a circuit of the street, taking in the sights and attempting to orient herself. The architecture was different than where the Crimson Keep stood. The homes were lower, more angular with slate rooftops and a series of spouts to channel what must have been considerable rainwater or snow melt. He noticed the spouts all went below the surface so there had to be sewers and underground plumbing meaning they were sophisticated. That implied a level of technology that was not found in every other country. No obvious candidates came to mind although he had to admit, geography was not something the Master prioritized, not beyond the nearby lands two days' ride from the Keep.

A gurgle from his stomach broke the silence and caused Klaria to focus on his eyes.

"He should have fed us," she said.

"Not that he ever fusses over such details," he said. She nodded in agreement and then began patting her robes. He did the same, hoping one of them might have a forgotten coin or two for a stew and maybe even some cider.

Both came up empty.

Athis began scanning the area, seeking options while trying not to seriously contemplate panhandling. His eyes were drawn to a steady stream of people heading to their left, where the sounds of commerce drifted toward them. Barkers, salesmen, peddlers. There was a market in that direction and perhaps a solution to their hunger.

The sky above them was filled with birds, some chasing one another, others seeking food, while one perched atop a vendor's stall and seemed to look right at them. He shuddered a moment and tilted his head in that direction and after a pause, she nodded in assent and began marching, automatically taking the lead. As they walked, he considered how unprepared they were. No spells could be used, no coin or weapon was on hand, and their clothing was not suitable for prolonged exposure. They had to find Achrios' castle quickly but the first order of business was survival and that meant food.

Less than a minute of walking took them to a town square that was ringed with stalls, carts, and peddlers hawking their wares from trays hung from their necks. Fruits, nuts, vegetables, and baked goods competed for coin and attention. People in thick capes and overcoats milled about, chatting one another up or haggling over prices. Barrels overflowed with a veritable rainbow of edible goods and the cheerful tones led Athis to conclude the harvest had been a plentiful one. Everyone would profit but it also meant a stray piece of fruit or two might not get noticed. After all, their training did include legerdemain, making their hands and arms quick. He spied a stand off to the side where the sole proprietor, a very young boy clearly minding the shop for his parent, was engaged in filling an order.

He moved over, conscious of trying to appear casual and willing his shivering hands to stop moving. Carefully, he pulled open a small pocket in his robe, a space big enough for a few vials of potions but little else. He eyed several bright orange pieces of sweet fruit and moved directly toward them. With his left hand, he picked one up to squeeze, then bring to his nose for a prolonged sniff. Meantime, his right hand had snatched a second piece and had lowered it from sight. The examination would mask the theft, or so he hoped. Success! So, he placed the fruit down and selected a second piece to scrutinize and repeated the theft. Two pieces of fruit would not support them for long, but would at least be a start.

In triumph, he whirled about to let Klaria know he had succeeded at procuring lunch.

She was nowhere to be seen. He hurried from the stall, feeling somewhat guilty about stealing from a boy and hoped the gods would forgive him.

"Oy, he stole my fruit!" the boy shrieked before Athis had gone three feet. So much for the gods' forgiveness.

Athis broke into a run, zigging and zagging, a survival skill he learned early in life and had way too many times to practice since. His movements and the cries of the youth brought him unwanted attention so he tried to slow down and lose himself in the crowd. It would be hard given his blue robe was a distinctive shade, with nothing else like it in the crowd of blacks and browns and tans.

He stepped between two stalls, hoping to avoid notice, worrying what became of Klaria when a strong hand grabbed his collar.

Athis was pulled inside a tavern which had an entirely different set of cries to drown out the commotion he caused. As he regained his footing, he caught the strong scent of pork stew which got his mouth watering so much that he reached into the pocket for one of the pilfered fruits. His hand felt a pulpy, stick mess.

"Fool!"

Blinking, he realized the person who grabbed him was Klaria, who was glaring at him, a look he recognized as that learned from their Master. "What have you done now?"

His hand withdrew, the orange mess in his palm.

"I brought you some lunch."

"Stole it and got caught is more like it," she said, clearly displeased.

"Well, what have you been doing?"

"Ascertaining what we can do for some spending coin so we could have a proper meal before risking our lives to retrieve the gem," she said. She cocked her head towards the tavern's interior. He looked past her and spied the table in the room's center. Two men were arm wrestling, sinews and tendons popping from muscled arms, sweat pouring from the brow of a bald man and a grunt emerging from an older, heavier competitor. They were surrounded by a throng that was yelling their encouragement, protecting their bets.

"I take on the winner," she said as if she were making a dinner reservation.

"You what?"

"I will wrestle the winner, is that so hard to understand?"

"No, but what did you have to bet with?"

"I believe you saw it," she said and cut her eyes back to the competition.

Athis swallowed hard and began calculating how on earth she thought she could beat someone so much more muscular, so much stronger. He imagined the worst, having to give up his life to defend her virtue, which she foolishly offered up. Lifting the food would have been so much easier, especially if she had been nearby to distract the kid.

His thoughts were interrupted by the eruption of cheers and boos as the bald man proved victorious. Coins were exchanged, as were wrapped fish, a live chicken, and three gold teeth. The victor had a small pile of gold and copper coins heaped before him and someone placed a tankard of ale before him.

"How—how do you propose beating him?"

Klaria had been studying the competition and clearly had her mind at work on the solution to that very dilemma. The bald man gestured for her to take the now vacant bench opposite him as he drank nearly half the tankard in a single, noisy pull. It made a loud thunk as it was slammed atop the wooden table.

"C'mon sweet meat, I have worked up quite a thirst," he said to the guffaws from his allies. There was genial laughter and the mood seemed light, seeing her as nothing more than a distraction, not even worth betting a single coin in her favor. "Let's get this over with so I can end this day with a bang." More laughter.

"Or a fizzle," she said, swinging a leg over the bench and taking her place. She made an elaborate show of stretching her fingers, cracking a knuckle then two. She rolled her neck and adjusted her feet, all a show for her opponent.

Athis couldn't watch, determining to do his part to save her. He began scoping out the tavern, making note of windows, doorways, and where the bartender likely kept a club to maintain order. It wasn't particularly large nor was it all that busy once you moved away from the wrestling table. Two bored looking prostitutes chatted at one end of the long, damp bar and a drunk was wheedling a refill from the equally bored barkeep.

He concluded that before the winner could take Klaria upstairs, he would have to pass the side door he entered from. He began calculating how best to trip him, breaking his presumed hold on her and getting her outside where they had room to maneuver. Three different spells vied for attention but he told them to get lost, they had the day off. Instead, he scanned the space for anything to use as a weapon.

Of course, once they escaped, they needed to find their way, with an imagined mob chasing them, out for blood or worse.

Two men were at a table, ignoring the action, clearly there to discuss some business matter. Assuming his most formal manner, he approached them and waited until he caught the eye of the man closest to him.

"Pardon me, good sirs, but I was hoping you could point me in the direction of Achrios' castle."

They both stared at him with hard, calculating eyes. They exchanged a glance and then studied him once more, taking in his robes, judging his threat or profit value. Finally, one spoke up, "If ye're asking, then ye're from elsewhere."

"Very astute, sir."

"Go east from town, clear the hills and you will see his castle. Do ye have business with his lordship?"

"I am on an errand," was all he would offer. There was a

loud cry behind him but Athis dare not turn and see what had become of his friend.

"Good luck to ye," the first man said and, seeing there was no more profit in the conversation, returned his attention to his drinking partner.

Free to turn without giving offense, he quickly looked over his shoulder and saw nothing but a crowd of men around the wrestlers. They were screaming and gesturing and he could not tell who was winning.

Easing his way over and then into the crowd, he saw the stalemate. Both participants were straining, tired, and no doubt sore. The bald man had been through at least one previous contest, likely more, and was clearly running out of energy. Klaria was trying to outlast him, her smaller but fresher muscles working to hold out. The clasped hands moved a bit towards her, eliciting one cry, then tilted away from the apprentice and a larger cry rang out.

Her strategy was failing because he did not look ready to collapse.

She then did something Athis had never seen before.

Klaria let her tongue slip between her lips, lightly running along her upper lip, pausing, and then running very slowly along her lower lip.

That caught the man's attention and as he studied the pink organ, his attention wavered just long enough for her to put her last reserves of energy into a final effort, yanking his hand with unusual force until it smacked against the wood. As it met the wood, she let out a victory cry that was primal. A smattering of birds took off from their sleep and made a lot of distracting noise while the cries from the spectators were mixed but definitely not in her favor.

"You cheated!" the loser cried. "I'll still have your quim!" He broke his hand free from her grip and rose, shoving the bench away. He was easily over six foot tall and his neck was thick, his shoulders broad, an overall impressive display of manhood.

"Like hell you will," Klaria said boldly, but her eyes betrayed the fear she felt inside. Maybe the man saw it, maybe not, but Athis recognized it and knew this was trouble.

With his trained eye, he studied the scene, his mind awhirl with planning, judging scenarios, rejecting the foolish course of action. Everything they had been taught for magic duels was brought to play in a heartbeat with the sole exception of the magic itself.

The man lunged over the table to grasp her in his massive arms. As he did so, immobilizing himself from further movement, Athis deftly swept his right arm across the table ostensibly to spill the tankards and scatter them, but his true goal was to collect as many of the coins as possible while he could.

Klaria, meantime, backpedaled and only one beefy hand caught her left arm. He pulled, throwing her off-balance, but also keeping him preoccupied. Athis, running entirely on adrenaline and training, pocketed the coins then reached for the tankards. With one in each hand, he scrambled atop the table and swung with all his meager might. The tankards collided with the man's temples causing him to do two things: howl with a bark and loosen his grip.

Someone reached for Athis and he knew his time was up, the mob would pin them both in a moment, the numbers were not in their favor. Instead, he released the tankards and did a somersault over the crowd, expertly landing on his feet away from them. He thanked the gods that they let him be at least good at one thing.

Klaria, now free, grabbed a candle and tipped hot wax on the hands that groped for her, keeping the table between her and the main attacker. She slid under their table and upended the bench on the opposite side, blocking the approach of several men. Pulling herself up, she swept a leg that brought another to his knees.

By then, everyone was in motion, including the far-less-bored bartender, now armed with his massive club. Athis knew this was their moment to flee or be caught. He spun to his right to avoid one man, grabbing another to help him block a flying bowl. Shoving the man away from him, Athis was now close enough to the main entrance to run.

Only once he was outside did he look for his partner. Klaria was emerging from a window, back first, legs kicking to keep free. He darted to her side and grabbed her waist and pulled, bringing her completely outside.

"Run!" they both ordered the other. She hurried south but skidded to a stop when it was clear Athis knew exactly where he was headed.

"Why east?"

"Because that's where the castle is," Athis replied.

"Thanks for the save," she said several minutes later, as they slowed down and were catching their breath, which was clearly visible in the cooling air. "Of course, I only agreed to the bet to pay for the fruit you stole."

"Of course," he agreed, believing none of it. She couldn't possibly have known he had stolen fruit for them at the time of the bet. Now, he had money to pay the boy back and more for a meal but the village was receding behind them. All that effort for naught. They were hungry and cold.

Which is when the rain began.

"The castle is visible past the hills," he said, spitting out water from the sudden deluge. "I swear, the Master is watching and did this intentionally."

"You give him too much credit," she shot back, shaking water from her nose. "He sent us away and will not think twice about us until we return."

"Or our bodies," Athis said glumly.

They trudged ahead in silence, both tired, wet, cold, and hungry. The sun was hidden behind clouds but the cooling air which threatened to turn the rain to snow indicated the day was rapidly waning. He withdrew the solid fruit from his pocket, and with trembling hands, peeled it deliberately. His task complete, he divided it in two and silently handed half to her which she wordlessly accepted. It was tart but never before had he appreciated something so fresh and tasty.

As it grew darker and colder and wetter, it had become clear the village was the last vestige of civilization for some time. The hills were foreboding shapes, looming over them, and filling Athis' head with images of monsters or demons. One shape even reminded him of Koliander, which made him violently shiver.

The hills were bisected by a well-worn path, wide enough

for a good sized wagon and team but there were no huts, storage units, outhouses, or other structures to provide them with any shelter. Even if he could do magic, he lacked knowledge of a spell to create a waterproof cloak and after the disaster with Koliander, he didn't want to go near a teleportation spell. So, by silent agreement, they continued to walk on rather than stop and just be rained upon.

Thankfully, the storm lightened up with each passing hour so as the skies shifted from pitch black to dark gray and the first birds could be heard, they were that much closer to their target. Of course, they were utterly exhausted, famished, and soaked through. It would be hours before either felt comfortable and their growing hunger would only sap their energies just when they would need them most.

"We have just over a day," Athis told her.

"Sounds right," Klaria agreed.

Athis looked through the gray, trying to make out shapes and failing so he continued to walk, trying to focus on the mission. As a result, he missed a shadowy form stepping through the lightening gloom.

"Hold fast," a guttural voice cried.

Athis stopped hastily, a heel slipping in the muck of a road, and fought to keep his balance, losing any semblance of dignity. Klaria, though, stopped and assumed a defensive stance. She was, after all, the better fighter.

"We have stopped, now what?" she challenged.

The shape seemed to divide in the murky morning air, complicated by the last of the rain, now a mere mist. There were two then three distinct, human shapes, wide and thick. He assumed they were highwaymen and Athis could only wonder where they had been and why they were on the road at his ungodly early hour. Unless . . . they knew someone was coming and were lying in wait.

"Where're your horses?" the voice asked.

"What horses?" she said.

"The ones pulling the wagon," it said after a moment.

"What wagon?" she said, her tone lightening which baffled him. Was now the time to be playful?

"The one bringing the supplies," the voice returned. It had stopped moving so Athis could not make out any detail. Three experienced criminals against two inexperienced interlopers—these were no favorable odds.

"What supplies?" she continued.

"Stop that!" the voice demanded.

"Stop what?" Athis swore she was having fun and that worried him. Had she lost her mind during their walk?

"That!"

"What!"

"That!"

"Oh shut up, dolt," a second voice said from the opposite side.

"Your friend's an idiot," Klaria challenged.

"That he is," the second voice agreed. "But he is strong and we need strong backs. Just as we need comfortable women."

Oh great, Athis thought. They were lying in wait for some wagon but will now kill him and rape Klaria to stay busy. That would not do but really, what were his options other than not dying?

"Aye, some may find me comfortable, but you'll be worm meat long before you find out," she said. He couldn't understand why she was egging him on. But then he heard it: a sound of a boot scrapping against the mud. She was stalling, making them angry enough to do something stupid while she was ready for them.

No wonder he was falling in love with her.

"I should warn you, we've been out here in the rain all night and are far from charitable. You could let us pass and keep waiting for the wagon or you could try and attack us and lose twice before the sun peeks through the clouds."

"You think you two could truly survive us?"

Klaria paused, and Athis could hear more mud being moved, now making soft sucking sounds. Whatever she was doing appeared to be deep.

"Indeed. Tell you what, come this way and find out how your chances are."

And with that, she threw a handful of mud like a snowball

in their general direction. Apparently fortune was smiling on her this dreary morning because they both heard the splotch of wet dirt hitting a target.

"I'm dirty, brother," the first voice said.

"That was unwise," the second voice said and with a low growl he moved. Athis heard the heavy footsteps quicken as they neared. Klaria took several steps back and planted her feet. She gestured for him to hold his position. He nodded in affirmation.

The man became visible, layered in thick leather and a cotton shirt beneath, both damp and dirty. He was maybe thirty, with coarse graying hair and fat jowls. His girth spoke of too much ale and too little work, so this thief would be nowhere near the threat he initially appeared. As his speed increased, he grit his teeth, reaching for a cudgel from his belt but he kept his eyes fixed on Klaria so he totally missed the six inch deep gap she had gouged in the soft ground.

He stepped into it, altering his momentum and his heavy top fell forward, his arms flailing unsuccessfully for balance. Klaria carefully timed his fall and when he was nearly a foot from the ground she twisted herself and let out a well-positioned kick that landed where this throat met his chest. The impact was loud, only to be drowned out by the expulsion of air and gurgle of pain. One down and decisively so.

It was a one-time trick but it did narrow the odds, although Athis was now convinced the idiot brother would be some superhumanly strong obstacle. He wanted to flee; not that there was anywhere to go, but standing still and getting beaten was not how he envisioned the day going.

"Bitch!" the previously unheard third voice cried and Athis was certain he heard a sword being pulled from a scabbard. They had no weapons. No protective armor. No cover.

He stepped backward and his heel hit a rock. In fact, it felt like a good-sized one so he crouched and fought the mud to free it. The sucking sound of the unforgiving mud was mixed with the gasping fallen attacker nearby but finally, he freed it, his action carrying to its natural conclusion, rising up and over his shoulder. The momentum did its part and the slimy exterior of the rock followed, slipping from Athis' grip and sailed nicely through the air until it struck the rushing attacker in the solar plexus. This halted his progress, knocked the wind from him, and made him skid on the slick road, now losing his balance. He fell first on his ass and then his back. Athis had already scrambled to his feet and grabbed his solid projectile. Firmly gripping it with both hands, he brought it swiftly down to the sword hand, cracking fingers and forcing the weapon from the man's fingers.

Two down and Athis's head was having difficulty registering their success.

They now stood side by side, ready for the simpleton.

Instead, they heard his footsteps receding into the mists.

Klaria let out a chuckle but cut it short when a new sound arrived: the steady clip-clop of hooves in the mud. The wagon, the intended target, was finally nearing and this meant they might have their way into the castle. She gestured for them to go back the way they came, putting some distance between themselves and the two aching criminals who still posed a threat.

Within a minute, the shape of the wagon, four horses, and two men driving the load appeared. One brandished a sword when the figures on the road became visible but Athis waved at them anyway. Klaria smiled, trying to put them at ease. She never smiled often enough in Athis' estimation.

"Ho," she called out. "There are three highwaymen just ahead. We've softened two up for you and chased the third away."

The wagon slowed to a halt and the men regarded the pair. A bird landed atop the wagon and seemed to intently seek a stray worm or watched the exchange. Slowly, the sword was returned to its home. "Why would you do that?"

"They are idiots and mistook us for you," she replied.

"Idiots indeed if they mistook a pretty young thing for a horse," the driver said.

She smiled but saw her eyes tighten and Athis hissed at her, a warning to keep things light. They needed a ride.

"Good sirs, is there a chance we could ride with you to the castle? We've been walking all night and are wet and exhausted."

The two men touched foreheads as they rapidly whispered among themselves and Athis hoped this wouldn't require payment or service. He wanted to keep the stolen coins until he absolutely needed spend them. Finally, they parted and he noticed the space between them was lightening; the rains had ended and dawn was coming.

"Better up here than risk your lives down there," the driver said. "Get in back and stay quiet."

That was far from difficult as they were asleep moments after settling between casks of wine and sacks of flour. They slept without a sound until the wagon's ride over the mud changed to the uneven roll over stone. Athis awoke, noticing Klaria's arm rested over his lap, and just let it lay there. He was still a little damp, but his stomach reminded him they had barely eaten since yesterday and that would become an issue. He hoped they got to the castle soon since he also had to pee.

As if the world was listening in, the wagon drew to a halt and he could hear voices. It sounded to him like this was a routine delivery with familiar drivers so there would no suspicions raised. True enough, after a few minutes of conversation, he could hear heavy chains pulling open the gate so, much as he hated to do it, he needed to wake up his companion.

"I'm alert," she said before he could shake her shoulder. The warm arm rose from his lap, much to his regret, and she stretched as the wagon moved. A few minutes later it stopped and they could hear the two men climb down.

The back of the wagon allowed dim daylight to pierce the darkness and the two figures were silhouetted. Klaria smiled her thanks and accepted an outstretched hand to help her down. Athis scrambled down on his own and reached out to clasp hands with the men.

"If you help us unload the supplies, you'll easily enter the castle if this is truly your destination," the driver said.

"It is," Athis said and turned to reach for a sack of flour.

He gamely followed the two men, neither of whose names was ever offered the travelers, from the wagon and through a huge set of wooden double doors that were charred and splintered in places. The quartet carried their goods into a dark passage giving Athis a chance to assess the castle's construction and defenses. So far it was ridiculously easy to enter the place and the guard appeared lax. There were no locks on the doors and the passage way was narrow, providing some defense if needed. Of course, who would ever think of attacking through the kitchen?

The corridor measured four dozen or so of his footsteps until it widened and they began passing wide round doors inset into the walls. Each was labeled, telling Athis things at this level were organized. They slowed and then stopped before one such door and the driver gave it a tug. It noiselessly swung open and he gripped the brazier set into the wall and waved it inside. Then he gestured at Athis, who shouldered the flour and carried it within. On wooden pallets stood a few other such bags, all identical. He laid his burden next to one and rolled both shoulders to work out the kinks.

They worked in silence for another twenty minutes or so letting Athis conclude that it was a smooth, well-run castle operation. Deliveries were made when supplies ran low but not perilously so meaning the chief cook paid attention. Things were clean and despite some dust and cobwebs, surprisingly tidy. The cook was also good, or Athis was so hungry that anything would smell delicious. His mouth watered at the frying meats and whiff of cinnamon from the porridge. No castle workers were to be seen, meaning there was a level of trust between the castle management and the local tradesmen. That could be turned against them, which was exactly what was happening although their intent was far from malicious.

As the last sack of barley was put in its place, the driver silently thanked his charges and turned to depart. Klaria cocked an eyebrow at Athis and he nodded in the direction of the kitchen, where there were minimal sounds of human activity.

He leaned close to her and at first she turned away from his foul, morning breath, but then twisted her head, her ear closer.

"We should swipe some food then proceed."

She nodded. "No kidding. But to where?"

They lacked directions. There was no mystic way or map to find the artifact. After all, if you lived and worked in the castle, you wouldn't need such information—you would just know.

"We're doomed," he moaned softly.

"Stop that!" she hissed. "First things first." She moved towards the wonderful, alluring aroma and they were rewarded with a large, well-lit kitchen. Huge stone tables were set at right angles to one another. One was clearly where meats were dressed while another was relegated to baking. It seemed a stack of bird carcasses were waiting to be cleaned for a meal. A heap of fresh, bright green leafy vegetables sat patiently waiting a chef's attention on yet another table. Beyond them was a massive walk-in fireplace where kettles happily burbled over low flames. A full cord of wood was neatly stacked to its right while the left offered a passageway from kitchen to elsewhere within the castle.

Klaria moved cautiously, quietly, and neared a platter that had once been filled with someone's breakfast. Scraps of fried meats and breads were on a metal plate and her fingers darted forward and snared the debris. Athis followed suit with a second such plate and soon he was chewing nosily, barely taking time to identify the contents of his mouth. It didn't matter, nothing lasted long in there after a few hurried chews.

Both were so busy scarfing down the remains of someone's meal that neither heard the footsteps that would have told them they were about to be found out. A young girl, barely into her teens, emerged near the fire, carrying another tray filed with dirty plates. She saw them and stopped, eyeing them, eyes wide with surprise then narrowing with suspicion.

"Flirt," Klaria said quickly.

Athis looked at her in shock. He never flirted, there was no one to flirt with in the Master's Keep. It certainly wasn't something taught.

"Who are you?" the girl asked, lowering the plate on the blood-splattered table. "Where's Giorg?"

"Who?" Athis spluttered, earning him a frustrated hiss from Klaria.

"I heard his wagon round the castle wall. And you have flour all over your clothes—are you a replacement?"

"Re-replacement? No." He felt like an idiot. If he was out of his element when they arrived—was it really only yesterday—then here he was truly lost.

"There were so many supplies Giorg asked us to help," Klaria spoke up. "Athi—Athosan is mighty strong and was happy to help." She gently shoved him, making him move closer to the girl.

"It was nothing," he stammered out. That seemed to earn him a smile. "So, where is everyone?"

"Cleaning from breakfast," the girl said. "Have you eaten?"

"Actually, we *were* hungry," Athis said.

"Come Athosan, there's extra boar," the girl said, pointing at a platter on a sideboard he totally missed earlier. She smiled at him and he naturally smiled back. Who was flirting with who?

Athis accompanied her and she gestured permission and he grabbed a thick, greasy slice. "Do you cook?" he asked as he chewed.

"I am in training," the girl replied. "I am Julianna, niece to Lupoff, chief cook to Achrios."

"How is it going?"

"Passable," she replied, gesturing he should take another slab. "I prepared this myself last night."

Athis smiled in appreciation, feeling a river of grease pour down his chin. He hoped such a display would be taken as a compliment for her culinary skills. Truth be told, it was tough and needed seasoning but he was never going to admit it.

"Where is Giorg?" she asked, handing him a rag to dab his face with.

"He, ah, he . . . ," he began before Klaria, finishing her food with less mess, said, "He's headed back to town."

Julianna stood still, eyeing the pair. "Then why are you still here?"

Athis leaned toward her, summoning up his best line: "I heard the women here had to be seen to be believed. They were right."

He heard Klaria's muffled groan but Julianna's cheeks went crimson.

"Truly?"

"Not really," Athis admitted. "We have come in search of something which was left here and needs to be retrieved."

She cocked her head quizzically and Athis loved the gesture. She was a cute, if young, thing. "Do you know where it might be?"

"I suspect Achrios has it in safe keeping. It's about the size of my fist," Athis said, raising an arm and making a fist, hoping there was a hint of muscle being flexed.

He pressed the advantage and leaned in towards her and whispered in her ear. She nodded once and he stole a look at Klaria, who was watching intently. Her eyebrows shot up quizzically, then she looked annoyed when Julianna's giggle carried across the room.

She reached out and took his hand, leading him toward the great hall. Her touch seemed to shield him as a line of serving men and women passed them, each laden with trays of leftover food and drink. Klaria followed behind, keeping close.

The great hall was empty, the diners clearly elsewhere, and the cleanup was mostly completed. It was an immense space, chilly and filled with braziers and lanterns with competing flickers and shadows. It was clearly the center of the structure with a variety of passageways leading off to other sections of the construct. High narrow windows were covered with stained glass and faded, frayed tapestries hung limply from the walls. A painting of some ancient battle between mages caught his attention and he slowed down to study it. One figure, in emerald robes, had his hands in the unmistakable position to unleash a spell of catastrophe. The other was brandishing some ward he didn't recognize in a defensive posture. Could it be? The eyes were definitely the Master's! Was this a portrait of the battle that resulted in Achrios obtaining their intended prize?

Athis' mind boggled and he tried to catch Klaria's attention, but she was studying the various entryways and missed it.

"My master keeps such things as you seek in vaults in the dark wing. Go down that path, two lefts and a right. But I'm told he has wards to keep out those with thievery in their hearts."

"My heart is pure," he said with a laugh, although he heard a derisive snort from behind him. He leaned once more towards Julianna and whispered, "Don't mind her, she's a jealous sister."

She stopped and turned to the pair. "I hope you find what you want but I am needed in the kitchen and in case you mean us harm, I need to keep my distance." Belying that statement, though, as she rushed past Athis she gave him a kiss on the cheek. "For luck," she said sweetly and kept moving.

"And none for me," Klaria said archly once the girl was well past them.

"I'll share my luck with you," Athis said and began marching in the proper direction.

"You wish," Klaria said, striding forward and taking the lead as they left the chamber. The first left was easily found but the second was nearly missed thanks to a particularly dark stretch of stone corridor. Athis missed the warmth of the kitchen although he was finally mostly dry and with a satisfied stomach. He was thirsty, though, but no water skins were within reach.

The second turn led them into an older, narrower, and far colder portion of the castle. He suspected the storage room was filled with magical artifacts and intended to be kept far from sight until needed. After walking several more minutes, they saw the right hand turn that should lead them to their goal.

Instead, there was rubble blocking their path and no light whatsoever beyond it.

"So much for her luck," she muttered. "We're lost."

"We'll just have to retrace out steps," Athis said.

"Yes, I figured that out. We must have missed the turn." With that, she hurried past him and kept moving so he had to hurry to keep up. As the air smelled fresher and the corridor grew lighter, his hopes rose.

They found their error and continued to move in search of the proper turn but the path was blocked by a large, armored figure. He was covered with bits of metal on his arms and legs, across his heart and grown, with everything joined by soft, flexible leather. It was well-maintained gear, as was the long, polished scabbard at his left hip.

"Oy, who are you? What's your business here?"

"We're lost," Athis admitted.

"You'll lose your heads if you don't explain yourselves," he said, withdrawing the sword, its steel catching the light of the torch directly behind him. The sound of steel sent several sleeping birds into the air, all save one, and they cawed and fled.

Before the sword was entirely free of the scabbard, Klaria was in motion. She hurled herself at the corridor walls, propelling herself from one wall towards the ceiling and suddenly was somersaulting over his shoulder and just like that, was behind him. As she touched down, she swept a leg at his knees, causing him to buckle.

He swatted at her but realized the corridor restricted his trained motions so he resorted to elbowing her in the side. She grunted and wrapped her legs around the sword arm and arched her back. His arm was now hyperextended and he let out a sharp cry, releasing his grip on the weapon. Klaria let go and back-peddled away from him. As the guard tried to rise to his feet, she suddenly charged him and was once more in the air, her right boot extended and making contact with the side of his head.

He crumpled in a heap and she hefted his sword and hurled it into the gloom where they had come from. It clattered with a satisfying sound.

"Nicely done," Athis said, applauding softly.

"You could have helped," she said, catching her breath.

"No, that was a fine display of training. The Master would be proud. I would have just been in the way," he told her.

"You just like to watch," she chided him.

"Actually, I missed most of your impressive skills," he added.

"Hiding your eyes?"

"No, I found our true course while no one was around to disturb us," he said with a grin.

"Nicely done," she said, clapping him on the shoulder. "Lead on."

He grabbed the torch and held it tightly with his right hand, letting the light guide them down one corridor, then another, until he pointed towards a passageway that was narrower than the one they walked. No wonder they missed it the first time, he mused. He gestured with the torch and dancing yellow light illuminated a large set of doors that were marked with runes he vaguely recognized. Ringing the frame were additional words written in a variety of tongues, only some he recognized. What he could translate seemed to invoke eternal damnation to thieves.

"If we're getting the Master's gem back, does that make us thieves?" he asked.

"That, Athis, is a matter of interpretation left to mages, not students," she said. "But I take your point."

"Well then, let me make this clear," a new voice added from behind them. "You are about to die."

Klaria and Athis slowly turned around and studied the three men that blocked their path back to the main part of the castle. All were attired in the same garb as the downed guard and they looked pissed.

"Don't you want to capture us and bring us to Achrios for questioning?" Klaria asked.

"Not particularly, no," the man said, and Athis noticed the dark red, angry-looking scar that ran from left ear to jaw. "He prefers when we simply kill intruders and not trouble him with details."

All three drew their swords in unison, an impressive display of discipline and training.

Athis broke into a cold sweat, his heart hammering within his chest. If ever there was a reason to break the rules and use magic, this was it. He began rummaging his thoughts for a good spell to cast when Klaria spoke up.

"We don't get a fighting chance?"

"This is not an arena for show," the man said. "You will now die."

"I'd rather not," she said and was in motion. She ran towards the trio, surprising them based on their facial expressions, and then she went into a slide and he heard her leathers rip on the rough stone floor. She actually went between the legs of the first and then popped up, using her motion to go into a roundhouse kick that took down one man.

Athis had no choice but to come to her support. He feinted left, drawing the lead man to the side, then pirouetted right so he was now between the lead guard and the downed man. He reached quickly for the sword but managed to withdraw only the dagger. At least he was now armed and could die a good death.

The twice-duped guard let out a roar of anger and swung at Athis, who backed away and to the left, away from the blade which whooshed far too close for his comfort. Klaria head-butted the third guard, pushing him backward and rendering him unable to properly swing his sword. She, like Athis, had determined the men were used to fighting with arms, while they had been trained to use their bodies. In the narrow confines of the corridor, that gave them the advantage—unless someone got in a lucky thrust. His job was to avoid that at all costs.

Later, he would replay the fight in his mind and as he recounted it to Belid, he would time it, estimating the entire struggle was maybe five minutes long, perhaps less. Right now, though, it felt an eternity. He elbowed, jabbed, kicked, and ducked. In fact, he did a lot of ducking. Klaria, though, was dancing with death and managed to avoid being hit, which impressed the hell out of him. Her best move, though, was when she reached out at one arm swinging the sword toward her and smoothly redirected it through another man's leathers. Then, the stone flood was getting slick with blood, thankfully none of it his.

With one man seriously injured and another down, she called to Athis. "We have to get free—now!" She lowered her shoulders and he understood, if they charged the last man standing, they had a chance of upending him or at least one of them getting free. He scrambled to be beside her and imitated her position while she was already in motion. Together, they crossed the three or four feet of distance while the man planted his feet to receive them. He dropped his sword and opened his arms wide, assuming he would snare them both. A second later, four bony shoulders smashed into his armored torso and he gave a little ground upon impact. But he began closing his arms, ensnaring Athis. Klaria, though, made a sudden drop and reached directly within the gap between metal and leather. She tightened her grip and the man howled in pain.

Athis squirmed loose and elbowed his attacker in the side of the head then joined Klaria in rushing down the corridor, back the way they came and further from their goal.

Breathing hard, they kept moving, blindly going down corridors, barely pausing to listen for the telltale boots of the castle guard. One thing about stone castles was that sound traveled and the sounds of a prolonged fight was sure to alert others.

Remarkably, each corridor was well lighted but devoid of life. Where was everyone, Athis wondered? It might be that the castle was sparsely inhabited, perfect timing for the Master to send in his students. Clever old man, Athis thought. Neither said a word, letting their gasping breaths do the talking for both. He ached from the battle and realized he was bruised here and there but surprisingly whole. Now, if only he could stay that way.

Sooner or later, he knew, their luck was sure to run out so the trick was to find the gem and be gone before that time came. Luck, like the fates, was unpredictable and that irritated him no end. The Master had been trying to train him, with little progress, not to dwell on that which could not be controlled but to accept it as a part of life and react to the flow of events. While that sounded nice in principal, it really sucked right about now.

A hissing sound was nearly missed but it grew louder and became unavoidable. He raised a hand to slow Klaria, but she had also heard it and was craning her neck in search of its source. Both heard stone against stone and a section of the wall seemed to open as if by magic. A pale, slender hand became visible, then a dark gray sleeve making the hand appear to be floating in the air.

Julianna emerged just long enough to gesture for them both to follow her. Without question they did and once they entered the very constricted space, the wall was tugged back into position. Athis began to speak, but Julianna placed a gentle hand on his mouth and he smelled spices. She had been baking while he had been trying not to die.

Her lantern and Klaria's torch lit the tiny hallway, making this the brightest part of the castle since the kitchen. They walked a full minute at a brisk pace until Julianna began to slow down and then turned to face them.

"Did you find your treasure?"

The two stared at her. "You got lost, didn't you?"

Athis nodded. Julianna sighed.

"We used to play hide and seek through these hidden passages," she said as they resumed walking. "Lupoff was raised here and showed me when I was four. Achrios thinks no one knows about them but the royal family and the original engineers, but he has no idea how many know of his 'secret' escapes."

"I can't thank you . . . ," Athis began when she shushed him.

"Whatever brings you here cannot be good, otherwise the guards wouldn't want your heads. You've caused no amount of trouble, but . . . I can't explain it, but something tells me to trust you."

"It's his winning smile," Klaria said, cocking her head toward Athis.

Julianna blushed a bit at that. "I lost time trying to find you but you made enough of a racket it wasn't hard. I can get you close to the chamber but the path doesn't go that far. You will have to hurry if you ever want to find your prize and escape."

"Our latest battle may misdirect them," Klaria mused. "We're going in the opposite direction now I think."

Athis nodded, surprised at how fortune continued to favor them. Surely, it would not last.

"What do you want for your silence?" Klaria then asked in a serious tone. "We have no money of note."

"You want to buy my trust?" Julianna sounded genuinely hurt by the accusation. Athis moved closer to her, placing what he thought was a comforting hand on her arm.

"We're strangers and don't know your customs. We certainly want to reward you with whatever coin or token we can bestow upon you."

That seemed to calm Julianna down and her hand covered his and held it in place.

"It gets lonely in the castle," she said. "When everyone is away or . . . busy."

"Kill me now," Athis heard Klaria mumble to herself. He swatted the air behind his back, shutting her up. Athis then moved even closer to her, enfolding her hands in his.

"I would very much like to end your loneliness but Klaria and I are on errantry and time is pressing. Might I return and . . . visit?"

She nodded and smiled. He could sense Klaria's agitation behind him and ascribed it all to Julianna's innocent ways. Growing up in a kitchen, he doubted she knew much of the greater world and even a student like him must have seemed exotic. Still, he needed her help and needed to make her feel worthwhile. Worth getting to know better.

"Where is the exit," he asked, refocusing her on the task at hand. They kept moving, now in silence, and a short while later, Julianna stopped. Her supple fingers felt along the wall for a seam then depressed a hidden stud, unlocking this door.

Athis thanked her, then leaned in and gave her a kiss. Not a peck, but one he had hoped to bestow upon another. He put his effort and will into the kiss, forcing himself to stay steady and gentle. But the firmness and its duration made its intent clear.

"That way," Julianna gestured after a gasp.

Klaria gave her a curt nod as she passed and with that, the door sealed closed and Athis doubted he would see her again.

"Did that make you feel good? She's barely out of diapers," Klaria noted, her tone low. He couldn't read the emotion in it and that bothered him. Normally, he knew her well enough to read her every word. Usually it was derision and scorn, that is until this mission.

"Look, you told me to get her help, I did what I could."

"You need practice," she said.

"Yeah, with most everything. I've never seen you move like that before. I need more time in the athletic room."

"Yes."

They trudged on but with every passing step, he felt the mood lighten which made him glad. Athis was finally starting to feel comfortable around Klaria. Almost losing your life once or twice will get people past the awkward part of having seen one another naked. As they sought a true path, he spoke up.

"Can I ask you a personal question?"

She let out a sigh then said, "I suppose."

"Why are you hairless below the chin?"

That seemed to catch her by surprise. She was silent for minute and Athis now felt like a moron, ruining whatever good will he had earned since their arrival in this forsaken land.

"You do know how magic works, right," she asked in her patented arch tone.

"Of course," he said, trying to sound as confident as possible.

"Everything about what makes us unique beings contains power that can be used against us. It's why we do not know our Master's name. Well, anything from our person might be used against us, empowering a spell directly aimed at us. I keep my hair short so there's less of a chance strands can be found. I do the same everywhere else, disposing of those hairs and my monthly blood in private, minimizing the chance of such an attack."

Athis nodded, stunned none of this had occurred to him. And she spoke with such matter-of-factness that clearly she had been at this for some time. She had a point and he reactively reached up to feel a soft curl over his right ear.

"Do you think I should follow such a practice?"

She chuckled at that, a happy sound he thought he'd never hear from her again. "I suppose you could, although you have far more to remove and would have to do it far more regularly. Don't come looking to me for help. And of course, that presumes anyone will ever target you."

"Hey!" he said with a hurt tone.

She merely grinned and turned away, leading them further into the gloomy catacomb.

They recognized certain corners, places where the stone arrangement was unique, confirming they were on the right path. He pointed up ahead to the juncture he found when Klaria was making short work of the first guard.

"This way," he said and waved a torch inside the new corridor, its light sending birds scurrying out of the way.

"I smell something . . . foul," she said slowly, loudly sniffing the air.

He took a deep breath and mentally agreed. It was fetid air, dank and unlike anything he had previously encountered. But it was organic and he feared what it might be. He poked ahead with the torch and this time he made out a shape.

"Ah, crap," he said quietly.

"What is it?"

"A what sounds about right."

She shouldered past him and aimed her own torch ahead. The comingled flames cast enough light to indicate a beast of some sort. Large, with four paws each ending with lengthy, sharp claws. It had a spiked tail, which curled around the sleeping form.

"Do you recognize it?"

"Not at all," she replied. She continued studying it when she spotted something and pointed with her free hand. "Its neck."

Athis focused and found the golden glitter encircling the thick, gray-green neck. It was a necklace of some sort. At that, his stomach fell away, certain he knew what was being worn.

"A fine place of safekeeping," he said. "Now what?"

She was silent, studying and mentally weighing their options. It was a stone corridor and they knew there were no more secret passages. The corridor ended at the doors to the storeroom but clearly that was no longer an issue. How on earth would they, without weapons or gear, going to lure the creature out and then make it give up its prize? More than that was the matter that the palace guard now knew the castle had been invaded. That would no doubt bring more human foes to deal with.

Fortune, it seemed, had its fill of Athis and was taking the rest of the day off.

Klaria withdrew the dagger she kept from earlier and weighed it in her hand. She practiced parrying and thrusting, testing the weapon. It was sharp and pointy and might pierce its hide but that meant getting very, very close to the beast. He did not like her odds.

"Can you run?"

She turned and looked at him if he were mad. "Are you really that much of a coward?"

"Not at all," he said sounding much surer than he felt. "But, I have an idea."

"Oh, this is going to be good," she said.

That stung. "Look," he began, "I'm trying to do my part and I have an idea and it would be nice if you actually heard it before dismissing it."

"If you keep your voice down and not wake that thing, I'll happily listen."

"If you can wake it up and keep it interested in only you, we can lead it away from the doorway. In fact, get it back to the juncture and I can be hiding in that last secret doorway so once it goes past, I can come up from behind and snag the gem."

She was nodding along with his plan, clearly picturing it in her mind's eye until the last part. "And how will you do that?"

He hesitated.

"I haven't figured that out yet."

"Good plan," she snorted. Then she smiled which surprised him. "It's ill-formed like so many of your notions, but there's a germ of an idea within it. I can lead it to you and yes, we'll use that doorway. But, I want it to go inside."

"Inside? But it's too big and would get caught . . ." He stopped himself. His eyes went wide and he nodded breaking into a smile of his own. " . . . and would get caught so I could grab the gem and go down the passage—out of reach."

"We'd rendezvous in the kitchen and leave that way."

He frowned, not liking the idea of them being separated for so long but he didn't see a better option. They were fighting time and with luck against them, they needed to make some of their own and the odds for success improved when one became two. He nodded.

"Ready?" she asked, gripping the knife tightly.

"Not really," he admitted.

"Excellent," Klaria said and began stalking the slumbering beast. He watched for a moment until she turned and waved him in the other direction. Once it woke up, things were likely to move quickly and he first had to find the trigger from this side of the wall.

He backed up steadily, watching as he neared the beast, which really needed a name but that was an issue for another time. Right now, he had to find the secret doorway and so far, he'd been very good at little but excelled at getting lost.

She later told him that when she got within five feet or so, something, perhaps her scent, woke up the beast. It opened its eyes, spotted her, and was up on its paws, snuffing in the still, foul air. Klaria had suspected it was not chained in place and was proven right when it began to paw the ground before it. Its mouth opened revealing a lot of mucous, slobber, and two rows of sharp teeth. Its tongue was thick and black, beginning to lick its very wide chops.

"Nice kitty," she said to it, holding still, watching intently to spot its muscles coiling for action. Rather than antagonize it, she kept the dagger at her side, just in case it recognized the threat.

Its intelligence was certainly a mystery.

As it moved, she told him later, it revealed the ruby quartz gem, wrapped in a lattice of gold and silver affixed to the golden collar. Getting it off looked problematic as it had no latch. She spied a space where the metal was marred, soldered into place, and therefore presented a weak link.

While the creature was preparing its initial attack, Athis hurried, having heard its movement. He began running his fingers along the stony surface, trying to find the exact space where the hidden door was. Thankfully it was hard to miss once you knew what to look for since it was rough, uneven. He felt his breath quicken as he traced the wall with both hands, knowing the latch released couldn't be *that* well hidden.

It was about this time he later learned the creature, whom he had taken to calling Ned, made its first approach. Klaria was able to back peddle at a good pace, staying away from the creature. She was always observing, and that's what made her a superb tactician. As a result, if she kept her wits about her and her feet on the ground, she'd be fine.

Still, once Ned rounded the corner, they would both be in danger, so he hurried and retraced his path until finally, a pinky felt something different, out of place. He stabbed at it with two fingers and there was a muffled click from the other side. He pulled and the door swung open so he stepped in and began looking down the corridor.

Athis didn't have to wait long as the he heard the sound of footsteps. Klaria was running hard, putting as much distance between her and Ned as possible. Then the creature rounded the corner with a roar that made the hairs on his neck do a shimmy. She passed him without a word and suddenly it was his turn. He took a deep breath, visibly swallowing his fear and stepped into the corridor, his arms waving.

Ned couldn't help but see him and their eyes met. There was a cold hunger in Ned's gaze, freezing Athis in place until the beast was two paces away. Finally, he willed himself to move and went within the secret passage.

The beast slowed to follow, sniffing the air before it, roaring and feeling with a paw all at the same time. It was a predator, either by birth or training and Athis never wanted to know which. He held the torch so it would see it him and try to fit its entire bulk in the doorway.

As Klaria estimated, it was too big and Ned wedged himself into the space gaining inches with every effort but it would never get all the way in. One forepaw was caught between body and doorway but the other continued to swat the air, reaching in vain for Athis. All he had to do now was somehow avoid that sharp paw and get the necklace.

Ned was making so much noise that Athis couldn't tell where Klaria was and hoped they'd see one another again.

With a furious howl, Ned was trying to move backward and wasn't having much success, angering it further. A wounded or trapped beast was the deadliest kind so he had to be even more cautious than he usually was. The torch sputtered once, its fuel almost spent which was a complication he really didn't need right now. When fortune left, it took everything with it he concluded.

Watching Ned's movements, he figured out there was a habit he could exploit so he grit his teeth and counted down. This would take an act of courage the likes of which he never thought he could perform but had little choice. Belid or Klaria would have done it and laughed but he was scared. A misstep and the creature would shred him like cloth. Dying was not an option, he heard Klaria say in his mind. If he died, they would both fail the assessment and while he was used to failure, she was not and this would crush her.

With a roar of his own, he rushed forward, brandishing the sputtering remains of the torch. Thrusting with his left hand, he singed the waving paw which thumped on the ground and he stomped hard on it with his boot. Meantime, the right hand reached under the snarling mouth and yanked with all his might. The soft gold cut into the beast which reared up its head, putting more strain on the metal and it gave with a snapping sound.

Athis fell backward from the force of the unhappy creature's movements, almost far enough away to avoid being killed. As he settled on the unyielding floor, the pain was obscured by a warm, sizzling feeling in his right hand. The gem, upon contact with his flesh, softly glowed, casting a crimson light around the tight space. It was warming to the touch but didn't burn and somewhere first deep in his chest and then in his mind, he could sense the power emanating from the mystical artifact. He was fascinated and wanted to experience it to the fullest extent possible.

Reality, though, had other ideas.

The waving, burned paw, though sliced through the air and two sharp claws pierced his old leather boot and dug deeply into his foot. He shrieked with the shock and pain and as the paw rose up for a second pounding, he crab-walked backward just far enough to avoid the paw. He left behind a thin trail of red blood, its scent further enraging the beast.

That was when the torch exhausted its fuel and went out, plunging the secret passage into blackness. Athis knew which direction to travel in but it hurt to walk and hobbling in the dark with an angry Ned on one side of the wall (actually halfway between, to be exact) and the castle guard on the other side was far from ideal.

With little choice, he kept moving, happy to clutch the heartfelt warmth of the gem in his hand, refusing to let go or even pocket it. It was slow, painful going and he was thankful he had no arteries in his foot otherwise he feared he would bleed to death before reuniting with Klaria.

It was painful going and he alternated between trying to understand how the gem was affecting his body since within, he was feeling good, the best he ever felt. Paradoxically, every other step reminded him of the oozing wound in his foot and it hurt, almost fighting the gem's influence for attention. He imagined it yelling, "Hey you, I'm leaking this guy's lifeblood. If you can't fix it, leave him alone!"

Athis began to wonder if he was in shock.

Clearing his head for a moment, he examined his progress. The glow illuminated the passage several feet before him and he got the sense he was going in the right direction. More than that, he could sense Klaria. His mind registered her presence, her well-hidden curves and steely core. He was aware of her in ways he never imagined but it also served as a beacon and he used it to limp forward, narrowing the distance.

While it felt like an eternity, it clearly wasn't because the pain was a constant reminder of his physical condition. He was pleased to see the red trail he left behind was thinning, the wound starting to congeal, preparing to scab over.

Klaria grew brighter in his . . . heart . . . his mind . . . and he suspected the kitchen was now only a few minutes away. Behind him, the roaring creature's voice had diminished, pleasing him. Things must have been improving, a bird was actually flying carefree behind him. Finally, he saw the switch that would release the locks to let him enter the kitchen. As he expected, it worked silently, a well-oiled mechanism that implied frequent use. There was Klaria, pacing, a drumstick in her hand. He thought of surprising her, but she suddenly stopped pacing and turned in his direction.

"About time," she said.

He gestured at his foot, which was a darkening mess and he couldn't tell boot leather from blood from flesh. Then, he triumphantly hoisted the gem in the air.

"It's funny, but I knew you found it," she said, tossing the gnawed-over drumstick onto a counter.

"Yeah, it's the gem," Athis said. "It helped me keep track of you."

"Well, that certainly explains why you didn't get lost this time," she said. "Maybe it tapped into the Master's spell which monitors our use of magic."

Any further conversation would have to wait because a racket from the great hall indicated the castle guard was finally approaching after having searched everywhere else. At best they had half a minute before they were outnumbered, out-armed, and clearly doomed.

"Shouldn't something be happening?"

Klaria looked at Athis' grimacing face. The Master implied once the gem was in their possession, his spell would automatically return them to the Crimson Keep. Nothing was happening other than the approaching guards making a lot more noise.

"Maybe it's the gem," she suggested. "He didn't count on

its power affecting the spell."

"But he's the Master! How on earth could he make such an error?"

"He's old. He's human. Take your pick, but we need an exit," Klaria snapped.

That was when the guard emerged into the kitchen. Achrios clearly trained them well because as they filed in, they knew the layout and expertly surrounded them. It didn't take long and the two stood in place, unsure of what to do. The gem glowed and filled his soul but it wasn't emitting the advertised hellfire, the very thing they could use right now.

"Our lord will want his property back," the guard in the neatest, cleanest uniform Athis had ever seen, said. He held out a gloved out, clearly expecting his open palm to receive the gem.

"We have to use our own magic to escape," Athis hissed into Klaria's ear.

She shook her head once. He knew this meant failing, violating the terms of the test, but it was either fail and try again or most likely die. If the pain in his foot was any indication of what that would feel like, he was perfectly happy to postpone the experience.

"Athis, the gem helped you find me, right?" she whispered.

"I'm waiting and won't wait much longer," the guard said.

"Excuse me, but we're having a conversation here," she snapped at him.

"Your options are fairly limited so it should be a pretty short discussion," he replied.

"What if you could use the gem to find us a way home?"

"Do you think this came with an instruction scroll? Yes, I feel something, but it acted on its own."

"No, it pointed you to me, it connected with your mind on some level we don't know," she said, holding up her index finger to further stall the guard.

"You want me to think about home and expect the gem to just transport us there?"

"As he said, our options are limited, so indulge me and try it," she implored him.

There didn't seem to be much of a choice so he gripped the gem tightly in his hand and shut his eyes, which had the positive effect of removing the guards from his sight. Instead, he thought of the Keep, the thick clouds that never seemed to escape its reach. He pictured the tower where the Master's chamber was, where they last stood.

A blindingly brilliant flash of red-white light burned through his eyelids and caused spots to appear. As it faded, Athis cracked open one eye and looked about him. It worked! They stood exactly where they were when the mission began.

He smiled at Klaria but then clutched his stomach and wretched, a spattering of vomit landing first on the thick carpet and then on the approaching slippers that belonged to the Master.

"That was not supposed to happen," the Master said, looking at the mess on his feet. His gaze then wandered across the similarly spoiled carpet to Athis' injured foot and traveled up until the gaze rested on the gem, still tight in Athis' fist.

"But retrieving this item was exactly the goal. A shame you used magic," he began but Klaria cut him off.

"You said we couldn't perform magic and we didn't."

"How did you return in this manner? I could tell when the return spell was activated and I am still waiting. Do you happen to be in two places at once?"

"Is that even possible?" Athis interrupted.

"Of course it is," the Master said in an irritated tone, sounding as if he were scolding a child. "I have chosen not to teach that to you yet."

"Still, sir, we used none of the magic you taught us," Klaria continued. "Athis used the gem and its magic did the actual work. Technically, we returned without violating the terms of the test."

"What sort of a test is it for magicians to go into enemy territory and steal for you without being able to use all the spells we have learned?"

"Not every test need be about magic manipulation," the Master told Athis then turned to Klaria. "I concede your point. Maybe you should consider a career in law."

She blushed at that and lowered her head. "I would rather continue my studies if I . . . if we have passed the test."

There was a long silence then the Master spoke as he gestured for the gem. Athis was reluctant to let it go, fearful the void without the gem's presence would be a terrible one. Still, with some hesitation, he handed it over only to see the gem vanish within a hidden pocket of the Master's robe.

Belid knocked and ended, a bucket of water in one hand and a first aid kit in the other. He bowed before the Master and, with a stunned expression, took in the messy presence of his friends. Athis tried to smile reassuringly, but without the gem he did truly feel a void in his soul. It was as if he shared his body with another spirit which was now gone. Instead, the searing pain of standing on the injured foot was now commanding all his attention.

"Belid, please attend to the . . . debris from their return. I shall dress Athis' wound."

Belid hesitated a second then nodded and got down on his knees and began scrubbing at Athis' vomit. While that made the others smile, Athis couldn't help but wonder what Belid may have done to be punished in this manner. He knew this chore all too well, spending many an evening on his own knees to clean things after displeasing the Master. It was a tale for another time.

"You see, Klaria, Athis, this was an assessment of how you could handle yourselves. You rarely leave the Keep and that will be changing. More, you were given a set of challenges to see how you would fare."

"The village without money," Klaria said.

"So far from Achrios' castle," Athis added.

"The highwaymen," she said.

"The beast," Athis said. "You knew about the beast."

"And more," the Master agreed. "I was monitoring from afar and was most pleased with how you handled yourselves."

"The bird," Athis cried. "That silly bird seemed to be everywhere!"

"Yes, it acted as my eyes," their teacher said.

"So, we were never really in danger," Athis said as the Master finally got the boot worked off his foot and was now clearing away the clotted blood. It stung and Athis grimaced a lot but he refused to let out a single pained sound.

"No, you could have died any number of times. I was power-less to help you, just observing."

"You're a dirty old man," Klaria said coldly. "You watched us apply the runes."

"I needed to see if you could truly trust one another and starting you with such an intimate act was the very first test. I have seen naked women before, my dear, and not once have I ever touched a student. There are rules, you know." He sprinkled a variety of powders over the wound, said a few soft words.

Klaria bowed her head once more but Athis didn't need to have the gem in his possession to know that this still troubled her.

"Speaking of the runes," the Master said as he wrapped soft, white gauze around the wounded foot, "it is time to wash them off. No need to glow here in the Keep. Athis, keep the foot dry and let me check the dressing tomorrow. Now go clean up. Well done."

A "well done" from him was the equivalent of a medal from a King or better. Athis' heart swelled with pride.

With a suddenness that confused Athis, they were dis-missed and they walked past Belid, who was now required to clean the Master's slippers. They left the chamber and began walking towards the baths. It was a companionable silence, the likes of which he had never felt with Klaria before. That's when it hit him. With the mission over, he was able to relax and noticed that he was no longer uptight in her presence. They were allies, rivals, fellow students, but more importantly, they were truly friends.

"Those runes are all over," Athis said in a tone brimming with newfound confidence. "What if I wash your back if you wash mine?"

She nodded in agreement then stopped walking, tugging on his arm. The movement caused him to put weight on his ban-daged foot and he winced.

"Athis, I want to be clear about one thing: what I have seen will never be inside me. Do you understand?

He considered her tone, tried to read something in it. Was she playing hard to get or was she truly offended at an unspoken comment?

While he may have passed a variety of tests over the last few days, ones involving women seemed insurmountable.

With a mental shrug, he committed himself to further study.

TURN TAIL AND RUN

by Glenn Hauman

"TAILS."

Belid pulled another coin out of his pouch and tossed it. Athis looked at it, said "Tails," and put it in his pile.

Belid pulled out yet another coin, looked at it, and then focused his gaze on Athis. "There is a point to this flipping thing, isn't there?" He tossed the coin up in the air. It landed with a soft clang.

"Of course there is. Tails."

"Care to tell me what it is?" Toss.

"Have you forgotten? Tails."

"Other than lightening my coin purse?" Toss.

"Well, that's always worthwhile in and of itself. Tails."

"Yes, but why are we here?"

"Oh, now we're getting into existentialism, are we? Tails."

"You know what I mean."

"If I knew what you meant, that wouldn't be existential-ism— tails—it'd be solipsism."

"I mean, why are we sitting here in the hallway spinning coins?"

"I told you. This is my final project, a magic spell that warps the laws of probability to an extreme. Tails, by the way. Seventy-six to zip."

"How do I know you're messing with probabilities? You could have just rigged the coins."

"Well, that's why we're using yours. Tails."

"We? I—" Belid sputtered for a moment, then regained his composure. He stood up and started to pace, jingling a few coins in his hand. "The law of averages, if I have got this right, means that if an infinite number of monkeys were thrown up in the air they would land on their heads about as often as they would land on their—"

"Tails," Athis said. Belid looked down. He had dropped a coin. And it, too, had landed "tail" side up. He looked back up at Athis, who smiled wanly. Disgusted, Belid took all the coins in his hand and threw them at his classmate. They bounced off, and Athis looked at the coins.

"Tails, tails, tails, tails, tails, tails... and the last one . . . oh!"

Belid perked up. "Heads?"

"No, tails. I was just trying to give you a sense of hope. Eighty-five in a row."

"Is that as far as you're prepared to go?"

"What do you mean?"

"Have you considered the potential havoc that you're causing to the probability plane?"

"How so?"

"Just consider the cosmic balance, as our Master always warns us to. Think about it— because you worked your magic here, there could be two men sitting in a castle far away from here tossing coins, except all of their coins are coming up heads to counteract all of the tails thrown here."

"Aw, c'mon. What are the odds of that happening?"

Belid just stared at him.

"What are we doing here, Athis?"

"We're proving my spell works."

"We can do that anywhere. In fact, we should be doing it in the workshop. Why are we sitting in a hallway, working on something that should've already been done and with the graduation ceremony later this afternoon?"

"Because— shhh!"

"What the—" Belid was interrupted by Athis slamming a hand over his mouth. So silenced, they could hear footsteps coming down the hall. Peering out from the alcove, they espied Klaria in an elegant gown. Belid looked at their shapely classmate, and then at Athis, who looked positively pathetic as his eyes followed her walking down the hall.

"Oh, now I understand," Belid said softly to himself. "You don't care about working the probability plane. You just want some tail . . . s." He scooped up his coins and left quickly before Athis came to his senses.

■ ■ ■

"Y'know, I don't think I've ever been here before," Belid commented as the three of them followed the Master down a narrow brick hallway, with not a mouse stirring. Nor, for a change, were any of the corridors shifting or new doorways appearing. It was eerily quiet.

"I know I haven't," Klaria agreed. "Where are we going, Master?"

Their mentor laughed but didn't bother to stop or turn around. "You shall see," was all he answered. Athis exchanged glances with Klaria and Belid, and they all shrugged. All these years of study had taught them that the Master was as enigmatic as he was powerful, and he was the mightiest wizard in existence. Some said of all time. They doubted he meant them any harm, though—at least, no lasting harm—so they continued to traipse after him.

At last he reached a large, paneled oak door. Producing a key from his sleeve, the Master inserted it into the carved brass lock plate, gave a twist, and then pushed the door open. "Enter, enter," he instructed, gesturing past him with a sweeping bow.

Once inside, the three senior students paused to marvel at their surroundings. It was a large room, tall as well as wide and deep, its walls covered in stacked balconies around three sides facing what was plainly a raised stage complete with columns and a roof over an additional recessed balcony. "It seems you've brought us to a theater?" Klaria asked.

"Seems, madam! Nay, it is; I know not 'seems'," their master replied, stroking his long beard as he wandered to the edge and looked out onto the currently empty seats. "This is the Proscenium Room, once used for large demonstrations of magical expertise." He treated the trio to a mock glare. "Now it is where we hold the final student exhibitions. Verily, have we fallen upon hard times." No one was certain if he meant the small size of the senior class or the quality of the students, neither option was appealing. Still, their years of training were drawing to their inevitable conclusion and if they passed, they would become active participants in the final stages of the Demon War; not necessarily the best graduation gift one could have hoped for.

"Oh, that doth cut to the quick," Belid retorted. Then his eyes got very wide, as if he couldn't believe he'd just said that.

"Yes, perhaps you should warm up a bit first," their mentor warned with a grin. "Klaria, does Athis look a bit pale to you?"

Klaria looked over at Athis and affected a regal accent. "Good my lord, how does your honor for this many a day?"

Athis, taken aback, started to stammer. "I-I-I humbly thank you—well, well, well."

Belid's face puckered. "What dost thou?" he whispered to Athis.

"I know not!" Athis whispered back. "I never gave—"

"Are you kidding me?" That shut Belid up, which was a rarity indeed. He frowned, then glared at their Master. "You cast a spell on us?"

"Oh, no," the old wizard replied, chuckling. "I didn't need to. The room did. This castle, as you know, has absorbed traits from its many early occupants. An architect, a baker, an actor. Everyone who enters here has an urge to speak in just such a fashion. You can resist it, especially once you know the compulsion is there, but it takes effort." He laughed again, louder this time "Or strong emotion." He let them stew on that a moment, then clapped his hands. "Now, come, let's get on with it. Klaria, why don't you begin?"

"Verily, my lord, I know no wise to protest," she answered, curtseying at the same time. Then her gaze sharpened, her jaw set, and she continued, "my final project was on . . ."

❦ ❦ ❦

". . . an interesting exercise in vanity, certainly," the Master concluded, "and thus particularly well suited to you, Belid, though I'm not sure I can see any practical application beyond the, ahem, salacious. Still, well reasoned and solidly executed." Belid bowed and stepped off the stage, moving across the gallery floor to the first row of seats, where Klaria had already taken a spot on the bench beside their mentor. "Athis, I believe the stage is yours."

"Sooth then I shall endeavor to deserve it," Athis replied. He gulped, forced down the couplets struggling to burst from his lips, and continued, "I chose to study probability, and the means by which one could subvert its normal laws. Behold!" He reached into his robes and produced a large coin pouch, heavy with currency.

From the cheap seats Belid gasped. "You rotter, that's my coin purse!"

With a grin, Athis acknowledged his classmate's generous donation before flinging the pouch up toward the room's high, arched ceiling. The coins leaped free, shooting skyward, only to begin plummeting back toward the ground a second later. "When they land," Athis explained, "every last one of them will land on tails. Which is statistically impossible, of course, but by manipulating probability I have—"

"Hold, enough!" The Master gestured with one hand and the coins froze, still spinning, in mid-air. "Your rash habit of care-lessness is as costly a habit as thy purse can buy. Know not what you have done?"

"Clearly not," Athis answered, flustered. Belid and Klaria hadn't had to endure interruptions like this! "Prithee, sirrah, explain if thou must."

"Indeed, I'll speak to it, though Hell itself should gap and bid me hold my peace," his master replied. "There is a divinity that shapes our ends, that frames us within its cosmic scope, and though dress ourselves differently we might, it is not given to us to alter our place. Each move is dictated by the previous one—that is the meaning of order."

"Really?" Athis couldn't believe what he was hearing. "You're saying we shouldn't mess with the laws of chance?"

"Indeed."

"Why, what should be the fear?" Athis demanded, stomp-ing forward to the very edge of the stage and glaring down at his mentor and his fellow students. "We're wizards, are we not?

Who dares tell us what to do? Who decides?"

"Decides?" The Master thundered back, floating up into the air until he was a full head above Athis. Clearly he did not like being talked down to, literally or figuratively. "It is *written*! And you, you idiot, have made a mess of the order of things, blundering about like a very child, forsooth like an addlepated knave, knowing not what you do and yet determined to break all that you should touch! You are oft to blame in this, 'tis too much prov'd."

"You're slipping back into speech, Master," Belid murmured from the cheap seats, and the old wizard visibly controlled his rage.

"Here is the problem," he told Athis no less harshly but at least more cogently as he held up one still powerful hand and counted off on his fingers. "One: probability is a factor which operates within natural forces. Two, probability is now not operating as a factor. Three, we are now within un-, sub- or supernatural forces. If we postulate, as we just have, that within un-, sub- or supernatural forces the probability is that the law of probability will not operate as a factor, then we must accept that the probability of the first part will now operate as a factor, in which case the law of probability will operate as a factor within un-, sub- or supernatural forces. Do you understand?"

Athis didn't understand a bit. As near as he could figure half of what the Master had just said meant something else, and the other half didn't mean anything at all.

Klaria, on the other hand, had turned pale beneath her usually tawny complexion. "You're saying that normally chance doesn't work on magic, but because Athis used magic to alter chance, it can now affect magic?"

"Aye, there's the rub." The Master harrumphed at Athis and tugged on his own beard. "At least someone pays attention around here!"

"Okay, so there's a chance that chance can affect magic now," Athis said. "So?"

"So?" His mentor's tugging was starting to look a little frenzied. "Think it through, you simple fool! Chance means it's possible for anything to happen, no matter how ridiculous. If it be now, 'tis not to come; if it be not to come, it will be now; if it be not now, yet it will come. Our wills and fates now so contrary run that our devices still are overthrown; our thoughts are ours—"

"—their ends none of our own," Athis finished.

Even as he said that, a door to the rear of the stage flew open, revealing a colossal room beyond. Said room was filled with monkeys, he noticed, and each one was seated at a desk before a writing device. There were traditional quill pens. Others pounding away on something with keys. One was painting pictograms. Another few were tapping at something with glowing screen. It was a fascinating variety of communications tools. They were all busy writing (or painting) away, except for one near the front who got up to close the door, shouting, "Oy, a little quiet, please! We're only up to the start of Prince Hal!" Then the door slammed shut and the students and their master were once more alone within the theater.

Belid looked boggled. "How did the monkeys learn . . . ?"

"How? Infinite faculty. Cancel the spell!" the Master shouted. "And most rapidly!"

"I can't!" Athis hollered back. "It's a cascading effect—if I try to cancel it now it'll just set loose a counterwave with even higher peaks and lower troughs but less predictability!" He shrugged helplessly. "The best thing to do now is just ride it out."

The Master considered that, but finally nodded. "That is the wisest course," he agreed. "And after it has run its course, you will never attempt such a spell again!" Athis nodded fervently. "Very well. We must then hope the effect ends before the worst can occur."

Athis gulped but couldn't stop himself from asking. "What's the worst?"

"Look around you, boy," his mentor replied. "Think about where you are—and what it does. What it means. Then think about your spell, your silly little coin-tossing spell. And put the two together."

Athis did, but even as his brain began recoiling at possibilities Klaria, ever the clever one, let out a small gasp. "The demons," she all but whispered.

Belid got it next. "There was always an extremely slim, nearly nil chance one or more of them could get free. But if something is a virtual impossibility—"

"—then logically it must be a finite improbabilty," Athis finished, his mind finally catching up and really wishing it hadn't. "And if we reach that level of improbability, then every demon ever imprisoned in the Keep could be freed. Because of me."

"Well, if it makes you feel any better," a new voice offered, "you'll all be dead soon, so you won't have to think about it much longer."

Athis turned, as did the Master, Belid, and Klaria beside him. There, standing upon the balcony above the stage, was a most foul, strange, and unnatural demon.

"Angels and ministers of grace defend us," whispered Klaria.

"Our hour is almost come, when in sulphrous and tormenting flames we render up ourselves," the demon said in a foul and pestilent congregation of vapors. "Tis now the very witching time of night, when churchyards yawn and hell itself breathes out contagion to this world."

And then behind him were at least a dozen more. Including one who was all too familiar.

"You!" Koliander the Undying bellowed, pointing at Athis. "I will tear you limb from limb before I devour your flesh and consign your very soul to eternal torment!"

Athis gulped. Behind him, he heard Belid mutter, "O horrible, O horrible, most horrible!" To which he could only agree wholeheartedly. And Klaria added, "Death followed by eternity . . . the worst of both worlds. It is a terrible thought."

But, surprisingly, Athis found that he was not afraid. Or, rather, yes, he was terribly afraid—he was practically quivering from fright, his limbs nigh unto jelly, his forehead sodden, his eyes tearing, his jaw limp, each particular hair standing on end like quills upon a fretful porcupine—but somehow it did not control him. Perhaps it was that Klaria was there, and Athis realized that while he had no desire to die he would actively fight to save her life. Perhaps it was anger at the injustice of it all, a simple parlor trick turned into the greatest prison break in history. Or perhaps it was simple annoyance at yet another interruption in his final presentation. But whatever the reason, Athis found himself stepping forward and raising his hands before him, shouting, "You scullions! You rampallians! You fustilarians! I'll tickle your catastrophe! Thou art unfit for any place but hell!"

The demons did in fact pause, if only to laugh. "What is this quintessence of dust?" one of them, a big hulking brute with five double-jointed arms, sneered. "Tender yourself more dearly; or—not to crack the wind of the poor phrase, ruining it thus— you'll tender me a fool. Give thy thoughts no tongue!"

"I would a tale unfold whose lightest word will harrow up thy soul, and by heaven, I'll make a ghost of him that lets me!" Athis answered, standing as tall as he could muster. He reached behind him and plucked a pair of coins from the spinning display there, then held them up for the demons' perusal. "These, these shall destroy thee."

"Two coins?" Another demon, this one with a head like an alligator's covered in a horse's mane and sprouting boar's tusks, chortled. "What, you intend to bribe us into killing ourselves? What a piece of work is a man! I doubt some foul play, for our night has come!"

Some of the demons had yet to partake in the hilarity, Koliander among them, and it was to those that Athis directed his next remark. "You dull and muddy-mettled rascals are magical beings," he told them, "and can sense the fabric of reality around you. Surely, then, you felt the laws of chance alter and free you from your bonds." He thought he saw one or two of them nod faintly, but none argued, so he continued. "Think upon what that must mean. The laws of chance have changed, and you now suffer the slings and arrows of outrageous fortune as you suffered the Keep mere moments before. Whatsoever those laws decree, so it shall come to pass."

He walked one coin across the back of his left hand. "Oh, there has been much throwing about of brains. What odds would you say there were that all of you should suddenly discorporate, your very existence torn to dust and scattered across reality?" He flipped the coin and smiled as it thunked against the stage floor at his feet. "The same odds, perhaps, as yet another coin landing upon tails?" His smile widened and he held up the second coin.

"Or, perhaps, the odds of still another following suit?" And he spun the coin around his index finger, balancing it there with his thumb wedged beneath, ready to be tossed.

"Wait!" It was Koliander. "There is no need to test the probability of such a conjecture. We shall abandon our resistance and allow the Keep's restraints to reassert themselves." One of the demons behind him muttered "Words, words, words," but was cut off even in the blossoms of his sin as Koliander's fist smashed into the lesser demon's mouth, silencing him and removing him from consciousness at one and the same time. "I could be bounded in a nutshell and count myself a king of infinite space," the powerful demon reminded his gathered brethren, "so long as I am still awake, for in that sleep of death when we have shuffled off this mortal coil must give us pause."

Athis nodded, and bowed to Koliander, the coin still firmly pinned against his flesh. "Wise words from a wise demon," he complimented.

The look Koliander gave him was equal parts respect and warning. "My honored lord, I will most humbly take my leave of you," the demon called out, his tone and bearing making it clear that no true humility was involved, and that this leave-taking was intended as only temporary at best.

Yet it was the best answer Athis could hope for, and so he replied: "You cannot, sir, take from me anything that I will more willingly part withal."

The demons vanished, sucked back into the Keep's tight embrace, and Athis let himself slump, the tension leaching out of him now that the crisis appeared to be over. With his muscles now lax, the last coin dropped from his grasp, and rolled clattering across the stage floor until it collided with a pillar and wobbled over onto its side.

"Well played, lad, well played," the Master complimented, slapping Athis heartily on the back. "You kept your head and your courage, and for that alone I'd grant you a passing grade even if your spell, however ill-advised, had not proven most puissant. Let the doors be shut upon them, that they may play the fool nowhere but their own house."

"Yeah, good job with that one coin, two coin thing," Belid

added, joining them to pump Athis's hand. He looked at Athis's coin purse, filled with what had been his coins. "Beggar that I am, I am even poor in thanks."

Klaria stepped up beside them then, and Belid fell silent, he and the Master both gliding back instinctively to give her and Athis space. "That was easily the stupidest, most foolhardy thing I've ever seen in my life," she told him heatedly. Before he could so much as frame a reply, she grabbed him by the shoulders, hauled him down, and kissed him soundly on the lips. Then she shoved him away. "Don't ever do that again!" she shouted, and stormed out through the stage door.

Athis watched her go, bemused but delighted, his lips still tingling from the touch of hers. *The lady doth protest too much, methinks.*

"Guess you got lucky after all, eh?" Belid teased him, elbowing his classmate in the side as they, too, headed for the exit. The Master merely harrumphed and marched on ahead.

"Lucky?" Athis glanced down at the pillar as they passed, and at the coin still lying beside it. "Yeah, I guess I was. We all were."

"What?"

Athis put an antic disposition on. "It was heads."

■ ■ ■

A deep bow to Bill S., Tom S., and Aaron R.

GLISK OF THE KEEP

by Mary Fan

SUNSET DRAPED A RUBY VEIL UPON THE DEEP RED stones of the distant fortress, making the structure's hue appear even richer. Meilin stared at the distant walls and turrets, a smile tugging at her lips. Relief and joy swirled through her heart. At last, after months of travel, she'd found the legendary Crimson Keep.

Impatient, she urged her gray-and-white stallion to gallop faster. Stray wisps of black hair blew free from the twin knots on the sides of her head. She didn't care, though she briefly wondered whether she should tidy up before knocking on the Keep's door. Her tunic had faded from its original blue color to something grayish, and her loose pants were ripped in a few spots from all those times she'd had to cut through untamed forests. If Mother could see her, she'd scold Meilin harshly. But traveling alone into the West had meant abandoning any semblance of vanity. Particularly since time was short.

Little Feng, Meilin's baby sister, had been given only one more year to live—and that had been before Meilin had set out on her journey. The strange disease that had eaten away at Little Feng's small body, weakening her until she could barely sit up, for the past half year would kill her if Meilin didn't return in time. Though Mother and Father were both respected purveyors of medicines back home in their seaside kingdom of Huihai, even their combined skills hadn't been enough. Only the blood of a powerful wizard would be potent enough to heal Little Feng. And so Meilin had left home to seek the one known only as the Master, who was rumored to be the most powerful wizard of all.

Meilin had no idea how she would convince the Master to

give up a few drops of his blood—especially since she presently resembled a beggar. She doubted he'd be interested in what few possessions she had in the rough pack tied to her back. Though her parents had sent her off with a number of valuable herbs and spell ingredients to trade, they'd all been stolen a while back. Despite her stocky build, Meilin had never been physically strong—she'd spent most of her days in Huihai reading or helping her parents in the shop. She'd hardly been able to put up a fight when she'd encountered a knife-wielding robber.

Meilin scowled at the memory. She was no weakling, she reminded herself. She'd made it across an entire continent by herself, even though the furthest she'd traveled before then was to the neighboring town. Neither Mother nor Father had wanted her to make the trip, but since they had no sons, they'd had no choice but to send a daughter. At sixteen, Meilin was the second eldest of five sisters and the only option, since her married older sister was pregnant and her younger sisters all under twelve. Not that any of them would have wanted to go anyway. None of them seemed to share Meilin's thirst for the unknown.

As Meilin drew closer to the Crimson Keep, anxiety wrapped its icy fingers around her heart. What if the Master wouldn't help her? What if she'd come all this way for nothing?

The horse stopped at the edge of a wide moat surrounding the Keep. Scarlet rays glittered upon its frenetic ripples. Meilin jumped down and regarded the enormous building, her black eyes so wide, her narrow brows nearly reached her hairline. On the road, she'd heard many stories about the enchanted castle and its ever-expanding walls. This close, she felt as if she stood before a living, breathing giant. The groans and creaks of shifting rock peppered the air, and something about its multitude of dark windows made her feel as if it were staring at her. But whichever way she looked, she found no doors or gates.

"Is this the Master's way of keeping me out?" she wondered aloud. The words emerged in the Western tongue, which she'd been practicing nonstop since she'd left home. It had almost become as familiar as her own language.

A high-pitched giggle fluttered across the breeze.

Meilin whirled. "Who's there?"

Only the wind's song answered her.

Narrowing her eyes, Meilin wandered along the moat. "Hello?"

The giggle wafted by again, as if the breeze itself were laughing. But whichever way Meilin looked, she saw no one. She guessed that a spirit of some sort was present.

"Over here!" a quick voice whispered in her ear.

Meilin spun toward the sound. Again—no one.

Then she noticed that the moat's glittering ripples seemed to be getting brighter. And gleams were no longer red—they were purple and white. The sparks leapt from the water like a million fireflies, darting up and up until they formed a glittering line from the moat's shore to one of the Keep's third-story windows.

Meilin was no stranger to magic, but the unexpected enchantment left her stunned.

"What are you waiting for?" The voice whispered to her again. "Come in! Come in!" The line of sparkles shone brighter, inviting Meilin to approach.

Curious, Meilin drew closer and cautiously reached toward the sparks. To her surprise, her fingers met something solid, like rope.

"Climb up!" The voice sounded eager—perhaps too eager. Though it was reminiscent of a child's, Meilin reminded herself that magic was not to be trusted.

"Who are you?"

"Climb up! Climb up! You'll find no other way in!"

Pursing her lips, Meilin considered the Keep's door-less, gate-less wall, which seemed endless in either direction. She could ride along the moat seeking another entrance, but what if this mysterious spirit was right, and this was her only opportunity to enter?

Deciding she'd rather risk falling into a trap than riding uselessly around the Keep for who-knew-how-long, Meilin seized the sparkling rope and pulled herself up. The pack shifted on back, and she lifted her shoulder in an attempt to adjust it. Her arms screamed at the exertion, and sweat trickled down her round cheeks. Though the rest of her had become significantly leaner from her travels, her face had kept its full-moon shape.

Part of her wished she could have kept her moon-like pallor as well—mostly to avoid Mother's inevitable lecture when she returned home—but mostly, she didn't care that the sun had gilded her complexion. Besides, with all the blisters this climb was giving her hands, she could hardly pass for a lady anyway. Not that she'd ever want to marry into a higher-class family as her older sister had. Nor marry at all, for that matter.

"Hurry up!" The voice, impatient, zipped past Meilin.

She suddenly felt herself moving upward at a rapid pace. Gasping, Meilin realized that the glittering rope was retreating into the window above, pulling her along with it.

The spirit's laughter tinkled from the direction of the window, though Meilin couldn't tell what lay beyond it.

She soon found herself stumbling onto a cold stone floor illuminated by twisting gold chandeliers that dangled high above a wide hallway. The purple-and-white sparks streamed toward one of them and swirled around a little girl perched between tall white candles. She looked even younger than Little Feng—five, maybe six. Snowy white pigtails sprouted from her scalp, above her pointed ears, and brushed her full, lavender cheeks. Bare legs dangled from beneath a loose blue dress decorated with ribbons so colorful, Meilin wondered if the girl had torn apart a rainbow to make it.

"Hello!" The little girl spread her lilac lips into a wide grin and jumped off the chandelier.

Alarm flashed through Meilin before she recalled that this was a *spirit*, not a child.

The sparks formed a pair of butterfly wings on the girl's back, and she hovered several feet midair. She peered into Meilin's face with a pair of large, bright eyes whose irises seemed to hold every shade of blue in the world—pale ice, rich azure, deep indigo, and a hundred hues in between.

"Who are you?" the girl asked.

"You first." Meilin crossed her arms. "You brought me here, after all."

"I'm Glisk!" The spirit twirled midair, delighting in the sound of her name. "I was born of the wind, and like it, I am eternal. But eternity can get *boring*. That's why I like it here in the Crimson Keep... It's always changing, and it's always bringing me new people to play with." She grinned. "Like you!"

"I'm not here to play." Meilin adjusted the pack on her shoulder. "I need to find the Master—he's the only one who can save my little sister's life."

"Oh?" Glisk cocked her head. "You look different from most people who enter the Keep. You must have come from very far away."

"I did."

"Where? Where? And you still haven't told me who you are!" Glisk pouted. "I won't help you unless you answer my questions!"

Though having three younger sisters had taught Meilin how to be patient, Glisk was testing her limits. But she didn't dare wander through the Crimson Keep alone. While on the road, she'd heard many tales of how even the Keep's residents found its enormous, changing interior impossible to navigate. People were known to vanish for months, years—sometimes forever. A guide was essential, and Glisk seemed to be the only one available.

"My name is Meilin. I come from a kingdom called Huihai on the other side of the continent."

Glisk gasped. "You came all the way from the East? That's amazing! I've always wanted to go."

"Why haven't you? Can't the wind blow wherever she pleases?"

"Sure, but I don't know the way. And the journey would take *forever*! What if I got lost somewhere boring?"

Meilin nodded, recalling the miles upon miles of dull landscapes she'd ridden across. "The road is indeed long... and mostly uninteresting. Though I'm sure there was plenty that I missed... I haven't stayed more than a night in any one place."

"Why not?"

"Because I had to get here as fast as I could and return just as quickly. My sister is very ill... She probably only has half a year to live by now. My parents need a few drops of the Master's blood to create a potion strong enough to heal her. I fear I've already been gone too long."

"That's so sad." Glisk lowered herself to the ground, and the butterfly wings dissolved from sight. "What's your sister like?"

Without the sparks, Glisk appeared almost human—in fact, she looked a lot like a purple-skinned, pointy-eared version of Little Feng. The sight sent a pang through Meilin's heart, and she gave a wistful smile. "Her name is Meifeng, which means Beautiful Wind. But we call her Little Feng. She's a lot like you—playful. She loves to dance... or she did, before she got sick."

"I like dancing too!" Glisk jumped up.

"If I fail, Little Feng will never dance again. Will you help me?"

"Of course! Of course!" Glisk's eyes twinkled, and Meilin sensed mischief behind them. "I'll take you to the Master! I know the way!"

"How? Aren't the halls always moving?"

"Yes, but the more you use them, the more they hold still. *Everyone* uses the kitchen, so it's always in one place. Even the Master has to eat—and it's almost dinnertime! He'll be there, I promise!"

The mention of dinner reminded Meilin of how long it had been since she'd last eaten something other than a crust of bread here and there. Glisk's plan sounded logical enough, and a place with food sounded like an excellent destination.

Meilin gestured down the hall. "Lead the way."

A look of glee filled Glisk's face. She leapt into the air, her glittering wings returning. Meilin sprinted to keep up as the spirit soared down the corridor and turned into another. Though Meilin was a decently fast runner, she found herself clinging to the sparks Glisk trailed behind her.

"Slow down!" Meilin nearly tripped as she followed the sparks through an open doorway. But by the time she entered the cavernous room, the spirit was nowhere to be seen. "Glisk?"

The spirit's disembodied giggle bounced off the red stones. Meilin shivered. Something wasn't right—she could sense it.

Seizing one of the burning torches from the wall, she panned her gaze across the high ceiling, the dim chandeliers dangling from long chains, the wooden tables spanning the space, the high-backed chairs scattered across the floor. Deep gashes marred each surface. Something monstrous had attacked this place.

A large, circular window lay on the opposite wall. The sun must have already retreated below the horizon, for shadows filled it, obscuring the view. Wondering if Glisk had gone outside, Meilin took a nervous step forward. "Glisk?"

The shadows spread across the wall, and more appeared to seep from the stone. Meilin froze. It wasn't night outside—and that was no window.

She stared, wide-eyed, as the shadows spread to the floor. A hundred long, spindly fingers extended toward her. Though it had no eyes, she could sense it—whatever it was—staring at her. An uncanny feeling frosted down her spine. "Glisk! What is this?"

Only a faraway giggle answered.

Like a viper striking, the shadow shot toward her and seized her ankles. A shocked cry burst from Meilin's lips as she fell. The next thing she knew, she was being dragged across the floor and toward what she'd mistaken for a window. Now, Meilin could see that the dark circle was a black vortex that swallowed light and was waiting to swallow her. A column of shadow extended from the wall and took the form of an enormous, grasping claw.

Alarmed, Meilin swiped the torch at it. A hideous shriek ripped through the air, and the claw recoiled. But the shadows still had her by the ankles, drawing her closer to that vortex. Though it looked like no mouth she'd seen before, she was certain that it was just that. These shadows formed a shapeless monster, and it wanted to consume her whole.

Terror coursed through her blood. Friction burned her back and limbs. She frantically swiped the torch this way and that, hoping to repel the darkness, but though the claw stayed back, the grip on her ankles remained. Though she extended her arm as far as she could, she was unable to reach the shadows that held her. The vortex was only a few feet away. Soon, that blackness would be all she knew—

I didn't travel all the way across the continent to be a monster's snack!

"Let me go!" With a burst of rage, she hurtled the torch at the vortex.

An earth-shattering screech rang out, so loud it shook Meilin's bones. Like a creature covering its wounded face, the shadow withdrew into the vortex, freeing her.

Meilin scrambled to her feet and sprinted toward the entryway. An ominous rumble reverberated in her ears. Glancing back, she saw two arms explode from the vortex and dig their claws into the floor. Whatever the monster was doing, she didn't have time to stop and watch. The moment she was out of the room, she seized the heavy, wooden door and slammed it shut.

The noise of metal scraping stone, ear-piercing even through the door, squealed behind her. It was coming for her—and that door wouldn't hold it. Meilin rushed to grab another torch and raced down the hallway. Her bulky pack bounced against her back. She had no idea where she was going; all she knew was that she had to get as far as possible.

Behind her, the sounds of splintering wood and breaking stone crackled. She chanced a look back. Shadows spilled through chinks in the door and wall. They rapidly spread across the deep red stone, wrapping the entire corridor from floor to ceiling. Black tendrils exploded toward her with a rasping cry—it still wanted her, and it was more determined than ever.

Spikes of fear pierced Meilin's chest, and her breaths grew short. Her lungs burned from effort as she forced herself to keep running through the dread. Questions churned in her mind. What *was* that thing? And where was Glisk? Had the childlike spirit led her to the monster on purpose?

Meilin darted around a corner. It wasn't until she'd run several yards into it that she realized that it led to a dead end—no doors, no windows, no intersecting hallways. She started back the way she came, but had barely taken a few steps before the shadow monster appeared at the end of the corridor.

It clung to the walls, floor, and ceiling, leaving the space between hollow but for a single great claw extending toward her. Meilin brandished the torch. The claw briefly recoiled, then shot forward and seized her middle. What felt like ice exploded in her stomach. With a cry of shock, she drove the torch's flame into the claw.

The creature screeched. The shadows retreated into a single round swath against the ceiling, its edges quivering. That swath seemed to hold all the darkness in the world, and Meilin realized that it was the same vortex she had mistaken for a window before. That was the monster's core, it seemed.

But the respite was short-lived. Tendrils sprouted toward her once again, this time spreading along the ceiling and down the walls. The monster was trying to surround her. Even if she could attack part of it, another part could grab her again.

Meilin waved the torch this way and that, wishing she could turn herself into a ball of flame. The ground trembled. She stumbled into the wall, which abruptly gave, as if nothing had been propping it up. The hallway widened around her, its floor stretching and its walls growing taller.

The Crimson Keep was shifting again, with her in it. Stone popped from mortar, and new stone grew in its place—except in one spot, where a hole gaped wider and wider.

The Keep's movements appeared to disorient the monster. Shadows extended and withdrew seemingly at random. Meilin punched the torch at any that drew too close. She eyed the end of the corridor, wondering if she dared trying to get out of this dead end. But the vortex still gaped directly above it, and shadows covered the floor ahead.

The wall's new opening, though, was right beside her. It was now large enough for her to climb through. A staircase lay on the other side. Wherever it led, this could be her only chance.

As Meilin scurried through the opening, the torch's flames licked a stray wisp of her hair. Startled, she grabbed the burning strand. Pain lanced her palm, but at least that put the fire out.

She landed on a stone step—one of many that formed a long, twisting staircase. Except for the hole she'd emerged from, the walls on either side were featureless. Shadows lay above and below, with the only light coming from her torch.

With two directions to choose from, Meilin picked the easier one. She scurried down the stairs, nearly tripping several times. A hollow, rumbling noise from behind told her that the monster was following, and a quick glance over her shoulder confirmed it. Sweat trickled down her face, and her heart hammered. The creature would catch up any second—even with the torch, how long could she hold it off?

A tremor shook the stones, and the ground tilted. Meilin stumbled into the wall. The Keep groaned as its walls and floors stretched. It was shifting again. Pebbles rained down from newly formed gaps in the ceiling. The shaking steps tossed Meilin into the opposite wall, and she lost her balance, landing hard with a startled cry.

The stairs below her crumbled away, leaving her stranded above an enormous room several feet in the air. Meilin peered over the edge. Broken rock littered the ground, and metal chandeliers, covered in tiers of white candles, dangled from the ceiling. She was too high up to jump to the ground—she'd certainly break a limb in the attempt.

She glanced back up the stairs. A black tendril along the wall reached into the light of her torch—the creature was still coming, and she was trapped. Trembling, she looked over the edge again. Jumping down seemed to be the only choice.

She was about to force herself over when her eyes caught on the nearest chandelier. It was only a few feet away and about the same height from the ground—maybe a bit lower. And all those candles might discourage the monster from following.

The black tendril wrapped around Meilin's ankle. She screamed and drove the torch into the shadow. It released her with a screech. She stood quickly, forcing herself to act before fear could stop her, and leapt at the chandelier.

For a moment, the rush of flight filled her chest. She reached out to grasp her target, dropping the torch. Her fingers found one of the metal rings forming the tiered chandelier, and her body crashed into the levels below. Heat seared her arm as candles caught her sleeve. She gritted her teeth against the pain and managed to find footing on the chandelier's lowest ring, then quickly patted out the flame. She looked herself up and down to make sure nothing else had caught fire and found another flame on her pack. She blew until it vanished.

Panting, she looked to the staircase—or what remained

of it. Shadows covered the stones, and she knew the creature was watching her. Yet it remained still, hesitating. She was surrounded by fire, and it didn't dare follow.

Meilin hoped the creature would retreat, but instead, the shadows spilled over the edge of the crumbled steps like a waterfall of tar. It pooled on the stone floor below. The central vortex made it look like a wide hole in the ground, with thin threads of shadow leaping from its edges.

Meilin bit her lip, dismayed. It was waiting for her. She couldn't stay on this chandelier forever. But at least she'd earned a moment of respite.

Anger churned in her stomach. Had Glisk intentionally led her into a trap? Meilin cursed herself for having been so foolish. Then she cursed the shadow beast for its unrelenting pursuit. No matter which way she ran, the thing seemed determined to consume her.

"Why won't you leave me alone?" she yelled.

A low rumble filled the room. The monster's wordless reply carried menace, and she knew it was a threat.

A new wave of determination swelled in Meilin's chest. If she couldn't escape it, she'd have to confront it. She already knew its weakness—there had to be some way to exploit that. Flame forced it to retreat—maybe she could drive it into some kind of trap. But what? Doors and walls had little effect on it. It seemed to need only the slightest crack to escape.

Meilin glanced around the wide room, hunting for inspiration. Her eyes caught a square of metal on one of the walls. Upon closer observation, she realized it was a small door with a handle that allowed it to open downward. Maybe metal could do what stone and wood couldn't. If she could open that door, force the creature inside, and close it quickly enough, the thing might not be able to get out.

After searching for other ideas and finding none, she decided it was worth a try. But first, she had to get off the chandelier.

She looked down. The torch she'd dropped lay on the floor, its flame flickering weakly. Calmer now, she realized she wasn't as high up as she'd thought. If she climbed down to the lowest ring and hung by her arms, her feet would only be about a person's height from the ground. Of course, the monster would seize her the moment she left the safety of the candles.

The candles . . .

Meilin seized one and hurtled it down at the vortex. The creature barely had time to let out a screech before she'd hurtled another in its direction. The black circle slid away, just as she'd hoped. Its cries echoed against the cavernous walls, buzzing in her ears and shaking her bones. She cringed but kept throwing candle after candle after candle, forcing the thing back and back and back. Each time it recoiled, it drew closer to the metal door—just as Meilin intended.

She grabbed the last candle and swung down from the chandelier, launching herself toward the torch. She landed hard. Snatching the torch, she rushed to reignite it. The flame roared back to life.

Black shadows crawled along the floor, reaching for her, but she wouldn't run from them anymore. She drove the fire into each one that drew too close and sprinted to the metal door. Grabbing its handle, she yanked down. Blackness lay beyond, and she sensed some kind of magic swirling within.

Whatever it was, she hoped it would hold the creature. It lashed out with its black tendrils, and she fought back with her flame, driving it toward the open doorway.

The central vortex now lay against the wall directly beside it. With a cry, Meilin shoved the torch into it, ramming the end against the stone. The creature's shriek seemed to crack the Keep's walls. As it withdrew, a part of it fell into the doorway. Meilin rushed to drive the flame into it again and again, until it was all the way inside. She shoved the door closed on its last shriek.

Startling silence rippled through the air.

Meilin watched the metal door in case the thing came surging back, her blood still pumping from the rush of action.

High-pitched laughter pealed across the room. Glisk appeared in a shower of purple and white sparks. "You flushed it down the toilet!" she exclaimed between fits of giggles.

Meilin cocked her head. "What?"

"That sluice was made for dumping chamber pots! The pipes

are enchanted to get rid of poop and keep it from reforming! It's a toilet!"

An incredulous laugh escaped Meilin's throat. At least she'd been right about that metal door being her salvation. Then anger bubbled through her veins as she glared at the spirit who'd gotten her into that mess in the first place. "Why did you lead me to that room? Did you know the monster was in there?"

"Of course I did! I wanted to see what would happen!"

"*What?*"

"An apprentice called Belid made the creature by accident—I think he was trying to bring his shadow to life. The Master trapped it in that room and forbade anyone from entering this part of the Keep in case it escaped. I always wondered what would happen if it did, so I lifted the enchantment and led you to it." Glisk grinned. "It was so much fun to watch you fight it!"

Meilin scowled. "What kind of monster are you?"

Glisk's smile fell. "I'm not a monster! *It* was!"

"You nearly got me killed just so you could watch what would happen. That's not fun—that's cruel."

Glisk knit her brows. "But you're okay. Why are you mad at me?"

Meilin shook her head. There was no point in arguing with the wicked little thing. Adjusting the pack on her shoulder, she strode away.

"Wait!" Glisk zoomed ahead of her, her butterfly wings fluttering. "Where are you going?"

"Away from you."

"You'll never find your way around the Keep without me!"

"I'll take my chances."

"Stop!" Glisk landed in front of Meilin and stamped her small foot. "I want to play with you!"

"By feeding me to another monster?" Meilin brushed past the indignant purple girl. "Go bother someone else." She exited the room and strode down a corridor. "Hello?" she called. "Is anyone here?"

"*I'm* here!" Glisk appeared before her in a burst of sparks.

Meilin gritted her teeth. "Anyone *else?*"

"Why are you mad at me?" Glisk ran to follow Meilin. "It was just a bit of fun!"

"You tricked me! I could have *died*."

"So? It was just a game!"

"Not to me. Why won't you leave me alone?"

"Because I like you! You're fun! I want you to be my friend!" Glisk grabbed Meilin's sleeve. "You have to play with me!"

Meilin yanked her arm back, her temper rising. "Go away, you little demon!"

Glisk's eyes widened, and her lip trembled. A tear fell down her lavender cheek, and guilt stung Meilin. She was about to apologize when she reminded herself that Glisk was *not* a human child. For all Meilin knew, the spirit was manipulating her to draw her into another trap. She wouldn't fall for it again.

She continued on her way, choosing to ignore Glisk. "Hello? Master? Anyone?"

A shrill wail ripped through the corridor. Meilin glanced back to find Glisk in the throes of a tantrum, bawling and stamping her feet.

"I *hate* you! I hate you I hate you I *hate* you!" The girl's wails followed Meilin down the hall.

A buzzing noise filled the space around Meilin, low but frantic. She froze and held the torch out before her, wondering if the shadow monster had escaped the sluice despite the enchantments.

A large drop of glowing liquid dripped from the ceiling, so blue and so bright, it looked as if a piece of the sky had liquefied and fallen. Meilin jumped back as it splashed to the floor. Droplets bounced up, but instead of returning to the ground, they hovered several feet above it. The buzzing intensified. Fluttering wings sprouted from the droplets, and they zipped toward her. Meilin brandished the torch, but the droplets flew right through the flame. She ducked.

More liquid dripped from the ceiling. Against the backdrop of Glisk's wails, it was as if the Keep itself were crying. Each blue drop transformed into the tiny winged creatures, which swarmed around Meilin. When her attempts to swat them away with the torch proved useless, she spun and ran back toward

Glisk—only to find more liquid dripping around the girl.

Meilin held up her arms to protect her face. Tiny pricks pierced her hands and arms, sharp and relentless.

"Glisk!" she cried. "What are those?"

"I don't have to tell you!"

Something sharp pierced Meilin's side. She doubled over with a cry. Her tunic was apparently poor armor against these things. "*Glisk!* Please!"

"They're bluebugs!" Glisk's high-pitched voice pierced through the crescendoing buzz. "They're drawn to sadness, and they eat people! And now, they're going to eat you! Because you made me sad, but they can't eat me! So they're going to eat *you!*"

Meilin realized with horror that each of those pricks was a tiny bite. They were miniscule enough to hurt no more than a thorn's prick, but the cumulative effect was becoming more and more painful by the moment. The bluebugs were nibbling on her, bit by bit eating her alive. More poured from the ceiling— how long did she have before there was nothing left of her?

From every direction, the vicious creatures pierced her skin. Meilin clenched her jaw against the pain. "Please, stop crying! I'm sorry!"

"No, you're not!" Glisk cried between sobs. "Nobody's ever sorry for me! N-Nobody wants to be my f-friend! The M-Master tried to banish me . . . The apprentices cast spells to k-keep me away… I just want to play!"

"Maybe more people would play with you if you didn't try to kill them!"

"I didn't mean to! I-It was a game!"

"Is this a game too?"

"No! *You* did this! You made me sad! I didn't know they were here, but now that they are, I hope they eat every bite of you!" Glisk screwed up her face and screamed. After stamping her foot once more, she vanished from sight. But the sounds of her sobs remained, reverberating against the stone.

"*Glisk!*" Through cracks in her fingers, Meilin looked around for someplace she could escape to. But the bluebugs filled the entire corridor, and more kept raining down. None of her swatting, even with the torch, did any good. Hoping to find shelter, she ran a few steps forward, then quickly realized the futility. There was no place to go—the bluebugs would consume her before she made it very far. And she couldn't drive them back as she had the shadow monster.

Panic swirled through her. This was it—she'd crossed a continent for nothing. She'd fought the shadow beast for *nothing*. Little Feng would die, and her family would never know what became of her, never realize how close she'd come to saving her baby sister.

Tears streamed down her face. The buzzing was so loud now, she could barely hear her own thoughts. That infernal noise would be the last sound she'd know before she died. Even Glisk's cries had faded away—or maybe she'd disappeared to some other place entirely.

That little demon! I hope I come back as a ghost so I can haunt her for killing me!

A calmer part of Meilin reminded her that Glisk hadn't *made* the bluebugs appear. Yet her tantrum had attracted them.

The bluebugs draw to sadness...

Meilin realized with a start that her own panic was worsening the situation. She wasn't dead yet—she still had a chance. But what could she do?

An idea hit her. If the bluebugs were drawn to sorrow, then perhaps the opposite—joy—would repel them. Maybe if she could fill her head with thoughts of happier times, they'd leave.

She squeezed her eyes and pictured her hometown—the waves kissing the sand, her sisters running along the shore chasing kites shaped like swallows. Little Feng dancing as Meilin played a merry melody on her xiao—a vertical bamboo flute.

She still had that flute—it was in her pack. She'd turned to it for comfort during those long days traveling alone. Each time she felt homesick, she'd pull it out and play a familiar tune, and it would, for a moment, transport her back to Huihai.

The stinging bites seemed to be abating—or maybe she'd just grown numb. Whether her idea was working or not, Meilin decided that if this was the end, she'd rather leave the world thinking of better times. And she'd rather hear the song of a xiao again than go out with only that horrible buzzing filling her ears.

Struggling to ignore the repeated bites, she took the pack off her shoulder and pulled out her xiao, navigating by touch since she had to keep her eyes squeezed. She brought the instrument to her lips and played an old folk melody her mother had taught her. It was Little Feng's favorite. In Meilin's mind, she could see her youngest sister twirling and leaping to the bouncing notes. Her heart warmed at the image. For too long, she'd only carried memories of Little Feng sick in bed. She'd almost forgotten how happy the girl could be.

Meilin's fingers flickered against the bamboo flute's round holes. The high, boisterous tune skittered down the hallway.

The buzzing diminished, and her skin stopped stinging. Meilin cracked open one eye. To her relief, the swarm of bluebugs was much thinner. They dropped into the ground, and, instead of springing back up, sank into the cracks between the stones.

A delighted giggle wafted toward her. Anxiety seized Meilin—she recognized Glisk's laugh. But she kept playing, kept picturing her family as they'd been before Little Feng's illness. Mother and Father tending the shop where they sold medicines and herbs, satisfied with their success and the respect they'd earned. Meixiang—her oldest sister—joyfully telling her that she'd found the man she was going to marry. Meirong and Meihua—the two sisters between her and Little Feng—showing off their skillful embroidery and boasting of their ambitions to sew for noble ladies. And, of course, Little Feng, whose smile outshone the sun.

The bluebugs had all but disappeared now. Yet the song wasn't finished, and Meilin didn't want to stop halfway through. And so she played on, her heart skipping with the tune.

Glisk's giggle rang out again. Purple and white glitter showered down before Meilin. When the little spirit reappeared, she was in the midst of a dance of her own, her bare feet spinning on the floor, her small arms waving above her head, her blue dress twirling into the shape of a bell. The grin on her face and the glee in her eyes were so reminiscent of Little Feng that Meilin momentarily forgot that this was the same trickster who'd led her into the jaws of a monster.

By the time Meilin finished her song, the last of the bluebugs had disappeared. Glisk, who'd been spinning like a top, landed in a heap of skirts and ribbons and sparkles, her face bright.

"Play another! Play another!" She clapped her hands excitedly.

Meilin twisted her mouth, annoyed. She glanced at her hands—they were covered in red welts from the bluebugs. She imagined the rest of her looked just as bad and was glad there was no mirror nearby.

"Do your hands hurt?" Glisk gasped. "Is that why you won't play?"

Meilin shook her head. She didn't dare respond, in case the little spirit got upset again and the bluebugs reappeared.

"What's wrong?" Glisk tilted her head. "Here, I can help!"

She vanished into a whirl of glitter. Before Meilin could say anything, the sparks surrounded her, and a warm wind wrapped around her entire body, hugging her.

Moments later, the sparks retreated, and Glisk reappeared. "Is that better?"

"What did you do?" Meilin glanced at her hands. To her surprise, the welts had vanished. She touched her face and found neither wounds nor the stinging she should have felt.

"I fixed you!" Glisk smiled. "Now will you play another song? Pretty please?"

Meilin gave her an incredulous look. "First you try to kill me, then you leave me to be eaten by bluebugs, and now you heal me? What do you want?"

Glisk looked at her feet. "I told you—I want you to be my friend."

Meilin shook her head. But if the spirit had healing powers, perhaps it was worth putting up with her antics. "How did you fix me? Can you fix more serious wounds? Like those caused by disease?"

"No." Glisk twisted her mouth. "I can only fix things that are a little bit broken. I can't fix your sister... You'll still need the Master's blood for a cure."

Meilin pursed her lips. She'd still have to find her way through the Keep somehow, and Glisk was still her best chance. Meilin reminded herself that if walked away, not only might the spirit throw another tantrum, but she could wind up wandering the shifting hallways for years. Now that her anger had been given time to abate, she realized that Glisk wasn't wicked—just selfish and inconsiderate. Like a child. An immortal child with great magical powers, but a child nonetheless. And driving her away would be a foolish thing to do.

"How about this," Meilin said. "I'll play for you *after* you take me to the Master."

"After?" Glisk pouted.

"Yes, after." Sensing Glisk's hesitation, Meilin added, "And I'll give you my xiao and teach you to play. That way, you can have all the songs you want."

Glisk spread her mouth into a wide grin. "I'd like that! Let's go!" She sprang up, her butterfly wings shimmering.

Meilin caught her hand before she could fly off. "No tricks this time?"

"No tricks. I promise."

Meilin narrowed her eyes, then released the girl's hand. She took a moment to put her xiao back in her pack. To her relief, Glisk waited, hovering, until she was finished.

The two traveled down winding corridors and curving staircases, passing carved doors and strange statues of mythical creatures—creatures with wings and fangs and claws. Now and then, they passed a wandering denizen of the Keep—an apprentice carrying a stack of books or a worker with a belt of tools. Other than an odd glance here and there, none paid any attention to the lavender-skinned spirit or the young traveler from the East. Meilin supposed that those who lived in a place as enchanted as the Keep must be accustomed to seeing unusual faces.

As they made their way through the castle, Glisk chattered about her past adventures—tricks she'd played on the Master and his apprentices, pranks she'd pulled on unsuspecting visitors. Her babbling words rolled past Meilin's ears like the rush of a brook, but Meilin didn't mind the company. Actually, it was rather nice to *have* company for a change—as long as that company didn't throw another tantrum or lead her into another death trap.

"Nobody seems to like my games, though." Glisk sighed. "They keep trying to chase me out of the Keep."

"Have you ever thought about what your tricks might feel like if they were played on *you*?" Meilin asked. "How would you like it if someone told you they'd help you, then led you into danger?"

"I wouldn't care." Glisk shrugged. "I can just turn into wind and escape."

"Well, the rest of us can't. Keep that in mind before you play another 'game.' It's not as fun when you could actually die. That's probably why people keep trying to chase you away— they're trying to protect themselves from you."

Glisk twisted her mouth. "I never thought of that... I thought people were just being mean to me."

"If that's so, why have you stayed in the Keep for so long?"

"It's fun here, and I don't know where else I'd go. Before I found the Keep, I spent forever blowing across a desert, and it was *boring*. I hated it. I'm afraid if I leave, that will happen again."

"Maybe you need someone to lead you." Meilin paused. Something was calling her attention—invisible yet powerful. It was as if a magnet were pulling her toward a wide, open door a few steps ahead. Curious, she approached.

A great library lay beyond the doorway, with books stacked on wooden shelves that stretched from the floor to the high, vaulted ceiling. A wide window threw golden light upon the colorful spines and gleaming letters. Meilin stared in awe. She'd heard about the great libraries of the West, where words were bound in stacks instead of rolled into scrolls, and she'd hoped to see one on her journey. But the small villages she'd passed through were scarcely literate enough to possess such a thing, though, and she'd given up hope.

Now, her wildest dream was standing before her. More than anything, Meilin loved to learn. It was why she'd already read every scroll on medicine and magic that her parents possessed, and why she'd begged them to let her make this journey. Yet her travels had proved disappointing—she'd had to spend all her time surviving and scarcely had a chance to explore the new places around her. Though she was literate in three languages—that of her home, that of the West, and an obscure tongue from the far South that she'd picked up from a fellow traveler she'd spent several weeks journeying with—she hadn't had a chance to read more than a signpost in months.

Meilin wandered into the library, drawn by all the promises of knowledge and enlightenment. A rational voice in her head warned her not to waste time here, but she could barely hear it through her excitement. A deep-seated craving built in the pit of her stomach. She had months of travel ahead of her, and the thought of all those long, empty days on the road back to Huihai made her blood churn with discontent. If she only had something to fill her mind, maybe the journey home wouldn't be as dull as the trip to the Keep had been.

"You can't go in there!" Glisk's frantic voice chased after her. "Come back!"

"Just a moment." Meilin walked between the shelves, overwhelmed by a sensation of belonging. She couldn't explain it, but it was as if the library were drawing her into its embrace.

"Come back! Come back!" Glisk's voice grew frantic.

Somewhere in the back of her mind, Meilin found it odd that the spirit hadn't followed her. She ran her fingers along the spines of cloth and leather. The titles, stamped in metallic lettering, enticed her with tales of adventure and secrets of how the world worked. The Keep had so many tomes... surely they wouldn't miss just one...

"Don't touch them!" Glisk cried. "Come back!"

Even Glisk knows that stealing is wrong. Meilin chastised herself for even considering taking something. But it couldn't hurt to look...

She pulled a random book off the shelf, eager to see what lay inside.

"How dare you!" A deep voice rumbled through the library.

The floor shook, and Meilin wondered if the Keep was shifting again. Then, the shelves and all their books—including the one in her hand—evaporated into mist. The entire space shrank as the ceiling lowered and the walls drew in.

A fog seemed to clear from Meilin's head, and she suddenly realized that this place was trying to trap her. Alarmed, she ran back the way she came, but found that the door had vanished.

"You have violated me!" The voice spoke again.

"I'm sorry!" Meilin spun, searching for any way out. But every way she looked, all she saw was stone. "I-I wasn't going to steal it! I just wanted a look!"

"You strayed from your path to pursue your own desires. You are unworthy."

"Who are you?"

"I am whatever would cause you to stray. The worthy ignore my calls. You chose yourself over your quest. Now, you will stay here forever."

"No! Please!" Meilin pressed against the walls, trying in vain to push the back. Only a thin shaft of light from a crack in the ceiling broke through the shadows.

What had been a great library was now a small cell, hardly tall enough for Meilin to stand. If she stretched her arms, her hands would touch both walls.

"Let me out!" she cried. "Glisk! Somebody! Let me out!"

Only silence responded. After several minutes of calling, searching the cracks in the stones, and pushing against the walls, Meilin realized how useless her actions were. She couldn't escape, and no one would find her here. Worse, she'd gotten herself into this situation. Glisk had tried to warn her, but she'd fallen into the trap nonetheless.

"Somebody! Help!" Her own shouts bounced back into her ears.

Dejected, Meilin sank down to the floor. She was going to die here, and it was her own fault. She'd just escaped death twice, and yet here she was again—except this time, she had nothing to fight with. How could she have made it so far, fought back so many adversaries, only to lose her focus and let herself be drawn into a trap? She could say it was because some spell had entangled her mind, but the truth was, she'd done nothing to resist it.

"I'm sorry," she whispered.

Her eyes stung as she pictured her family back home. They would forever wonder what had become of her. She almost wished she'd been consumed by the shadow monster or the bluebugs instead. At least then, she would have been a victim instead of a fool. For a moment, she wondered if her sorrow would draw the bluebugs out of the walls. She'd rather be eaten in a matter of moments than spend days wasting away in darkness, until her body failed from hunger and thirst.

Tears rolled down her cheeks, but no glowing blue droplets answered. She must have followed Glisk far enough from their part of the Keep that they couldn't sense her anymore. She wondered how close she'd gotten to the Master, how near she'd come to succeeding in her quest before she'd let herself be fooled.

"I'm sorry," she repeated. "Mother, Father, I'm sorry I failed you after you put your trust in me. Meixiang, I'm sorry I'll never get to meet your child. Meirong, Meihua, I'm sorry I'll never get to see you grow up. Little Feng... I'm sorry I couldn't save you. I hope you all know how much I love you and miss you... how much I wish I could tell you..." She buried her face in her knees and cried.

A soft whimpering filled the tiny cell. For a moment, Meilin thought it was an echo of her own sobs.

Purple and white glitter poured through the shaft of light. Meilin looked up with a start. "Glisk?"

When the little spirit materialized, she had her face pressed into her hands and was weeping into them.

"Glisk? What's wrong?"

"I don't want you to be sad." Glisk wiped her eyes and looked up. "And I don't want you to die in here, but I don't know how to get you out. My magic isn't strong enough."'

A faint smile lifted Meilin's lips, and she found herself unexpectedly touched by the girl's concern. "You tried to warn me. I should have listened."

"I wish I knew how to help." Glisk shuffled her feet. "No one's ever stayed with me as long as you have without trying to chase me away."

"Maybe that's because you keep leading them to monsters?"

Glisk grinned sheepishly. "Sorry about that."

Meilin reached into her pack and pulled out her xiao. "Here. You kept your promise. As long as I'm not dead yet, I can still teach you to play."

Glisk grabbed the bamboo flute and bounced on her toes. "Show me! Show me!"

Meilin instructed the girl on how to hold the instrument, where to place her fingers, and how to blow across the top. She was surprised when Glisk was able to produce a sound right away—usually it took weeks of practice. But she supposed it made sense that a wind spirit had uncommon control over the flow of air. And she was glad for the distraction.

"I changed my mind," Glisk said suddenly. "I want to leave the Keep and go to Huihai." She waved the xiao. "I want to see the land where things like this came from. And I want you to take me there so I don't get lost."

Meilin shook her head. "I'm trapped, remember?"

"There *has* to be a way out." Glisk transformed into sparks, and a strong wind filled the cell.

Meilin watched, heart too heavy to hope, as the sparks frantically bounced against the stones.

"There has to be! There has to be!" Glisk's disembodied voice surrounded her. Moments later, she reappeared, her eyes wide. "I have an idea!"

Before Meilin could ask what, Glisk yanked a hair from her head.

"*Ow!* What was that for?"

Glisk vanished again without replying.

Meilin stared at the spot where the spirit had stood, wondering what she'd meant. The xiao lay on the ground—she supposed Glisk couldn't carry anything that wouldn't fit through that tiny crack. But what could she want with Meilin's hair?

Minutes ticked by. Meilin picked up the xiao and fiddled with it as she paced, her mind rattling between wanting to hope and not daring to. Maybe Glisk would find a way to help her—or maybe she'd get distracted with her next "game" and forget all about her.

A sudden gust wrapped her in a cold blast. For a moment, Meilin thought it was Glisk returning, but then she noticed the absence of purple and white sparks. She squeezed her eyes against the wind's sting, wondering what was going on.

The wind ceased. Meilin blinked. To her shock, she was no longer in the cell, but was instead standing in the middle of a wide kitchen. Fire roared in a wide hearth, and the smells of roasting meat and simmering vegetables wafted around her. A large table stood before her with a strange structure of colored sticks upon it. Beside it, a stocky old man with a white beard scowled as he snatched something from the giggling lavender-skinned girl hovering beside him.

"It worked!" Glisk flew up to Meilin, throwing sparks like confetti. Her blue eyes flicked down to the xiao in Meilin's hand. "Oh, good, you brought it!" She grabbed the instrument and twirled it like a baton.

"What—What happened?" Meilin asked.

"I gave the Master your hair, and he used it to cast a summoning spell on you!"

"*You're* the Master?" Meilin stared at the cross old man and noticed that the thing he'd taken from Glisk was a yellow stick that looked similar to the ones in the structure on the table.

"I am." The Master crossed his arms. "And I was just about to solve this enormously complicated puzzle when that little pest stole the last piece. She said she'd throw it into the moat unless I helped her summon you." He glared at Glisk. "I should have turned you into a newt!"

"You don't know ho-ow!" Glisk teased in a singsong voice. "Just like you don't know how to banish me!"

"Quite unfortunate," the Master grumbled.

Meilin's head was still whirling at her sudden change in fortune. She rushed up to the Master. "Master, I've traveled across the continent to find you. My little sister is very ill, and I need a few drops of your blood for a cure. Will you help me?"

The Master frowned. "That is an enormous favor you're asking. A wizard does not part with a piece of himself lightly."

"I understand, but—"

"Help her! Help her!" Glisk interrupted. "You have *so* much blood, and she only needs a little bit, right?"

Meilin nodded. "A few drops—that's all."

The Master's frown deepened. "As I said, a wizard—"

"You *have* to help her!" Glisk exclaimed. "Because she won't go back to Huihai without it, and I *really* want to go with her to see Huihai."

The Master raised his white brows and stood. "Is that so?" He reached into his cloak and produced a small, empty vial. With a flick of hand, he conjured a needle, then pricked the tip of his finger and squeezed a few drops. After corking the vial, he handed it to Meilin. "Here you are, my dear. I hope you have a safe journey home. In fact, let me help you make it faster." He pointed at Meilin's pack, which suddenly grew heavier. "There. I've supplied you with enough provisions for a few weeks so you won't have to stop as often. I'll even transport you back to your horse—I assume that's your beast that's been grazing by the moat."

"Yes, it is." Meilin stared, flabbergasted. She'd thought she'd have to do a lot more persuading. "Thank you. I'm afraid I have nothing to offer in return."

"On the contrary, you've already done me a great favor by ridding my Keep of a wicked creature that's plagued me for far too long."

Meilin knitted her brows. "You mean the shadow monster your apprentice created by accident?"

"Oh, you got rid of that too? That's fantastic, though I was actually referring to Glisk."

Glisk stuck out her tongue at the Master.

Meilin laughed. "At least the journey back won't be boring."

"Now, if you don't mind, I'll speed you away so I can finish my puzzle." The Master flung out one hand, sending a powerful gust at Meilin. "You'd better join her, Glisk, if you want to see Huihai."

Glisk burst into sparks and dove into the swirling air, surrounding Meilin with her giggles.

A moment later, Meilin found herself standing by the moat once more, just a few feet from where her horse stood grazing. The sun was long gone, and a full moon lit the night sky.

Meilin tucked the vial of the Master's blood into a hidden pocket of her tunic. Meanwhile, Glisk flitted beside her, her glowing sparks providing a convenient source of light. She blew into the xiao, experimenting with notes as Meilin mounted her horse.

"Not bad for a beginner," Meilin said. "Ready to go?"

Glisk grinned. "Yes!"

Meilin rode into the night with the little spirit flying beside her, trailing purple and white sparks and playing a merry tune.

DOOM RAIDERS

by Peter David

ALBERT WIPED HIS BROW AS HE GLANCED UP AT the relentless sun that was beating down upon him. It was hard to believe that it was so vicious simply because he and his cronies were in Egypt. It was the same sun, after all, that shown down upon them whether they were in Cairo, New York City, or Pismo Beach. What was it about the Egyptian desert that made it so utterly nasty? He had no answer for that question, but figured there wasn't really a reason that he should. He was, after all, an archæologist, not a weatherman.

He heard the steady, delicate chinking noises from nearby, courtesy of Karen and Boris's small pick axes. Their dedication to their work was simply amazing. At that moment, Albert simply wanted to kick back, perhaps crack open a bottle of some sort of soothing liquid, and take a break from his efforts. But Karen and Boris didn't even appear to understand that it was possible to not work for every hour of every day. It seemed as if they were immune to the sun's rays and the unending heat.

Then again, he supposed he shouldn't have been surprised. They were off in their own little world. They'd been working together for a year in a strictly platonic fashion, two thirds of a reliable team of explorers. But then one drunken night while celebrating too hard in Turkey, one thing had led to another and they'd woken up the following morning in bed together.

But instead of having the good sense to realize what a huge mistake it was, what do they do? Go at each other again. Albert could scarcely believe how screwed up their priorities had become. Yes, granted, when they were out in the field, they were totally focused on what they were doing. But at night, when the day's work was completed, it might as well have been that Albert had ceased to exist. Which was not the way it had used to be with them.

Maybe it'd be better if I'd been drafted.

It would have been a worthwhile way of spending his time. This Adolf Hitler individual was indisputably becoming more of a threat. Every passing week, newsreels in the theaters would talk about how his Nazis were making noises about advancing here or invading there. It might well have been better for Albert if he had been sent off to join the army and fight for democracy and all that important stuff.

Yet there was no point in his thinking about it. His asthma struggles had wound up with his being rated 4F, rendered unsuitable for service just as utterly as Boris's flat feet had left him excluded as well. Sometimes they referred to themselves as the 4F Squad when they were feeling humorous or had just had too much to drink. Except the drinks helped to soothe the frustration that was gnawing away at him.

Forget it. Concentrate on your job.

"How's it going?"

It was Boris, and it was only at that point that Albert realized that the chipping and digging noises he'd heard earlier had ceased. Karen was coming up behind Boris. Apparently they were taking a rare break to check in with him and his section of the dig.

It was their third week at the excavation and Albert was still uncertain what it was they were digging up. He'd been crouching, but with Boris and Karen there, he allowed himself to tilt back and sit. He tipped his pith helmet back slightly so he could see them better.

"I found some symbols," he said. He tapped the ground in front of him. "Right here."

Boris cocked an eyebrow. "Really?" He immediately made his way down a nearby incline, Karen right behind him. "What do they say?"

"I haven't the slightest idea."

"Is it hieroglyphics?" Karen asked.

"If it is, it isn't any system that I'm familiar with. And I'm familiar with most of them."

Boris scratched his chin as he studied it. Albert knew that Boris's habit of knowing everything about everything was a forced part of his personality; that typically Boris could be as clueless as anyone and simply loathed admitting it. In looking at these markings, however, even Boris wasn't capable of coming up with any sort of convincing explanation. "Any idea of the century, at least?"

"None."

This entire business was just the latest frustration in what had been an exceedingly annoying dig. They were simply the latest team to explore the set of ruins that had been found in the middle of the Armana sites, a fairly popular source of Egyptian archa eological research. Fifteen centuries earlier it had been constructed by Pharaoh Akhenaten to be the capital city. It was then subsequently abandoned for reasons that no one really knew for sure. It was their hope that they would be able to discern some reason for why the Pharaoh and his people had departed their newly built city.

"There is, however, one symbol that I do recognize," said Albert. "Come here."

He got up and strode across the compound, stepping carefully around other areas where they had been digging. Boris and Karen followed him, ready to see what he had come up with.

He stopped at the edge of one large circle carved into the ground, about five feet on each side. There were various spirals decorating it and there was a symbol set off in the middle. "Is that it?" said Boris. Albert nodded. "Okay, well . . . what does it say?"

"Loosely translated? It says, 'Do not touch.'"

Boris and Karen exchanged confused looks. "Do not touch . . . ?"

"Yeah. I figure it was rendered in the more common glyphs of the time so that no one would have any trouble reading it. Must have been important to them that no one touch it."

"All right, so . . . what do we do?" said Karen.

"Isn't that obvious?" said Boris with a ready grin. He strode toward the hieroglyph. "We touch it."

"Now hold on," said Albert nervously. "Maybe it's there for a reason."

"A reason that's still valid fifteen centuries later? Please," he said disdainfully. "What's going to happen? Am I going to unleash a mummy or something?"

"No, but . . ."

"That's your problem, Albert. You're always so damned afraid of everything."

"I'm not afraid! I'm just being cautious!"

"No, you're overcautious, which is the same thing as being afraid of everything."

Albert felt heat starting to pound behind his eyes, and it only got worse when he heard Karen chuckling. It was bad enough to have Boris razzing him, but the fact that she found it amusing was enough to push him over the edge.

"Fine!" He strode toward Boris with unaccustomed determination and, as he drew close, yanked his pickaxe out of its holster on his hip.

Boris's eyes widened in alarm when he saw that. "Hey, I was kidding!"

Albert realized that Boris thought he was about to attack him. For some reason the notion that Boris was filled with a sense of satisfaction that he had suddenly intimidated Boris. "Move aside," he said brusquely and Boris promptly did as he said. Moments later Alfred was standing astride the circle and, swinging his arm back, he brought the hammer down onto the inscription. It made a loud clink on contact and his arm shook in response.

Then he turned and said, "Happy?"

That was the last word he got out before the circle crumbled beneath his feet.

He heard Karen cry out his name in alarm and then he was gone, plunging down into blackness that enveloped him like a shroud.

For half a heartbeat, wild imaginings slammed through his head. He thought that he had fallen into some sort of bottomless pit and would wind up plummeting all the way to the Earth's core. But before his fancies could continue to spin in that direction, he hit something hard. It knocked the air out of him as he slumped back onto the floor, the light from above flooding down on him and illuminating the area around him.

"Albert!" Karen was continuing to scream. "Albert!"

"I'm fine," he managed to gasp back. He had fallen about twenty feet, near as he could tell. It wasn't an easy drop, but at least it wasn't life threatening. He stretched his arms, his legs, to make sure that everything was intact, and then slowly got to his feet. "I'm okay."

"We'll lower some rope to get you up!"

"No hurry." He unslung his backpack and extracted a flashlight. He flipped the switch, lighting up his surroundings.

It was the damnedest thing. It looked as if he was standing in the hallway of some sort of castle. But that was completely wrong for the area that they had been exploring. His surroundings didn't bear the slightest resemblance to the typical buildings of Egyptian structure. This area seemed like something out of Europe constructed during the Medieval period. It was making no sense at all.

That was when the torches lit up.

He hadn't even seen them at first because they were mounted on the wall and naturally had been long since extinguished. Somehow, for some reason that Albert couldn't even begin to fathom, they had lit up. They ran the length of the corridor, illuminating it quite effectively.

"What the hell . . . ?" he whispered.

"Albert! What's going on down there?"

"Damned if I know. Wait there."

"Wait . . . ? Where are you going?"

Albert didn't respond. Instead he was already cautiously walking down the corridor, exploring it with the additional light of his flashlight. He was seeing more of the indecipherable markings that had been above ground. They were lining the ceiling and floor and he felt as if they were trying to put forward some sort of story or narrative. He did not, however, have the slightest idea what that narrative might be.

There was a corner just ahead of him. He turned it and stopped dead.

There was a young man staring at him.

He wasn't wearing anything remotely modern. Instead, just as the environment surrounding him, he was wearing something that looked as if it would be more at home in the middle ages: a brown jerkin, green leggings, brown boots. He looked as if he were part of Robin Hood's band, save that he carried no weapons.

"Who are you?!" said Albert in confusion.

The young man slowly approached him. He had a thick shock of red hair and his skin was quite tan. His blue eyes widened as he whispered, "You can see me?"

"Of course I can! You're standing right there!"

"It's worn off! The translocator spell . . . it's worn off! I can't believe it!"

Albert had no idea what the hell he was talking about. "Who are you," he said again, "and what are you doing here?"

"Me? I live here! What are you doing . . . ?" Then his voice trailed off and he stared in confusion at Albert. "You!"

"Me?"

The young man strode forward and grabbed him by the shoulders. "Athis!"

"Who?"

"What do you mean, who? You! Don't you know your own name!?"

"I have no idea what the hell you're talking about!"

"And what is this clothing you're wearing?" He plucked at the shirt in confusion and then stared at the flashlight. "Is that some manner of torch in a canister? I'm unfamiliar with this magic."

"It's a flashlight! And my name isn't Athis! It's Albert!"

"Albert? What type of strange name is that?"

"Look, what are you doing down here?"

"I live here," said the young man in confusion. "As do you. As do Belid and Klaria and the Master Wizard and . . . are you ill, Athis?"

Albert took a deep breath and let it out slowly. "What's your name?" he said at last.

"You have forgotten me?"

I never knew you. Albert cleared his throat. "Remind me."

"Randall! I'm Randall! I tried the translocator spell and ever since I've been wandering the corridors, trying to get back, and it hasn't done me any good. But what happened to you?"

Albert still had no idea what Randall was going on about. Translocator spells? Did the poor boy fancy himself to be some sort of magician? That was ridiculous.

But how had he wound up there? How had he come to be wandering around inside an archæological dig? In a sealed-up area, no less? It just made no sense at all.

"Okay," Albert said slowly. "How about you come with me. My partners have probably lowered a rope by now and—"

"Holy crap."

It was Boris. He and Karen had descended into the pit after Albert and were approaching from behind. Boris was looking around in wonderment. Karen was focused on Albert. "Are you all right, Albert? And . . . who's *that?*"

"This is Randall," Albert said in an off-hand manner as if they were long time friends. "Apparently he lives here. Randall, this is—"

"Klaria!" Randall cried out in obvious joy. "Belid! All of you are here!"

Boris and Karen exchanged confused looks. "Who?" said Boris.

Randall's face fell. He was clearly incredulous. "I don't understand! How can you not know who you are! Unless . . ." And his voice dropped to a worried hush. "Of course. This is the action of demons. Demons have erased your memories. It's the only thing that makes any sense."

"That makes sense?" Boris said incredulously. "Demons? There are no such things as demons."

"There are always demons," Randall replied.

※ ※ ※

Colonel Schmidt lowered his binoculars, squinting against the heat of the sun. He glanced behind himself and saw that his men were likewise wilting under the pounding from the sun, but he was hardly in a position to express any sort of sympathy.

He was seated in the back of the jeep that was leading the procession. He cursed to himself—always to himself—the name of the Fuhrer for assigning him to this dead-end job. Hitler had been convinced that there had been some sort of artifact buried here in the vast Egyptian desert that could aid him in the coming battle. That was Hitler's way: to be obsessed with magical objects. Which was ridiculous, of course. Schmidt knew as well as anyone else that there was no such thing as magic, but it was impossible to convince the Fuhrer of that simple reality.

So now Hitler's advisors had told him of a formidable eldritch force that was supposed to be rising up in Armana. The advisor had been quite certain of his declaration, basing it on a stack of cards that he endlessly manipulated and some sort of prognostication that was buried in a book somewhere in the Berlin library. And because of that stupidity, Schmidt and his men had been sent to excavate. They hadn't received permission from the Egyptian government, figuring that there was no point in asking about something that they would doubtless be refused. Instead they had simply traveled to Egypt and were now in a convoy toward Armana, led by locals who were perfectly happy to do whatever it took in order to earn some spare money. It was a mindset that Schmidt was able to understand.

"Muller!" he called to his second in command. Muller, a short, bald man who was nevertheless one of the most formidable hand-to-hand fighters Schmidt had ever seen in action, was riding in the preceding jeep. Muller was also an archæologist, or at least had been before he joined the army. Not only that, but his interests and field of studies was steeped in mystical relics that were along the lines of what the Fuhrer was interested in. So Muller's presence on the excursion was invaluable. Muller turned, eyebrow raised. "How much longer?"

Muller repeated the question to the guide who was driving the jeep he was riding in. Muller spoke in Egyptian flawlessly, and the guide readily responded. He turned back to Schmidt. "Less than an hour, sir."

"Good." Schmidt had removed a handkerchief from his jacket and dabbed at his forehead. *The sooner we get out of this heat, the better.* "What are we looking for again?"

Muller shrugged. "The Fuhrer says it is some manner of talisman that will enable us to summon demons."

"Demons?" Schmidt could scarcely believe it. "And what will that accomplish?"

"Presumably they will fight for us."

"I would very much like to see that," Schmidt said with a laugh. "And what does this talisman look like?"

"The documentation is unclear," Muller said. "But I have been assured that we will know it when we see it."

Schmidt rolled his eyes. There was nothing about this assignment that he liked. Even worse, it had no termination date. They weren't given a specified period of time in which to find this mythical talisman and return home. They were only supposed to come back to Berlin once they had their hands on this allegedly mystical device that the Fuhrer wanted and none of them knew what it was.

Not for the first time, Schmidt found himself wondering if he was on the wrong side of the war.

But there was no point in allowing his thoughts to wander in that direction. He was what he was.

■ ■ ■

Randall drank deeply of the water from the canteen that Karen had handed him. Then he lowered it and looked around, not for the first time, at their arid surroundings. There was clear disbelief on his face. "No forest," he said for what seemed the hundredth time. "When I think of all the times that the four of us would wander about, just for exercise. What happened to it?"

"There was never a forest here," said Albert. "This is the desert. To the best of my knowledge, it's always been desert."

Randall looked around the dig in amazement. He was still squinting, having trouble with the sun's rays even though they had given him a hat to try and protect him against it. Albert supposed that made some degree of sense. There was no telling how long he had been underground, so naturally his eyes would have acclimated to his darkened surroundings. "I still don't understand how you survived down there. There's no food. How did you survive without eating or drinking?"

"The translocator spell took care of that. Or it did until it wore off, obviously. And at least I've figured out why you have no idea who I am or who you are."

"Really," Boris said, not even trying to keep the sarcasm from his voice. "And why would that be?"

"Because the three of you have obviously been reincarnated."

"Oh, well, of course!" Boris declared loudly. "I mean, that makes perfect sense! We've been reincarnated! We're actually wizards from another time and we've been reborn into these bodies, and we just happened to wind up together but with no recollection of our past lives! Why didn't that occur to me?"

"Well, probably because it's outside of your normal realm of experience."

"No, because it's ridiculous!" Boris looked at his companions in disbelief. "Why are you even listening to this idiot? He's obviously some young American who wandered into the middle of our dig and got lost below!"

"How did he wander into it?" Albert demanded. "There was no direct entrance to it. Not until I fell through that circle with the 'Do not touch' label on it. And by the way, next time we see something that says 'Do not touch' on it, I suggest we don't touch it!"

"I didn't wander into it," said Randall. "I was trapped there. But I don't think you understand the 'there' of it."

"Meaning?"

"The Crimson Keep connects to many lands, many times. That was part of why I cast the translocator spell: to try and travel to one of them. And I obviously succeeded beyond my wildest dreams. It just took me far longer than I would have . . ." His voice trailed off. "Wait. This 'Do not touch' symbol. What did it look like?"

"Like this. I picked it up as we were climbing back up." He had tucked it into his sack and now carefully extracted it. "See?"

He handed it to Randall and was shocked to see every trace of blood drain from the boy's face. Then he looked up and said, "We have to get out of here. Right now."

"What?" They exchanged confused looks. "Why?"

"Because whatever you think this means, it means far more than that. It . . ." Then he frowned. "What's that noise?"

At first Albert had no idea what he was referring to, but then he heard it as well. It was the sound of motors in the distance. Some sort of vehicles were approaching quite rapidly. "Engines."

"Engine? What is an—?"

Albert didn't bother to wait and answer the question. Instead he quickly climbed up a nearby ridge so that he could have a clear view of the surrounding area. What he saw literally made his blood run cold.

Quickly he slid back down the embankment and scrambled back to his friends. "We have to get out of here. Right now."

"Why?" said Karen. "What's wrong?"

"Nazis."

"*Nazis*?!" Her voice rose in alarm. "Why would they be coming here?"

"I don't know, but I have no interest in waiting around to find out."

"What are Nazis?" Randall said. He was clearly confused.

Albert's mind raced to find a way to explain and he decided that the simplest response was the best. "They're bad guys. Very bad guys. You know how you were talking about demons? These are them."

"Perhaps your magic can stop them."

"We have no magic!" Albert practically shouted at him. "What part of that don't you understand?"

"Yes, you do! Deep down! I can sense it within you. You just need to tap into it."

Deciding that continuing the conversation wasn't going to get them anywhere, Albert turned to his compatriots. "We need to go. Get our stuff."

"We don't have time to get everything . . ."

"Then get what you can, Boris! I don't want to have to deal with damned Nazis!"

"These Nazis are not what you have to worry about," said Randall.

Albert stared at him with open disbelief. "You don't know them."

"And you don't know the seal that you removed." He pointed to the piece of rock that he was holding in his hand. "Perhaps in your language it means 'Do not touch.' But it's originally from a far older language than that. And it warns that if the circle is shattered, then demons will be unleashed."

Boris rolled his eyes even as he hurriedly gathered up their things. "I don't believe this. Why are we even listening to him? Albert, go start up the jeep!"

Albert grabbed the circle of stone back and shoved it into his back, even though he bristled at taking orders from Boris. Randall followed him, speaking as fast as he could. "You need to listen to me! You need to restore the circle! You need to put the seal back! Otherwise—"

"There is no otherwise! We are leaving! Do you understand? We are leaving!"

He clambered into the jeep. The keys were hanging in the ignition. They'd left them there since there seemed little point in worrying about someone coming along and stealing their vehicle. He shoved the gas pedal as he turned the key.

There was no response from the engine. He might as well have not been turning the key at all.

"What the hell—?!" he shouted as he turned the key again and again. There was still nothing from the motor. He tried putting on the headlights but got no response. "Boris! The car's dead!"

Boris was heading toward him with as much of their equipment slung over his shoulders as he could manage. He skidded to a halt upon hearing Albert's declaration. "Are you kidding me?"

"The battery's dead."

"So now what are we supposed to do!"

"You can use magic," Randall started to say.

"*Shut up!*" they both shouted at him, neither in the mood to hear any of his preposterous claims.

The Nazis were now only minutes away. Albert scrambled out of the jeep and they ran toward Karen, who was standing there looking puzzled, and quickly apprised her of their situation. "What do we do?!" she asked.

"Hide somewhere," said Albert.

"Where?"

He only had one response: "Down there," and he pointed at the hole that he had fallen into. The rope that they had scaled down to get him was still in place. "Unless you've got a better idea."

None of them did.

Quickly they scrambled down the rope, Randall leading the way. They dropped to the bottom and then Randall abruptly took charge. "This way," he said with confidence.

"Are you sure?" said Albert.

Randall looked annoyed for the first time. "Considering how long I've been wandering around here in a state of being out of time, I'd think I'd know which way to go." That was clearly his final word on the subject, because he started down the corridor and the others followed.

As they walked briskly, Albert said, "So otherwise what? You were starting to tell us before. What happens if we don't put the seal back?"

"Then the demons will spill out into your world."

"What demons? You keep talking about them. What demons are we supposed to worry about?"

Randall kept moving as he spoke. "There was a final invasion. It was many years after I'd wound up getting myself stuck in a nether state in the castle. We thought the demon wars had been settled, but no. Instead there was a new rebellion and the final battle spread over into the Keep itself."

"And what happened?"

He turned and stared at them, his face impassive. "You died, Athis. I saw it. You were a fully powered wizard; this was long after your training had ended. You and Klaria and Belid and so many others, and you fought a great and wonderful battle, but in the end, it was not enough. But the demons, they took a heavy toll as well. Fatalities on both sides. And eventually it came down to the Master, making a last stand against the demon leader, Drazil. The final battle raged through the castle, and everything was laid waste. Drazil's demons were transformed into this sort of black goo that seeped into the bricks of the walls, and Drazil and the Master . . ."

"What?" Despite the absurdity of what Randall was saying, Albert found himself caught up in the narrative. "What happened to them?"

"I do not know. There was a massive blast of eldritch flame and I ran from it. And because the castle is so vast and confusing, I never found my way back. I have wandered ever since. I—" His voice choked and he stopped walking, staring down glumly at the floor. "I am so sorry, Athis. If not for my own incompetence, I would have been there for you. Instead I am here." Suddenly he blinked in surprise. "Wait. That symbol you have . . . the Master! He must have created it! It is the only answer. He must have survived the battle but felt that the only course left to him was to seal up the Keep forever, so that no one in any realm—including this one—would ever have to be threatened by it! It's the only thing that makes any sense!"

"To you, maybe," Boris said sarcastically.

Albert wasn't listening. Instead he kept looking at the walls. He was sure he was imagining it, but it seemed as if there was some sort of tar that was seeping out from between the bricks. That was ridiculous, of course . . . until he remembered what Randall had said about demons being transformed into goo. Then his pulse began to race. *What if everything he said is true? What if we really are surrounded by some kind of demons?* He wanted to voice his concern, but was certain that Boris would just disdainfully shut down any such conversation.

"Where are we going, anyway?" said Boris.

"There is a room of safety. A special place where we can take refuge. It is just ahead."

"You're sure? I feel like we are going in circles."

"I'm absolutely positive. There! Right up there, up ahead!"

A door was sitting there waiting for them. It didn't seem especially heavy; just a standard sized oaken door. Randall ran straight to it, threw it open and ran in. There was nothing but darkness on the other side, but Albert didn't see any other option. He ran through after Randall, with Boris and Karen right on his heels.

The door slammed behind them. They skidded to a stop.

They were back outside.

The sun had set.

And there were Nazis everywhere.

One of them was already holding Randall from behind. Randall was struggling in his grip but was unable to free himself.

"And what is this?" said one Nazi who, from his uniform and air, was clearly in charge. "More interlopers?"

"We're not interlopers!" Albert said defiantly. "We're Americans and we have as much right to be here as you do!"

"Is that what you think? How very charming." The Nazi snapped to, tossing off a sarcastic salute. "I am Colonel Schmidt, on a special mission for the Fuhrer. And if you are interfering with it . . ."

"We're not interfering with anything," Albert said. "If anything, you're interfering with us."

"Indeed." Schmidt did not seem the least bit deterred by Albert's protests. "And may I ask just exactly what you were doing inside this dig? What did you find through there?" He indicated the door through which they had just exited.

"Nothing," Albert told him. "As a matter of fact, that door wasn't there before."

This prompted amused chuckles from the Nazis. "Then where was it?" asked Schmidt. "Where did it come from?"

I have absolutely no idea. "That's none of your business."

"Well then, perhaps I'd best check."

He strode toward the door.

"No!" Randall shouted. "You mustn't!"

His urgency caught Schmidt's attention. "Why ever not?"

"Because you're not a sorcerer. You were never a sorcerer. You have no inner defenses. The demons will swallow you whole!"

The result was predictable: outright laughter from the Nazis. "I will take my chances," said Schmidt.

He strode toward the door, indicating that several of his men should follow them. As he approached, Randall kept shouting at him so furiously that the Nazis shoved a cloth in his mouth to quiet him.

Schmidt pulled open the door. The dimness within prompted him to shine a flashlight into the interior, and then he strode in, followed by three of his soldiers.

This is not going to end well, thought Albert.

And that was when the screams began.

Schmidt and his men were screeching in clear terror. Something was going on that was petrifying them, and no one had any idea what it was. No one except Albert, who remembered the black ooze that seemed to be seeping from the bricks for no reason.

The Nazis were looking at each in confusion and worry. One of them, a short, bald individual, strode forward. "Herr Schmidt!" he called. "What's wrong!"

The screaming stopped as abruptly as it began. For a long moment there was no response and then Schmidt's voice floated out. "Everything is fine, Herr Muller. Everything is more than fine. Come here, would you, please?"

Muller frowned in confusion but slowly walked toward the door.

At that moment, Randall managed to spit out the cloth that had been stuffed in his mouth and he shouted, "No! Back away! Don't go near him! Run the other way!"

Much to Albert's surprise, Muller actually stopped approaching the door. He seemed confused and concerned. "Why should I?" he said to Randall, but there was no challenge in his voice. Instead he sounded as if he was genuinely looking for a reason for Randall's concern.

"He sounds wrong. Can't you tell he sounds wrong? Have him come out here!" When Muller didn't immediately respond, Randall said again, "Have him come out here. You'll be able to tell!"

"Tell what?" asked Muller, but then he didn't wait for the answer. Instead he turned back to the door and said, "Colonel, would you mind coming out here instead?"

"I believe I ordered you to come here, Herr Muller," his voice floated out. There was now a grating sound to it that hadn't been there before.

Muller took several steps back. "I'm afraid I must insist, Colonel."

"I am in charge!" Schmidt's voice shot back. "You do not get to insist!"

"And yet I am."

Very slowly and deliberately, Muller had removed a gun from the inside of his jacket. There were stunned expressions on the faces of the other Nazis, but no one made a move.

For some reason, Albert took deep pleasure in the notion that Nazis could appear as concerned and frightened as he was.

And then something exploded from the door.

It was Schmidt, but it wasn't. Long, curled black horns extended from his forehead and he had a pair of batwings mounted on his back that were propelling him at impossible speed. It had Schmidt's face, but it was twisted into a demented sneer. The most horrifying were his eyes, which no longer contained anything resembling a human soul but instead burned a deep crimson.

The other soldiers were directly behind him, and they had been likewise transformed. They had a variety of horns, and some had wings but others didn't. Their eyes, however, were uniformly similar to Schmidt's.

Muller fired without thinking, pumping bullet after bullet into Schmidt's body. It didn't even slow him down. Instead he leaped upon Muller and, as the other soldiers screamed in shock, sank his teeth deep into Muller's throat. He yanked his head back and blood fountained from it. Muller tried to shriek but couldn't inhale, his lungs too quickly filling up with blood.

Schmidt's head snapped back as he swallowed the huge chunk of flesh whole, blood pouring down either side of his face. Muller sagged in his arms, already dead, and the creature that had been Colonel Schmidt tossed him aside.

The other demon soldiers were descending on the remaining Nazis. They yanked out guns from their holsters and opened fire, just as Muller had upon Schmidt. The result was exactly the same: the creatures staggered slightly from the impact of the bullets but otherwise were not slowed. They leaped upon the Nazis, literally ripping them apart. Some of them managed to avoid being shredded in the initial attack, and their response was to turn and run for the jeeps as quickly as they could. They gunned the engines, backing up and spinning around so quickly that they almost tipped the jeeps over.

Albert stood there, paralyzed. The men who'd been holding him had been among the first ones to run, and now he was left there but couldn't think of how to respond. Boris, Karen, and Randall had likewise been abandoned. When it came to trying to save one's life as opposed to following orders, apparently there was no contest.

The former Colonel Schmidt drew his arm across his mouth, wiping away the blood. His red eyes narrowed as he focused on Albert. "Athis," he breathed.

Oh God, here we go again. "I'm not Athis!" Albert said and he pointed at his companions. "And that's not . . . Belid, I think and that's not Klaria!"

"But this is Randall," Boris said, sounding a bit too eager. His legs were visibly shaking. For some reason, Albert took solace in that.

Schmidt frowned. "I do not remember you."

"Well, I wasn't around much."

Schmidt glanced around. "I," he said with a great deal of self-importance, "am Drazil." He thumped his chest. "So where has your sorcery taken us? What land is this?"

"My sorcery didn't do anything," Randall told him. "I wasn't part of the fight. Whatever was done to you, the Master did it."

"Then bring him forth!"

"He's gone," said Randall. "They're all gone. You managed to survive. You win. You demons won the war."

"Congratulations," Karen said, obviously having no idea what to contribute to the conversation.

Schmidt's voice dropped to a deep, threatening level. "And you survived as well. You wizards . . ."

"We're not wizards!" Albert said desperately. "I mean, okay, okay, maybe we look like some wizards from back in your time. But we're not them, I swear!"

"Then you are what? Humans? Modern humans?"

"Yes, that's all we are."

"Then why," said Schmidt, and he slowly walked toward Albert, "do I sense great magic coming from you?"

He backed up as Schmidt approached. "I have no idea."

"You are possessed of power. Power that can be a threat to

me. That cannot be tolerated."

As Albert backed up, he felt something jostling on his back and remembered what it was. A desperate idea occurred to him and he had no comprehension of why it did. Quickly he unslung the pack on his back.

"What are you doing?" demanded Schmidt. "What do you think you're—"

Albert thrust his hand into the pack and yanked out the piece of stone that had the prohibit symbol on it. He was so nervous that his hand was trembling. "It's probably this," he said.

"And what is that?"

Shove it. Against his chest.

The words slammed through his mind, and he had no idea where they came from. It was not his own thought, of that much he was sure. How in God's name another voice was speaking through his mind, he didn't have the faintest idea. And yet he was certain of it.

"Why don't you find out for yourself!" Albert shouted and, against his better judgment, he charged at Schmidt.

The movement caught Schmidt completely by surprise. Albert had been shaking in fear only seconds earlier and so seemed the very last person who was a threat to launch an attack. So it was that, rather than defend himself, Schmidt simply stood there with his red eyes wide, clearly uncomprehending of why Albert was running at him or what he hoped to accomplish.

And Albert lunged forward with the tablet and slammed it against Schmidt's chest.

And then he screamed, for the tablet literally lit up with power.

It burned so quickly that Albert was unable to yank his hands clear, with the result being that it seared into his flesh. He screamed, falling back, shoving his hands under his arms in a desperate effort to cool them.

Schmidt was howling even more loudly, however. Somehow the piece of etched rubble was adhering to his chest, and his desperate efforts to pry it loose came to nothing. He shrieked and kept pulling, but it did no good. "What have you done? *What have you done?!"*

Albert shook his head. He didn't have the faintest idea, even though a voice had come from nowhere and urged him what to do.

None of the other demons were trying to help Schmidt. Instead they seemed to be having their own problems. They were violently trembling, some of them even having fallen to the ground and continuing to shake as if they'd lost all control of their bodies.

Schmidt continued to yank at the stone, which was now visibly glowing. Blue energy was cascading from it.

"Get back!" Albert shouted as he scrambled toward the others. They attended his warning, running backwards as fast as they could, getting clear of the phenomenon that they didn't understand.

With a high-pitched shriek, Schmidt stopped pulling on the stone and instead threw his arms wide.

A thick black ooze seemed to explode out of his body through his open mouth, his ears, the very pores of his skin. Everywhere it hit the ground, it sizzled, as if the earth itself was burning it alive. The same thing happened to the other demons as well, and as the black goo left them, their outward demonic attributes departed with them. Their horns shrank, their wings disappeared. The ooze bubbled furiously on the ground and a stench like brimstone filled the air.

As the last of the goo seeped out of Schmidt, the redness from his eyes vanished. He took several steps forward, swaying from one side to the other, and suddenly he was bleeding from the bullets that had been fired into him. He pitched forward and was dead before he struck the ground. The same thing happened to the other Nazis as well and seconds later the only living things left were Albert, Randall, Boris, and Karen.

Karen clapped her hand over her nose because it was the only way she could deal with the stench. Slowly Albert walked toward the stone that was lying on the ground, having fallen off Schmidt's chest. He passed his hand over it and could detect no heat rising from it. It had cooled instantly and now he picked it up, turning it over as he stared at it.

"I think," he said slowly, "we've found a mystic talisman. This thing made the demons go away."

"Away where?" said Boris.

"They're dead," said Randall. "They couldn't survive outside the Keep without host bodies. And when you shoved the tablet onto Drazil . . . well, he was the center of their power. When the tablet shut him down, the rest of them went with him."

"So you're sure they're dead?" said Albert.

"Absolutely," said Randall. "One hundred percent sure." Then he paused. "Ninety percent at worst. Maybe eighty, but that's an absolute worst case—"

"I'm getting one of the Nazi jeeps!" Boris said immediately and dashed away from the scene.

Karen watched him go and then walked over to Albert. Putting her hands on his shoulders, she said, "That was very brave, what you did." And she stood on her toes and kissed him warmly.

"Thanks." He paused and then added, "Boris looked scared out of his mind."

"He really was," she said, and laughed.

Albert turned and looked at Randall. "Athis, huh?"

"Athis, yes," said Randall.

"This may sound weird, but I think I have him rattling around inside my head. Which is interesting because I've never heard him before."

"Maybe he was waiting for the right moment."

"How about you come with us and maybe you can help bring him out again."

"It'd be my honor," said Randall, and he bowed deeply.

Seconds later they had piled into the jeep, taking only the minimal amount of time required to gather their belongings. Boris floored the gas and seconds later they were speeding off across the Egyptian desert.

And behind them, the black ooze began to bubble . . .

ABOUT THE AUTHORS

RUSS COLCHAMIRO is the author of the hilarious scifi backpacking comedy *Finders Keepers*, and the pulpy sci-fi adventure *Crossline*, both from Crazy 8 Press. He claims to be writing the first of two *Finders Keepers* sequels, but that could just be the galactic delusions talking, given that he was exposed to a jar of the Universe's liquid DNA. To learn more about Russ and his ongoing tales of cosmic lunacy, you can visit his website at russcolchamiro.com, and follow him on Twitter @authorduderuss, on Facebook at www.facebook.com/RussColchamiroAuthor, and Goodreads. Russ is married with two children, and a kooky dog, and lives in West Orange, NJ. But if he suddenly vaporizes before your eyes and reconstitutes in another part of town, don't take it personally. It's just how he is.

PETER DAVID is a *New York Times* bestselling author with works ranging from science fiction to fantasy. His media tie-in works include his corner of the *Star Trek* universe, New Frontier, along with novelizations of *Hulk*, *Spider-Man*, and *The Rocketeer*. His original works include *Artful*, from Amazon, the now-back-in-print Sir Apropos trilogy (plus the new *Gypsies, Vamps & Thieves*), *The Camelot Papers*, and the Hidden Earth triology from Crazy 8 Press. He's also written for animated and live-action television as well as film. Follow Peter at www.peterdavid.net, @PeterDavid_PAD, and Facebook.

MARY FAN is a YA and SFF author based in Jersey City. Her books include the *Jane Colt* space opera trilogy, comprising *Artificial Absolutes* (2013), *Synthetic Illusions* (2014), and *Virtual Shadows* (2015), and *Starswept* (2017), a YA sci-fi novel. Her latest book,

Flynn Nightsider and the Edge of Evil, is a YA dark fantasy releasing 2018 from Crazy 8 Press. In addition, she is the co-editor of the *Brave New Girls* YA sci-fi anthologies about girls in STEM, which aim to encourage more girls to explore STEM fields and raise money for the Society of Women Engineers scholarship fund.

MICHAEL JAN FRIEDMAN is one of the founders of the publishing juggernaut known as Crazy 8 Press, and therefore at least partly culpable for the mystical, magical, motley tomfoolery that regularly occurs within the boundless bounds of the Crimson Keep. Mike is also the author of seventy-one books of fiction and nonfiction, eleven of which have appeared on the prestigious *New York Times* primary bestseller lists. His latest novel, *I Am The Salamander*, is about a teenager coping with the usual teenage problems—girls, school, spending money, and the sudden, terrifying onset of super-powers. Mike has also written for network and cable television, radio, magazines, and comic books, the *Star Trek: Voyager* episode "Resistance," which guest-starred Joel Grey, prominent among his credits. He continues to advise readers that no matter how many Friedmans they may know, the vast probability is that none of these people is even remotely related to him; what's more, they are better off that way.

ROBERT GREENBERGER is a writer/editor/teacher with an extensive array of credits ranging from media tie-in fiction to adult non-fiction. He has worked for Starlog Press, DC Comics, Gist Communications, Marvel Comics, and *Weekly World News*. He was instrumental in relaunching Famous Monsters of Filmland as a brand and briefly served as News Editor at ComicMix.com. He is the co-creator of the *Latchkeys* and *ReDeus* series, and one of the founders of Crazy 8 Press. His novelization of *Hellboy II: The Golden Army* won the 2009 Scribe Award. He continues to work as a comic book historian when not writing original fiction. Additionally, he is a high school English teacher in Maryland, where he resides with his wife, Deb. To learn more about Bob, you can visit his website at bobgreenberger.com, and follow him on Twitter @bobgreenberger and Goodreads.

GLENN HAUMAN, alternately known as "Da Big Guy,","G to the H," "Crazy 8's Shabbos Goy," and "Party Of The First Part," made the mistake of asking his friends during a *Cards Against Humanity* game, "What's missing from my biographical blurb?" The responses included "Spectacular abs," "A low standard of living," "The secret formula for ultimate female satisfaction," "Pretty Pretty Princess Dress-Up Board Game," and "Some god-damn peace and quiet." You can find out more at www.glennhauman. com, @glennhauman, or at his day job at ComicMix.com.

PAUL KUPPERBERG is also the author of the mystery novel, *The Same Old Story* and is a co-creator and contributor to the *ReDeus* anthology trilogy from Crazy 8 Press, and *Kevin* (a young adult novel featuring the first openly gay character in Archie Comics' history), *Betty & Veronica* and *DC Superheroes Mad Libs* (all from Grossett & Dunlap), and a regular contributor to R. Allen Leider's *Hellfire Lounge* anthology series (Bold Venture Press). Paul wrote the groundbreaking *Life With Archie* series for Archie Comics (including the controversial "Death of Archie" storyline), which has been nominated for the 2012 Eisner Award, the 2013 Harvey Award, and the 2014 GLAAD Media Award for "Outstanding Comic Book." He has written close to 1,000 stories for DC Comics, Marvel Comics, Bongo Comics, 2000 A.D. and others, from Batman to Johnny Bravo and Superman to the Simpsons, as well as his own creations, *Arion, Lord of Atlantis, Checkmate,* and *Takion,* and newspaper comic strips (*Superman* and *Tom & Jerry*), children's books, short stories, non-fiction, essays, and humor. Follow Paul online at PaulKupperberg.com and on Twitter @PaulKupperberg.

AARON ROSENBERG is an award-winning, #1 bestselling novelist, children's book author, and game designer. His novels include the best-selling DuckBob series (consisting of *No Small Bills, Too Small for Tall, Three Small Coinkydinks,* and the forthcoming *Not for Small Minds*), the *Dread Remora* space-opera series, the epic fantasy *Bones of Empire* with Steven Savile, and, with David Niall Wilson, the O.C.L.T. occult thriller series. His tie-in work contains novels for *Star Trek, Warhammer, WarCraft,* and *Eureka.*

He has written children's books, including the original series *Pete and Penny's Pizza Puzzles*, the award-winning *Bandslam: The Junior Novel*, and the #1 best-selling *42: The Jackie Robinson Story*. Aaron has also written educational books on a variety of topics and over seventy roleplaying games, such as the original games *Asylum*, *Spookshow*, and *Chosen*, work for White Wolf, Wizards of the Coast, Fantasy Flight, Pinnacle, and many others, and both the Origins Award-winning *Gamemastering Secrets* and the Gold ENnie-winning *Lure of the Lich Lord*. He is the co-creator of the *ReDeus* series, and one of the founders of Crazy 8 Press. Aaron lives in New York with his family. You can follow him online at gryphonrose.com, on Facebook at facebook.com/gryphonrose, and on Twitter @gryphonrose.

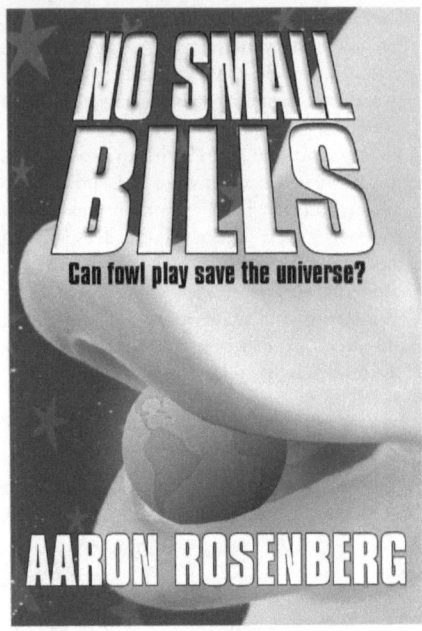